The Warriors

The Girl I Left Behind Me

A Novel

by

Robert Cubitt

The Warriors - The Girl I Left Behind Me

A novel by Robert Cubitt

Published by Ex-L-Ence Publishing a division of Winghigh Limited, Gloucester, England.

ISBN: 978-1-909133-80-8

"I'm lonesome since I crossed the hill
And over the moor that's sedgy
Such lonely thoughts my heart do fill
Since parting with my Betsey
I seek for one as fair and gay
But find none to remind me
How sweet the hours I passed away
With the girl I left behind me."

Anonymous popular song of the American Civil War, based on an older European soldiers' song, possibly originating in Ireland.

Contents

British Military Terminology

This novel uses a number of military terms. I have tried to introduce them gently and explain them wherever possible, but I have also taken the liberty of placing a Glossary at the end of each chapter to some further information if you are interested. The glossary is repeated in full at the end of the book if you would like to read it before you start.

Author's Note

The Middlesex Regiment

Throughout this novel the names of both infantry and cavalry regiments have been taken from units that no longer exist. Once proud regimental names have disappeared as the army has been reformed, reorganised and then reorganised again.

The selection of the Middlesex Regiment as Sergeant Lofty Lofthouse's unit is not an accident. Not only does it provide a geographical anchor to attach two of my main characters to, but it was also this regiment that my father joined as a boy soldier in 1938. My father later joined No 3 Army Commando and spent five years of World War II with them, before returning to the Middlesex Regiment in 1945 when the Army Commandoes were disbanded. He continued to serve with the Middlesex Regiment until he left the army in 1963 and I still have family connections with the London Borough of Enfield, which was once in the county of Middlesex.

The Middlesex Regiment started out as two regiments of the foot soldiers, the 57th and 77th. The 57th were raised in 1755 as the 51st Regiment, but were retitled in 1756. In 1782 they became the 57th (West Middlesex) Regiment of Foot. The 77th were raised in 1787 as a regiment of East India Company soldiers recruited from Britain and Ireland. On returning to England in 1807, after being absorbed into the regular army, they were designated the 77th (East Middlesex) Regiment of Foot. It is from the 77th that the regiment earned the right to incorporate the Prince of Wales feathers and the motto Ich Dein into their cap badge.

From the 57th Regiment the Middlesex earned their nickname the Die Hards. In 1811 at the Battle of Albuhera on the Iberian Peninsula their mortally wounded Commanding Officer, Lieutenant Colonel William Inglis, exhorted his men to "die hard the 57th, die hard" as they battled against superior numbers of Napoleon's army. A further tradition from the same battle was adopted from the 57th, that of the silent toast. After the battle the surviving officers are said to have melted down some of their silver accoutrements to make a cup. They and the NCO's of the battalion then passed the cup from hand to hand as each man present silently toasted the "immortal memory" of those that had fallen. The cup still exists and has the medal of the battle's longest living survivor, Colour Sergeant Henry Holloway, mounted within it. At the Battle of Albuhera Henry Holloway was an 11 year old drummer boy.

The links to the now defunct county of Middlesex were re-asserted by the 1881 army reforms which joined the two regiments together and gave them the title of Duke of Cambridge's Own (Middlesex Regiment), which was to become The Middlesex Regiment (Duke of Cambridge's Own).

The Regiment's Depot was at Inglis Barracks, Mill Hill, now part of the London Borough of Barnet. The regiment recruited from the heavily populated areas of North and West London, as well as from the smaller towns and villages of the county. Following the disbandment of the regiment the barracks was home to the British Forces Post Office (BFPO) until they moved to new accommodation at RAF Northolt in 2007. The Barracks is to be sold off for redevelopment. The county of Middlesex itself disappeared under local government reforms of 1965 and was mainly swallowed up by the neighbouring London boroughs, with some towns being absorbed into Hertfordshire and Surrey.

Under a reorganisation that took place in 1966 the Middlesex Regiment became the 4th Battalion of the Queens Regiment, joined by The Queen's Royal Surrey Regiment, The Queens Own Buffs (The Royal Kent Regiment) and The Royal Sussex Regiment. A further reorganisation in 1992 saw the Queens Regiment combine with the Royal Hampshire Regiment to become the Princess of Wales Royal Regiment (Queens and Royal Hampshires), the title by which they are known today. Albuhera Day, the anniversary of the battle on 16th May, is a significant day for the regiment when the silent toast is still drunk.

The Princess of Wales Royal Regiment have conducted a number of operational tours in Afghanistan. None of the events described in this novel are attributable to them in any way.

This story is entirely a work of fiction and any errors of fact made within it are mine alone.

Other titles by Robert Cubitt

Fiction

The Deputy Prime Minister
The Inconvenience Store

Non-Fiction

I'm So Glad You Asked Me That
Writing A Book That Sells

Dedication

In memory of my father
Company Sergeant Major Robert (Bob) Cubitt
Middlesex Regiment
21st February 1921- 17th January 2011

1 - Accident Of War

Death crept into Pakistani airspace at the relatively slow speed of 170 knots. From the ground far below it was invisible to the naked eye. So small was it in comparison to its height that it didn't even cast a shadow on the sides of the mountains.

In the air conditioned control room at Creech Air Force Base, Nevada, Captain Cory Duncan of the United States Air Force checked the position of his aircraft.

"OK guys, we are now in Pakistan air space." He flicked his radio switch. "Achilles One Zero this is Catcher Five. What is the status of hostile aircraft?"

"Achilles One Zero, we have six PAF aircraft in the air at present. We classify them as two pairs of Chengdu Sevens and one pair of Mirage Threes. All are deployed along the frontiers with Kashmir and India. No hostile aircraft in your sector." The radar operator of the E3 Sentry aircraft, flying high above the Indian Ocean, signed off with a cheery "Have a nice day".

"OK guys, we have 400 miles to target. No hostiles in the area." At the current cruising speed of their aircraft it would take more than two hours to reach the target.

The mission specialist sitting at the next console raised his head. "We are under radar surveillance, but no missile signatures at present."

Their General Atomics MQ-9 Reaper RPV would show up brightly on the Pakistani air defence radar systems, and no doubt half a world away a radar operator was tracking their 170 knot progress across his airspace. It was well within the capability of the

Pakistani Air Force to locate and destroy a Reaper, but for reasons best known to themselves they had never tried. They raised merry hell every time a mission such as this was carried out, but never raised a finger to stop them. In the meantime mission Catcher Five flew on towards its target at 50,000 feet.

* * *

In the far off city of Abbottabad in North West Pakistan a man settled himself onto a roof to carry out his part of the Catcher Five mission. He was born in Pakistan and regarded himself as a Pakistani patriot, but his wages had been paid by the United States of America ever since he had returned home from his short trip to that country.

In this town the leader of the Al Qaeda terrorist movement had been tracked down and killed by U.S. Navy Seals. Now it was his mission to bring about the end of another enemy of Uncle Sam and, as far as he was concerned, an enemy of his own country.

From his battered rucksack the man pulled out a metal clad attaché case. Opening it he withdrew a rectangular object from its foam rubber packing. It was painted in a camouflaged pattern and had an aperture at one end housing a lens. He laid it gently on the parapet of the roof and took out the other object in the case, a collapsible tripod. The tripod was screwed into the base of the device, the legs were extended then the whole assembly set down carefully behind the waist-high wall that surrounded the roof. On hot nights people slept up here and it wouldn't do for a sleepy child to fall over the edge of the roof.

The man sighted along the device and lined it up carefully on the house that was providing temporary accommodation for the second in command of the Taliban in North West Pakistan.

A check on his watch showed it was still a long time to go before the aircraft would be in range. No point in wasting valuable battery life by switching the device on too early.

* * *

Trying to overcome his boredom Cory remembered back to when he had joined the United States Air Force and had imagined himself screaming across the skies in a jet fighter, dog fighting with whatever enemies Uncle Sam asked him to fight. For a while that is what he had done, flying F17s in Germany and then South Korea, though he had never been engaged in a dog fight. On 20th March 2003, Cory had flown his F17 into Iraq as part of Operation Iraqi Freedom. He was disappointed when the Iraqi air force refused to take to the skies to fight him and his comrades.

Now he was posted to 432nd Fighter Wing at Creech, and wore his flight suit only as a way of distinguishing himself from the ground staff at the base. The aircraft he flew was controlled by signals bounced off satellites while he sat at a console in Nevada and the Reaper was high above the mountains and plains of Afghanistan and Pakistan and, more rarely, Iran.

This mission had started out as a routine tasking to detect the incursion of terrorists along the Pakistan-Afghanistan border. It was a search and destroy mission, and they were 'weapons free' to engage any hostile targets they encountered. About an hour into the mission they had been re-tasked to this new operation, a missile attack on a house in a city a third of the world away.

"OK, target is confirmed at location." The intelligence analyst announced, looking up from his computer screen.

"What is our target?" Cory asked out of curiosity.

"A house." The analyst replied.

"No shit Sherlock. That's so helpful."

Staff Sgt Willy Westheimer blushed in acknowledgement of his gaff. "Sorry, Sir. It's a senior figure in the Taliban, that's all they've told me."

It was the job of the intelligence analyst, the third member of the Reaper flight team, to confirm the nature of the target before they released any weapons. It was his responsibility to decide if they were the enemy or just a bunch of kids on their way to school. In this case, however, he wouldn't even see the human target, so this time he wouldn't be responsible for identifying him when the time came. That was the responsibility of a man risking his life on the ground in Pakistan.

Time ticked by and the crew chatted to relieve the boredom. An imaginary line in the sky was finally passed and Lieutenant 'Ace' Vincent, the weapons specialist, announced that Catcher Five was within range to begin the attack sequence.

"Taking us down to attack height." Cory pushed forward the joystick mounted on the arm of his leather chair. It was hardly any different from that used to control a games console. In the sky above Pakistan the Reaper's nose dropped and the aircraft began to descend to 20,000 feet.

* * *

On the sweltering roof in Pakistan the man checked his watch again. The mobile phone in his hand vibrated to indicate that a text message had been received. The message contained only one word, the code word for the mission to proceed.

The man flicked a switch on the side of the rectangular object, then sighted along it again. Half a mile away a miniscule green dot appeared on the side wall of a house.

* * *

"We have laser lock." 'Ace' informed the team. Like Duncan he had joined the Air Force to fly in fast jets, but now flew a technology driven operating console instead. Still, it wasn't too much of a hard life, playing computer games at Uncle Sam's expense, and just down the road was the city of Las Vegas. For a gambling man like 'Ace' that could only be good news. Meanwhile, the Raytheon sensor systems aboard the Reaper had picked up the electromagnetic signature of laser light being reflected from the target, which was all that 'Ace' needed to carry the mission through to its conclusion.

* * *

The man turned as he heard voices approaching up the stairs that led to the roof. The house was supposed to be empty, and he had paid hard American dollars for it to be so. The door at the top of the stairs was jammed shut from the outside, a stout chair wedged under the handle, but if someone wanted to gain access to the roof it wouldn't take much effort. The voices faded and the man relaxed a little. The tiny nudge of his foot against the tripod that held the laser target designator went unnoticed. Over the half mile space between the roof and the target the tiny angle of error was magnified so that it now shone its slender beam not on the original house, but on a very similar one a few metres further along the street.

* * *

"I have visual." Ace called, informing his pilot that the on-board camera had aligned itself to the source of the laser reflections and was now providing a visual feed to them. The TV screen showed an oblique angle view of a typical concrete and cinder block building arranged in a square around a central courtyard. The same pictures were being viewed in an operations room on the other side of the country, just outside Washington DC. There were no people visible in the house, even when Ace zoomed the camera to get a close up. In the heat of the day all sensible Pakistanis sought the cooler interiors of their homes or workplaces. The lucky ones would have air-conditioning, but a lack of vents on the exterior walls suggested that this house wasn't that lucky.

"Visual identification confirms target. You are weapons free." Willy announced as his computer screen displayed a fresh message. "I repeat, you are weapons free."

Raising the safety guard Ace pressed the weapon release button. "Missile launched." He stated flatly, as though they were engaged in a practice drill rather than actual warfare.

It took 1.2 seconds for the electronic command to reach the Reaper and release the missile carried on one of its external stores pylons. The AGM-114 Hellfire missile streaked away under the power of its solid fuel rocket. The aircraft lurched slightly as it reacted to the sudden loss of the 100lb weight.

The missile's electronic brain adjusted the angle of attack as it responded to the laser signal that originated on the ground and the missile powered the final 2 miles to its target. Dropping from 20,000 feet it hardly needed the power of its rocket, which only served to speed its descent. The sonic boom created as it broke the sound barrier wouldn't be heard above the blast of its explosion.

* * *

Youssef left the Madrassa at the end of his school day and headed for his father's house. He felt quite elated; his tutor had just told him that he was making good progress in his studies. It would soon be time for him to start repaying some of the cost of his education by teaching English to the younger students.

It was about a mile from the school to his home and the heat made him uncomfortable. He hadn't yet become acclimatised. When his parents had returned to Pakistan to manage the building they had inherited from Youssef's Grandfather the boy had remained behind in Britain to finish his education. Now that he was here he was finding it difficult to adapt to some features of his new home.

Keeping to the shade the man on the roof went unnoticed by Youssef, as did the laser designator that directed its needle thin beam across the rooftops of the quiet suburb. The sun glinted off the Reaper's wing as it went into a turn to maintain its position, but that too went unnoticed.

* * *

"Target destroyed" announced 'Ace', as the view at the centre of his TV screen disappeared in a bright flash of light. As the burst subsided the TV screen showed a cloud of dust and flying debris. The blast of the metal augmented 18lb explosive charge had left only one wall standing. Along the street debris crashed to the ground, risking the lives of anyone in the open at that moment. In a richer country glass would have shattered, but here there was no need of it and little money to pay for it even if there had been a need.

"Taking us home." Cory announced. By home he meant back into Afghan airspace. Their mission to Pakistan might be complete, but their patrol still had several hours to run. He pulled the joystick backwards and to the right and the aircraft at once climbed and reversed its course. With the Reaper capable of staying aloft for up to 42 hours it wouldn't be them that landed the aircraft back at Bagram Air Base.

* * *

On the roof the man stared aghast as the dust cloud cleared to reveal that the wrong house had been destroyed. His ears were still recovering from the blast of the detonation, so it was some minutes before the noise of panic in the streets reached him. Running men, some of them armed, drew his attention. Rats leaving the sinking ship.

The man returned his gaze to the place where a house had once stood. He hoped that it was unoccupied, but knew in his heart it was unlikely to be so. Women and children had been observed at that house and any hope for them was already lost. He offered up a fervent prayer for their souls, then dismantled his equipment. A few minutes later a text message was on its way to Islamabad, telling of the terrible mistake that had been made.

Turning his back he didn't see the drama unfolding at the stricken house. A young man being physically restrained from throwing himself into the wreckage to search for survivors. It was a sensible precaution as the last remaining wall of the house collapsed inwards into the space the man had been heading for.

* * *

Youssef felt the blast before he heard it, the vibration travelling through the earth in a straight line as the sound bounced and ricocheted off the walls of the buildings to assault his ears a split second later. Smoke and dust rose in a plume. He had been in Abbottabad long enough to have a good sense of the source of the plume. His eyes opened wide in fear and he started to run. The heat of the day no longer mattered as he built up his stride to his full bowling pace and then beyond. He bounced off walls as he refused to slow down to round corners.

As he rounded the final obstacle between himself and his father's house he was left in no doubt. Where there had once been a happy home where he had lived for the past several weeks. Now there was just a heap of rubble, the dust settling back onto it. He howled in anguish at the loss of his family. He continued his headlong run towards the rubble, desperate to start searching for survivors. Surely someone must be alive. There was no time to waste.

Strong hands grabbed at him, the first few slipping off as his weight and speed carried him forward. But they slowed him enough and other hands completed the job, holding him back. He was forced almost to the ground and pinned in place.

"No brother. It isn't safe. You'll get yourself killed." Youssef heard the words but his brain refused to comprehend their meaning.

"My Father. My Mother. The children. I must help them." The men struggled to restrain him.

"No, brother. They are beyond your help now. Let Allah take them."

Youssef collapsed onto his knees, his body wracked with sobs, his laboured breathing combining into wheezing gasps. Satisfied that he wouldn't attempt to approach the wreckage of the house again, the men relaxed their grip. Sirens indicated the approach of rescue vehicles and they moved out of the way, anxious not to become casualties themselves. Youssef reluctantly went with them.

A lone man approached the distraught Youssef and he felt something hard bang into his side. He registered the presence of a weapon. They weren't unusual in this part of Pakistan, but he wasn't used to seeing them in this quiet neighbourhood.

"After you have buried your family, look for me outside the mosque." The man said, then turned and walked away. Youssef saw him climb into the front of a pick-up truck that already held half a dozen other armed passengers in its cargo space. As the rescue vehicles arrived the pick-up drove away at a pace that wouldn't attract attention.

Glossary

PAF   Pakistan Air Force.

RPV   Remotely piloted vehicle, a drone. Predator drones are unarmed, while Reaper drones can carry bombs, rockets and/or missiles.

2 - Bright Futures

Four Months Earlier

Youssef left the mosque with a broad grin on his face. Huddling into his coat in the sharp March breeze he hurried along Seven Sisters Road towards his home, anxious to share his news with his family. He felt the urge to skip, but resisted it. He was nearly twenty, a man, not some silly boy.

Sun glinted off the rain slicked roof tiles of the terraced houses. Traffic splashed along the road beside him, wetting Youssef's feet as they passed. Already the weather men were forecasting a hose pipe ban and Youssef chuckled at the absurdity of it on such a damp day. Weak sunshine struggled to break through the clouds as the rain slid away northwards.

Arriving at the small house, he let himself in and called out to see who was at home.

"Ssh, Youssef," His aunt scolded, coming down the stairs. "Your nephew is still sleeping."

Youssef's cousin Ata had come late in his aunt's life, much to the joy of the whole family, but his demands placed a great strain on his aunt and her only periods of respite were when the child slept.

"Good news, Auntie, I've been accepted."

"Please, Youssef, you know I prefer Aunt Aaleyah." She spoke with mock severity.

"Sorry, Aunt Aaleyah, but did you hear what I said? The Madrassa has accepted me. A full scholarship."

"Oh my." His aunt ran across the room and took his face in her hands and placed a sloppy kiss on Youssef's forehead. "That's wonderful. Your uncle will be so pleased. Have you told him yet?"

"No, he left the mosque straight after prayers to go back to work. It'll have to wait till this evening."

"Oh, so much to do. Now, go and get all your laundry, I must get it washed." Aunt Aaleyah flapped around the room, going from one corner to the other, not knowing where to start. The kitchen was her pride and joy, her private fiefdom. While her husband's rather traditional tastes dominated the rest of the house, this one room sparkled with stainless steel and the sheen of hardwood veneers. She had designed the whole edifice herself and nearly driven the salesman insane with her changing demands and specifications. She spent little time in the other rooms of the house, except to sleep.

"Easy, Aunt Aaleyah. I've got a couple of weeks before I have to go. There's plenty of time for you to do the laundry."

"My nephew the Imam." Mrs Ibrahim squealed with delight.

"No Aunt Aaleyah, your nephew the scholar. If I do well then perhaps I may be allowed to study to become an Imam. Now, are you sure that father and mother are expecting me?

"We've already agreed it with them. I knew you would be accepted. It is Allah's will. We spoke to your father last week and they are so excited by the prospect of you going home to live with them. They have a big house, so there is plenty of room."

"I can hardly think of it as my home. I've never lived there myself. But I'm so excited Aunt Aaleyah.

13

Going to Pakistan, studying at the Madrassa. It's going to be so wonderful." Youssef paced around the room, a dreamy look on his face.

"Remember Youssef, Pakistan is very different from England and Abbottabad isn't Finsbury. It's not just the heat, but a whole different culture. You must speak with Mumtaz Faraj. He lived longer in Karachi than he has lived here. He'll be able to advise you on how to behave. I don't want you disgracing the family name and nor will your father." She took her nephew's face in her hands again. "I'm going to miss you so much." Her face expressed a mother's love even though he was a nephew.

"You'll have the baby to keep you occupied, Aunt Aaleyah. You'll hardly know I've gone. I bet I'll be hardly through the door before Uncle Rafiq has my room rented out."

She tapped him playfully on the cheek. "Don't be rude about your uncle. He works hard and is careful with money. Other families would be happy to blessed with a man as good as him."

Youssef accepted the telling off in good heart. "Now, I'm just going to visit Mr Rahman to give him the good news."

"Are you sure that its Mr Rahman that you're going to see?" His aunt asked archly. While Mr Rahman was a good family friend she was quite sure that Youssef was far more interested in sharing his news with his daughter, Fatima.

Youssef just smiled and put his coat back on. "I'll be back in an hour." He announced, as he left the house.

As the door slammed shut behind her nephew, Mrs Ibrahim sat down at the kitchen table and wept. She was so happy that he had been accepted at the madrassa, but she was also going to miss him so much. She could feel the pain of her loss already, and he hadn't even gone yet. For almost ten years, since his parents returned to Pakistan, she had nurtured him and cared for him. He had been her whole universe. Now he was going to Pakistan and it might be years before she saw him again. She still had her baby, her own child, but losing her nephew would be like losing her firstborn.

* * *

Youssef was dismayed when Fatima didn't appear to share his happiness. They sat in the living room of her home, accompanied by an aged aunt who was acting as chaperone.

The aunt appeared to be engrossed in a TV show about antiques, but was keeping a careful eye on her niece at the same time. More importantly she was keeping a careful eye on the boy. She knew about boys and what they got up to when they thought no one was watching. Well, nothing would happen if she had anything to do with it. She looked across at her niece. Such beauty, not even her hijab could hide it. So like herself at that age.

"I'm sorry, Youssef. I know this means so much to you, but what if you forget me? What if you meet someone else?"

"It won't happen, Fatima." He longed to take her in his arms, to give her a hug of reassurance, but knew that it would result in him being evicted from the house for his boldness. "Firstly I'm going to be studying at a Madrassa, and there are no girls there. And you know that in Pakistan the families of girls never let them go out alone, so how can I meet any? Besides, I have no desire to meet anyone else."

Fatima pouted. "Maybe not now, but when you've been away for a few months, who knows how you might feel. Maybe your father will have plans for you."

"I promise you Fatima, I'm not interested in meeting other girls. The only girl I'm interested in is you. My father knows this and accepts it. I'll spend all my time studying, and when I get back, perhaps, you know…"

She smiled shyly. "Are you proposing, Youssef?"

"You know that wouldn't be right. My father has to speak to your father, and that can't happen until I come back. Actually he will probably ask my Uncle Rafiq to talk to your father. Then, if I can get a job, a position at a mosque, maybe your father will agree." He paused and spent a long time looking at his finger nails. "But if I were to propose…"

"I would say yes. I wouldn't even need to think about it." She looked across at her aunt, hoping that she might have dozed off, but was disappointed to find that she was still engrossed in the TV programme. Fatima was a good girl, but she would have been willing to risk a quick kiss if her aunt wasn't watching.

"I'm going to miss you so much, it will break my heart when you go."

"I'll phone every week. I promise."

"It isn't enough."

"My father has a PC, maybe we could Skype."

"If I see any Skyping going on there will be trouble." The aunt said, not understanding what the word meant.

The two youngsters laughed. "Auntie, Skyping is talking to each other using a computer." The girl explained, thinking 'Oh for a few minutes of privacy'.

"That better be all it means." The old woman grumbled, but returned to watching her TV programme.

"It always amazes me that you want to become an Imam, Youssef. You were such a mischievous little boy. Pulling my hair and getting into trouble all the time."

"I know, but that was when I was nine or ten. I've grown up a lot since then."

"But an Imam, a holy man. It's such a big change. Cricketer I could understand. You love cricket."

"But I love Allah as well. You remember old Mr Chaudhri who used to live three doors down from us?"

"Yes. I remember him. He was such a good man."

"Exactly. He was a good man. He didn't just go to the mosque on Friday like a lot of other people. He really tried to live his life by the words of the Prophet, all blessings be upon him. When he became ill, before he died, I used to take meals round for him that my auntie made. I would sit with him while he ate and talk with him. It was inspiring to listen to him."

"So he was a good man. I don't see your point."

"That's because I haven't made it yet. He inspired me to try to live like him, but to do more. If Mr Chaudhri had been an Imam, he could have changed so many lives for the better. He set a good example of course, but he could have taught our people so much about what it really means to be a Muslim."

"Don't you think that our Imam does that now?"

"He teaches the word of the Prophet, blessings be upon him, and that is what he is required to do. But I never feel that he really gets the message across about

17

what it means to be a Muslim in today's world, especially in a country like Britain. Not in the way Mr Chaudhri explained it. The Imam teaches the way he would, if we lived in Islamabad."

"Give me an example."

"Well, you know that the Prophet advises against the drinking of alcohol. It makes men do stupid things. But in Britain alcohol is freely available. Look at Seven Sisters Road. How many shops are there that sell alcohol, and I don't mean pubs or restaurants? There must be a dozen or more and that doesn't even include the big supermarkets. Some of them are even owned by Muslims. So there is temptation at every turn. Can it therefore be a surprise that young Muslim men drink alcohol? Of course not. They are curious, so they try some. Maybe they like it, so they try some more. Then one day they find out what the Prophet really meant, when they drink too much and are ill, or end up in a police cell because they did something stupid while under the influence of alcohol. Maybe they will learn the lesson and maybe they won't."

"So what was Mr Chaudhri's answer? Did he have one?"

"Of course. He said you should take these young men into a room and give them alcohol. Let them have their fill and let them do stupid things. But make sure you capture it on video and play it back to them when they are sober again. Let them see how stupid they have been, but in a controlled way, where they can't do harm to others."

"I don't think the mosque committee would approve of that."

"Of course they wouldn't, but that doesn't make it a bad idea. Sometimes telling people that something is wrong just makes it more attractive. Look at the number of Muslim boys who chase after English girls. We are told to respect women and that sex before marriage is wrong, but that doesn't stop those boys wanting sex, and if they can't get it from Muslim girls they will go and get it where they can, just like the alcohol."

"So are you suggesting that you also put boys in a room with girls and let them see what happens?" Fatima shot a glance across to her auntie, fearing she might react to what she had said, but the auntie was engrossed in her TV programme.

Youssef went red, realising that he had been caught out by the logic of his own argument. "Perhaps there are things that will work in some circumstances and not others. But you see what I mean. Show people rather than tell them."

"But they can see what happens when people drink alcohol. They can see it any Friday or Saturday night outside the pubs and nightclubs."

"And Mr Chaudhri had an explanation for that as well. It's like drug users. Drug users say that they can control their habit, even when it is clear that the habit controls them. It's the same with alcohol. The young men who drink think that they are in control when they aren't. You must show people that they can't control themselves when they are drunk. It's almost the definition of being drunk.

The people that are seen outside of the pubs and nightclubs are unbelievers. No Muslim would dare allow himself to be seen that way for fear of what his family would say. But it doesn't stop young Muslim men from drinking and it doesn't stop them doing stupid things. Anyway, it's only a theory. Maybe it wouldn't work, but it was a practical proposal. Just telling people not to do something doesn't seem to work by itself."

"So that's what makes you want to become an Imam."

"I think so. Yes, trying to find new ways of dealing with old problems, but at the same time keeping Allah at the centre of our lives, where he should be. I'm not saying that Mr Chaudhri was right in all things, but at least he was thinking about the issues, not just reciting prayers."

"Well, I think I understand now, at least a little better. It is hard to live in a modern world. I should know. Look at the rows I have had with my father about going to college."

"Exactly. We forget that this is a modern country which grew without the benefit of Islam to guide it. If we want to fit into it and also retain our faith we have to view things differently. Just before I came over here my auntie reminded me that there are cultural differences that we have to deal with. It doesn't mean that we have to abandon our faith, but we do have to consider how our children view the world which we expect them to live in."

"We don't have any children. Not yet."

"But that doesn't mean that we won't have any, does it?"

The elderly auntie's antenna twitched at the talk of children. "I think Youssef has been here long enough." She announced. "Perhaps it is time for you to let him return to his family now."

* * *

In a side street not far away from where Youssef sat with Fatima and her aunt, 'Lofty' Lofthouse was getting out of his car. He hauled his rucksack off of the back seat and walked the few paces to the front door of a house. It wasn't his house, but he did have a front door key which he used to let himself in. It had an empty feel about it, as though it had been waiting for someone to arrive. Emma was at work at that time of day, so Lofty would be on his own until she came home.

Emma had been lucky to have a place like this to herself. With London property prices the way they were, and rents so high, few single women could afford such luxury. Most women of her age either lived at home or shared with others. It was the joint benefit of an inheritance and indulgent parents. They had inherited it and Emma had nagged them into letting her rent the house at well below the market rate. Her sister was furious at not having thought of it herself.

He dropped his rucksack onto the floor of the hall and headed towards the kitchen. Hunger nagged at him after the long drive from Wiltshire. Searching the fridge he found the makings of a sandwich. Bread, ham and cheese were quickly assembled, accompanied by a large mug of tea.

Emma would be surprised at his early arrival. Pleasantly surprised, Lofty hoped. Normally the weekend didn't start until the late afternoon, depending on exactly what time the Battalion stood down, but this weekend they were dismissed immediately after the morning parade. Apparently they were in for a busy time, starting from Monday, so the CO wanted everyone to have one last full weekend break before the pressure was applied.

Lofty made himself comfortable in the familiar living room. The room reflected Emma's tastes perfectly. The furniture was inexpensive but comfortable and the walls were decorated with framed photographs of her family interspersed with modern prints and black and white images of street scenes. The room was uncluttered by ornaments or bric-a-brac, though she had allowed some carefully selected books to decorate the large coffee table. Books were as much a part of Emma as her hair style. The room was spotlessly clean, as though dust never dared to show itself.

One day they would buy a house together and would furnish it in a way that suited them both. That was what marriage was all about. But this had been Emma's house before he had even met her, so he didn't want to make his mark on the place.

Lofty was dozing on the settee, the TV showing a programme on house hunting, when he was roused by the sound of the front door opening.

Emma spied the rucksack lying in the hall and went straight into the living room. "Lofty darling," she cried out, rushing to give him a hug. "What a lovely surprise. I wasn't expecting you till this evening." She was as neat and tidy as her home, from her carefully shaped auburn hair to the patent leather flat heeled shoes that she wore.

Lofty gave her a lingering kiss before explaining. "We were stood down early. Apparently we're going to be working hard for the next few months, so they stood us down this morning. Now, how are you?"

"Missing you madly, lover. Come on, let me show you how much." She grabbed his hand and pulled him towards the doorway. Lofty didn't resist as she led him up the stairs. Downstairs was off limits for what Emma intended.

* * *

"Is it significant, letting you go early for the weekend?" Emma was curled up in Lofty's arms, snuggled up beneath the sheets.

"I can only think of one reason. It's no secret that we're due for a tour, so I'm guessing they're going to announce it on Monday, then we'll start the training programme."

"Afghanistan?" She whispered the word, almost frightened to say it more loudly in case it brought bad luck.

"Where else? It's a six month tour, so if we start training now we'll be ready to go at the end of September. That includes embarkation leave as well, of course. Roulement months are April and October."

"You'll definitely be going with them, the Battalion I mean?"

"Of course. I'm a Platoon Sergeant. Where my platoon goes I go."

"And you'll be away six months. What will I do without you?"

"Get through a lot of batteries I expect."

Emma slapped his arm, then pulled it closer around herself. "Cheeky. I don't have anything like that."

"I'll buy you one as a going away present."

"No you won't" The hard edge to her voice told Lofty she wasn't joking. He grinned behind her head. He'd do it just for a laugh. Maybe post it to her the day he flew out. And a big box of batteries to go with it.

Emma drifted into thought as Lofty dozed off. She had known Lofty was a soldier when she had met him, but as she got to know him better she started to think of the army as a competitor for her man's affections.

At first she had thought things might change when they were married, that she would learn to love the army just as he did, but she couldn't quite get the hang of it. He enjoyed being a soldier so much that she felt excluded. He had asked her to move down to Wiltshire to be closer to him, but she hadn't fancied the idea. Maybe that had been a mistake.

During the few weekends she had spent down there with him, attending Sergeants' Mess functions and sports events, she found she had little in common with his friends or their wives. They were so wrapped up in the army life that it was all they seemed to talk about. And the jargon! She thought they were talking a foreign language half the time. Like just now; what the hell did roulement mean? Perhaps you had to live in a garrison, surrounded by other soldier's wives, in order to understand how it all worked. The idea still didn't appeal. Down there she wouldn't be Emma Lofthouse, she knew. She would be Emma, wife of Sgt Lofthouse. That was how every woman she had met had been introduced: "wife of".

Then there was the politics. Everyone had a rank, and the wives and girlfriends seemed to take on the rank of their men. Emma recalled a conversation she'd had in the Sergeants Mess one night and the embarrassment it had caused. She had been introduced to the wife of the Regimental Sergeant Major (RSM) and they had been chatting when one of the other wives had come up and mentioned an excursion that was planned for the next day. Emma had said that it sounded interesting and that she would love to go along as well. She had been rewarded with a cold look and a flat statement that it was only the Warrant Officers' wives who were going, before the woman turned and walked away. The RSM's wife had tried to smooth things over but Emma knew she had committed a serious social gaff.

Emma briefly considered putting her foot down and asking Lofty to come out of the army and get a proper job. One where they could live in London and he would come home at nights and not just at weekends. One where she wouldn't have to wait six months for him, dreading the phone ringing in case it was bad news, but also dreading it not ringing in case he had grown tired of her. She dismissed the idea. Lofty loved the army and she loved Lofty. It wasn't his fault that she didn't seem to fit the mould of a military Stepford wife.

But there had to be something she could do, or she was faced with a life of loneliness with him down in Wiltshire, or Afghanistan, while she stayed up here in Finsbury Park. That wouldn't work either. Friday night was curry night, so they would talk about it at the restaurant, over dinner.

Maybe she should have a chat with her Mum. Mum always seemed to know what to do. When she had cried over her first boyfriend, it had been Mum that had helped her to heap up the photos of him and set fire to them in the BBQ, laughing about how he would regret dumping her one day. When she had been trying to decide what to study at college it had been Mum who had encouraged her to follow her heart, not her head. There was no point in studying a subject that you have no feeling for, she had said, and she had been right.

Unlike some of her friends she hadn't had to struggle to maintain an interest in her studies.

Mum liked Lofty. That was a good thing. She would have the best advice to offer on the subject.

* * *

Lofty could feel the tension between them. It had started as soon as they got out of bed to get ready for their regular visit to the Indian restaurant, and had grown ever since.

He could understand it, to a point. He was going to be up to his ears in work for the next few months and then would be half way round the world for another 6 months, their only contact being by e-mail and the odd telephone call. Emma would worry about him, she was bound to. He wondered what he could do to make things easier for her.

Lofty glanced across the table at his wife, nibbling unenthusiastically at a poppadum, and realised how much he loved her. All week long, back at the barracks, he longed for the weekend so that he could be with her again. Drinking in the Sergeants Mess or down at the pub with blokes from the Platoon just weren't what he wanted any more. He wanted to be with Emma. Sundays were torture. The whole day marred by the prospect of having to leave in the evening to return to his solitary room in the Sergeant's Mess.

They had met when he'd gone to see an old school friend. The plan had been to go out for a drink with him, but he'd already made arrangements to meet his girlfriend. A phone call later and the girlfriend had set up a blind date, with her old school friend Emma as the other party.

Lofty and Emma had both been nervous, but Lofty told a silly story about an incident at school and that had broken the ice. By the end of the evening Lofty knew that he had to see Emma again. He stood on the steps of the pub and nervously asked her out. She agreed and a date was set for the following weekend, this time just the two of them. They had eaten in that same Indian restaurant and had done so ever since, almost every Friday night for three years. Six months before, they had got married, with Lofty in his best dress uniform and Emma looking like she had stepped out of the pages of a bridal magazine.

"You look a bit distracted, Emms. Something I should know?"

"I'm sorry Lofty. I'm afraid that your news about Afghanistan has knocked me sideways a bit."

"I thought it might, but you knew it had to come sometime."

"But that was a bit like saying it's tomorrow, and knowing that tomorrow never comes. Now it has though, hasn't it?"

"It goes with the territory. You know that."

"Your territory Lofty, not mine, at least not until now. And it's not just Afghanistan. That's bad enough. But when you come back you'll still be in Wiltshire and I'll still be here." She waved her hand to take in the neighbourhood along with the restaurant.

"We've talked about this before. You could move down there. We're entitled to a married quarter and I reckon you could get a job on the garrison, or maybe in Trowbridge. But you said you didn't want that."

"Well maybe it's time to think about it again. How long have you got left on your current engagement?"

"Three years. I can give a years' notice to leave, but it wouldn't make any difference. Once we're put on warning for Afghanistan we can't leave until we come back. It would be bad for morale otherwise."

"Have you thought about leaving?"

"To tell you the truth, no I haven't. You know how I feel about the army. It's my life."

"You've told me that enough times, but I've never really understood why. It's just a job, after all."

"Not to me. To me it's a way of making a difference."

"How do you mean?"

"Well, my Dad died doing it. I've told you how he died in Northern Ireland. Well, the army were there to keep the Nationalists and the Loyalists apart. To stop them killing each other."

"They killed your father."

"I know. But he died doing what he believed in. Now it's my turn. This isn't just a job to me, it's a way of making a difference. Look at what we did in Bosnia and Kosovo. We saved hundreds of thousands of lives just by being there."

"And Iraq?"

"Well, maybe we shouldn't have got involved in that one, but I think we made a difference there as well. Saddam Hussein killed anyone who opposed him."

"And hundreds of thousands died in the war and afterwards."

"True. I can't argue against that, but it wasn't because of the military. We did what we were told to by the politicians, as always. It was them that got it wrong."

"And Afghanistan. What are we doing there?"

"Well, first of all we're stopping it from becoming a safe haven for terrorists. That was where Osama Bin Laden had his base, remember. Secondly we're stopping the Taliban from taking over the country and making people's lives a misery."

"But it's not our country. It's not for us to say who should govern it."

"No it isn't. But the Afghans should be able to decide that for themselves, but they can't if the Taliban are running the show. They've never stood for election, and they never will, because they know they wouldn't win. So they're trying to take power regardless of the what the people want. It's our job, my job, to make sure that doesn't happen."

"Well, it's hard to argue against that. You sound very sure about it all."

"If I didn't believe what we were doing was right, I couldn't stay in the army."

"Well, I can appreciate that. So where does that leave us? When you come back you'll still be in Wiltshire and I'll still be in London."

"We could get a married quarter within weeks. You can move down and there will be plenty of time for you to settle in, make friends, before I have to go. Maybe you'll feel less lonely if you're surrounded by other people in the same boat."

Emma considered his answer as she toyed with her starter, pushing a slice of cucumber round her plate. She didn't have much of an appetite.

"I'm a London girl, a city girl." She said at last. "What would I do in the middle of the country?"

"I was a London boy before I joined up. Half the wives are from this part of the world. I wouldn't be surprised if you went to school with some of them.

They seem to fit in alright. It's a Garrison, not Emmerdale Farm. It's got its own shops, its own cinema. A big gym, a swimming pool, and all within walking distance. If you want somewhere bigger with more shops then you get in the car and go to Bath."

"I went to Bath once. It's nice."

"There you go. So it's not all bad, is it?"

"I'm not sure about a married quarter though. It sounds a bit institutionalised."

"OK, we could rent somewhere, or even buy a place of our own. Close enough for me to get to work, but somewhere you'd feel more at home. There's some nice towns in that part of the world. You've seen it. It's very pretty."

"You'd be happy to buy a house?"

"It would make more sense than renting a place. I've got enough savings for a deposit and to buy furniture. There's some real bargains to be had right now. It would mean you could get more involved in the social life, the Sergeants Mess. Meet some new people and make new friends."

"What about work?"

"They have librarians in Wiltshire as well, you know, and in Somerset. Besides, with your qualifications you could walk into a job just about anywhere. You never know, there might even be something on the Garrison."

"I'll tell you what. I'll meet you half way. I'll look for a job, and if I can get one then I'll move down there. We'll give it a try." There was no way, Emma felt, that she could contemplate moving without being sure of employment. It wasn't the money, but it was the independence that a wage gave her. She wasn't going to be anyone's 'wife of'.

Lofty stretched his hand across the table and placed it over one of Emma's. "I love you Babe. We'll make this work, I promise you."

"It better had Lofty. My sister will be waiting on the doorstep for me to move out, so there'll be no coming back here."

With the short term future decided Emma's appetite returned and she started a methodical demolition of her chicken chat.

Glossary

Barracks The permanent base of a military unit, comprising domestic accommodation for both single and married soldiers, administration and training buildings, armoury, storage buildings and workshops. Very often named after a significant military figure, eg Wellington Barracks in London. A building providing domestic accommodation for unmarried soldiers is a barrack block, while SNCOs and Officers live in the Sergeants and Officers messes respectively.

Garrison A geographic area providing infrastructure, eg barracks, for a large number of soldiers, usually in different units. It may consist of a number of different estates spread around the geographic area and can be quite extensive. Catterick Garrison, for example, houses around 12,000 soldiers and their families.

Roulement The routine deployment of troops on operational duties, usually to relieve a unit already in place.

RSM	Regimental Sergeant Major, the senior most NCO in a battalion or regiment. He is responsible for discipline within the unit and also for the organisation of ceremonial occasions.
Sgt	Sergeant.
SNCO	Senior Non-Commissioned Officer, NCOs (see above) of Sergeant or higher rank.

3 - War and Peace

The briefing room buzzed with conversations. The mood was tense as the officers and non-commissioned officers of the battalion speculated about the purpose of the briefing. The fact that they were going to Afghanistan was an open secret, but that didn't inhibit speculation about what they would be doing there, what dangers they might have to face and how many of them might not come back.

Sgt 'Cobber' Bruce squeezed himself in beside Lofty and turned to give him a broad grin. "Here we go again, Lofty old son. Back to the sharp end. I hope we see some action this time."

"Be careful what you wish for Cobber. Remember the last lot?"

Cobber was Lofty's oldest friend in the battalion, perhaps his oldest friend anywhere, come to think of it. He had been Lofty's Section Commander when he had arrived from the training depot with no more than fluff on his cheeks, and had been his Platoon Sergeant when they had gone to Afghanistan four years earlier. It had been he that took Lofty under his wing when he found out that, like himself, Lofty was a keen footballer. It had also been Cobber that had pulled Lofty up short when he nearly triggered the trip wire of a roadside bomb near Musa Qala.

"You just remember what your Uncle Cobber taught you and you'll be alright."

"Well, you just keep you head down, Cobber, or you'll never live to issue the Colonel with his parking ticket."

Cobber was twelve years Lofty's senior and was now the C Company QM Sergeant. He had risen about as far as he ever would, but was happy with his lot. This would be his last tour of duty before completing his twenty two year engagement and leaving the army to take his pension. He joked about becoming a parking warden in Barnet and clamping all the officers cars at Inglis Barracks. Lofty knew he would miss him.

The RSM appeared next to the lectern at the front of the room and the volume of noise began to reduce. As he cleared his throat the remaining conversations immediately ceased. "Parade, Parade attention." His words of command could have been heard in the next county. The soldiers stiffened in their seats, backs upright, their fists clenched and resting on their knees. There was insufficient space for them to stand, which would have been normal practice when the Commanding Officer entered the room, but the numbers of people packed into the briefing room on this occasion prevented such formality.

"Thank you RSM," The CO said. "Good Morning ladies and gentlemen. Please sit easy." Around the room shoulders dropped a fraction and palms unclenched, but otherwise there was no visible relaxation. Note pads were lifted off knees and pens made ready.

Lieutenant Colonel Max Gascoigne arranged his papers on the lectern and nodded towards the back of the room. The most junior soldier present, a clerk from Headquarters, switched on the ceiling mounted projector and a picture of the Regimental Badge appeared on the screen positioned to the Colonel's left, the maroon and yellow background provided by the regimental colours casting a warm glow across the room.

The symbolism of the badge wasn't lost on the soldiers. Nearly three hundred years of history were encapsulated in the image. Three hundred years of heroism and sacrifice on behalf of the their country. Now the battalion would add a new chapter to the story. The mood in the room was summed up by the motto engraved on either side of the Prince of Wales feathers: 'Ich Dein', I Serve.

"I don't think it's any secret," he opened, "that the Battalion is overdue for a tour and it wouldn't take the brightest mind to work out that it would probably be Afghanistan. I am therefore pleased to confirm that we will be deploying on Op Herrick as part of 109 Mechanised Brigade. This briefing is to provide the details and outline the plans for the next few months as we undertake the training programme in preparation for our departure. Please make sure that your loved ones have up to date photos to remind them of what you look like, because they're not going to see much of you in the up-coming weeks."

A ripple of polite but dutiful laughter went around the room.

"The good news is that the Battalion will stand down for two weeks in September to give you all time to be with your families before we head off." He turned a page and the clerk clicked the mouse of the lap top to bring up the first slide, which showed a map of the part of Helmand province that they would deploy to.

For the next hour the CO outlined the training plan and the individual assignments for the four rifle companies that made up the battalion, filling in the minutiae of military preparations for war. Lofty forced his mind to concentrate on taking notes so that he could brief his own men when he saw them later that morning.

After the briefing was over Lofty joined Cobber in his office in the QM Stores, where Cobber oversaw his small empire. They drank tea from oversized mugs, lounging in a pair of salvaged arm chairs.

"That's what soldiering is about." Cobber commented on the briefing. "Making sure that the people get democracy."

"Is that what you think we'll be doing there? I thought it was mainly about not getting ourselves killed." Lofty replied. He had heard this lecture from Cobber before.

"There is that as well, but the people really want us there, you know. I remember the first time I went, not long after it all kicked off. The people were so pleased to be rid of the Taliban. They had made their lives miserable. No music, no entertainment, nothing. All they could watch on TV was mullah's ranting at them or rotten drama's in which the hero always strayed from the true path and where Mohamed guided him back onto it."

"Well, isn't all drama like that, a bit? You know, loss and redemption?"

"Yes, but you don't want that every time you turn the box on. Anyway, it's not just about the TV programmes. The people had no say in how their country was governed. The Taliban did whatever they wanted, and if anyone argued they were put on trial under Sharia law, usually on some trumped up charge. You know they stoned little girls to death for witchcraft. Nine year old girls."

"Really?" Lofty was astounded by this revelation.

"Oh yes. I met the mother of one of them. Her daughter had attracted the attention of the local Imam, but the mother thought she was too young to marry, so she wouldn't allow it. Quite right too. Nine year olds can't get married, can they? Anyway, in retaliation the Imam accused the little girl of witchcraft and she was stoned to death."

"Wow, I must admit I'd never heard of that."

"And it wasn't an isolated incident either. If women didn't come across for the right people they'd be accused of adultery. If men didn't pay the right bribes then they would be accused as well. It was archaic, the way things were run. Like they were living in the dark ages."

"Well, I can see why the people would be glad to see the back of the Taliban."

"And that, Lofty me old son, is why we have to be there. Someone has to look after those people until their own government can take over. And that someone is us. You and me and those lads out there."

Lofty looked at his watch and swallowed the rest of his tea. "Time I was over at the training room to brief my lads. And if any of them ask what we're doing there I'll tell them what you just told me."

* * *

As Lt Col Gascoigne drew his briefing to a close, 116 miles away in one of the cafeterias at the University of North London, Youssef met up with Fatima to spend a few stolen minutes together. One of Fatima's friends sat close by, reading a book, close enough to count as a chaperone but not so close as to intrude on the couple's privacy. They sat a few feet apart in order to maintain the correct level of propriety. The buzz of student life eddied around them as the students gathered at the start of the academic day.

"So what will you do while I'm away?" Youssef asked as a conversation starter.

"I'll carry on studying, of course. If I don't finish my course then I can't qualify."

"I admire how hard you work. I think we'll make a great team."

"How do you mean?" She asked.

"Well, faith is a matter for the heart. But if your head is troubled then your heart can never be at peace. You will look after the head while I take care of the heart."

"I hadn't thought of it that way." Fatima smiled at him. "That's so clever."

"Not really. I stole it from Mr Chaudhri. But there's more to it than that. If it's possible to understand why people behave in certain ways, understand their motivation, then it is so much easier to work out how to help them spiritually."

"That is very true. Advertisers spend huge amounts of money to work out what makes people buy things and how to tap into their sub consciousness, so why shouldn't an Imam use the same techniques."

"Precisely. See, you have worked out my own motivations already."

Fatima laughed and Youssef was pleased to have lifted her mood. Both of them were filled with thoughts of his departure and it saddened them both, even though they knew it was necessary.

"My father was pleased to hear about your scholarship." Fatima said quietly.

"That doesn't fill you with delight, I can tell."

"No, it doesn't. He thinks that a spell at a Madrassa will make you understand the role of women in the world of Islam, and you'll persuade me to give up my studies. Maybe even not let me work when we get married."

Youssef was pleased by her choice of the word 'when', rather than 'if' in relation to the prospect of marriage.

"It is difficult for him. He was raised in Pakistan and is used to the Pakistani view of the world, and women's place in it. I'm of a different world and a different generation. You are clever, you have ideas and ambitions. I think it would be wrong of me to stand in your way. The Prophet's own wife, peace be upon them both, was a business woman. She employed him to do the things she wasn't allowed to do under the constraints of the times, and that was even before he had heard Allah's words. I can't imagine him being so opposed to women working."

"Did Mr Chaudhri have anything to say on the subject."

"Oh yes. He said that on a farm it makes sense for the woman to stay at home and mind the children, to make the meals and mend the clothes. It is a division of labour. He also said that to do such tasks a woman didn't need an education. But we aren't on a farm. We live in an expensive city. If men and women don't both work then the children go hungry."

"Mr Chaudhri was a man ahead of his times."

"No, he was a man who understood that the same rules can't be applied in London as they are in a village in Pakistan. If women just stay at home and make the chapattis then pretty soon there will be no money to buy the flour."

"So that's my role is it? To work to buy flour to make your chapattis." Fatima teased him.

Youssef was just about to snatch at the bait when he saw the twinkle in Fatima's eye."

"Yes, woman." He reposted. "You will work to keep me in the style I am accustomed to. You will have to take my auntie's place when we're married, and she waits on me hand and foot."

"And if you think that, then you have another think coming, Youssef Haq Ibrahim."

He laughed. "We will share the chores. But first I have to be educated, so I must go to Pakistan."

Fatima lowered her eyes, struggling to hold back a tear. "I will pray for your safe keeping."

"That is selfish." Youssef responded. "Pray instead that Allah keeps all his children safe."

"Always thinking of others, aren't you Youssef. That's why I love you."

The young woman acting as chaperone looked up sharply at the mention of love. It didn't do to use such words in public. Fatima caught her look and lowered her voice. "I'm sorry. That is a very bold thing to say."

"I think there's nothing wrong about talking of love. So long as we keep the laws we will remain pure in both our bodies and our hearts."

"But it is so difficult, Youssef. You have no idea....."

"I think I do." He interjected before she could compromise them again. "I have feelings too. But we must stay pure as the Prophet, all blessings be upon him, has told us that Allah commanded."

At that moment Fatima had a few words she would have liked to have said to the Prophet, had he been there, but she recognised the wisdom of Youssef's words. It would serve no purpose for her to bring shame on her family. She had enough difficulties at home without adding that to her burden.

"There are other things I'm worried about." She said, deftly changing the subject. "I have heard how men who go to Madrassas can become radicalised. They end up as terrorists, or fighting in foreign countries."

"Yes, I've heard that as well, and I'm sure it happens. But I have chosen this Madrassa not just because it is close to my family in Abbottabad. I also chose it because it doesn't teach that Allah wants us to kill."

"That isn't the only way that young men become radicalised." Fatima countered.

"I know, but I remember the words of our prayers. Every time we pray we praise Allah and call him the most compassionate and the most merciful. If he is compassionate then he doesn't need mortal men to kill for him, and if he is merciful then he would forgive men anyway, not have them killed. I could never worship Allah if he asked me to kill for him."

"You would deny your faith?"

"No. I would still believe in Allah. I just wouldn't worship him. However, that will never apply. Allah doesn't wish me to kill, I'm sure of it."

"Is that more of Mr Chaudhri?"

"No, that is more of Youssef Haq Ibrahim."

Fatima looked at her watch and gave a gasp of surprise. She stood up abruptly. "I'm sorry, Youssef, but I'm late for a tutorial. You will visit me this evening?"

"Of course."

She gave him a wave and she and her friend hurried off across the crowded cafeteria.

"I love you." Youssef whispered towards her receding back.

Glossary

CO   Commanding Officer, normally of a battalion or regiment.

Op HERRICK   The codename applied to the overarching military operations being conducted by British forces in Afghanistan.

QM or Quartermaster   The officer in a unit, usually a Major, responsible for providing the equipment that soldiers require to live and fight. He is also responsible for accommodation and catering. QMs are often long serving soldiers promoted from the non-commissioned ranks. Most units also have a quartermaster of Sergeant rank in each company to allow them to operate independently.

4 - Jihad Justified

The tent was loud with the sounds of men sleeping. Youssef lay in the dark, aching in every muscle from the unusual punishment his body had experienced over the recent weeks. It would soon be Fajr, the first prayer time of the day, and the sleeping men would wake, but sleep was eluding Youssef once again.

Youssef liked lying in the dark, remembering his former life. It had been so wonderful to be with his parents again and his little brother and sister. Wahid had been a toddler when he had last seen him and Noor hadn't even been born. Tears stung his eyes as he recalled the last time they had been together.

He had been dripping with sweat as he and Wahid came back from their game of cricket. Wahid was mad to play and was always waiting at the door for Youssef to arrive home from the Madrassa, bat in hand. They played in the street using a box with stumps painted on it as a wicket. Other children would gather and join in, while Youssef coached them as they played. "Hold the bat this way.", "When you release the ball just give your wrist the slightest of twists.", "Always throw the ball to the end where the wicket keeper is if you want to be sure of a run out." They had followed his advice and he was pleased to see how much they enjoyed their games.

From a loose group of children they had started to form themselves into teams, this street against that. The children were used to the heat but Youssef struggled with it, but he had fun and the children seemed to appreciate his coaching.

"And how was my opening batsman today?" Youssef's father asked jokingly as they entered the house.

"He's coming along well, father. Aren't you Wahid?"

"I scored twenty runs, and then Youssef made me retire so that someone else could bat."

"It's only fair, Wahid." Youssef commented. "The other children need their turn as well if they are to become as good a batsman as you."

The child gave a beaming smile, basking in the glow of his big brother's praise.

"Youssi, Youssi, play with me now." Hearing their voices Noor came running into the room. She was jealous of the time her big brother spent with Wahid and always demanded her share of his attention.

"In a moment, Princess. I must shower first. You wouldn't want to play with someone who was all smelly, would you?"

The little girl's nose wrinkled in mock distaste. "OK, I'll get the things ready."

It would be another doll's tea party, Youssef knew. She loved that game and never seemed to tire of playing it. Youssef had yet to work out all the rules, but Noor had very strict ideas on what should happen and when. He wondered where she had learnt them.

"And how was the madrassa today?" Youssef's father asked.

"Very good, father. We debated the role of women in the world. I had no idea that the Prophet, peace be upon him, had such an enlightened view of women."

"For God's sake don't tell your mother that or we'll all be in trouble." He joked.

"Don't tell your mother what?" Mrs Ibrahim asked as she entered the room, passing through on her way to the kitchen.

"The Prophet's view's on women."

"Ah yes, so much more enlightened than your father's." Mrs Ibrahim gave his father a look, then winked at Youssef behind her hand. "What would you like for dinner tonight, Youssef."

"See, you get a choice. I get what I'm given." Grumbled Mr Ibrahim. Youssef laughed.

"I'll have whatever you're making for Daddy." Youssef called after her. He wondered if he and Fatima would one day be like his parents. So much in love that they could grumble and moan at each other without ever taking offence, and incapable of being separated for more than a few hours. Was that what all marriages were like after twenty five years? Youssef hoped it was. It felt comfortable.

Youssef went for his shower. Once more refreshed, he played Noor's game with her until it was time for the children to go to bed. After dinner Youssef and his parents watched some television, though Youssef found the programmes bland compared to what he had watched in the UK. He realised that TV companies in Pakistan operated by more rigorous rules than they did back in England, but this made the plots of the drama so tame compared to something like Holby City or Midsummer Murders. He had never thought he would, but he even missed the constant gloom of Eastenders.

Youssef cried at the memories, realising now how wonderful those few short weeks had been, getting to know his family again, getting to know his little brother and sister. He felt a pain in his chest that had no physical cause but hurt just as much.

And then there had been the days after they had died. It was Islamic custom for the dead to be buried before sunset on the day they died, but it had taken two days for the work parties to recover the bodies of his mother and father, of young Wahid who was such a promising cricketer and Noor, the little princess, as her father, his father, had called her. After burying them Youssef returned to the mosque and sat on the steps. He had never felt so alone. Neighbours had sheltered him for the last two nights, but now Youssef was unsure what to do. Perhaps the man with the gun might have an answer.

As the sun moved across the sky Youssef shifted his position to make best use of the small amount of shade. Flies buzzed around and the energy sapping heat bore down. Passers-by cast curious looks but the boy's melancholy demeanour discouraged conversation. The young man took his Koran from its place of safety inside his clothing and sought some comfort from its teachings, but none came.

It was past the midday mealtime when the man appeared and sat down beside him. He was unarmed on this occasion.

"From your accent you aren't from around here, are you Youssef?" The man crossed his legs to make himself more comfortable.

"You know my name?" Was the surprised answer.

"It is essential for our safety that we know who our neighbours are. When you first came we asked a few questions. But our security was compromised never the less."

"The missile was meant for you?" Youssef frowned.

"Not for me, but for an important man in our organisation. He is safe now, well away from here."

"My family is dead though."

"Insha'Allah, it is the will of God. Where are you from?" The man's tone was light, even friendly, and Youssef found himself warming to him.

"London, England. A place called Finsbury Park."

"A Mujahedeen brother once preached at the mosque in Finsbury Park. Did you ever hear him?"

Youssef was surprised by the reference to Abu Hamza but then, he supposed, they had TV and the internet even here. "No. I moved from another place, Slough, and by then the mosque authorities had stopped him preaching inside. My uncle wouldn't let me attend the prayers that he led outside the mosque. And then Abu Hamza was arrested and put in prison. Now the British have sent him to America."

"Why did your uncle not let you attend the prayer meetings?"

"My father believed that Islam is a religion of peace and love, and Abu Hamza preached hatred. So my uncle acted as he believed my father would have done. I discussed it with my father when I arrived here and he said my uncle did right."

"Is that what you also believe?"

Youssef's brow furrowed in concentration. He stared out across the sunlit, dusty square in which the mosque was situated, trying to decide what he believed and what he didn't. "I have always believed that Allah would never ask us to kill. He is the compassionate one, there is no need for him to ask that of us. But now, all I can feel is anger. Anger towards the Americans for firing the missile. Anger towards Pakistan for providing refuge for men such as you. Anger against myself for not being able to save my family."

"You desire revenge for your family?"

"I don't know. Maybe. Is it ever right to kill?" Youssef turned to look at the man, searching his face for the answer.

"If one is engaged in Jihad, then it is not only right, it is essential. The enemies of Allah must be destroyed."

"I have heard it said that Jihad can be carried out by non-violent means."

"But not when the enemies of God are violent. If they kill Muslims, then Muslims must kill them. The kuffar's (unbelievers) own bible tells them 'an eye for an eye and a tooth for a tooth'."

"Will that bring my family back?"

"No, it will not, but it will assure you of a place beside them in Paradise. Youssef, we must free our Muslim brothers of the oppression of the West. We must once again return the world to the worship of Allah."

"The whole world?"

The man's face became sombre and his deep brown eyes willed Youssef to hear his message. "One day, yes, but for now we will settle for freeing Afghanistan. Then Pakistan, and from there we will send out our armies to defeat the infidels. It is Allah's will and it is what the Prophet, peace and blessings be upon him, tells us in the Koran."

Youssef pondered the man's words in silence for a few minutes and wondered which Sura of the Koran told of Allah's will with such clarity. It certainly wasn't one that Youssef was familiar with.

He had been raised by his father and uncle to be a man of peace. His destiny was to be an Imam, so his father had believed and so believed Youssef. But his parents and siblings had been brutally murdered, and that changed everything. If being an Imam was to serve Allah, then surely doing Allah's work to free Afghanistan from the infidels must be an even greater service?

"What is your name?" Youssef asked the man.

"You may call me Abisali."

The name meant warrior, and probably wasn't the man's real identity. "Abisali, even in my anger I'm not sure your way is the way for me. I still cannot believe that Allah would ask men to kill for him. That is a message from the past. When the Christians and the Jews were massed against us, taking the holy places from us, then it was right for us to defend against them, but that isn't the case now. I have read the western press. I know of the horrors that have been inflicted against the British and Americans by our people. That can't be right."

"It doesn't make it right that they should invade our lands, take our wealth and destroy our faith."

"An eye for an eye, brother. You said it yourself. They had to avenge their dead. I don't think it was right, but I can understand it. The men who instigated that act were up there." Youssef gave a nod in the direction of Afghanistan. "The Americans had to go and get him and to do that they had to defeat the Taliban who were giving him a safe haven. Would you have not done the same if the positions were reversed?"

"But they stayed. They are still there now. They conquered the country and now rule it through a puppet."

49

Youssef noted that Abisali didn't say 'our country', and wondered briefly what nationality the man might be. "They stay because they say the people don't want to be governed by the Taliban. They say that the people want democracy. So they held elections and now stay to protect the government that won those elections. They say they will leave when the government is capable of looking after the people without them."

Abisali spat on the ground. "They have done a good job on you, Youssef. You believe their lies."

"Why should their words be more lies than your words? By what right do you claim to do Allah's work?"

"The Prophet, all peace be upon him, has told us what to do. It is in the Holy Book. You have a copy in your hand."

"Show me." Youssef offered Abisali the green covered book.

The man turned away contemptuously. " I don't need to read the words to know they are true." Youssef suspected that Abisali might be illiterate and so couldn't back up his rhetoric by showing Youssef any examples.

The man seemed to have an idea. He gave Youssef a shrewd look, gauging the young man's beliefs and calculating how he might use them. "You are a clever young man, Youssef. Our cause could benefit from your intelligence. If I can't persuade you then perhaps there is someone who can. Will you meet me here tomorrow, at the same time?"

"If you like. I don't seem to have anywhere else to go at the moment."

Youssef bid the man good bye, then made his way back to the Madrassa. They offered him a bed in the students' dormitory for as long as he needed it, though they made it clear he would need to pay for his food. Youssef accepted gratefully.

* * *

The next day Youssef was taken north into the mountains. He knew that he was entering territory where the Government in Islamabad held little control, but with Abisali and a couple of armed guards in the pick-up truck with him he felt no fear. After a couple of hours of travelling they arrived in a small town in a lush green valley, high up in the mountains. Youssef thought it was the prettiest place he had seen since his arrival in the country

Abisali helped Youssef down from the back of the truck and took him towards a non-descript looking house. It was similar to Youssef's own family home in Abbottabad, though smaller. Four rooms were built around a courtyard, with flowers and vines growing on trellises. It had a feeling of coolness and calm, Youssef thought.

An old man came from one of the rooms and Abisali greeted him, kissing him on both cheeks and grasping his hands. Clearly Abisali respected the man. They conversed in low tones for a moment and then the man went over to sit cross legged on a rug in the most shaded corner of the courtyard. Abisali led Youssef across to join him and they also sat down on rugs and crossed their legs.

"This is Mohamed Dost Mohamed and he was once an Imam. He trained at the Islamic university in Cairo." Abisali introduced the old man. Youssef recognised the pre-eminence of the school where the old man had studied and bowed his head out of respect for the preacher. "He speaks only Arabic. Do you know that language?"

Youssef replied that he didn't. "I will interpret for you both then. Feel free to challenge what he says and to ask questions. If he cannot persuade you of the justice of our cause then I will take you back to Abbottabad and leave you in peace."

A young boy, the old man's grandson or great grandson thought Youssef, brought a tray of tea and sweet cakes. He smiled shyly at Youssef before hurrying away back to the safety of his mother.

For the next two hours the old man lectured Youssef, pointing to Sura in the Koran to illustrate his points. The Sura were written in Arabic, but it was easy enough for Youssef to find them in his own Koran, which was printed in both Arabic and Urdu.

"Firstly, my son," The old man began, "you must remember that there are four types of jihad. There is Jihad al-nafs or jihad against oneself, where one continuously strives to live by the teachings of the Prophet, all blessings be upon him, and to tolerate the burdens placed upon us by Allah. Secondly there is jihad al-Shaytaan, where one continuously strives to resist the temptations that Shaytaan places in front of us and which will condemn us to Hell if we submit to them. These two are obligatory for all true believers and failing to undertake them means not being able to enter Paradise. There is also jihad against the hypocrites, which we must undertake as a community to save the believer from himself. Finally there is jihad against the unbelievers and the tools of Shaytaan, which may become obligatory for some or for all under certain circumstances."

"I understand this, Sheikh." Youssef broke in, almost abashed at interrupting such an important cleric. "We have debated this in the mosque many times. However, I still don't see how this justifies killing."

"You will come to understand, my son." The cleric continued to outline his argument, building up from the personal jihad to the greater fight against evil. It took some time and Youssef found himself growing impatient, though he sensed that it would be fruitless to try to hurry the man. At last he got to the point.

"At first the Prophet was commanded by Allah not to fight. For ten years he obeyed that command. But then Allah commanded him to fight those who would fight him, but not those who left him alone." More tea arrived and the Imam poured cups for himself and his guests.

"Then it was commanded to the Prophet wage fard kafayyah, which places the obligation for jihad on the community as a whole. This is written in Sura al-Mughni, 9/163. What this means is that if not enough of the community wage jihad then they are all guilty of sin, but if sufficient do then the obligation is dropped. Too few people undertake the fard kafayyah so our whole religion is in jeopardy."

"Sheikh, I still don't understand why jihad is justified against the kuffar." Broke in Youssef, his frustration and impatience becoming more apparent.

"Ah, now I come to that. There are four justifications. First, when the Muslim is present in a jihad situation. Secondly when the enemy has come and attacked a Muslim land. Thirdly when the ruler mobilizes the people they must respond and finally when a person is needed and no one else can do the task except him.

Now, you are present in a jihad situation, for it is happening here and in Afghanistan. Allah says that you cannot turn your back on an enemy, for it is a sin to do so. Clearly the kuffar have attacked Muslim lands, and many of them. Clearly also leaders have mobilized the people to jihad. You may ask which leaders and I will answer: the Imams, the leaders of the Taliban, and many others. The Prophet said 'Listen and obey, even if your master is an Abyssinian slave'. So if a man becomes a leader then his words must be obeyed. Even I, humble as I am, am a leader and I too command people to jihad.

And as for you, young Youssef, you are needed. Fard kafayyah becomes fard 'ayn, a personal obligation, when you are needed. There are too few people obeying the fard kafayyah, but you can change that. You can change it by recruiting more people, or you can change it by engaging in jihad yourself. If you do neither than you do not obey the words of Allah as spoken to the Prophet, all blessings be upon him. If you don't obey then you place your soul in peril."

Youssef considered the Imam's words with care. He had indeed pointed out the passages of the Koran that described jihad and its justifications, but he already knew that they could be interpreted in many ways. The words of the Prophet were not always clear and in many ways they appeared like the writings of Nostradamus, the Frenchman that many Europeans considered to be a seer. Youssef knew that, but how could he argue with an Imam who had studied at the great Islamic university of Cairo? But he had one more question.

"Sheikh, when the jihad was first commanded the Muslim peoples were few and the kuffar were many. It is clear that the people of Islam, of the true faith, had to protect themselves and their lands. But now the people of Islam are many. We are dominant in Africa and in many parts of Asia. So how is jihad still justified?"

"You are a clever young man, you ask all the right questions. If you were to study at the great university in Cairo you would do well. To answer your question, the word of Allah does not give us a number. It doesn't tell us that when we are a million, or ten million or even a billion then jihad is no longer justified or permitted. It says only that when our lands are threatened or when we are killed by the kuffar, then jihad is not only permitted, it is a requirement. So the kuffar come to our lands and they take the oil and the minerals and leave our people poor. They send their soldiers and their tanks and they tell us it is for our own good, but it is a lie. So jihad is justified."

"There is still one thing I don't understand. Sheikh. The fighters who undertake jihad are killing Muslims as well as kuffar. How can this be permitted?"

"You forget jihad against the hypocrites. Any Muslim who doesn't undertake the fard kafayyah is a hypocrite, because they do not follow the teachings of the Prophet, all blessings be upon him. Therefore it is justified to punish them by killing them, just as it is justified to kill the kuffar."

Youssef realised that he had no argument against the old man. He was not wise enough or knowledgeable enough to do so. He was still not totally convinced, but he bowed his head in acknowledgement to the cleric. Abisali thanked the old man for his time and the two younger men made their way back to the pick-up truck.

"Did he convince you, Youssef?"

"I'm not sure. There are still questions unanswered." He shared his feelings with Abisali.

"I can see your confusion. But do you agree that the Sheikh made his case.

"He did that. Even if I still don't agree with his case." Youssef needed to buy himself some time to think, so he changed the subject. "What is an Egyptian Imam doing so high up in the mountains of Pakistan?"

"He wrote a pamphlet in support of the Muslim Brotherhood in Egypt, which brought him into conflict with the kuffar puppet Mubarak. He had to flee. With some help from us, he ended up here."

"Mubarak is no longer President. He could return now."

"No, the new man, Abdel Fattah el-Sisi, is just as much a puppet as Mubarak was. He would still be arrested. Besides, he is an old man, he has two young wives and four young children. Egypt is unstable yet, so he chooses to live here. He has said he will return if he is called, but until then he is content to live out his old age in this beautiful place."

As Youssef stared out over the valley, he agreed that it was a beautiful place.

"So what do you want to do now?" Asked Abisali. Youssef knew he wasn't just asking him what his plans for dinner might be.

"What choices do I have?"

"Easy. You can join us if you wish, join the jihad and gain the blessings of Allah, or you can go back to the Madrassa and continue your studies in peace. Or you could even go back home to England."

"If I choose the jihad?"

"There is a camp in the mountains, not far from the border with Afghanistan. You would be trained to fight as a warrior of the Jihad."

Youssef pondered his future. Could he, in all honesty, return to the madrassa and resume his studies? Would that be what his father wanted? Was it what Allah wanted? Youssef thought in both cases that it might not be. He made a silent bargain with his God. If he fought the jihad then Allah would allow him to take revenge on his family's killers.

So it had started. He went into the mountains of Waziristan with the man, he and a dozen other recruits. The roads had become narrower and eventually petered out into tracks. They finished the journey on foot, carrying their few possessions on their backs. That had been three weeks ago and now Youssef ached all over.

He had learnt many things. How to field strip an AK-47 assault rifle in under two minutes and reassemble it in under 90 seconds. He also learnt how to fire it, though he wasn't a great marksman. Soon, he had been told, he would be taught to fire the RPG7 rocket launcher. He had also learnt how the kuffar soldiers raped the women of Afghanistan and burnt the mosques and piled the Koran into bonfires.

The thought of the desecration of the Holy book made him reach out to touch his own copy and make sure it was safe.

They taught him how the kuffar weapons maimed the children and killed the peasant farmers in their fields. Each thing he learnt made him more angry and he hated them more for what they had done to his family, and what they continued to do to his Muslim brothers and sisters.

Electronic feedback split the night and the call to prayer was shouted by one of the sentries, acting as the camp's muezzin. Around him the other recruits stirred and coughed and farted their way into wakefulness. Youssef reached for his clothes and made ready to start another day.

Glossary

AK-47   An assault rifle capable of single shot or automatic fire. 7.62 mm calibre fed from a thirty round magazine. The weapon of choice of most of the world's terrorist groups.

RPG   Rocket propelled grenade. An unguided explosive projectile fired from a tube that is rested on the shoulder for firing. Originally of Russian manufacture it is in common use by terrorist groups.

5 - The First Casualty

In the Sergeant's Mess at the barracks in Wiltshire the steward pulled the bar shutters down. Lofty tried to voice a protest but it fell on deaf ears. "You've had enough, Sgt Lofthouse. Everyone else has gone. Why don't you go to bed?"

"Fuck bed. Don't want to go to sleep ever again." Lofty slurred.

"Well, I do I'm afraid. Goodnight Sergeant." The steward left through the back door of the bar, turning the bar lights out as he went. Lofty was left in the gloom of the lounge, lit by a single table lamp.

"Fucking civvies." Lofty called after the man, but he was no longer there to hear it.

It was unusual for Lofty to get so drunk, but on this occasion he felt he had cause to. That day they had buried one of his platoon. There would be an inquiry, of course, but he knew that the man he considered responsible for the death of Private Chris Wood was unlikely to be called to account for his negligence.

The platoon had been on the rifle ranges and Lofty had been with Catfish 1 section. They huddled in the drizzle waiting to be called onto the range for their turn to fire their weapons. The crack of rifle fire from inside the range had ceased, meaning that Catfish 2 and 3 sections had completed their practice and were carrying out their unloading drills before vacating the firing point.

The door to the firing point opened and Company Sergeant Major Smith came out, lighting a cigarette. Through the open doorway Lofty could see Davie Tomlinson, Catfish 3's Corporal, going from man to man checking that their weapons were correctly unloaded.

Lofty felt a wave of annoyance flow through him. It was the Range Officer's job to carry out that task, and CSM Smith was the designated officer for the day's firing. He wondered whether he should say anything but decided against it. He had never really got on with the CSM and it wouldn't do to antagonise him over protocols like that. From previous encounters Lofty knew that the CSM didn't allow young sergeants to challenge his authority.

Lofty called Catfish 1 together and lined the men up in single file by the open door, ready to march onto the firing point as soon as it was vacated. He had just turned back towards the door to wait for the other two sections to file out when the crack of a rifle shot rang out. At the front of the file Chris Wood fell backwards onto the man behind him. The man, Kenny Hill, recoiled in horror as gore spattered across his face. Woods hit the ground with an audible thud, his rifle clattering to the concrete beside him as it dropped from his lifeless fingers.

"Stop fucking about, Woods." Lofty bawled, even as he realised that Woods wasn't play acting.

Shouting erupted from within the rifle range and as the smoke from the weapon's muzzle drifted away on the chill breeze Lofty could see Cpl Tomlinson berating the man whose rifle had gone off. Jones was obviously unaware that the shot had caused a casualty.

It didn't take long to establish that Chris Wood was dead. In the front of his head, just below the rim of his Kevlar helmet, was a small hole about 5.56 millimetres in diameter. The back of Wood's head , where the bullet had made its exit, was mainly spattered across Kenny Hill's face and upper body. Kenny Hill had only missed becoming a casualty by a faction of an inch, as the bullet had continued its flight for nearly half a mile until gravity brought it to earth in the tangled gorse of the heath.

Lofty called into the range. "What the fuck happened Tomlinson?"

"Pvt Ward had a jam, Sarge, and his weapon went off. Fucking idiot." He blurted before gasping in surprise as he saw the huddle of men gathered around Chris Woods, lying on the ground just outside the door to the range. Realisation of what had happened dawned on him.

The Corporal grabbed Ward's rifle off him and pointed it down the range before completing the unloading drill himself. He lay the weapon on the ground and ordered Ward's neighbour, 'Nosey' Parker, not to let anyone touch it. The weapon was now evidence and would have to be subjected to an examination to make sure it had been working correctly. Tomlinson then grabbed Ward by the arm and dragged him down to the far end of the firing point. Better he didn't get too close to the casualty. Ward lowered himself onto the ground and slumped into the corner.

Lofty looked towards the CSM, expecting him to take command of the situation, but the man had the slack jawed look of someone who had lost the plot. Lofty stepped onto the range and used the telephone to summon an ambulance and the MPs. Until the MPs decided that Woods' death was an accident the range was now a crime scene.

Lofty went along the range again checking each man's weapon was unloaded. He didn't want there to

61

be any further accidents. He then marched the shocked men of 2 and 3 sections off the firing point and out into the rain to wait for the MPs to arrive. Finally Lofty strode over to where Ward was sitting slumped in the corner and made sure that he was OK. His face was pale and his hands shaking. He was clearly in shock.

Lofty crouched down so that he was at eye level to the distraught Ward. "The MPs are going to want to talk to you. You have to be prepared to answer questions." Lofty tried to keep his voice even, dispassionate, but it was hard. The shock of the death had hit Lofty as well.

"He's dead, isn't he Sarge?" Ward whispered.

"Yes, I'm afraid he is." Lofty stated flatly.

"Who was it? Cpl Tomlinson didn't tell me."

"Chris Woods."

"Oh my God. Not Chris. Not him." Ward started sobbing heavily, his head cradled in his arms.

Lofty remembered that the two men were friends, having been through recruit training together before they arrived with the battalion. Sergeants weren't generally selected for their caring side, but Lofty knew he had to handle Ward carefully.

"Can you tell me what happened Len?" He asked softly, placing a reassuring hand on the young man's shoulder.

"We'd finished the drill. We'd been taking snap shots at the targets as they appeared, Then the CSM ordered us to cease fire and unload. My rifle jammed. The cocking lever wouldn't move so I couldn't eject the round that was up the spout."

"And then what happened?" Lofty encouraged.

"I turned to ask Nosey what to do. He was next to me. I must have squeezed the trigger because it went off."

Lofty stared along the firing point, trying to envisage the scene.

"Are you right or left handed Len?"

"Left handed. Why?"

"Nothing, just checking." Lofty didn't want to draw any conclusions in case he influenced Ward's story and planted a false memory, but Lofty knew the answer was significant.

If Ward had been right handed the angle of his weapon across his body would have kept it pointing towards the open front of the firing point as Ward turned, albeit it at an angle to the safe direction of the butts 300 yards away. The bullet would have disappeared into the expanse of Salisbury Plain without harming anyone. Instead, with the butt of the rifle held under Ward's left arm the barrel traversed to angle in towards the firing point as Ward turned to talk to his neighbour. If the heavy steel door to the firing point had been closed, as it should have been, Chris Woods would still be alive. He was killed because the CSM had wanted a fag and couldn't wait the few minutes that were needed to make sure all the weapons were safe.

If the CSM had been on the range, as he should have been, could the accident have been avoided? It was difficult to know, but a more experienced NCO might have been aware of the dangers and spotted Ward's unsafe behaviour in time to stop the accident happening. The door would certainly have been closed, reducing the risk.

So Lofty mourned the loss of one of his men. Well, two actually. Ward wouldn't be allowed to stay in the Battalion after this. Even if he was exonerated by the inquiry the bad feelings within the Platoon would make it untenable for him to stay. No doubt he would be posted out, probably to a non-combatant roll somewhere, as much a victim of the accident as Wood.

Lofty blamed himself to a degree. If he had tackled CSM Smith perhaps the accident might not have happened. The rules were clear. No one leaves the range until all the weapons have been declared safe, and it's the Range Officer's job to make sure they're safe. The findings of previous Boards of Inquiry into other deaths on rifle ranges had shaped the rules so that accidents like this one shouldn't happen.

After the ambulance had left the CSM had pulled Lofty to one side.

"OK, Sgt Lofthouse, Lofty, let's get the story straight, shall we?" The CSM had snarled.

"There's hardly a lot to get straight Sir. Ward pointed his weapon in the wrong direction and pulled the trigger. It's not rocket science."

"Not that, Lofthouse. I mean where I was at the time he fired. I was inside the range checking someone else's weapon. Got it? At the far end of the range where I couldn't see Ward."

"You mean you want me to lie for you?" Lofty was taken aback by the nerve of the request, no, demand.

"If you want to put it that way sunshine, then yes." The CSM leant forward till his face was almost touching Lofty's, eyeball to eyeball. "And if you aren't happy about it then remember, I can make your life difficult, *Sergeant* Lofthouse. Very difficult indeed.

Remember Cpl Timmins and the lost rifle? How do you think he lost it?"

Cpl Timmins had been Guard Commander when a rifle had gone missing from the Guardroom and it had always been rumoured that he had been set up by someone with a grudge against him. A Court Martial had demoted him to Private and sent him to the glasshouse for a month.

Lofty considered his options and didn't like what he saw. It wasn't just him that would have to lie, but the whole of his platoon. But the alternative was the living hell of being in the CSM's bad books and that wouldn't bring Chris Wood back to life. The CSM was spiteful enough to take out his revenge on the platoon as a whole, which Lofty knew would be even worse.

"Just make sure all your lads are singing off the same hymn sheet and everything'll be hunky dory, OK. Now, I've got to get back to RHQ and make my report. The Redcaps will want to speak to you and your lads. Make sure when you're called your report matches mine." He turned on his heel and marched off to his Landrover.

Lofty hurried after him. "Sir, I'm not going to lie for you, and I'm certainly not going to ask my Platoon to lie for you."

The CSM stopped in his tracks, his shoulders rigid with tension. He slowly turned to face the Sergeant.

"Don't cross me, Lofthouse. Don't you dare cross me."

"I'm sorry Sir, but I can't lie like that. Maybe the accident would have happened anyway, and maybe it wouldn't, but it's the Range Officer's job to check the weapons, not the Corporal's. You weren't where you should have been."

"That's insubordination, Lofthouse."

"You may think so Sir, but I call it the truth. I'm not going to lie to protect your back."

"You're going to fucking regret that." The CSM snarled, before turning back and continuing his journey to his Landrover. There was a clash of gears and the vehicle roared off in a spray of gravel and rain water.

Lofty knew he was going to pay a high price for that bit of defiance, but that was another matter. He made his statement to the MPs, which contradicted the CSM's, as did the statements of the twenty three surviving members of 1 Platoon.

An inquest was opened and adjourned to allow Chris Woods to be buried. The full formalities of the court procedures wouldn't take place until after the Battalion came back from their tour. The witnesses were needed elsewhere and even justice sometimes has to be delayed in the National Interest.

After the funeral they had drunk tea and eaten sandwiches in the Garrison Community Centre with Chris Wood's grieving family, then Lofty had taken the platoon out to say goodbye in their own way. He had already been drunk when he returned to the mess to find he was the only member still interested in drinking.

Lofty slid off his bar stool and staggered towards his room, finally defeated by the amount of alcohol he had drunk. The next week Emma would arrive in Wiltshire and they would start their married life together properly, though that wasn't in the forefront of his mind at that moment.

* * *

The next morning Fatima walked into the local library to try to find one of the books she needed to support her studies. The librarian in the University library had apologised, but all their copies of the work were out on loan. With the help of the internet they had tracked down a copy in the public library.

"Can I help you?" a member of the library staff smiled at her. Fatima was relieved that it was a woman. It would save her having to decline a man's help.

"Yes, I'm looking for a copy of this book." She handed over a slip of paper with the title and author's name written on it."

"Will you want to borrow the book?"

"Oh yes. I need it for my studies. I'm not a member of the library though."

"That won't be a problem. I'll show you where you can find it, then I can sign you up as a member."

The woman's name badge showed that she was called Emma.

"Thank you. May I call you Emma?" Fatima asked, pointing at the badge.

"Of course. We're very informal here." The woman gave her another smile. She was tall and quite pretty, with a thick mop of auburn hair. The woman had that confidence that many English women exuded. She knew her place in the world and was comfortable in it. After checking the library's catalogue the two women walked along the rows of bookshelves until Emma indicated that they should take a turning. She stopped midway along the row of shelves and Emma quickly scanned the spines of the books until she found the one they were looking for.

"Here you are." Emma said, as she pulled a thick volume from between its neighbours. "I don't envy you having to wade your way through this." She handed the book over.

"Fortunately I only have to read a couple of chapters; the ones that relate directly to my studies."

"What are you studying?" Emma chatted, as they returned to the front desk.

"Psychology. I want to be a counsellor."

"That sounds interesting. Will you specialise?"

"There is a shortage of counsellors for Asian women. A Muslim woman couldn't possibly go to a male counsellor to discuss her problems and, I'm sorry to say, most women counsellors simply don't understand our culture well enough to be able to relate to us."

"I hadn't thought of that as being a difficulty, but I can see what you mean. What sort of problems do Asian women have that are different from ....." Emma sought the right word to describe white British women without causing offence to a British woman from a different ethnic group, "different from what a non-Asian woman might have? That require the help of a counsellor I mean."

They had reached the front desk and the librarian sat down at her computer, ready to begin the enrolment procedure.

"In essence they aren't really any different from the problems of any other women, but they have to be understood against the backdrop of the Islamic religion. It places constraints upon women that non-Muslim women simply don't experience. For example, if you want to marry a boy then you are able to go out with him whenever you want. You can be alone with him and you can really get to know him. In our culture that would simply not be allowed. So even if a woman has known someone from birth they find themselves in marriages to men they hardly know at all, which places a great deal of strain on them and there isn't anyone that they can talk to about it."

Emma asked the questions necessary to complete the form. "I hadn't really thought of that. We take a lot for granted I suppose."

"I'm not complaining, of course. We behave as the Prophet, all blessings be upon Him, has said we must if we are to be held in the grace of Allah. But sometimes it causes problems."

"Well I wish you well in your studies." Emma stamped the library book and handed it across the counter to the young Asian woman. "You can keep it for three weeks, but if you need it longer you can renew it over the telephone or via the internet. There's full instructions printed inside."

There was a lull after the girl had gone and Emma took some time to sit back and relax. It was her last week working in the library and she would miss it. One of her colleagues walked by, taking care not to catch Emma's eye and get dragged into a conversation. The woman was carrying a dog eared buff folder. Emma recognised it as the one that was used to transport greetings cards around the building for signature by members of the staff before being ceremonially presented to the recipient. Over the previous years she had lost count of the number of birthdays, weddings, promotions, births and retirements she had marked in that way, always struggling to find the right words to inscribe on the card. Now, no doubt, the folder contained her farewell card, which is why her colleague had so pointedly ignored her, not wishing to give away the surprise-that-wasn't-a-surprise.

It had been easier than she expected to find a new job in Wiltshire. A brief search of the MoD's recruitment web pages had revealed that the Garrison where Lofty was based was seeking to recruit a senior administrator for the Garrison Education Centre. Emma had completed the on-line application form, attached her CV and a fortnight later travelled to Wiltshire for an interview. It all seemed too easy really, but it turned out that she was the best qualified candidate to apply and her charm at the interview had done the rest.

Since then life had been a bit hectic. There had been a weekend of house hunting with Lofty, which had resulted in them putting in an offer on a semi-detached house in a quiet suburb of Bradford on Avon. Despite the low offer the seller had been only too keen to accept and the deal was done. Now her little house in Finsbury was piled high with cardboard boxes containing all her worldly goods, ready for Lofty to arrive with a rented van and whisk them away to their new house. Her sister had already started to move her own possessions in, much to Emma's annoyance.

Emma was nervous. Despite the prospect of living a normal married life with Lofty she wondered how she would cope with them living under the same roof, seeing each other every day, eating together and watching TV.

She had never lived with anyone other than her family before. Lofty blew into town on a Friday evening, they had two days of fun and then he was gone again. She had liked that arrangement, up to a point. She missed Lofty when he wasn't there, but that made the weekends more exciting. The anticipation of his arrival, the preparations for their love making and the things they did together during their brief co-habitations. It all worked. They hardly ever argued, and when they did they made sure they never went to sleep without making up. Would it be the same from now on? She doubted it. Maybe it would be better. She could only hope that it was.

* * *

Saafir sat in his bedroom nibbling on a slice of pizza. He worked his way through all the 'friends' he had on Facebook. He had over 500 now and they were very useful to him.

Had anyone analysed the list of friends that he was viewing they would have been surprised to find that they were all members of the armed forces. Mainly soldiers and marines, but some RAF and Navy personnel as well. They would also be surprised to see that on Facebook his name wasn't Saafir, it was Tracey Temple.

It had been easy to set up, of course. On Facebook you don't have to prove who you are, so you can be anyone you choose. So Tracey sought out members of the armed forces and invited them to be her friends, claiming to have known them at school. No one ever challenged her. The picture on her profile page showed a pretty brunette wearing a bikini, and there had been a rush to accept her invitations.

Once he had been accepted as a friend by one person Facebook's algorithms had offered him more and more people that he could be friends with, so Saafir selected those that matched his particular requirements. All he had to do to maintain his cover was to keep posting pictures of Tracey partying with groups of girls just like herself. Photoshop was an invaluable tool when it came to maintaining the fiction. Even female members of the armed forces weren't immune to Tracey's charms, and the jewel in Saafir's crown was a very indiscrete female sergeant in the Intelligence Corps.

He clicked on another face. Interesting. According to Ronnie King, one of his friends had been killed on the rifle ranges the previous week while training to go to Afghanistan. He scrolled down his other posts. Bingo!

Private King's company were to take over a Forward Operating Base (FOB) at Nâd'Ali called Camp Elizabeth. Saafir took a memory stick out of his pocket and plugged it into the USB port of his PC. Memory sticks were such useful things in Saafir's opinion. If his PC were to be seized it meant that there would be very little incriminating evidence on it. If the house was raided then he could drop the stick on the floor and stamp on it, so that even the best forensic experts could never read the contents. If, somehow, his PC was hacked then the information he held would be safely separated from the machine and the hacker would find nothing of use.

Finding the file he wanted Saafir opened up the spreadsheet and scrolled down to find Pvt Kings details. Ronnie had been quite a prolific poster over recent months. So Saafir now knew that C Company, 2nd Battalion Middlesex Regiment, were to deploy to Helmand province, and one of their FOBs would be Nâd'Ali, currently occupied by the Royal Hampshire Regiment. No doubt the Middlesex would take over all the remaining FOBs occupied by the Hampshires, which meant that he could pinpoint where each company would be located. From these locations individual platoons would mount patrols or combine with Afghan military or police units to conduct joint operations.

Saafir studied the rest of the data he had gleaned on Ronnie Walker. He was married with no kids, lived in a married quarter close to the barracks and, according to Facebook's location functions, was currently in a public house in Trowbridge. If Saafir had access to a gun he could go down there right now and shoot him, if he wanted to. That wasn't his role, of course. Not only did he not have a gun he was nearly 200 miles away in the North West of England. He was serving the cause far better by gathering intelligence on soldiers and forwarding it to those who could use it to best effect.

Opening up his e-mail account Saafir composed a very carefully worded message. Drawing on information held on another file on the memory stick he selected code words to disguise his meaning. The recipient, now sleeping in Islamabad, would have no difficulty understanding the communication.

Glossary

Civvie(s) Slang: civilian personnel. Often used as a derogatory term. Can also be applied to a soldier's non-uniform clothing as in 'wearing his civvies'.

Cpl   Corporal.

CSM   Company Sergeant Major, Warrant Officer II rank.

FOB   Forward operating base.

MoD	Ministry of Defence, the arm of Government responsible for administering the British armed forces.
MP	Military Police. On military bases they have similar powers to civilian police officers. Off base in the UK they would normally act through the local constabulary.
NCO	Non Commissioned Officer. There are seven NCO ranks in the army which are, in ascending order: Lance Corporal, Corporal, Sergeant, Staff Sergeant, Colour Sergeant, Warrant Officer II (CSM, see above), Warrant Officer I
Pvt	Private, the lowest rank in the army. Trooper is used for cavalry soldiers and there are other terms that stem from the specialist nature of the soldiers work, eg Sapper for an engineer, Signaller for a member of the Royal Signals, etc. There are also terms used as a matter of regimental tradition, eg Fusilier for soldiers in Fusilier regiments.
RAF	Royal Air Force
Redcaps	Slang: Military Police. So called because their peaked caps have a bright red covering. When they wear a beret it is crimson in colour.
RHQ	Regimental Headquarters

6 - Disappointments

It had been weeks since Fatima had spoken to Youssef. She was relieved when her father called her to the 'phone and told her who it was.

"Youssef, Oh, how I've been longing to hear from you. How are you?"

"I'm OK. Look, I can't stay on the 'phone for long. I'm in a place where it isn't safe to use a telephone." He had walked for two days to find the nearest public telephone. As a stranger he stood out and had received curious glances. It was only his ever present AK-47 and his two armed companions that had prevented him from being accosted.

"Where are you, Youssef? You make it sound dangerous. Are you still in Abbottabad?"

"No. There was nothing for me there. I am with friends in the mountains."

"What on Earth are you doing there? It's dangerous there."

"Too many questions Fatima. I just rang to say that I'm OK and that you shouldn't worry about me."

"But what are you doing in the mountains. That's where the Taliban are."

"It's true that my brothers in the Taliban are close by." Youssef dissembled.

"Youssef, you haven't done anything stupid, have you?"

"No, I haven't done anything stupid. I have only done what Allah asks of me."

"But what is it you have done?"

"I have taken up the jihad, just as Allah commands us to."

"Oh, Youssef, please tell me you're joking. You're a man of peace. You told me so yourself."

"The errors of my ways have been pointed out to me. I was a hypocrite, pretending to be a true believer but not wishing to behave as one. It's something that I couldn't see when I was in London, but my eyes are clear now."

"Youssef, these aren't your words. Where have you been? What have you been doing?"

"No more questions woman. It isn't the woman's place to question the man."

Fatima was stung by the vehemence of Youssef's words. What had come over him?

"Youssef, please listen to me. Come home to England. We must talk."

"My home is here now. I have no place in that land of kuffar. It's my destiny to make holy war. If you love me then ask me no more questions."

"But what of us? I thought we would be together one day, as man and wife."

"And we shall. When my duty is done I will send for you and we will live together in peace here in Pakistan."

"But what about my career? All our plans?"

"It is unseemly for a woman to work. I know that now. It is also unseemly for a woman to be educated. When I have time I will write to your father and tell him my views."

Youssef could hear Fatima's tears down the telephone. The machine bleeped at him to tell him to insert more money, but he had no more coins.

"I will telephone when I can." He said curtly, before replacing the handset in its cradle. He went in search of his companions and the supplies that they had come to purchase for the training camp.

Far away in London, Fatima stared at the handset of her own telephone as though it had just bitten her. Her world had just come to an end. Tears streamed down her face. No, that hadn't just happened. It must have been some sort of joke. Perhaps Youssef was drunk or on drugs. Yes, that had to be it. He had got drunk and in his drunken state had played a joke on her. When he sobered up he would ring to apologise and they would laugh about it.

Fatima lied to herself, convinced that Youssef was unchanged. Later that night, as she lay in her bed, she replayed the conversation in her head, still trying to deny it. Bit by bit she realised that what she had heard was no drunken prank.

It had been weeks since they had last spoken. He said then that he wasn't going to take up his studies again; that he had some things to think about. That had concerned her. Youssef had always been so clear in his plans, so a sudden change of heart was a cause for concern. It would seem that her fears had been realised. He had been talking to someone, perhaps several people, and they had altered the way he viewed the world. He was no longer the Youssef she knew.

Fatima's fears increased as she realised where he may have been and what he may have been doing. On the telephone he had referred to his Taliban brothers. He would never have identified with them in that way before. Two words blazed in her head even though Youssef hadn't actually said them: Training Camp.

* * *

Abisali had returned to the camp and the trainee insurgents sat in a semi-circle around him on the hard packed earth of the training camp. Each held his AK-47 rifle across his knees. The weapons had been their constant companions since their arrival in the camp, even before they knew how to use them.

"The instructors tell me you have done well, brothers. They tell me you are ready to fight in the cause of Jihad."

The men's faces lit up with delight.

"In Helmand province some of the kuffar soldiers will soon be going home. Other brothers of the Taliban are arranging a few farewell surprises for them." There were nods of approval from around the semi-circle. "But other soldiers are coming, so we will wish to give them a suitable welcome and then send them on their way. That will be your task."

Excited chatter broke out around the group and Abisali had to call for quiet. "I'm glad you are all so keen but don't forget, brothers, that these are professional soldiers. They will not die easily. You must prepare yourselves for the possibility of martyrdom."

The euphoria evaporated as the warrior's words sank in.

"Some of the soldiers are from your part of the world, Youssef. They are the Middlesex Regiment."

Youssef looked up in surprise.

"Will it cause you problems to have to go to war against men that you might know?"

Youssef shook his head emphatically. "No, Abisali. It won't be a problem. This is jihad. It is sanctioned by Allah. If I were back in England right now I would gladly place a bomb in the middle of the Emirates football stadium."

He paused, an idea occurring to him. "In fact my knowledge of the local dialect may come in useful." He switched to English, raising his voice to the level of a costermonger. "Oi, Frankie, cumin dahn the Arsenal Sat'day?" A ripple of laughter went round the group, even though none of them had understood a word of what Youssef had said. He tried another one. "Cum on yoo Spurs!" He was rewarded with more laughter.

Abisali's usual stern expression softened into an indulgent smile. "Thank you, Youssef. I'm sure your talents will be useful." He cast a glance around the small assembly. "Now brothers, gather your possessions together. We have a long journey ahead of us."

As the men returned to their tents to gather their meagre possessions Abisali watched Youssef with particular interest. He had showed all the promise that he had hoped of him, and the next part of the process would ensure that there was no going back. Youssef had to kill, or at least take part in combat where killing might take place. Once Youssef was fully committed he could then move the plan forward to fruition.

* * *

"Is this what it's going to be like, Lofty?" Emma placed a glass of water and two paracetamol tablets on the kitchen table in front of her husband.

"What do you mean?"

"You standing at the bar yarning with your mates while I sit with the wives making small talk. Me making a glass of wine last three hours because I'm going to have to drive you home when you've finally had enough."

Lofty groaned. Not that conversation again. "Sorry love, but the Mess is the place for the soldiers. Wives are guests."

"You're supposed to entertain guests, not stick them in a corner and ignore them."

"None of the other blokes wives' complain about it."

"More fool them then!" Snapped Emma.

"Did I do anything I have to apologise for?"

"Apart from ignore me all evening? No, not really. You and Cobber got into a Sambuca drinking contest for some unknown reason. You picked one up, blew out the flame and then keeled over backwards. Cobber says you owe him a tenner."

Lofty let out another low groan. At least that accounted for his hangover.

"I'm sorry, Babe. I should have spent more time with you last night."

"It isn't just last night. Its nearly every night. Either you go down to the Mess with your mates and I have to pick you up, or I go with you and spend the evening with the coven." It was the word Emma had taken to using to refer to the wives of the other SNCOs. It wasn't meant maliciously, but they did seem to spend an awful lot of time gossiping and back biting. She said it was only a matter of time before they started casting spells. Lofty had laughed, but didn't really understood what she was getting at.

"I thought it would be different down here." Emma continued. "I thought we'd have time to be together. Time to get to really know each other."

Lofty got to his feet and took his wife in his arms. She laid her head on his chest.

"I know, it's just that we've been so busy lately. If we're not on the ranges we're in the classrooms and if we're not in the classrooms we're out on the plain on manoeuvres. By the time we get back at the end of the day all I feel like doing is having a few beers and kicking back."

"You could kick back here at home, with me."

"You're right, of course, but it's good to talk things over with the other guys. Talk about who's shaping up and who's not pulling their weight. Talk about what we need to do better and what we're good at. There's not much time left before we go and if we get it wrong when we get out there then it could cost someone their life."

"And what has that got to do with you and Cobber having Sambuca drinking contests?" Emma remarked dryly. "Besides, talking to the other wives it sounds like that's what you blokes always do, regardless of whether you're preparing for Afghanistan or not."

"That was just things getting a bit out of hand. I promise, we'll spend more time together. Now, I've got to get my kit together. It's the inter-company football final this afternoon and I'm team Captain."

Lofty released Emma from his embrace and went off to sort out his football kit. Emma slumped into a chair and buried her face in her arms, quietly sobbing to herself.

Life with Lofty, she had discovered was soldiering, drinking and football. He had almost no time for her. She couldn't remember the last time they had made love. At least when he had come up to London for the weekend they had done that. You can't have sex with a man that isn't there, or if he is there he's so pissed he couldn't raise a smile.

Emma dabbed at her eyes with a tissue then blew her nose. She wasn't going to create a scene with Lofty, not now. He was right, there was too much to do and too little time in which to do it. She had to allow him to stay focused, but when he came back they would have to talk. If she had to endure more of this then she couldn't imagine their marriage surviving.

"Where are my shorts?" Lofty's voice drifted down from the bedroom.

"In the drawer with all your other shorts. Third one down." She called back, managing to keep the sobbing out of her voice. Don't worry, Master, she said silently to herself. I'll wash your filthy football kit for you. I'll make your dinner and iron your shirts ready for work. I'll do it whether you're a soldier or a civilian. But I need more. I need you to be a husband to me.

Yes, they would have to have that conversation eventually.

* * *

Lofty shouldered his way across the crowded room, bearing a tray of drinks aloft like a trophy. Once the place had been called the NAAFI but it was now run by a private company who fed the soldiers as well as providing them with somewhere to drink. The catering company called the bar "The Place To Be" but most of the single soldiers disagreed. They would rather have been in one of the local pubs.

Eager hands claimed glasses and the tray was emptied. Lofty returned to the bar to collect the next portion of the large round. Able to take his seat at last he tried to catch up with the conversations that had been taking place while he had been fetching the drinks.

"Why are we confined to barracks?" Asked Frankie Morgan. "We ain't done nuffin' wrong."

"The CO would like you all to be at the buses on time, Frankie." Replied Lofty. "We can't keep the crabs waiting while we bail you out of the local nick."

"Seems a bit harsh. This place serves rotten beer."

"Hark at the con-oo-sewer." Chipped in 'Nosey' Parker. "Since when have you drunk anything other than the cheapest lager on the pumps?"

"I might fancy a change." Frankie replied grumpily.

"Ere' Sarge, you've been out there before so maybe you can tell us. Is it true that the Afghan women will cut your bollocks off if you get taken prisoner?" Dennis Allen asked him.

"I don't know about that. Back in the old days there were stories of it happening, when a whole British Army was massacred in the Khyber Pass." Lofty paused to take a generous sip of his beer. "Mind you, that was two hundred years ago, near on."

"You don't have to worry about that anyway." Chipped in Mickey Flynn. "They'd have to wait for your balls to drop first."

There was a general chorus of laughter at the discomfiture of one of the youngest members of the platoon.

"I think the best thing you can do, young Dennis, is to make sure you don't get captured." Lofty winked at him. "You know the rules. Stay together and back each other up."

"We're going to tear those Taliban bastards new arseholes, ain't we Sarge?" Justin Green challenged.

"Do you know much about Afghanistan and its people, Justin?" Asked the Sergeant.

"Not really. Only what they've told us in the indoctrination classes."

"Well you couldn't have been listening very well. If you had been you would know that no Western Army has ever conquered the country. We've been there twice and had our arses kicked, and the Russians were chased out when they started taking so many casualties that not even the Soviet press could keep it quiet anymore."

"Only 'cos the Yanks were giving them weapons though." Chipped in Mickey Flynn.

"They ain't civilised like us though, are they?" Continued Green, warming to his theme. Around the group there were nods of agreement. "They're 'ardly even yuman, some of them."

"If you think that then you're in for a big surprise, Green." Lofty responded, annoyed at hearing racism of that type from within his platoon. "True, they weren't well equipped until the Americans started supplying them, but it still needed a hand on the trigger and the balls to keep shooting when they had tanks coming straight at them. The mujahedeen didn't have any armour or air cover, but they created havoc. The Soviets didn't know how to deal with them, and nor do we."

"Lofty's right." Cobber Bruce joined the Platoon. "They're probably the best irregular fighters in the world. They're tying down over a hundred thousand of the best trained soldiers available, and there's probably no more than a thousand of them fighting at any time."

It was a sobering thought and the group went quiet for a moment. Someone took up a kitty and more beer was ordered at the bar. Cobber nodded towards a quiet corner and Lofty followed him across the room.

"How was Emma?"

"Tearful. No surprise there."

"Is she coming to wave you off in the morning?"

"I guess so. She didn't really say, but with most of the Garrison there I can't see her staying away."

"My Sam was the same. Poor lass was in bits."

"It's tough on them. We know what we're getting into but they don't."

"That's what Sam said when we went last time. Seems like a lifetime, but its only just four years ago. Sam's promised to look in on Emma from time to time to see how she's getting on. She'll also make sure that Emma gets invited to any events that are organised for the wives. You look a bit down." Cobber concluded, seeing Lofty's sombre expression.

"I sometimes wonder if we should be there at all." Lofty commented.

"Think what it would be like if we weren't." responded Cobber. "The Taliban would drag the country back into the 7th century. Did you see that interview with Malala Yousafzai? Poor girl was shot in the head just because she wanted to go to school. That's what this is all about Lofty. The right of a little girl to go to school."

"You're right I guess."

"I'm not often right, Lofty, but I think I am this time. Anyway, that wasn't what I wanted to tell you. I picked up a bit of intel today from the RAO. The CSM's been disciplined over the death of Chris Woods. The CO gave him an official reprimand. He won't make RSM now, not with that on his record."

"If the inquest finds him negligent he might even get the chop." mused Lofty.

"Yep. Anyway, I wanted to give you the heads-up. The CSM's going to be on your back like Frankie Dettori on a Derby winner. Every time he gets the chance he's going to try and do the dirty on you."

"Thanks Cobber. I appreciate the warning. Best I make sure he's never standing behind me with a loaded weapon when there are no witnesses about."

"Ain't that the truth. Shtum now, we've got company."

Mickey Flynn bore down across the room carrying three pints of beer. He handed one each to Lofty and Cobber.

"Tell me something, Sarge." he said to the QM Sergeant. "Why do they call you Cobber?"

The Sergeant laughed. "It started when I joined up. Some wag in the Platoon said that all Australians were called Bruce, so I must be an Aussie. Someone else called me Cobber and it stuck."

"And are all Australians called Bruce?" continued Mickey.

"I haven't got a clue. Bruce is an old Scottish clan name, as in Robert the Bruce. My Dad was Scottish and came down here to join the Scott's Guards. He married a London girl and stayed here after he was discharged. I'd have joined the guards as well but I didn't make the height restrictions they had at the time. So I'm stuck with you bunch of wankers instead."

Mickey laughed good naturedly and they made their way back to the rest of the platoon. Cobber went off to share a joke with 2 Platoon on the far side of the room.

"A Company must be in-theatre by now." Mickey Flynn commented to the group.

Lofty looked at his watch and calculated the local time in Afghanistan, four and a half hours ahead of them. "I reckon so. And B Company will be just about leaving Cyprus to join them."

"Lucky bastards. Getting in ahead of us and grabbing all the glory."

"Just remember, when they're on their way back we'll still be out there. First in, first out and last in, last out. Those are the rules."

"Poor old D Company then. Last to go out and last to get back." commented Mickey.

The talk turned to football and the traditional rivalry within the battalion around the seven Premiership and Football League clubs that fell within their recruiting area meant that things could get a bit heated. As the Captain of the battalion's football team Lofty was called upon as an expert witness as each faction made its claims for superiority, though as a lifelong Arsenal fan he was hardly impartial.

As his mobile phone rang Lofty made a grateful exit and went to find somewhere quiet to take the call. The display told him that it was from Emma, and Lofty was relieved that she had decided to phone.

"Hi Babe, missing me already?"

"Hi Lofty. I had to ring, just to say goodbye. No, I don't mean goodbye. I mean...."

"I know what you mean love. Don't worry. I'll be OK."

"I'm going to miss you, you know that."

"And I'm going to miss you too. I love you, you know."

"Yes, I know that. You've told me enough times. What are you doing?"

"In the bar with the lads. Last night booze up. Doing my best to keep them out of the clutches of the Regimental Police. I don't think I'll get much sleep tonight."

"I'm guessing you'll end up in the Mess bar with Cobber and the others. Why you booked a room I don't know. You're not going to see much of it. Anyway I just phoned to wish you all the best and to tell you that I love you too, and that I'll be thinking of you, night and day."

Lofty heard a catch in Emma's voice and suspected that she was crying. "I'll be thinking of you too, Babe. Are you coming to wave us goodbye in the morning."

"I guess so. I'm sure they'll give me time off work. You better come back safe and sound, you big idiot," Emma gabbled, "or I'll never speak to you again." Unable to control her emotions any more Emma broke the connection.

Lofty took a few minutes to compose himself. He wasn't quite in tears, but they weren't far away. Memories of the good times with Emma filled his mind. They had managed to settle their differences for the time being at least, and that was something. During the leave period Lofty had taken Emma away for a week in the Lake District and they had talked a lot. Not about the big thing in their life, but about the small things. Lofty felt he knew Emma better, and hoped that she understood him a little more as well.

The sound of breaking glass and a raucous chorus of cheers brought Lofty back to the present and he steeled himself to go back into the bar. There would be a few sore heads in the morning, which didn't worry him, but he didn't want any of his platoon to fall victim to the RP.

Entering the crowded bar again he was in time to see Dennis Allen being lifted onto a table as someone chanted the first line of Zulu Warrior. Someone else started to hammer out the beat on the table top and the chant was taken up by the rest of the platoon. Time to slow down his own alcohol consumption, Lofty thought, so he could better maintain a watch over his men.

The chant was taken up around the overcrowded room. "Get 'em, down, you Zulu warrior. Get 'em down, you Zulu chief, chief, chief." Lofty moved forward to make sure Allen didn't come to any harm, but didn't intervene. Let them have their fun. For some of them it might be the last fun they ever have.

Glossary

Crabs	Slang name used by the Army and Navy to refer to the Royal Air Force.
NAAFI	Navy, Army and Air Force Institute. Employed by the IMoD to provide leisure facilities. Replaced in the UK by contract catering companies.
RAO	Regimental Administration Officer or Regimental Administration Office.
RP	Regimental Police. Members of the battalion given some police training in order to act as constables within the barracks. They hold powers of arrest over military personnel of junior rank but not civilians.

7 - Arrival In Theatre

The platoon had been working at full tilt since their arrival at Camp Elizabeth FOB, and the camp was starting to look more shipshape.

It had once been a police barracks, but bore little resemblance to the sort of establishment that any of the soldiers had seen before and some of them were quite familiar with police stations. Someone compared it to the sort of cavalry fort seen in Western films, only made of mud instead of logs.

Foot thick mud walls faced outwards and also formed the outer perimeter of the accommodation buildings. These in turn formed the boundary of a broad square. Cinder blocks were interspersed with the mud where repairs had been done since the arrival of the British. The parade ground provided space to park the Company's vehicles.

According to the official version the camp had been named after the Queen, but rumour had it that the Lieutenant Colonel of the Coldstream Guards who had first used the location as a base had named it after his wife. Lofty didn't really care either way, but he knew which version was more likely.

The pale mud reflected and amplified the heat, so even in the cooler temperatures of October the intensity of the sun was sufficient to burn exposed skin. The buildings on three of the sides of the square had been allocated as sleeping accommodation while along the remaining side stood the Company HQ, the kitchen and the dining area. Wheeled trailers provided shower units and latrines and were parked in one corner of the square. The flat roofs of the buildings created a fire step and parapet should the FOB come under attack. Sand bagged emplacements stood at each corner to house machine guns and act as sentry points. Above the roof a Union Flag occasionally fluttered on its pole as the breeze ruffled it.

The whole compound was accessed by a single solid gate which sat in the middle of the Western wall, splitting the offices from the catering section. It was barred against intruders. Beyond the walls a barrier made of giant wire bins, known as Hesco, filled with rocks and mud surrounded the whole camp, designed to prevent a suicide bomber crashing a truck into the walls and killing the occupants of the buildings.

No 1 Platoon had drawn sentry duty as the remainder of the company carried out a range of tasks to improve living conditions. Since the dawn of time no army departing its barracks has ever left them in a condition that met with the approval of new occupants. A lot of work was required to improve the defences as well as the living quarters.

The three Catfish sections had taken turns to stand guard, two hours on duty and four hours off. Fortunately no attack had come, but the soldier's necks had prickled as some sixth sense told them they were being watched.

The departing company of the Royal Hampshire Regiment had suffered badly at the hands of the insurgents during the last few days of their residence. Two men had fallen to road side bombs, with another six seriously injured. The Company Commander had to be evacuated with a sniper's bullet lodged in his back. They hadn't been sorry to leave.

At the end of their week of sentry duty, or stag as they called it. 1 Platoon handed over to 2 Platoon. The soldiers returned to their allocated bed spaces while the Company Commander held a briefing for the Company's officers and NCOs.

"It's time the company made its mark with the local population, so I'm sending 1 and 3 Platoons out to conduct patrols in the area. 4 Platoon will act as a reserve in case either platoon runs into difficulties." Major Hardcastle went on to provide the details of what he required each platoon to do, and how he expected them to do it.

"In a nutshell that's it. 1 Platoon will deploy at 06.00 hours local tomorrow morning to carry out a long range patrol to this area." He tapped his map at a place marked Zābol. "3 Platoon will depart 30 minutes later and carry out a foot patrol in the local area. An extended sweep around the local farms and the villages close by. I'll leave the detailed planning to Platoon Commanders and Sergeants, and I'll want to attend the Platoon briefings so I know what you're up to.

1 Platoon's briefing will be at 21.00 and 3 Platoon at 22.00. OC 4 Platoon will also attend both briefings with his Platoon Sergeant. Make sure that your briefings contain strong words with regard to the treatment of local civilians. They are not our enemy; they are our allies. They may look like murderous ruffians, but they're on our side unless they prove otherwise. Any questions?"

After dealing with a few minor queries the three platoon commanders went into huddles with their sergeants and started the detailed planning for their missions.

* * *

Saafir carried out his daily task of checking out the Facebook postings of his current favourite 'friends'. One from Ronnie King caught his eye.

"Our first patrol tomorrow. Out at 06.00 to some place called Zābol. Not a clue what it's like, but if its anything like the other places we've seen then it's bound to be a shit hole. LOL."

Saafir smiled and started to compose an e-mail.

* * *

The party of Taliban didn't get much time for rest. They chose a remote farm as their temporary base, locking the farmer and his family into one room while they converted the remainder of the house into a small but effective fortress. Their single heavy machinegun was set on the flat roof so that it could be easily moved around to provide a 360° field of fire. Furniture and food sacks were stacked at the windows to provide protection from incoming fire, while still leaving loop holes through which fire could be returned.

Abisali called Youssef across to him, out of hearing of the rest of the band.

"Your instructors told me good things about you, Youssef. I need a second in command; would you like the job?"

"But I've never even been in a battle. I hardly know how to fire my rifle."

"You are educated and a quick learner, Youssef. I have been told that you can scan a piece of ground and work out the best way to cross it without being seen. I was also told that you set up an ambush that even your instructors failed to detect. Is that true?"

"Well, I do seem to have some skills, but I still lack experience."

93

"In the first battle I led I had only ever fired my weapon in anger once before. Look, the other men are good fighters, or they will be I think. But they are simple people. Most of them can hardly write their own names. I need someone who has been trained to think, and that is you. You were a student. Does the word Taliban not mean student? What better leader could I choose? Besides, you're popular with the men. That counts for a lot."

"If you're sure, then OK, I'll do it."

"Thank you, Youssef. You will be good, I'm sure of it. So, now I'll tell the others, then I want you to come with me to choose the place where we will teach these kuffar soldiers what war is like in Afghanistan."

Abisali allowed himself a small smile of satisfaction. Youssef's pride had not permitted him to refuse the promotion, and that sealed his fate. With responsibility for other men Youssef would have to put the lives of others before his own.

To Youssef's surprise there was a general acceptance of his appointment as second in command of the twenty strong band of fighters. After the announcement he oversaw the completion of the defensive arrangements, then picked out four of the men to act as an escort for their reconnaissance mission.

* * *

In the cool light of dawn Lofty went from man to man checking their equipment. Water bottles were opened to make sure that they were full, and also that they contained nothing but water.

"Idiot." Lofty cursed one of the men as he found coffee in one of the canteens. "Weren't you told that coffee increases your thirst. It contains caffeine and that makes you pee more. Now get rid of it."

The man looked sheepish and hurried away to do as he was ordered.

"OK, Parker. How are you feeling." Lofty asked the next man.

"Good Sarge. It's good to be getting a bit of action."

"I hope the most action we see today is to ride around the countryside for a few hours."

"Oh, Sarge, surely we'll get more than that."

"Only if we're unlucky, Parker. We're here to stop a war, not to start one."

Lofty understood the desire of his men to get stuck into the Taliban; the enemy. He had felt just the same way when he had first arrived in Afghanistan four years earlier. The desire soon evaporated when AK-47 rounds started whizzing past your ears. Part of it already felt like an eternity.

Rifles were checked for cleanliness and spare magazines checked to ensure that they were fully loaded and wouldn't jam. Lofty jerked on straps to tighten body armour into place and reduce the gaps that made men vulnerable to bullets. Section by section Lofty dismissed the men to gather at the back of their allotted vehicles for a final cigarette before departure. They would not be allowed to smoke again until they were back in the safety of the FOB.

The patrol was using five vehicles. In the lead would be a Jackal fire support vehicle in which Lofty would travel along with the two man crew. Behind that would come three Mastiffs, each armoured truck carrying an eight man section plus its crew. Finally a Panther command vehicle would carry the Platoon

Commander and one of the two translators, Cpl Debbie Moon from the Intelligence Corps, who had been trained to speak Pashtun. The other translator, an Afghani by the name of Mohammed, travelled with Catfish 3 so as not to offend his cultural attitudes towards women. Private Griffiths of Catfish 3 travelled in the Panther to make room in the Mastiff.

The small convoy was more than capable of defending itself if necessary.

Near the front gate Captain Trent, 1 Platoon's CO, stood chatting to the Company Sergeant Major. Lofty marched briskly across to report. The CSM gave Lofty a mocking look, sure of his power over his subordinate.

Ignoring the CSM, Lofty neither stood to attention nor saluted. There was no point in showing a hidden enemy who the leaders were by offering the standard military courtesies. "Sir, 1 Platoon assembled and ready to depart."

"OK, thank you Sergeant. Get them mounted up. All further orders will be issued over the radio."

"Roger, Sir." That was standard practice once the patrol went into the field. Again, no point in letting the enemy know what you're doing by shouting commands back and forth. Lofty wondered how they had managed in the bad old days when each platoon would only have one radio between them. Besides, a significant part of the journey would be in noisy vehicles so radio was the only effective means of communication between them.

Lofty toggled his radio and relayed the order to the Section Commanders. Along the line of Mastiffs the corporals ushered their men into the air conditioned, armoured protection of the interiors. Lofty climbed into the passenger seat of the Jackal and ordered the driver to start the engine. Behind him the air thickened with diesel fumes as the other drivers followed suit.

At 06.00 hrs to the second the CSM ordered the sentry to open the gate and the small convoy moved off. As Lofty's vehicle passed him the CSM gave the sergeant a sour look. He had wanted to come along on this first patrol but Lofty had protested.

"Taking him will mean leaving someone else behind, Sir. We can't afford to lose a rifleman, so that would mean leaving either you or me. With due respect, Sir. I think I should be with my men for this first patrol." The Captain had politely declined the request and so the CSM stayed behind.

If Capt Trent knew of the enmity between his Platoon Sergeant and the CSM he took care not to show it. 3 Platoon would have the dubious honour of the CSM's company instead. Unconstrained by the size of vehicles the foot patrol could accommodate him without making compromises.

The plan for the Op was quite simple, as Capt Trent had explained at the briefing the previous evening.

"We will head due West towards the small town of Zãbol. As we pass farms and isolated dwellings on route we'll stop and try to engage with the local people, firstly as part of the hearts and minds campaign that is the mainstream of the mission, but secondly to try to gather intelligence on enemy movements. I'll take Mohammed to talk to the men, while Cpl Moon will try to engage with the female members of the household."

This was a new initiative for the British forces in Afghanistan, but it was bearing fruit. The Afghan women were curious about the female soldiers and had lots of questions to ask them. In return the interpreters asked them questions, supposedly innocent but designed to reveal if strangers were in the local area and what they might be doing there. It was also useful to be able to gauge the women's feelings towards the British and their Afghan government hosts.

"Once in Zābol," The Captain continued, "the Platoon will dismount to conduct a foot patrol through the village, showing the flag, as the saying goes and handing out sweets to the children. Mohamed will seek out the community leaders and they will be invited to come and discuss their concerns with me in an impromptu durbar. After a decent interval the patrol will be recalled and the convoy will make its way back to Camp Elizabeth to arrive before dusk. I'll go through individual assignments in a moment, but any questions so far?"

That had been the previous evening. Now the Jackal set a slow pace along the dirt road towards their destination. This was partly because it was uncomfortable to drive faster, but mainly because it gave the driver and Lofty more time to spot the tell-tale signs that might indicate the presence of IEDs. These roadside bombs caused more casualties than direct attacks, as well as effectively ending any patrol so that casualties could be evacuated.

* * *

Abisali and Youssef lay on the ridge overlooking the road and watched the small convoy pass slowly by below them. "A full platoon, about 24 men plus officers and the vehicle crews." The leader commented. The sun beat down on their backs, creating rivulets of sweat, but they didn't dare wipe

98

them away in case the movement betrayed their presence.

"The Jackal is the weak point. Its only lightly armoured. If we can stop it we can kill the crew before they can respond." mused Youssef.

"The platoon sergeant normally travels in the lead vehicle. It's a good target." Abisali whispered his approval.

"What will the other vehicles do?"

"The machine gunners will return fire, of course, but they daren't leave the road for fear of our bombs. They will be pinned down while we fire at them. They have two choices. Stay inside the vehicle or get out and fight. If they get out we can rain fire down upon them and we will kill them. If they stay inside we keep firing RPGs at them until we either destroy the vehicles or we run out of rockets"

"What about air cover?"

"If there is a helicopter already up then we may only have a few minutes. If not then ten, maybe fifteen minutes." Abisali looked at his second in command shrewdly. "Where will we do it?"

Since they had taken up the position Youssef had been scanning the ground with that question in mind.

"There." He pointed at a defile along the road to the West. "We place a mine on the road, which will force them to either stop and try to clear it or which will blow up the lead vehicle. Either way the whole convoy is stopped. Then we pour down fire from above. Their guns will have to fire upwards, which will make them much less accurate. We attack from both sides, of course."

"A good plan. That is exactly where I would do it. Now, let's return to the farm and gather the men.

According to our intelligence they're headed for Zābol. If they follow their usual routine we have at least four hours before they return, and probably much longer.

Glossary

Hesco ™ Large diameter wire mesh baskets, 3 to 4 ft tall, that can be filled with rubble to form a defensive barrier.

HQ   Headquarters.

IED   Improvised explosive device, which includes roadside bombs and booby traps. There is no set design for an IED and each bomb maker will design his own.

Jackal   A lightly armoured patrol vehicle with a crew of two, a driver and a gunner and room for a passenger.

Mastiff   An armoured truck capable of transporting a complete section. It also has a crew of two, a driver and a gunner.

Medivac   Medical evacuation.

OC   Officer Commanding, usually of a formation smaller than a battalion.

Panther   An armoured command vehicle.

Stag   Slang. Sentry duty.

Theatre   The main geographical area where military operations are being carried out, eg Iraq, Afghanistan.

8 - First Contact

The patrol had gone pretty much as planned. There had been one scare when Pvt Scott of Catfish 3, patrolling on foot, had thought he had seen a man with a gun in hiding behind a house in Zãbol, but when the section had caught up with him it had turned out to be no more than an old man carrying a stick to help him walk. Profuse apologies and the gift of some cigarettes smoothed matters over.

The Platoon Commander ended his discussions with the town's elders and ordered the return to Camp Elizabeth.

Capt Trent and Lofty had seen the significance of the defile when they had examined their maps the previous evening. A line of hills running from the South West to the North East was cut by the road they would use. The tightly packed contour lines flanking the road indicated steep slopes.

"Ideal place for an ambush, Boss." Lofty had commented.

"That's where I would put one if I wanted to stop a convoy." Agreed his OC. "I don't think we have to worry on the way out. Between us leaving the FOB and reaching the defile no one would have time to set up an ambush. But on the way back it will be a different matter."

They developed a counter ambush strategy.

Lofty called the convoy to a halt a short distance from where the ground started to rise on either side of the road and which signified the entrance to the defile. He raised his binoculars and scanned the road and the slopes on either side. The ground rose steeply for about forty feet and a man would need to use his hands as well as his feet if he wanted to climb the near vertical faces. Above that the slopes started to level out and climbed more gently to the summits of the flanking hills. No doubt the gash in the hills had been caused by water, perhaps the seasonal rains, but the builders of the road had spotted the opportunity to pass through the gap.

The heat haze rippled and danced making it difficult to identify features even with the aid of the glasses. A sudden breeze swept the haze away and Lofty thought he saw something lying in the middle of the road, but the curtain descended again before he could be sure.

Lofty toggled the microphone of his radio. "Sunray this is Sunray Minor. I can't see anything much. There might be something on the road but we're too far away to get a good look. Request permission to carry out a recce?"

"Roger Sunray Minor. All Catfish call signs hold your positions while the recce is carried out. Keep your eyes peeled in front and behind."

One by one the section commanders acknowledged the instruction.

Lofty showed the Jackal's driver the route he wanted him to take and the vehicle edged off the road and onto the slope on the Southern side. The Jackal's air-bag suspension helped to keep the ride comfortable, but still the vehicle swayed wildly over the rough ground as it climbed up to the summit of the nearest hill.

Behind Lofty's head the machine gunner tracked his weapon from side to side, searching for any possible threat. Back down on the road the gunners in the 'top cover' positions of the Mastiffs kept an equally vigilant lookout. The sweat dripped off the soldiers' faces as the heat was reflected back off the armour of their vehicles to sear their faces. Inside the vehicles the section commanders watched their Situational Display Units (SDUs), the CCTV system that allowed them to see outside the vehicles by selecting from the six external cameras. A halted convoy makes for a very inviting target.

From his vantage point Lofty was able to scan the area on both sides of the defile. Unfortunately his position prevented him from seeing the road as it passed through the gap. Nothing suspicious was seen, so Lofty ordered the driver to descend the slope until he could see along the road.

From above the road the distortion of the heat haze was less intrusive, and Lofty was able to see what he had only suspected before. In the centre of the road was a black disc.

"Sunray this is Sunray Minor. There is a suspected landmine in the middle of the road. I believe we have an ambush situation." Lofty reported over the radio.

"Sunray Minor, have you seen any Tangos?"

"Negative Sunray. All quiet up here."

"Roger. Deploy as planned and recce the ground. Once we're sure it's all clear we'll deal with the mine. Catfish 1 and Catfish 2, this is Sunray. Catfish 1 deploy your section to the South of the road. At the top of the rise de-bus and proceed on foot, line abreast. Catfish 2, deploy to the North of the road and do the same. Sunray Minor find a vantage point and be ready to give fire support. Over."

The Catfish 1 and 2 section commanders acknowledged their orders and their Mastiffs rolled forward and off the road to the North and South. Lofty took the Jackal back to the top of the hill where he could fire over the heads of Catfish 1 and 2 sections if it became necessary.

Catfish 1 commander was the first to halt his vehicle and the eight men climbed out of the rear doors, taking time to stretch their arms and legs before loping into position. The men formed a line starting above the road and extending away from it towards the summit, each man about ten yards from his neighbour, making the line about 90 yards long in total. A few moments later Cpl Norris of Catfish 2's deployed his men on the other side of the road.

The two sections started to make their way forward, searching for any signs of the enemy. Their Mastiffs chugged along a few yards behind them.

* * *

Abisali was grateful to the unknown commander of the Jackal that he had chosen to climb the Southern hill. From his concealed position on the Northern side of the road he was able to observe without being seen himself. The decision to stop and recce the route was unfortunate. He hadn't expected newly arrived troops to be so cautious. Normally they were quite gung-ho until they had learnt a hard lesson. Perhaps they had an experienced commander.

No matter. He could counter their reconnaissance. It might force the soldiers out from the protection of their armour and give his men softer targets to aim at. He didn't have state of the art encrypted radio systems like the British, but the simple two way walkie-talkie radios that he had purchased in Pakistan would meet his needs.

"Youssef. Take your men and retreat about 200 metres. Keep well hidden. Nasif, you also must pull your men back 200 metres."

By the time the Jackal had come to a halt on the summit of the hill the insurgents were already concealed once again.

As the reconnaissance proceeded Abisali decided on his tactics. Of his twenty strong force, five had been left behind to guard the farm that was their rallying point. Five men were on his side of the road including Nasif, their temporary commander, while on the other side Youssef commanded the other nine. They didn't have the heavy machine gun. Had they brought it with them it would have hampered their withdrawal and it was too valuable an asset to leave behind. They would have to fight with AK-47's and RPGs.

"Youssef, Nasif. Let the kuffar get past you, then when you think the time is right fall on them from the rear. Remember to aim for the legs and arms. When you have done what you can you may retreat and make your way back to the farm. May Allah protect you."

He watched as the two skirmish lines, followed by their armoured trucks, made their slow way across the exposed faces of the hills.

* * *

The sudden crackle of rifle fire drew Lofty's eyes to the North side of the road. A haze of smoke indicated where the firing had come from. The soldiers of Catfish 2 had instinctively gone to ground as the first shots rang out, but they were in a poor position to return fire. Their line was at right angles to their attackers, so only the nearest soldiers were able to bring their rifles to bear.

Lofty focused his attention on the emerging battle. "Contact, contact, contact." Lofty heard Harry Norris's voice in his earphones, notifying all of his platoon that his section was under attack.

"Catfish two one this is Sunray Minor." Lofty responded. "You need to turn to face the attack. I will lay down covering fire. Order your fire teams to pivot left and right."

Glossary

Capt	Captain.
CCTV	Closed circuit television.
Recce	Reconnaissance. The process of gathering intelligence through direct observation of the enemy or terrain.
SDU	Situation display unit, a TV screen inside a Mastiff vehicle that the section commander uses to display views from any one of six external cameras, including infra-red capability for night use.
Sunray	Radio call-sign used to identify the local commander. Sunray Minor identifies the second in command. These may be used with or without the unit's own call-sign, eg Catfish Sunray or just Sunray.
Tango	Radio code word for target.

9 - A Woman's Fear

Emma answered the door wondering who could be disturbing her on a Sunday morning. Facing her on the step was Sam Bruce, brandishing a bottle of Cava.

"Sunday brunch, lovey. Bucks Fizz and smoked salmon bagels." She announced, a broad grin forming on her scarlet lips. She stepped past the bemused Emma and headed for the kitchen

"What, erm. Oh, I'm sorry." stammered Emma. "Come in. Please."

"Taken you by surprise, have I? Good. Surprises are fun."

Sam Bruce described herself as a brassy blonde from Haringey who was sent from heaven to liven up the Sergeants' Mess, which she tried to do at every opportunity. She was one of the few soldiers' wives that Emma had taken to. But still and all, invading someone's house on a Sunday morning! Well, she was here now and trying to put off a force of nature such as Sam was like trying to stop a tsunami with a tea spoon.

"I'll take care of the fizz, love. You get to work on the bagels." commanded Sam tossing a carrier bag of food onto the kitchen work top. "Glasses?"

Emma indicated the appropriate cupboard.

"Nothing better than a bit of Buck's Fizz on a Sunday morning, preferably naked, in bed with the man of your dreams. Unfortunately George Clooney lives too far away so it has to be Cobber." Sam laughed uproariously at her own joke and Emma couldn't prevent a small chuckle from escaping.

"So to what do I owe the pleasure of this visit?" asked Emma, trying to get control of her life back.

"Well, if things are running to form, you'll just about be bursting into tears because Lofty's been away for over a week. Am I right?"

"Well....."

"Thought so. So it's Auntie Sam to the rescue to cheer you up a bit. We'll drink the fizz and eat the bagels then I'm taking you to Cribbs Causeway for some retail therapy. Then this evening we'll go to the pub and get ridiculously drunk. Have you got a spare room I can stay in, so I don't have to drive?"

"Yes, but it's not very comfortable. We haven't really....."

"I'm sure it will do. I'm an army wife. I can sleep on a clothes line if I need to."

Emma sipped at her drink and continued buttering bagels. "Is it always as bad as this when they go away?"

"It never gets better, Emma. I remember the first time Cobber went away. We hadn't been married much longer than you. I was ten months pregnant with our Todd when Cobber was sent to Bosnia. Then four years later I'm ten months pregnant again, this time with Kylie, and he's off to Kosovo. He missed Iraq, thankfully, 'cos the battalion were training to go to Afghanistan for the first time, but this is his third trip there. I think the Afghans have seen more of him than I have."

"Don't you get fed up with it?"

"I used to, but in the end you realise that it goes with the territory. If you don't like it then you shouldn't have married a soldier."

Emma bit into a bagel and considered the older woman's words. Yes, it does go with the territory. Emma had known Lofty was a soldier, and he had never made it any secret that he would be away from time to time, sometimes for several months. He had been very honest with her about that.

"Don't you worry about Cobber? You know, that he might….."

"Get himself killed." Sam finished the sentence for her. "Of course I do. It happens, you only have to turn on the telly to know that. Top tip: Don't read the newspapers while they're away, and don't watch any news on the telly. If something happens, the army will let you know quickly enough, so there's no point reading the horror stories in the press and letting your imagination run riot. It'll just make you ill." Sam tipped her bleached blond head back and emptied the champagne flute before setting about re-filling it.

"So tell me, how did you manage to snare Lofty? I can tell you, there were some broken hearts around when he announced he'd got engaged, and not all of them single women."

"Lofty didn't go out with married women, did he?" Emma was shocked at the thought.

"Oh no. Lofty's not like that. But plenty tried to get him into bed. You've seen him in his football shorts. Who could resist something as hunky as that?"

Emma laughed. "I know what you mean. He's got lovely legs."

"And not just his legs." Sam let out a throaty laugh. "So how did you get him?"

Emma told her about the story of their blind date. "After that things just sort of happened naturally. He'd come up at the weekends and we'd go out, well, mainly go out. We did occasionally spend the whole weekend in bed, but only because the weather was bad. We went on holidays together and of course I came down here from time to time to watch him play football or go to a

Mess function. Anyway, when he proposed to me it just seemed like the right thing to do. I didn't have any second thoughts."

"Quite right. He's quite a catch. You'd have to go a long way to find one better. Apart from my Cobber, maybe, but his legs aren't as nice. When Cobber wears shorts they're like two sticks of celery poking through the bottom of a paper bag." Sam let out another roar of laughter and Emma smiled at the image.

Emma felt the champagne starting to take effect on her and it emboldened her to ask a question. "Are all the wives as rank conscious as they seem, or is it just me?"

"No, it's not just you. Lots of them are like that. They think they wear their husbands rank and throw their weight about accordingly. The CSM's wife, Brenda Smith, is one of the worst. She's a right bitch. She was just waiting for the day when her Dave made it to RSM so she could lord it over us. It won't happen now though."

"Why, what happened?" Sam filled her in on the aftermath of the death on the rifle ranges and the affect it would have on the CSM's career. "Don't be surprised if she's especially bitchy towards you now."

"Why? It had nothing to do with me. I wasn't even living down here at the time."

"Soldiers' wives and soldiers' ranks, lovey. She'll hold you every bit as responsible for Dave being disciplined as she does Lofty. Just watch your back. But if you want my opinion Lofty did exactly the right thing. That Dave Smith has been a liability for years. Thinks he's the big 'I am' but he's only got where he is by stabbing better men in the back. He's a right sneaky bastard."

"You seem to know Lofty well. How long have you known him?"

"Oh, since he first joined the battalion. Must be over ten years now. He used to baby sit our Kylie. Todd as well, but we didn't tell him that of course. Lofty taught Todd how to dribble a ball and how to take a free kick like David Beckham. He's practically our third child. Cobber took him under his wing a bit. I think it helped him get promoted. You know he's the youngest Sergeant in the battalion?"

"No, I didn't know that. I thought it was sort of normal to get promoted as young as that."

"No. Twenty eight or twenty nine is about right for a Sergeant. Cobber spotted him as being above average and recommended him for Lance Corporal and Corporal, much earlier than what was normal. Then the Company Commander started to take an interest in him. He got him onto some courses and he got his third stripe when he was only twenty five. That's young by any standard. But you have to be good or it doesn't matter what age you are."

"How do you cope when Cobber's away?" Emma wondered if there was some secret that she was missing out on. A magic formula that made the time pass quickly and without the constant worrying.

"Wine and chocolate mainly." Laughed Sam. "I'll probably put on two stone before they get back."

"Do all the wives do that?"

"Not all, unfortunately. There'll be a few that will find themselves boyfriends. The clubs in town are full of army wives at the weekends, those that haven't got kids or are able to get babysitters. It's not fair on the blokes and there'll be hell to pay if they find out, but young girls find it hard to stay celibate, it seems."

"Well, that's one thing Lofty won't have to worry about." vowed Emma. "I've never loved anyone the way I love Lofty. No other man could replace him."

"Good for you love. Now, what shops do you want to go to?"

Their talk turned to other things as they planned their afternoon excursion to the Bristol shopping mall.

* * *

Fatima lay on her bed trying to study, but her books lay un-read around her. She couldn't concentrate on what she was doing. Not now. The row with her father had been too severe and she had ended up storming from the room. Her eyes were still puffy with tears and there were streaks through the make up on her cheeks.

She picked up the printed copy of the e-mail that had been the cause of the argument. It had been sent to the computer at her father's place of work, so it had been necessary for him to print it out so he could produce the evidence for his daughter. The paper was wrinkled where she had crushed it in her hand. Just as Youssef had threatened, he had written to her father.

"Mr Rahman, I urge you to reconsider your decision to allow Fatima to study at an English college. The Prophet himself, all blessings be upon him, described women's brains as being deficient. It is therefore unseemly to try to educate them."

This chimed so closely with her father's view that he had at once told her that she was to quit the college.

"That is ridiculous, father. Everyone knows that the Prophet was a great champion of women, and gave them new freedoms that they had never had under the old pagan gods."

112

"Don't you call me ridiculous, child. I am your father. You will show me respect. What is the point of educating you. You will never be able to work. Youssef makes that clear."

And he had. She read the passage in the e-mail again.

"The Sura Al-Ahzab 33:32-33 makes it clear that a woman should stay in the home and only leave it with her husband's permission. In my enlightenment I doubt I would ever give Fatima permission to go out to work."

That simple sentence had nearly broken her heart. How could Youssef have changed his mind so completely? They had talked about this only days before he had left for Pakistan. He had said that she would care for people's minds while he cared for their hearts. Now he was saying that she would never be allowed to work.

Fatima cast her eye over her books. Somewhere within their pages, she felt sure, was the answer to why Youssef had changed so much. She flipped through the index of one of the heavy volumes, her memory speeding her to the correct entry. She found the reference to Kubler-Ross and turned the pages to read the psychologist's description of the five stages of grief.

Stages one and two she recognised quickly. Youssef had been in denial about his family's death when she had first talked to him after the missile attack. He kept telling her that he had to go and dig in the rubble for his family and help to rescue them. Then he had been angry. That was stage two. He had sworn revenge on the Americans for what they had done. He had practically been shouting down the telephone at her. The anger had still been in his voice when they had last spoken.

She read about stage three of the cycle: Bargaining. What bargain had Youssef made, she wondered. Clearly he couldn't bring back his dead family. Of course. He made a bargain with Allah for his chance to get revenge. And his side of the bargain was to undertake jihad.

So he had gone to a Taliban training camp.

But as well as teaching him how to fire a gun they had also taught him their version of Islam. The version that made women wear the burka and demanded that they remain within the home unless they had their husband's permission to leave it.

Fatima knew all about that version. There were some people at the mosque who advocated it. Fortunately, since the departure of Abu Hamza, they were not as influential as they once were.

Fatima quickly read about the final two stages of the cycle: depression and acceptance. The depression phase worried her the most. Would Youssef become so depressed that he might decide to take his own life? No, not take it, but perhaps sacrifice it. She shrank back from the words. *Suicide Bomber*. No, he wouldn't. Surely not. Not the Youssef she loved. But of course he wasn't the Youssef she loved anymore. He was now a stranger whose name she happened to know.

She cast the thought from her mind and focused on more immediate matters. At the moment Fatima wasn't speaking to her father, and her father was threatening to lock her up if she didn't obey his command to leave college. Well, there was something she could do about that. It would hurt her to do it. She would miss her parents, old fashioned as they were. She would talk to the student housing officer and see if she could find her a place to live, preferably sharing with another Muslim girl.

She went down to the kitchen where her parents were watching the omnibus edition of a soap opera.

"Father, I have reached a decision."

"Ah, you have come to your senses at last." Mr Rahman folded his arms and straightened his back, waiting for her to apologise for her behaviour.

"You could say that, father. I have decided to ask for a room at the college. There are many Muslim girls there that I can share with."

Fatima's mother raised her hands to her face and shrieked in protest.

"Don't be so stupid, girl." Her father said. "I forbid it."

"You can forbid it all you like father, but you can't lock me away. There are laws in this country. I'm over eighteen. I'm an adult, a free person. If you won't let me stay at college then I will have to go to the college and stay there."

"No, Fatima. Please, you mustn't." protested her mother.

"Father has left me no choice in the matter." Fatima looked at her mother, the distress she was causing etched into the woman's face. She hated herself for doing it. No, she hated her father for forcing her to do it.

"If you leave this house, child, you will never be allowed back into it again." His words had an air of finality about them.

"And if she leaves this house, Sa'id," said her mother, menacingly, "You will never be allowed in my bedroom again. I may not have much say in this house, but that little I do have."

Mr Rahman was stunned by his wife's open defiance of him. In the twenty five years they had been married she had never spoken to him like that.

"But a child must obey her father. And a wife must obey her husband."

"You will find it hard to gain my obedience from the wrong side of a locked door. Make no mistake, Sa'id. I mean what I say."

"Am I not master in my own house?" he shouted

"Yes you are, husband. But I am mistress of my own body. If Fatima leaves this house then you may as well become a eunuch."

Mr Rahman rose from his chair and grabbed his jacket from the peg behind the door. He stormed from the room, slamming the kitchen door behind him. The house shuddered as the front door was given similar treatment.

"He'll be back when he's calmed down, and I'm sure I can get him to see reason. Besides, I have no desire to become the first Muslim nun." The older woman said, patting the empty chair beside her. "Now my child, tell me what is going on."

* * *

Catfish two one gasped an acknowledgement into Lofty's headphones and Lofty ordered his machine gunner to open fire on the line of attackers. The first three round burst had barely left the gun's barrel when the Catfish 2's Delta fire team, the men nearest to the attack, rose and swung through 90 degrees to the left. As the new line formed they dropped to the ground and found fresh cover, however inadequate it might be.

They started laying down covering fire as the Charlie fire team stood and sprinted the greater distance towards the right flank of the new line. Lofty gasped with horror as he saw Catfish two one fall to the ground and lie still.

"All stations, this is Sunray Minor. Catfish two one is down. I repeat man down."

What the fuck was the Catfish 2 Mastiff crew doing? Why weren't they launching smoke grenades to cover the section's manoeuvres and why weren't they using their machine gun to support the redeployment? Lofty let off some invective over the net. It was a severe breach of radio discipline but it had instant results. Belatedly a flat pop sounded from the Mastiff and a thin trail of smoke traced the path of the canister until it hit the ground and started to spew out a dense cloud. At last the Mastiff's machine gun started barking.

"Sunray Minor this is Sunray. What are your intentions?"

From his disadvantaged position down on the road the Platoon Commander could only follow events by interpreting the radio traffic.

"Sunray, request air cover, and also suggest we get reinforcements out here."

They were seven kilometres from the FOB. It would take only a few minutes for 4 Platoon to reach them.

"Roger Sunray Minor. What can you do for the casualty?"

"I'm going to take my vehicle round to the other side and pick him up." Catfish 2's Mastiff was needed to maintain covering fire. Besides, the way the crew had apparently frozen suggested they weren't reliable enough to take care of a seriously injured man.

"Roger. Make sure you maintain fire support."

Easier said than done, thought Lofty as he surveyed the route to the other side. As they dropped to the level of the road to cross it they would lose sight of the battle on the slopes above them, and their 7.62 millimetre GPMG would be as useful as the walking stick that the old man had been carrying that afternoon. He would have to rely on the Catfish 2 Mastiff's crew to keep up the covering fire.

Lofty gave the driver his orders and the vehicle leapt forward. On the rough surface it wouldn't be able to reach anywhere near its top speed of 80 m.p.h. but Lofty urged his driver to get to the other side of the defile as fast as possible.

They raced past Catfish 1 as they crouched in cover. They weren't in a position to do anything for their comrades in Catfish 2. If they opened fire they were as likely to hit friend as foe. However, they were at risk from stray bullets fired from the far side of the road. Lofty noticed that they were still in their extended skirmish line.

"Catfish 1," He barked into his radio, "form a defensive perimeter at the top of the cliff." When they got back to the FOB he would give Mickey Flynn such a bollocking for not redeploying his section as soon as the first bullet had been fired. He turned to look back and saw the section hurry to form a semi-circle, each end of the arc anchored by the edge of the low cliff.

The vehicle bucked and jolted its way down to the road and sprinted across the smoother surface to the other side. As they started to climb again Lofty's radio crackled into life.

"Contact, contact, contact. This is Catfish one one, we are under attack."

Fuck. The enemy were on both sides of the road.

"Catfish 3 this is Sunray. Deploy as follows: Go South 500 metres and turn East to take the enemy from the rear. Sunray Minor, you take command on the North side and act on your own initiative and I'll take command on the South side."

Splitting the platoon wasn't a good thing to do, but with an attack from two sides it was the only option that the Platoon Commander had.

"Man down, man down. This is Catfish one one, man down."

Not Lofty's problem anymore. Sunray would have to deal with that. The Jackal bucked to the top of the rise and Lofty directed the driver to put the vehicle between the casualty and the firing. The vehicle skidded to a halt in a spray of dust and grit. The gunner swung his weapon to face North and re-started his short bursts of covering fire over the heads of Catfish 2. The driver threw himself out of his vehicle and ran round it to join Lofty beside the casualty. The two men worked together to staunch the flow of blood.

The bullet had hit Cpl Norris in the side, entering through an unprotected gap in his body armour, just below his right armpit. A lucky shot. Well, for Norris it was more of an unlucky shot. He was still alive, but barely conscious.

"Don't worry, Harry." Lofty reassured him. "You're gonna be alright. It's only a flesh wound." The amount of blood that soaked Norris's uniform said it was a lie, but there was no need for him to know that. Lofty heard the sound of air bubbling from the wound and knew that the bullet had pierced a lung. A sucking wound they called it. The driver stripped Harry's

Osprey body armour off him so that they could dress the wound.

Lofty fished in Norris's pocket until he found his field dressing. He jammed the thick linen pad into the wound then pressed his own field dressing on top. That at least should stop Norris's lung from collapsing. The driver tied the dressing into place.

"It's best not to move him." Lofty told the driver. "We'll wait where we are until a helicopter comes for him, unless the fighting forces us to move." The driver nodded his understanding and wriggled across to take up a firing position at the front of the vehicle. He didn't have any targets within view, but he would be able to protect that side if the enemy tried to attack them.

Lofty worked to make Norris more comfortable, talking to him and reassuring him that he would be alright. Privately Lofty hoped his optimism was justified.

A grenade from an RPG exploded against the armour on the far side of the Jackal, rocking it on its suspension. The gunner thudded to the ground as he was thrown from the vehicle by the blast. He narrowly missed landing on top of Lofty and the wounded Harry Norris. The gunner sat up, dazed but otherwise unhurt. Shaking his head to clear it he climbed back up onto his vehicle and started to return fire again. He let out a triumphal shout of vengeance as he saw an attacker drop to his first fresh burst of fire.

* * *

Abisali saw the Mastiff as it climbed the hill on a course that would take it behind his fighters and cut them off.

"Youssef, Nasif, you have done enough. Pull your men out and make your way back to safety. Take the wounded if you can." Abisali's radio crackled as his orders were acknowledged and he saw the first movements of his fighters as they broke cover and scurried away from the fighting.

"Cease fire. Cease fire. All stations cease fire." The RoE prohibited firing on the enemy if they were fleeing, even though they might still be armed and dangerous. Inside his command vehicle Captain Trent decided he couldn't take the risk of his men being led into another trap. He called off the pursuit, stifling his curses of frustration at having to let the enemy go. He used the Brigade radio net to notify his senior commanders of the different directions the enemy were taking. Brigade would direct a pursuit from the air. The priority now was the evacuation of casualties and getting the rest of his men back to the safety of Camp Elizabeth. Through the windscreen of the Panther he saw a growing plume of dust make its way Westward along the road. 4 Platoon to the rescue; a bit late but none the less welcome. He radioed his section commanders to make their 'after action' reports.

Glossary

GPMG   General purpose machine gun, 7.62 mm calibre, belt fed. See also jimpy

RoE   Rules of Engagement. A set of rules based on British and International law that describes the circumstances under which British forces may use deadly force. Other nationalities in ISAF may use different RoE based on their own law.

10 - After Action

Lofty waited patiently outside the Company Office. After the Lord Mayor's Show comes the man with the bucket of shit and Lofty had a suspicion it was going to be tipped all over him. Earlier the CSM had grinned at him. An evil grin that said he was going to take sadistic delight in somebody's suffering. Captain Trent and the Company Commander had been locked in discussion ever since.

The aftermath of the skirmish, it couldn't be called a battle, had been an anti-climax. Blood stains showed that the platoon had inflicted casualties on their attackers, but there were no signs of bodies. A medevac helicopter had arrived and taken Cpl Norris and Nobby Clark, the Catfish 1 casualty, off to the field hospital at Camp Bastion, while 4 Platoon cautiously chased after the insurgents, aided by an Apache attack helicopter. They had found nothing except a few droplets of blood, but too few to constitute a trail. As dusk started to fall they abandoned the search and returned to Camp Elizabeth.

Lofty had checked the men over to make sure there were no undeclared injuries, then stood them down to get some food and clean their weapons. He caught up with Micky Flynn as he headed for the latrine wagon.

"What the fuck were you playing at Mickey? Keeping your men in line abreast after the first contact."

"Sorry Lofty." Lofty wouldn't normally have allowed such familiarity, but he and Mickey had been friends for years, on and off the football pitch. First name terms were permissible in private, even during a bollocking. "I knew that I should have changed formation, but I couldn't make out where the firing was coming from. The echo of the shots confused me."

"Don't give me that, Mickey. You heard Harry Norris call the contact from his side of the road."

"Alright, I admit it, I should have re-deployed my men, but they had all taken cover and it seemed like more of a risk to make them move."

"That could have got your men killed if the enemy had tried to rush you. They'd have rolled your entire section up from one end. You had no protection on your open flank." Lofty lowered his voice. "Its basic stuff Mickey, you know it. You don't necessarily have to do the right thing, but you do have to do something. You know it makes sense."

"Sorry Lofty. It won't happen again."

"Make sure it doesn't. And just as a reminder you and your section can police up the parade ground this evening." A couple of hours picking up litter and fag ends would provide a salutary lesson.

"Lofty, look, I am sorry. It's the first time I've been under fire. It's OK for you, you've done this before, but me and the lads, this is our first time out here. I know I should have reacted better, remembered the training, but when that first round comes at you, well, I had no idea how shit scared I'd be."

Lofty remembered back to his first time. Mickey was right; it was scary. But Cobber had seen him through it. Mickey had been out on a limb by himself and he had to remember that.

"OK, but there aren't any more first times. If you get it wrong again it may be for the last time, if not for you then for one of your section. You can't afford to freeze."

"I hear you Sarge. It won't happen again."

"Make sure it doesn't Mickey."

Lofty turned on his heel and went in search of the Sergeant in charge of the vehicle crews. He had words for him as well.

The vehicle crews were on loan from the 17th/21st Lancers. They had been working with the Middlesex from March all the way to their training exercises in Kenya before the deployment. They had practiced anti-ambush drills before, and Lofty was severely concerned about the way the Catfish 2 Mastiff crew had frozen.

The driver and gunner had been contrite, but Lofty was insistent. He wasn't going to put his men at risk with a vehicle crew that froze when the firing started. He insisted that the Sergeant replace the two men. The Lancer Sergeant was reluctant to do it, but in the end he agreed to swap the gunner. He could use him elsewhere. The driver, who hadn't really done much wrong, would stay. Lofty accepted the compromise.

* * *

"Youssef, how good to see you." Ali greeted him, pushing his way into the crowded farm house. Youssef gave a smile of relief and a welcoming wave. Ali was one of the brighter of his men.

The stragglers were still coming in. Once the retreat started the men had split up, each finding their own hiding place, until darkness allowed them to return to their base. They reported hearing the helicopters overhead and the vehicles of the soldiers searching the ground. Boots had crunched close by but none had come close enough to be able to discover them

They had lost one man. His name was Qadeer and Youssef arranged a simple funeral for him in a shallow grave behind the farm. Two others had been wounded, one from Nasif's squad and one from his own, but neither wound was serious and both men would be able to travel.

The men chattered excitedly, still high on adrenalin. They told stories of their prowess with their rifles and of how many of the British Tommies they had killed. To hear them talk you would think that the battlefield was littered with dead bodies, Youssef thought, but he believed that there probably hadn't been any of the soldiers killed. Wounded, yes, but none killed.

Last to arrive was Abisali. He praised his men for their valour and accepted their stories of heroism. Later, privately, he told Youssef what he really thought.

"I only saw two stretchers being loaded into the helicopter. Both had their faces visible, so I doubt they were dead." Youssef nodded his agreement.

"But we bloodied their noses. They won't forget us in a hurry." he added.

Before midnight Abisali led his men South and West, heading for safer territory where his men could lay up until he decided on their next mission. By the time that 4 Platoon arrived to search the farm the next day they were many kilometres away. A fist full of Yankee dollars had bought the silence of the farmer and his family.

* * *

"So what's your version of events, Sergeant Lofthouse." The Company Commander, Major Hardcastle, asked him.

Lofty summarised the short battle. The communications log showed that it had lasted less than ten minutes, even though it had felt like an hour.

"Do you think you did the right things?"

"Well, I followed the plan, but in hindsight we could have done it better."

"Well, I heard your briefing last night, and the possibility of an ambush was covered. Hindsight is a wonderful thing. Pity we didn't have it last night." He paused. "The CSM thinks you cocked it up."

"With due respect, Sir, the CSM is entitled to his opinion, but I think I did the best I could have done considering the circumstances. The CSM wasn't actually there, Sir. He can't know all the ins and outs."

"He did hear it over the net. He's an experienced soldier."

"Hearing it on the net and seeing it on the ground are two different things, Sir. The rag heads had better field craft than we gave them credit for. That was a mistake. They also had the advantage of being able to watch us deploy and then react to what we did. It gave them the edge."

"And that is what Captain Trent and I told the CSM. Look, Sergeant Lofthouse, it wasn't all bad. I've discussed the whole patrol with your OC and you stuck to the plan, which was good. No plan survives first contact and you adapted successfully. I think you would have got bounced whatever you had done. Your attackers seemed to be one step ahead of you all the time. The big mistake that both you and Capt Trent made was to underestimate them, and you aren't the first to do that and I doubt you'll be the last. On the plus side your men performed well, even though there were some glitches. Have you spoken to the Catfish 1 leader and the Catfish 2 Mastiff crew?"

"I have, Sir. Cpl Flynn has had his card marked and you'll find the parade square a bit cleaner tonight. Sergeant Colthurst, the Lancers Sergeant, has agreed to replace the Catfish 2 gunner. I think that will help. It shows what standards the Middlesex expect."

"Good. We'll say no more about it for now then. Though I have had to concede to the CSM's request to go out with your patrols."

Lofty's cheeks burned. It was as good as a rebuke. "Very well, Sir. If that's what you want." He said through gritted teeth, his pride injured.

"It is, Sergeant." The Major allowed himself a smile. "Don't worry. I'll keep the matter under review, and if I think the CSM can be of more use back here then I'll reconsider my decision."

"How are Cpl Norris and Pvt Clark, Sir?"

"Well, Clark is OK. His Osprey stopped the bullet and all he's got is some bruised ribs. He'll do a week of light duties up at Bastion and be back with you next week. Unfortunately Cpl Norris is quite poorly. They're sending him back to UK on the next medevac flight. He's stable, but he lost a lot of blood. The doctors think he'll make it though."

"That's good news, Sir."

"OK, Thank you Sergeant Lofthouse. Dismiss."

Lofty threw up a salute, turned about and marched out of the office.

* * *

They had been at a meeting of senior Taliban leaders, held in the house of an opium farmer; One of the many who supported the Taliban in return for promises that

127

their activities would be overlooked once the Westerners had been thrown out of their country. Youssef realised how important Abisali was when so many of the others, many much older than his leader, deferred to his opinion and looked to him for counsel. Having devised their strategy for the coming months Youssef and his leader headed back towards the caves that they were now calling home.

Their dirt bikes bumped along the rough ground, a convenient method of travel across the terrain of the Afghan plains. If they were pursued the only effective method of following them was from the air and even the NATO air forces couldn't be everywhere at once.

Silence fell as the bikes' engines were switched off and they rolled them into a narrow opening in the wall of a wadi, covering the entrance with dried brush. The last few kilometres would have to be covered on foot and most of it was uphill.

Youssef heard the noise first. The unmistakable sound of a female screaming in fear. He broke into a run, covering the last few hundred metres at a hard sprint. The scream was repeated and it didn't take Youssef long to realise that it was coming from the cave that served as their refuge. There should be no women in there.

He ducked beneath the low entrance and then straightened as the cave opened out. Two of the fighters were struggling with a woman, no, a girl trying to pin her to the ground. She kicked out at them, but her sandal clad feet made no impact. Youssef shouted a protest and launched a kick at the nearest man, catching him in the ribs. The man gasped in pain and rolled away from his victim. The second man straightened and backed away before Youssef could assault him as well.

"What is going on here? Who is this girl?"

"She's ours. We found her and now she's our prisoner." replied the one who was able to breath properly. Youssef recognised him as Gamal. The other was his best friend Taj.

"What do you mean, your prisoner? She's just a girl."

"She's old enough." gasped Taj from where he was lying on the ground. "Come on, we only want a bit of fun."

"And when you've had your fun, what then? What happens to a girl who has been defiled?"

"Not our problem. That will be her family's problem." replied Gamal. "Look, she's not properly dressed, not like a true believer should be. Where is her Burka? She is already a whore."

Youssef looked at how the girl was dressed. As far as he could see there was nothing wrong with her clothing. She was in a plain coloured full length dress made of some rough material that covered her from her neck to her feet. No doubt the best that her family could afford. As he watched she adjusted her hijab so that her hair and throat were properly covered again so that only her face was visible. A glint of metal at the cuffs of her sleeves suggested gold bracelets, but that was nothing unusual. As in many cultures girls wore their dowries in the form of jewellery so that prospective husbands would know that the girl would bring a little wealth with her to her wedding.

By then Abisali had caught up with his subordinate. "Come on, Youssef." he said. "They only want a bit of fun. You can't keep men cooped up without women for long. It's bad for morale."

Youssef turned to face him. "We need to talk in private."

When the two men had released her the girl had scurried back to the relative protection of the cave wall. Youssef walked across to her and held out his hand. "Come, little one. You have nothing to fear from me."

The girl tentatively took his hand and stood up to go with him. She was about thirteen years old, but with her tear stained face she looked much younger. Youssef walked back out of the cave, jerking his head to indicate that he wanted Abisali to follow him.

"We can't treat our own people like this." he rounded on his leader. "This is the sort of thing Mohamed Omar raised the Taliban to put a stop to. If we now do it we become as bad as our enemies. If we start raping young girls then we are no better than the forces of Shaytaan who oppose us."

"Youssef, the men need some relaxation. So they have a little bit of fun, then we send her back to her parents with a sack full of Yankee cigarettes. They will be happy."

"How can you be so sure? How can you be sure they won't just send the girl away, so she ends up selling herself on Kandahar market. And what if she becomes pregnant? What then?"

"Gamal is right. She's dressed like a whore. Maybe she is one."

Youssef snorted in derision. "In Abbottabad you would pass her in the street unnoticed dressed like that. Where I live in England she would be regarded as being dressed as modestly as a true believer should be. Are you telling me you believe the only correct dress for a child is a burka? It is the role of the man to protect the woman, not to prey on her. Would you have us start to behave like beasts?"

Youssef gave a wry smile. "See, Youssef. I told you that you would become a good leader. You argue your case well, and you are willing to discipline your men. I agree. The girl must be returned to her parents at once. Will you do it or shall I?"

"I'll do it myself." snapped Youssef. Had Abisali been goading him, as some sort of test?

"In that case I shall go and deal with Gamal and Taj. They need to know how true believers behave towards women." Abisali turned back towards the cave. "Make sure the girl forgets where we are. We don't want any visits from the kuffar."

Perhaps that's something that Gamal and Taj should have thought about, thought Youssef. Or maybe they didn't think it would be a problem. Maybe the girl was never meant to go home. Just another of the young girls who turn up dead in Afghanistan, and for which the kuffar would take the blame.

Youssef turned his back on the cave and held his hand out to the girl again. "Come, little one. I'll take you home to your family."

She smiled shyly at him but declined to take his hand, remembering that contact between men and women who weren't related was forbidden.

Was this what they could expect if the Taliban were victorious once again and took over the running of the country? Youssef believed that he was fighting on the side of right, but how could he be sure? Men like Gamal and Taj would be rewarded for their part in the victory. They might be given senior posts. Would they use them to take whatever they wanted, whenever they wanted? Youssef had read the stories of how Saddam Hussein's sons had behaved in Iraq. How they took girls from their families and raped them, beat them and even killed them. After what he had just seen he wondered if it was possible for that sort of evil to become part of Afghanistan.

He shook his head in sorrow. The girl looked up, curious about the gesture. Youssef smiled reassuringly and helped her down a rocky part of the path.

Glossary

Apache   Boeing AH-64 ground attack helicopter used by the British and US armies. It's capable of carrying rockets and anti-tank missiles and is equipped with a 30 mm calibre M230 Chain Gun.

11 - Routine And Revelations

After the initial excitement of the skirmish on the road back from Zābol things settled into a routine for C Company. There was a constant round of sentry duties, foot patrols, mounted patrols and Vehicle Check Points (VCPs) to be carried out. In one way it was good. Idle soldiers get very bored very quickly and they often turn to mischief. Not so bad when its harmless stuff, like a mickey taking video for YouTube, but sometimes they turned to practical jokes, some of which finished with bad consequences.

As a whole the battalion didn't suffer too many casualties. B Company lost four men to two separate roadside bombs, with a number of lesser casualties. The Royal Warwickshire's, one of the other three infantry battalions that formed the Brigade, suffered more. Based up in the Musa Qala and Nahri Saraj districts, two of their FOBs came under simultaneous direct attacks which stretched their resources to the limit.

C Company had been plagued by a sniper that seemed to follow them around. 1 Platoon in particular attracted his attention. Fortunately he wasn't a great shot, but he didn't need to be. The sniper only had to get lucky once; 1 Platoon had to be lucky all the time.

Even having the CSM accompany the patrols hadn't been as bad as Lofty had anticipated. For the most part he had managed to steer clear of the Warrant Officer. If the CSM wanted to be at the front of a patrol Lofty would place himself at the back. If the CSM took a position on the left of the line then Lofty would be on the right. If they needed to confer then there was always the radio. It worked, though Lofty was very careful to make sure that the CSM was never behind him, which stretched his nerves even tighter than they already were.

Now the Battalion were into their second month in Afghanistan and the days were getting colder. Snow had appeared on the distant peaks and sudden rain showers had brought a green tinge to the otherwise barren plain. The spartan fields that were cultivated for grain and vegetables were ploughed and seeded ready for the next year's crops. Winter favoured the British. The Taliban preferred to retreat over the border into Pakistan to find themselves warmer places to hide, though C Company seemed to have a more determined enemy to deal with.

Lofty lay on his bed reading an out of date magazine and listening to music through headphones when he was disturbed by shouting from the long barrack room next door. Furniture crashed and more voices joined in. Not again, thought Lofty. It was the tedium, he knew. That and the constant tension of being in a combat zone. It made the men's nerves raw and their anger quick to rise. He levered himself off his bed and made his way out into the noise.

"OK you two, break it up." His voice bellowed over the hubbub. He saw it was Nosey Parker and Terry Griffiths of Catfish 3. That was bad. The two men were close friends and when close friends started fighting it meant morale had reached rock bottom. Lofty broke through the circle of on lookers and stepped into the gap between the pit spaces where the fight had taken place.

"Right, now who's going to tell me how this started."

The two men stared at the floor, neither wanting to be the first to speak.

"OK, if that's how you want it. Parker, what happened." Lofty snapped.

"It was his fault, Sarge." Nosey pointed at his friend. "He wouldn't give me my mag back."

Lofty spotted a much thumbed copy of a glamour magazine lying on the floor.

"And did you have his magazine?" Lofty asked Griffiths.

"He gave it to me, Sarge. I thought it was for keeps."

"Liar." shouted Parker. "You know it was only a loan."

Lofty recognised that it had been a silly dispute that had spiralled out of control. He retrieved the magazine and tore it down the middle. "Enough, both of you. There. Are you happy now?" He handed each soldier half of the magazine before turning to address the room. "You're like a bunch of kids, all of you, squabbling over your toys. Now, if I have to come here and sort you out again I'll have you all doing circuits round the parade square in full kit with your rifles above you head. It's bad enough the rag heads trying to kill you without you having a go at each other."

Lofty turned on his heel and stamped his way back into his tiny room, to find Cobber Bruce sitting on the packing case he used as a bedside table, swigging from a can of beer.

"All that fucking fuss over a girly mag." Lofty spat.

What next, he wondered. He didn't want to be too hard on them, they were just frightened boys, but if things got out of hand it wouldn't be long before something serious happened and someone would be on a charge, or worse, someone might get seriously hurt. Each man had a loaded rifle and a bayonet at his disposal and with such weapons came the risk of serious injury or death if it was decided that fists weren't enough to settle a dispute.

"Little things get blown out of proportion. You know that." Cobber commented. "Did you know that during the Napoleonic Wars a soldier might only face gunfire two or three times in a year?"

"Is that so?" replied Lofty, not really interested in 200 year old historical anecdotes.

"Yep. Then they all marched around the countryside, each side trying to gain an advantage, and maybe a couple of months later there'd be another battle. And they hardly ever fought in Winter. So maybe only three or four days fighting a year, unless they were really unlucky."

"Is there a point to this?" asked Lofty, wearily.

"I'm getting there. Then in the First World War the soldiers weren't in the trenches all the time. They'd maybe have a week in the front line, a week in the reserve trenches and a week working in the rear areas before going back to the front again. Even in the front line there was always work to be done, mending barbed wire, rebuilding damaged trench fronts, trying to kill rats or just trying to stay alive. So the men were always busy even if there was no fighting. Same in the Second World War. No one was exposed to fighting and danger all the time. But look at things here."

"Yeah, I get it. Here we're under non-stop pressure. We get shot at every day, never know when we're going to step on an IED, and never knowing where the enemy are. Then, as a reward, we get a week

136

on stag staring out at nothing and hoping we won't see anything."

"Yep. And never any time off. If you're lucky you might get a couple of days R&R in Cyprus, if there's a spare seat on an aircraft. So there's far more stress and far more fear about all the time. No wonder the lads get a bit skittish from time to time. Do you know Ben Sykes?"

"Corporal in B Company?"

"Yes, that's him. Word has it that he sat down in a corner last week and started crying. Nothing could stop him. Well, they took his rifle off him just in case, but they couldn't get him to stop. He didn't sleep for three days before they sent him to the medics. The shrinks up at Bastion are sending him home."

"But he's a great big bloke. Plays rugby for the battalion, and if I remember rightly he's something of a tae kwon do expert."

"Yep, just shows that you can't tell who's going to buckle under the strain and who's not. Some people can't take it and some of the most unlikely blossom under the pressure."

"Is that the end of the lesson?" asked Lofty sarcastically, regretting it instantly. Cobber was only trying to help, after all.

"Yeah, I reckon so. I've got a hot date with the stores inventory to sort out. See you later." He patted Lofty on the shoulder and sauntered away through the barrack room.

Lofty put his headphones back on and allowed Michael Bublé to calm him down a little.

* * *

In the Company Offices, Cpl Debbie Moon sat examining the latest contact reports. 1 Platoon again, she mused. They seemed to be dogged by bad luck. Another sniper attack while they were out on a foot patrol. Brigade G2 had even noticed that they suffered more than their fair share of attention.

She opened up a spread sheet on her laptop and entered the new data by date, type of incident, casualties, number of shots fired and a raft of other information. She tabbed between pages to compare Catfish with the other three platoons. The only time they seemed to get any peace was when they were on stag. Almost without fail they were subjected to attack when they went outside the walls of the FOB, whereas the other three platoons attracted much less attention. So, she mused, what was the difference between Catfish and the others?

Nothing sprang out of the computer screen at her, so she would have to slog through a process of elimination.

The first thing she eliminated was direct observation of the FOB. Firstly there was no high ground from which an observer could see what was happening inside the FOB and secondly any observation would affect all the platoons equally.

So, how about a spy inside the FOB? Well, there were a few Afghans who came and went, people such as the refuse collectors and kitchen hands, but again they would spy on all the platoons, not just Catfish. She shifted her attention to the two Afghan interpreters. They seemed more promising.

A few minutes later she discarded the idea of the interpreters being the source of the problem. They attended the briefings for the patrols they would accompany, but each patrol only took one interpreter with them at a time. The allocation of interpreters to patrols was random, and both men had been with Catfish on occasions when they had been attacked, but more importantly they hadn't been with them on other occasions. That meant they hadn't attended the briefings, which in turn meant they wouldn't have had access to the information necessary to mount an attack on the patrol.

So that left only one answer. The leak was inside Catfish platoon itself. And if that was the case then it wasn't leaking through direct contact with the insurgents. It had to be getting out by another route and that almost certainly meant an electronic route. She searched the office for a particular document, finding it on the CSM's desk. She quickly read through it.

The document was the record of who had made calls home using the MoD concessionary system. Each soldier was allowed up to thirty minutes of phone calls each week, and the CSM kept a careful record so that no one could abuse the system. The record came up blank. Once again the call log didn't match up with the pattern of attacks.

Debbie knew there were privately owned mobile phones in use, connecting through satellites to loved ones back home. It would be difficult to prove they were the source of the leak, but it could be done. She would have to get the telephone numbers of the phones and then obtain the call records from the service providers. It would need someone back in the UK to manage it all for her. It was something, but she would hold off of that for the moment. Besides, it wouldn't help her with the smart phones that connected through the internet.

An idea entered her mind as she thought of the internet. Why hadn't she thought of it before? It was so obvious.

Closing down the files on her laptop Debbie opened up the laptop's internet browser. She typed in the name of the site she wanted. Access denied. Of course, the MoD didn't like its assets being used for social networking. Debbie made a phone call to Camp Bastion and a few minutes later she was allowed to view the sites she wanted. She clicked on the 'Find Friends' link and started typing in the names of the soldiers of Catfish Platoon. Most of them had accounts, but the posts on them told her nothing she considered significant.

Rubbing the tiredness from her eyes Debbie was about to give up for the day but decided to try just one more name, placing a neat tick beside it on the nominal roll as she did so. The page opened and as she read the posts her mouth dropped opened as well. There was now no doubt in her mind about where the Catfish Platoon leak was.

* * *

Lofty was on his way from his accommodation block to the dining area when Debbie Moon called to him and beckoned him across to the Company Offices. They had worked together on a number of patrols and Lofty had developed a liking for the young Intelligence Corps soldier. He noted the serious look on the woman's face. This wasn't a social call.

"I think you need to see this." was her opening remark. Ominous. "Brigade G2 have been worried about the number of attacks that have been happening when we're out on patrol. The rag heads seem to be able to anticipate where we're going to be."

"Well, we do seem to attract a lot of attention. Do you think we have a mole in the unit? The only Afghans permanently inside the perimeter are the interpreters. Could it be one of them?"

"No. There's only two of them, and they only attend the briefings for the patrols they're going out on. So they can't know what all the platoons are doing. Look at yesterday. That bloody sniper again, but you didn't have an interpreter with you, did you?"

"No. We didn't need one. We were only escorting the re-supply convoy through the area."

"Yet you'd hardly been out there for ten minutes when the patrol was stopped by a suspect IED and when your EOD operative went to check it out he came under fire."

"Could have been a coincidence."

"No. There are probably less than 200 active Taliban in the whole province. OK, they get reinforced by hired muscle from the opium growers, from time to time, but they can't afford to sit out on a hillside just in case a patrol happens by. No, they're getting intelligence from somewhere."

"So what do you want with me?"

"Well, your platoon seems to be more prone to sniper attacks than any other. Then there was that ambush on your first trip out. It wasn't bad luck or coincidence. There were too many of them. They knew you were coming."

"So, you think you know where the leak is?"

"Abso-fucking- lutely. Its Ronnie King."

"Ronnie? No, you're having a laugh. He's not the sharpest knife in the drawer, but he's no traitor."

"I didn't say he was a traitor. I said I think he's the source of the leak. Come and look at this." She led him across to the laptop sitting on top of her desk. Waking up the computer she accessed what Lofty recognised as a Facebook page. She scrolled down until she found what she was looking for. "There you go. Read that."

Lofty read the post. "Out on patrol again tomorrow escorting a supplies convoy along the road to Bastion. Boring!"

"Shit."

"Oh, and there's more." Debbie affirmed, scrolling down to previous posts. Lofty read them one at a time. "I've cross checked them with your contact reports. Every time you were hit by the sniper King made a post like that one the night before. Usually straight after the O Group. This is the biggy, of course." She scrolled down to the post King had made about their first patrol. The one where they had been ambushed.

"Wait here." Lofty instructed. "I'll be back in a mo."

Lofty was as good as his word and returned a few moments later with a bemused Pvt King. The soldier was still chewing his last mouthful of dinner. Lofty pushed him in front of the laptop and told him to read his posts out loud.

"What the fuck are doing putting operational information on Facebook?" roared Lofty in his best parade ground voice. King flinched.

"It's harmless Sarge." He stammered. "Just telling my mates what we're up to out here."

"And how many mates do you have on Facebook?"

"Oh, I think I'm up to 200 now." King replied proudly.

"And you know each and every one of them personally do you?"

"Well, some of them are friends of friends, but they're still interested in what we're doing."

"Oh I just fucking bet they are. You attended the Operational Security training, didn't you?"

"Of course I did Sarge. We all had to. But what's that got to do with this?"

"What it's got to do with it, you muppet, is that anyone who is your friend on Facebook can read this and tell someone else. That's what OpSec is all about: Not telling anyone else what we're doing in case they compromise the operation."

"But like I said Sarge, none of my friends would do that."

"What about the friends of friends, or the friends of friends of friends, eh? Cpl Moon here has crossed checked your posts with the sniper attacks. Every time we got hit you've made a post on here, you fucking moron. Because of your posts Harry Norris is lying in hospital in Birmingham. Your little post nearly got him killed."

Realisation started to dawn on Pvt King, but he wasn't about to admit liability yet. "Could be just a coincidence."

"OK, if it's just a coincidence, why don't you put a post on here that says you're going to be walking around outside the walls tomorrow with no body armour on. Shall we wait and see if the sniper turns up and takes a shot at you?"

"You wouldn't do that, would you Sarge?" King sounded genuinely worried about the possibility.

"Why not. It's just coincidence, isn't it? Fancy your chances?" King clearly didn't. "Now, I'm going to tell you what's going to happen. Cpl Moon is going to give you some paper, and you're going to go through this list of Facebook friends and you're going to write down everything you know about them: names, addresses, how you know them, anything that tells us if they're genuine or not. You're not going to look at their profiles, you're going to get it out of here." Lofty rapped his knuckles on King's head, hard enough to make him gasp with pain. "Any of them you don't really know you're going to put a big question mark against. Got it?"

"Yes Sarge. Can I finish my dinner first?"

"No you fucking may not. Get on with it."

Debbie Moon provided paper and pencils and Lofty stood back as King started writing. Debbie joined Lofty and they conversed in a low tone.

"Do you think we'll find out which of them is the leak?" asked Lofty.

"Probably not just from King, but G2 will cross refer to other Facebook accounts in other units and see if any of the same names keep coming up. If we're right then we'll find out fairly soon. What makes it worse is that King hasn't disabled his location information. Every time he posts on his page his smart 'phone tells Facebook exactly where he is, and it continues to track him, all day, every day. Your platoon may as well have a fucking great neon sign hovering over it."

Lofty let out a groan. "OK, look, I'm going to have to tell the OC about this. He'll have me for breakfast if I don't. I suppose you're going to have to tell Brigade."

"Sorry," she grimaced. "but I can't keep something like this in house. Look, I doubt that King is the only idiot in the Brigade. They'll jump up and

144

down a bit and fire off all points bulletins to get thing back under control and close down the leaks, but there's not much else they can do. Dealing with King will be left in your hands. What will you do with him?"

"Pvt fucking King is in for a very long spell in the cookhouse, scraping plates and scrubbing tins. It will be a while before I allow him outside the FOB again." A thought struck him. "Look, maybe there's a way we can turn this to our advantage. If the rag heads are using Facebook to find out what we're doing, why don't we use it to sucker them in?"

"You mean post false information?"

"Yeah. Why not? The intel's been good for them so far, so why wouldn't they believe it if we got King to post some more?"

"I'll put it to G2. I'm guessing they'd want to control it, of course. They would take over King's page, and any other suspect pages they find, and they'd decide what to post."

"But maybe, just a for a change, we'd be one step ahead of them. With the right information we could even cripple them completely."

"I'll put it up the line." Debbie smiled reassuringly. In the stark light of the generator powered neon tubes Lofty thought she looked quite attractive. Some women suit uniform and Debbie was one of them.

"Thanks. Let me know when King's finished. We can go through his list together." Debbie said with an impish smile.

Lofty left the office and went to get his belated dinner. Bloody King. Bloody technology. As if he didn't have enough on his plate without an idiot like him to contend with.

145

* * *

"I see you've been crying again, Fatima." Mrs Rahman observed.

The girl looked up and gave her mother a wan smile. "I'm sorry, it's just that I'm so worried about Youssef."

"And what has that silly boy been up to, making my lovely girl cry like this?"

"That's the problem, Mummy. I don't know what he's up to." She pushed a newspaper across the kitchen table towards her mother. The headline reported the death of another soldier in Helmand Province.

"You can't know that he was involved." Her mother stated, knowing there was no evidence to say who had killed the soldier other than the fact that it was Afghan insurgents.

"But I also can't know for sure that he wasn't involved."

After the row with her father Fatima had told her mother all she knew about what Youssef had done following the death of his parents. Her knowledge was scant, and much of it had been deduced from what Youssef had said on the phone and, just as importantly, what he hadn't said. Her mother agreed that Youssef's behaviour was far from what they were accustomed to, but she refused to accept it as proof that he had joined the Taliban.

"He might just be hanging around the wrong coffee shops and being influenced by the sort of stupid men who have nothing better to do than gossip and drink coffee all day." she had concluded.

"But he said he had been in the mountains." argued Fatima.

146

"That's even worse. There's no one but ignorant peasants in the mountains. Stupid people with stupid thoughts. They think that woman are for two things only. Cooking food and making babies. And boy babies at that. If Youssef has been there then I'm not surprised he has come back with his head full of strange ideas.

Fatima had accepted the possibility, but in her heart she couldn't stop worrying about Youssef.

"I think I should go to the police, Mummy." she said in a low, fear filled voice.

"And what would you tell them? That you've had a row on the phone with your boyfriend in Pakistan over whether or not you should go to work after you get married. They would laugh at you."

Put like that Fatima had to acknowledge that she didn't have much proof to back up her suspicions.

For her part Mrs Rahman was more concerned about the attention Fatima might attract to them. The police might laugh, but they might also pass the Rahman name to people who would take the idea of a British Muslim fighting in Afghanistan far more seriously. People such as the SIS and Military Intelligence. Mrs Rahman had grown up on tales of how the British had behaved in India before independence and she doubted things had changed that much.

"I'm not sure you can trust the police, you know." Mrs Rahman voiced her doubts.

"Why not. We're British citizens just as much as any white person."

"That's not always how they judge us. Officially we're British citizens, but how many of them look at us and just see immigrants. And the way some of our

147

people behave, planting bombs and insulting people just because they aren't Muslim, who could blame them?"

"If you saw a man being beaten in the street, wouldn't you call the police?" Fatima reasoned.

"Of course. But this is different. This is about terrorism."

"It's still the right thing for a British citizen to do. If not then our citizenship is worthless. We can hardly claim the protection of the police if we're not prepared to help our country in return."

"My daughter the fancy philosopher." Mrs Rahman offered her sarcasm. "I'm beginning to think your father may be right about educating women. It makes you think too much."

"Mummy, what use is having a brain that can be used for philosophy if you are only going to use it to read recipe cards?"

Mrs Rahman gave her daughter a sour look , but privately conceded that her daughter might have a point.

"I think it might be an idea for you not to be reading the British press. You never see anything positive about Asians printed in there and stories about Afghanistan will only make you worry." To emphasise her words Mrs Rahman picked up the newspaper, flipped open the lid of the pedal bin and dropped the newspaper into it. "Now my child, dry your tears and help me set the table for tea. Your father will be home soon and we don't want to give the grumpy old man any more reasons to moan at us, do we?

Fatima smiled at her mother's description of her father. It was true that Mr Rahman had been in a sour mood with them both since he had climbed down over the issue of Fatima's education. He hardly spoke to

Fatima at all, and relations between him and her mother were frosty, to say the least. Her mother's good humour was the only thing making conditions in the house in any way tolerable.

Glossary

EOD Explosives ordinance disposal - bomb disposal.

G2 Staff officer responsible for intelligence and security.

O Group Orders Group – a briefing for soldiers about to take part in an operation.

OpSec Operational Security; the security arrangements for operating in the field including radio protocols.

Pit or pit space Slang: the bed space that a soldier has allocated to him in a barracks.

Rag Heads Derogatory term. Originally used to refer to Iraqis it is now also used to refer to Afghan insurgents.

SIS Secret Intelligence Service, also known as MI6, the foreign intelligence gathering arm of the British security services.

VCP Vehicle Check Point.

12 - Night Action

The Company Offices were quiet. Most of the soldiers that weren't on sentry duty were crammed into the mess hall watching a film, courtesy of SSVC.

"That's her." Debbie Moon clicked on Tracey Temple's Facebook page to show Lofty. "Or more likely that's him."

"How certain are you?"

"G2 are pretty sure. She's listed as a friend of all the idiot squaddies who've been making postings that are thought to have led to attacks. She's the only common denominator. They've hacked her page and she's got over 500 friends, all service personnel. Going back over the action reports for the last two years shows a number of them have also been in units that have been subject to a high level of attacks when they've been in theatre. G2 are checking her out now to see if her profile is genuine, but we can be pretty sure it isn't. Then it will be up to GCHQ to find out her IP address. Once they've got that it will only be a matter of time before they find out who Tracey Temple really is."

"Will they arrest her...him?"

"Probably not, at least not straight away. G2 likes your idea about turning the tables. They're taking it to the Brigadier to get the go ahead."

Lofty's head jerked up as a siren started to wail. Stand To; the alarm that summoned all the soldiers within the camp to prepare to defend against an attack. The lights went out as the main generator was switched off. No point in illuminating themselves for the enemy.

Lofty grabbed his helmet, his body armour and his rifle and headed out into the compound to assemble his platoon and await orders. None of his equipment was more than an arm's length away, even when he was in the shower trailers. Debbie Moon grabbed her own equipment and stumbled through the darkened office towards the command vehicle.

It was 2 Platoon's turn on sentry, so until the Company Commander took over the 2 Platoon OC would conduct the defence of the FOB. Lofty saw his own OC, Capt Trent, hurrying towards the command vehicle as the first men of the platoon jogged towards him, struggling to don body armour while also trying to keep their weapons under control. Lofty ushered them into the slender protection of the buildings on the Western side, their designated assembly point, then ordered them to spread out. A single artillery shell could take out a complete section of men if they were standing too close together. The Taliban didn't have artillery, but they might just have a mortar, which could be almost as deadly if it found the right target.

Lofty carried out a hurried radio check between himself and his section commanders then waited for his Platoon Commander to make contact and start issuing orders. Instead he saw the CSM running across from the command vehicle, obviously heading towards them. Lofty groaned. If the CSM had been released from his HQ duties then it couldn't be good news for him.

"Sarn't Lofthouse, you and your Section Commanders to me, Now!"

Lofty signalled to his two corporals and to LCpl Eddie Grayson who was acting Catfish 2 commander. They doubled over to the CSM.

"Here, hold this." The CSM thrust a torch into Eddy Grayson's hand. "Shine it down here." He indicated a patch of ground. Kneeling down he drew out his bayonet and used it to scratch a square outline in the dirt. The NCOs crouched down beside him to get a better look.

"There's rag heads over here." He scraped a line in the dirt parallel to the Eastern side of the sketch of the FOB. "They seem to be setting up a mortar in the rocks over there. The Company Commander has asked me to lead a patrol out to take them on."

The penny dropped. It was the CSM's bid for a commendation for bravery. It would look good in front of the inquest into Pvt Wood's death if he was wearing a shiny new medal. It might also cancel out the official reprimand that now lay on his service record. How he had persuaded the Platoon Commander to stand aside could only be guessed at. Perhaps the Company Commander had ordered it.

"We're going to exit through the gate," he stabbed the centre of the Western wall, "then circle North round to here, the old hut." He pointed to the place on his dirt map where a small building had once stood. Only the foundations and some debris now remained. "That will be our rendezvous. From there Catfish 1 and 2 sections will advance and take the rag heads from the side. Catfish 3 will stay in the RV and act as reserve. 2 Platoon will give covering fire from the walls at the same time. We'll have mortar cover to give us smoke and also to keep the rag head's behind cover. Any questions?"

"Sir," Lofty broke in. "Catfish 2 are a man short."

"Right, then they'll act as reserve. Catfish 3 will make the attack with Catfish 1."

"Where do you want me Sir?" Lofty asked.

"You stay with the reserve. I'll need you if things go tits up. I'll lead the attack with Catfish 1."

Effectively it was a slight. By rights Lofty should lead the attack. The commander should stay back where he could observe the bigger picture of what was happening and make tactical decisions as the situation unfolded, but there were no medals in that.

"OK, Catfish 1 and 3 sections will advance by fire teams until we're about 20 yards out then Catfish 3 provide covering fire while Catfish 1 rushes them. Catfish 1 and 3 will fix bayonets." With two sections attacking it meant that there would always be at least eight out of sixteen weapons engaging the enemy at any time. Fixed bayonets suggested that the CSM was expecting a close quarters fight for the first men to enter the enemy positions.

"It's going to be a doddle lads." The CSM grinned wolfishly. "Now, get your men over to the gate ready to go."

The impromptu O Group broke up and the junior NCOs hurried back to their sections.

"You seem very confident, Sarn't Major. Shouldn't we do a recce first? I could lead it for you."

In the light of the torch Lofty saw a sneer cross the CSM's face. "I know what I'm doing *Sergeant* Lofthouse. If I thought we needed to do a recce I'd do it. You just make sure you're ready to bring up the reserves if we need them." He turned on his heel and strutted back towards the command vehicle.

* * *

From his vantage point Abisali used his night vision glasses to observe the enemy stronghold. They were good glasses; British military issue. They'd been bought on eBay and air freighted to an address in Pakistan. No doubt there was a Quarter Master (QM) somewhere in the UK wondering why he was a set short. He hoped so. It gave him pleasure to use his enemy's weapons against them.

Turning the knurled knob the glasses were focused on the gate. His whole plan relied on them making a sortie against his men. Initially the majority of his force had assembled opposite the Eastern wall, making sure that the movement was spotted. Then two men were left to continue play acting while the remainder withdrew. Abisali wasn't stupid enough to risk his small force in a pitched battle with a much stronger enemy, so he had to use other tactics. He sighed with relief as the gate swung open.

Two soldiers dodged along the Hesco chicane to take up covering positions while the remainder filed out behind them. The platoon formed up into a loose V formation, the apex pointing North. They slowly advanced through the night. A mortar coughed and from beyond the camp Abisali saw smoke rising. Ah yes. They would cover their advance. Well, that wouldn't matter. A machine gun opened up from one of the corner emplacements, then a second joined in. A waste of ammunition as far as the insurgent leader was concerned. They were firing at ghosts.

* * *

Lofty wasn't happy. They were walking in the dark towards an enemy whose numbers they didn't know and with only a vague idea about their location. It broke all the rules. He had said as much to Captain Trent when he had come to wish them good luck.

"He wouldn't even let me do a recce." complained Lofty. "They're supposed to be setting up a mortar out there, but they've had nearly ten minutes so far and not a single round has been fired. You know how these rag heads work, Sir. Its quick in and out, hit and run, before we have time to react."

"I know Lofty, but the Company Commander's given him carte blanche to run this operation. I daren't interfere."

"OK, Sir, but at least see if you can persuade the boss to whistle up a chopper. They've got thermal imaging cameras which will tell us where the enemy is and how many of them we can expect."

"Seems fair. I'll see what I can do." The Platoon Commander wandered over to the Catfish sections to have a quick, calming word with his men, then strolled back towards the command vehicle. It wasn't the done thing to look like he was troubled by what was going on. Doubt tended to spread doubt and fear usually spread fear. On his way his path crossed that of the CSM as he returned to lead the patrol. They exchanged a few words, too quietly for Lofty to hear what was said, then the CSM arrived to take command. A second figure accompanied the Warrant Officer and in the darkness it took some time for Lofty to recognise Cobber Bruce.

"Sgt Bruce is coming along with us this evening." announced the CSM. "He seems to think he's spending too much time in the stores trailer and wants to smell some powder smoke. He'll go with Catfish 3."

Cobber leant towards Lofty and whispered in his ear. "Thought you might need someone to watch your back. Accidents happen in the dark. Besides, I really haven't had much trigger time since we've been out here."

Lofty smiled his acknowledgement. He appreciated the risk Cobber was taking on his behalf and was happier knowing that another experienced NCO would be looking after some of his men.

The gate swung outwards on well-greased hinges and two soldiers were dispatched to take up positions to cover the exit of the rest of the platoon. A few seconds later the order was given for the rest of the men to advance into the night. Lofty positioned himself at the outer end of the V formation, with one of the Light Machine Gun (LMG) carriers next to him. If they were bounced he wanted to have someone next to him who packed a good solid punch, and the heavier gun provided that.

The sickle moon provided little illumination. That was good in that the darkness hid them from view. On the other hand it prevented soldiers from seeing what was in their path and Lofty heard several curses as his men tripped and stumbled on the rough ground. Sound was their greatest enemy. A whisper carried like a shout and a shout carried like a rifle shot.

In the lead the CSM raised his hand to halt the patrol and then made a downward patting motion. The nearest soldiers to him saw the hand signals and lowered themselves into a crouch. One by one the remainder of the patrol came to a halt and dropped to the ground. Lofty signalled to the gunner to aim his weapon outwards into the darkness and turned himself to make sure no one was trying to sneak up on them from behind.

"Catfish one one this is Sunray." The radio sounded in Lofty's ears. "Take Charlie team forward and recce the hut." At least the CSM wasn't going to stumble in totally blind.

Mickey Flynn crept forward, his fire team spreading out to left and right to make themselves more difficult targets. The section commander took it upon himself to be the first to step over the wreckage of the wall into the middle of the hut.

"Sunray this is Catfish one one. All clear. Over."

"Catfish one one Roger. All Catfish call-signs advance."

With the RV declared safe the platoon made its way forward to take up positions in and around the disused building and prepare for the final assault. There were still no signs of a mortar attack from the supposed attackers. Lofty began to wonder if it was going to turn out to be a wild goose chase. He hoped so. There were no medals to be had for false alarms.

Lofty heard his heart thumping in his ears, his pulse rate climbing as his body sent adrenalin coursing through his veins. The noise sounded so loud he worried that he might not hear radio messages. He shook his head to try to remove the thought. It was his own natural instincts at work, trying hard to save his life. Anyone with an ounce of sanity would be curled up under their bed, pulling a blanket over their head and hoping the enemy would go away. Lofty knew he was fighting his own fear just as much as he was fighting the Taliban.

Taking up a firing position Lofty stared out into the night, seeking any sign of the enemy. His nerves twanged like banjo strings, but he took a deep breath and steadied his shaking hand. Remember the men, he told himself again and again. They're looking to you now, and if you break they'll break. And if they break the enemy will kill them the way a fox kills a flock of chickens.

* * *

Abisali watched the progress of the platoon with interest. He crept out of his cover and waved his two escorts to follow him. They worked their way through the darkness, keeping the rear most British soldiers within view. Once the British commenced their attack he would take the opportunity to circle behind them and take their reserve by surprise.

* * *

On the parapet of the FOB the spotter swept his night vision glasses across the countryside. Something caught his eye and he paused, returning to focus his attention on the slightest motion that he thought he had seen. There it was, a thin shadow on the pale dust of the ground. He knew this ground well and so knew that there shouldn't be a shadow there. It moved and resolved itself into the clear shape of a man. A man dressed in a perahan tunban, a heavy patoo (scarf) round his neck and a traditional turban. He was carrying an AK-47 which meant he wasn't just some stray shepherd. A second figure joined the first.

"I have a target." He muttered, just loud enough for the man crouching beside him to hear. "Just approaching the rabbits. Two men. No, three men."

The Dogfish platoon sniper consulted the sketch map taped to the wall in front of him. He adjusted the aim of his weapon so that he could see the small jumble of rocks that his spotter had directed him towards, some 400 metres away. In a certain light they did look like a small colony of rabbits, the nickname they had been given to help with identification. His night-sight made them stand out quite clearly.

A figure crawled forward and entered the limited field of view provided by the sight of his heavy calibre sniper rifle. It seemed he wanted to use the rabbits for cover. Bad choice; They concealed him from the patrol ahead of him, but not from the walls of the FOB to this side.

"I have a clear shot. Target designated Tango one." The sniper muttered, cradling the butt of his Long closer into his cheek. The rifle had a range of well over a kilometre, but the target in front of him was less than 200 metres away. The sniper didn't consider it a challenge to his skills.

The spotter had a brief exchange of words over the radio net. "You are clear to fire." He confirmed to the sniper. The man with a gun presented a clear and present danger to the soldiers of Catfish platoon, so the RoE allowed the sniper to take the shot.

The soldier took a breath and held it. As he gently squeezed the trigger he started to exhale. The weapon barked once, the discharge of the 8.95 mm calibre round making it buck. The muzzle flash from the weapon overloaded the optics of the night-sight causing a bright green bloom of light that obscured the sniper's vision.

The spotter made his report. "Tango one down. Tangos two and three have gone to ground."

No problem, thought the sniper. They can't stay there forever and I've got all night. He pulled back on the bolt of the weapon to eject the spent cartridge case. Pushing it forward again another round was fed into the breach, ready for the next target.

Lofty didn't hear the single shot of the sniper, masked as it was beneath the general cacophony of the covering machine gun fire. He arranged Catfish 2 into an all-round defence and they settled down to wait for the attack to start. He watched the eighteen men as the CSM took Catfish 1 and 3 sections forward. Two fire teams rushed forward as the remaining two lay ready to give covering fire. Then they advanced in turn, the sections leap frogging past each other until they were about thirty metres from the objective. The lack of gunfire from the objective suggested that the enemy were unaware of the approach of the soldiers, or were asleep on the job. Lofty's radio burst into life.

"Hello Shark, this is Catfish Sunray. In attack position." The CSM reported in to the Company Commander.

"Catfish, we have a chopper on its way in. Recommend you hold your position until they can confirm what's in front of you."

The throb of helicopter blades overhead confirmed the radio message.

"Negative, Shark. We're in position ready to go. Request you shift covering fire to the left, repeat left, and lay smoke in front of my position."

Re-directing the covering fire meant that the attacking force could charge through the smoke into the enemy position without running the risk of being hit by their own machine guns. The enemy, on the other hand, would almost certainly retreat straight into a hail of bullets.

"Catfish, I repeat. I recommend you hold your position until we get a report from the chopper."

"Negative Shark. We're going in now." How gung-ho was that! The CSM clearly wasn't going to be denied his medal.

"Roger Catfish." The voice on the radio sounded resigned. The Company Commander could over rule the man on the ground with a direct order, but had decided not to.

The cough of mortars sounded clearly across the open space in front of the FOB and smoke canisters struck the ground and started to belch fumes. They coughed again and flares rose in the night to provide illumination.

"Catfish 3, cover fire. Catfish 1, charge." The men of Catfish 1 rose to obey the command.

"Catfish abort, abort, abort." The shouted command in his headphones made Lofty wince, but it was already too late. The eight men of Catfish 1, with the CSM in the lead, were already running for the objective. If he had heard the command the CSM ignored it. To the left of the line of attackers Lofty saw one of the men hesitate, confused by the command he had heard over the radio. Realising the attack was being carried through the figure moved forward again, but now several yards behind the other men of the section.

The smoke lit up with a brilliant flash and then the blast tore it aside like an old curtain. It hit Lofty in the face like a well-aimed punch. An explosion had ripped through the attackers, throwing them aside like children's dolls. A line of flashes rippled across a low ridge to the East of the objective as the waiting Taliban opened fire to rake the already shattered section with small arms fire. An RPG round exploded to create further carnage.

"Catfish 3, shift fire right. I say again shift fire right. Fire on my tracer." Lofty opened up with a burst of automatic fire from his SA80, the bright incendiary rounds stitching a line through the night sky to show Catfish 3 where to aim. "Catfish 2," he summoned his own meagre force. "Form line ready to advance to the right flank of Catfish 3."

His men rallied to him and formed a line. They dashed forward. With Catfish 3 in front of them it was too dangerous to open fire, but they crossed the strip of ground at the double, bullets cracking past their ears, and threw themselves down beside their comrades, extending the line and finally able to add their firepower.

To Lofty it seemed to take an age to cross the narrow strip of ground between himself and Catfish 3. His legs felt heavy and each step seemed to happen in slow motion. To his left the section spread out in line abreast. Lofty felt sure they would be far ahead of him, outsprinting his pathetic lolloping run, but they were there alongside him, matching him stride for stride. Illusion, the analytical part of his brain whispered. You're running at normal pace. Just keep going. A bullet buzzed past his head like an angry wasp, then he was down on the ground. Dash, down, crawl. That was the drill. He done the dash, he was down on the ground now he had to crawl to change his location so that the enemy couldn't zero in on his last known position. Lofty scuffled forward to distance himself from the piece of ground he had dropped onto. He winced as a sharp stone stabbed into his thigh, then he started to breathe again.

A buzz like a chainsaw split the night and Lofty recognised the sound of the helicopter's chain gun firing on the enemy position. With their thermal imaging equipment the helicopter's crew would be able to pinpoint the enemy using the heat produced by their own weapons.

"Catfish 2 and 3, fix bayonets." Lofty drew the wicked knife and attached it to the barrel of his rifle. "Advance by fire teams." Lofty commanded.

At once the two corporals got their men to their feet, the Charlie teams rushing forward while the Delta teams provided covering fire. Lofty looked for Cobber and saw that he was in the middle of the line, where Catfish 2 joined up with Catfish 3. He looked to his front again, focusing on the next bit of ground he would try to reach. The men sprinted forward, gasping for breath and cursing the uneven ground, adrenalin driving them onwards. This was what they had spent six months training for.

The manoeuvre was repeated until the sections were about fifty metres from the sparkling muzzles of the enemy weapons.

"Shark, this is Catfish. Request flares. Call off the chopper, we're going in." Lofty panted into his radio.

The chain gun fell silent, as did the GPMGs firing from the FOB.

"Catfish sections charge." Lofty roared. No need for a radio this time. All fifteen men of the two sections, along with Lofty and Cobber, rose to their feet at his command and sprinted forward, firing their weapons from the hip as they went.

Flares popped into life above their heads and the scene in front of the two sections lit up. As the flares swung beneath their miniature parachutes the shadows flickered and jerked. The soldiers picked out individual targets at which to fire as the insurgents fled, only for them to disappear into the shifting shadows and re-appear moments later somewhere else.

Bringing himself to a halt Lofty picked out a running man, brightly lit under a descending flare. He raised his rifle and managed to get off a three round burst before the target disappeared from view. If he was dead or alive, Lofty had no idea. He launched himself forward again, an icy calm descending on him as he stepped over the line of small rocks that had been gathered to protect the front of the enemy's positions.

In the light of the flares the GPMG gunners on the parapet of the FOB were able to pick out the attacking soldiers, which allowed them to fire on the flanks of the enemy positions, cutting off the escape routes to the sides, but there was no way to prevent a retreat to the rear. The helicopter would have to do that.

A few rounds zipped past in reply before the men found themselves in the jumble of rocks that had already been vacated by the attackers. Every man in the platoon had practiced this manoeuvre a hundred times in training. This is what the infantry did. They charged towards the enemy and hoped that the enemy broke, because if the enemy stayed and fought then the soldiers would have to use the bayonet, just as their forefathers had done on the Somme a hundred years earlier. No matter how good the technology is, at the end of the day an objective is taken by a soldier with a rifle and a bayonet.

"Cease fire, Cease fire. All Catfish call signs cease fire." Lofty shouted into his microphone. "Form a perimeter. Catfish 2 take the left flank, Catfish 3 the right." Lofty immediately tried to bring his men under control, fighting against the adrenalin that coursed through their bodies and which could destroy their capacity for rational thought, taking them into more danger.

Reluctantly the men stopped firing as they responded to their training. They started to hurry to their new task, finding the best cover they could and to make ready for a counter attack. Lofty pulled two men from the thin defensive line and between the three of them they carried out an almost microscopic search of their tiny fortification to make sure there were no Taliban still lurking inside, ready to shoot them in the back.

"Shark, this is Catfish. Position secure. Request reinforcements."

"Roger Catfish. I'm sending Angelfish to secure the original objective. They will deal with the casualties." Shark had obviously worked out what had gone wrong, no doubt aided by visual reports from Dogfish platoon manning the parapet and the helicopter circling above.

"Swordfish will advance and help you secure your position. Settle in, it's going to be a long night."

With reinforcements on the way Lofty attended to his next task. Going round the perimeter he counted heads, making sure his men were all accounted for. Sixteen, he decided, tapping his own chest last. All present and correct. No, no, they weren't. Catfish 2 were seven strong, Catfish 3 were eight. So that was fifteen. He made sixteen and Cobber made Seventeen.

Who was missing? "Catfish 2, Catfish 3. Number off." Lofty commanded into his radio. One by one the soldiers reported in. All present and correct. All except for Cobber.

* * *

Lofty led the shattered remnants of his platoon back through the gates and into Camp Elizabeth. He stomped over to the weapons unloading bay and pointed the barrel of his SA80 into the sand filled drum before clearing the weapon. Turning on his heel he ripped his body armour off and threw it to the ground before removing his helmet and throwing it to one side. It hit the side of a mastiff with a dull thud before rolling across the dusty ground to the feet of Captain Trent.

Trent stepped forward, intent on giving Lofty a roasting for setting such a bad example, when Debbie Moon intercepted him.

"I think the rest of the platoon need your attention, Sir." She indicated the rest of the exhausted, smoke stained soldiers. "I'll take care of the Sergeant."

The OC was about to dismiss the woman's intervention when he saw what she was trying to do. Poorly chosen words at this moment could cause a lot of damage. "OK. I'll manage things out here then." He paused. "Thank you Corporal."

Debbie followed Lofty into the barracks before turning towards the small communal fridge. She pulled out a fizzy drink and ripped the ring pull open, then took it into Lofty's room. He was slumped on the ground, his back to the wall and his head in his hands. His shaking shoulders betrayed the muffled tears he had finally allowed himself to succumb to.

Debbie offered him the can, which he pushed away. Refusing to be deflected Debbie offered the can again. On the third attempt he took the can and sipped from it.

"He's dead." Lofty whispered in disbelief. "Cobber's dead."

"I heard." Debbie replied. Better to let the Sergeant take the lead and let his grief out in his own way.

"The bastards killed him. No, fucking Dave Smith killed him."

"The CSM's severely wounded himself."

"Serves him fucking right. He's pretty much wiped out 1 Section as well as getting Cobber killed. I told him we needed to do a recce. Bastard!"

Lofty took another pull at the can and handed it back to Debbie, who placed it carefully on the packing case before taking a seat on Lofty's camp bed.

"He shouldn't have been there." Lofty gasped between sobs.

"The Company Commander OK'd it."

"Not Smith! Cobber! He shouldn't have been there. It wasn't his place. I should have sent him back."

"There was nothing you could do. Cobber wanted to go. I heard him tell Capt Trent."

Lofty looked up. "What did he say?"

"Not much. Just said that in the dark things could be confusing, so best to have another experienced pair of eyes on things."

"I shouldn't have let him go. You know he was only trying to watch my back."

"I know. Pretty much everyone knows about you and Smith."

"What about the others?"

"Ripper Martin and Justin Green are both dead."

"Oh no. Green shouldn't have been here either. He only came in to replace Chris Woods. And Ripper. He was such a nice kid."

"Why was he called Ripper?"

"His first name's Jack. You know what squaddies are like with names. And the rest?"

"Harris probably won't make it. Clark, Hill, Morris and King are pretty bad, but they reckon they'll be OK. The medics don't think they'll ever see active service again."

"Mickey? What about Mickey?" Lofty asked, though he dreaded the answer.

"He got lucky. When the abort order came over the radio he hesitated, thinking that Smith would pull them back. It meant he was a bit behind the others. He was knocked off his feet but otherwise he's uninjured. His ears are ringing but he'll be OK. They took him up to Bastion with the others just in case." Debbie paused, not sure whether to ask the next question, but recognised that she had to get Lofty to talk about it. "How did Cobber die?"

Lofty stared down between his knees, his eyes on the ground between his feet, though in his mind he only saw the aftermath of the battlefield.

When Swordfish Platoon had spread a defensive screen around them Lofty had taken a fire team back across the ground searching for Cobber. Lofty hoped against hope that they would find him sat in the dust nursing a sprained ankle or something similar. The lack of a radio message suggested that it was unlikely, but radios had been known to fail. The worst possible scenario would be to not find Cobber at all, which would mean he had been taken prisoner. After torture and humiliation he would undoubtedly be executed in the most horrible fashion. Lofty had cast the thought from his mind and continued the search.

It was Jim Jones, Catfish 3's Lance Corporal, who found him sprawled face down in the dust, just as he had fallen. He had been shot through the throat, severing an artery. The pool, no the lake, of blood spread about him showed how he had died.

Lofty had managed to keep it together while they were still outside the FOB. The men needed a leader and he was all they had, but inside the anger grew. They shouldn't have been there. The fact that the CSM was injured was no consolation to Lofty. Had he been able to reach him he might have killed him with his bare hands for what he had done.

Of course Lofty knew it could have been him leading the attack, him that was now lying in a hospital bed. But then he knew it wouldn't have happened that way. He would have waited for the report from the chopper. The report that would have told him that there were no heat signatures in the objective, and so the Taliban weren't there. That knowledge would have stopped the attack there and then as far as Lofty was concerned. He would have crept forward and searched around to try to find out what the Taliban had been up to. He would have found the bomb's command wire, wouldn't he? If not he would have stayed well out of the objective until daylight provided the means to search it properly.

No, even before that it would have been different. He would have sent out a proper reconnaissance. A small team who could creep up close to the objective and make an assessment of what was going on, how strong the enemy were and how well dug in. But the CSM had refused to do such a thing. He had been in a hurry to win his medal and didn't want to give the enemy time to have second thoughts and withdraw. It had nearly cost him his life. Lofty wished he had paid the full price.

As for the mortar that was the whole reason for the sortie, a length of plastic drain pipe was found propped up on a bipod made of dead wood. In the dark it had looked sufficiently like a mortar tube to confuse a tired sentry at a distance of over 200 metres.

The clatter of boots and buzz of voices announced that the rest of the patrol had been stood down and sent to get some sleep.

"They need you Sarge." Debbie whispered, not wanting to intrude on Lofty's memories but knowing she had to.

"They need me like a hole in the head. If I'd stood up to Smith and insisted on doing a recce none of that would have happened."

"Yes it would, and you know it. He'd have ordered you to stay behind and taken Cobber anyway. There's no reasoning with men like Smith. It's his way or the highway."

"Do you think?"

"I know. I've heard him in the command vehicle. He thinks he's the only real soldier in the Company. There was nothing you could do to stop it. In fact if you hadn't been there it might have been worse. Catfish 2 would have been left leaderless and probably got themselves shot up as well. You did the right thing. You cleared the enemy positions so the enemy ran away. That saved the rest of your men."

"All except Cobber."

"All except Cobber, but he was only there because he wanted to be there."

"He was there because of me."

"And you were there because of your men. It could just have easily have been you that got it. That's soldiering. It's totally random who gets it and who

170

doesn't except when someone cocks up, like Dave Smith did."

Lofty continued to stare at the ground between his feet, but Debbie's words made sense. The enemy didn't pick targets out, they just opened fire and hoped to hit something. It wasn't personal. Only it was personal now. Whoever led that attack would pay for it, vowed Lofty.

He stood up and straightened his jacket. Picking up his rifle he walked into the main barrack room. The beds were arranged in pairs down either side. On the nearest bed Lofty found his body armour and helmet. Other than that the first four pairs of beds were empty. Further along the room the soldiers sat on their own beds or chatted in small groups.

"Listen up everyone." Lofty called. "We've had a rough night, so better get some sleep. Don't forget to clean your weapons first though."

"Any news on Catfish 1, Sarge." someone called.

Lofty brought them up to date with the information that Debbie had given him on the casualties. There were gasps of dismay as individuals felt the personal loss of friends as well as colleagues.

"Will we get a chance to hit back at them Sarge?" this time Lofty recognised the voice of Frankie Morgan.

"I don't know, but I'm going across to speak to the Company Commander now. We owe them big time." There were approving nods and a buzz of agreement.

Lofty picked up his body armour and helmet and left the barracks. Debbie Moon caught up and fell into step beside him. Lofty thrust out his jaw and marched on, forcing the much smaller woman to break into a jog to keep up.

Glossary

LCpl   Lance Corporal.

LMG   Light machine gun, 7.62 mm calibre, magazine fed.

Mortar   A small bomb fired from a tube that has its base resting on the ground. The bomb has a small explosive charge in its base to act as its propellant. The bomb is dropped down the barrel of the mortar tube and the striking of the cartridge on a firing pin fires it. Especially useful for indirect fire over objects such as walls, or for firing out of a trench. They can be used to fire explosive, smoke or illuminating rounds (flares). Ranges extend from 800 metres to around 5,500 metres depending on calibre.

RV   Also RVP, rendezvous and rendezvous point. A place to which soldiers will return if they are separated from each other.

SA80   The SA80 A2 rifle is the standard infantry weapon used by the British Army and can be used to fire single shots or in automatic mode to fire bursts. It has a 5.56 mm calibre and is fed from a magazine holding 30 rounds. The SA80 A2 UGL is fitted with an under slung grenade launcher. Each fire team will have one of these issued.

SSVC   Services Sound and Vision Corporation. An MoD owned organisation that provides radio, TV and cinema to military personnel serving overseas.

13 - Unwanted Burdens

Gamal and Taj were the last two of the fighters to arrive back at the refuge and with them they brought news of the death of their leader, Abisali.

"It was a single shot. A sniper no doubt. We were moving up behind the enemy ready to attack when you set the bomb off. That's when he went down. There was no more fire. We waited for the bomb to go off and then pulled back while the sniper was distracted. It has taken us two days to work our way here without running into their patrols."

"You're sure he was dead?" Youssef wanted absolute confirmation. There could be no doubt.

"Half his head was missing. No man could survive that."

That brought their total fatalities for the raid up to three; Abisali, of course, as well as Dawid and Salik. Salik had been killed by the fire from the helicopter, and Dawid had taken a rifle bullet in the back as the enemy made their final attack on their position. Uday had also been badly wounded as they withdrew and might not make it if they couldn't find medical help. That just left Imran unaccounted for. He had last been seen as the fighters had started their withdrawal, but no one had seen him fall. Youssef hoped he was dead. If he was dead he couldn't talk.

The group was despondent. They had paid a heavy price for the casualties they had inflicted. Abisali had been something of a talisman and his loss suggested their luck might be buried with him. Their original group was now down to sixteen with one of those seriously injured. Still a formidable force if they mounted a surprise attack, but worryingly small if they met the enemy in open battle. A British platoon numbered twenty four plus the officers. They were now easily outnumbered.

"I will make contact with the other leaders." Youssef declared. "I'll seek their instructions." With that Youssef waved the two men away.

Youssef felt another surge of grief sweep over him. Abisali had come to take the place of his father. He had nurtured him and made him grow. Now though, he had a target on which he exact his revenge. After his parents had died Youssef had wanted to kill Americans, because it was them that controlled the drones, but Abisali had brought him to the part of Helmand occupied by the British. Now the British had killed Abisali and Youssef knew exactly where to find them. Not just any British, but the very ones who had actually done the deed.

Youssef wondered if Abisali had foreseen his own death. Only days before the raid he had taken Youssef to one side.

"I need you to promise me something, brother." he had said.

"Just ask. If it is within my power I'll gladly do it."

"If I fall, you must take my place."

"You will never fall." Youssef stated with certainty.

"I am not so foolish as to believe that. My life is in the hands of Allah, and if he chooses it then I will fall. He may even choose that I fall so that you can take my place. You are a better leader than I ever was."

"That isn't true. You are a great and courageous leader."

"Courage alone isn't enough. You have qualities I have never had, Youssef. You are knowledgeable. You understand the world outside of here. You can plan and you can also fight. For these reasons you will always be a better leader than me. So promise me: you will take my place."

Youssef had reluctantly made the promise, hoping he would never have to fulfil it. But now, so soon afterwards he was about to do so.

"We need to attract new recruits." Abisali had continued. "We need a great victory to make them see that we can win here. You can deliver that for us, Youssef."

"What do you mean?"

"At some point the enemy will make a mistake. They will stretch themselves too thin, just as they did when they first came here. Then they will be vulnerable to attack. You must seize that moment and make them pay in blood. Other groups will follow you, Youssef. You have gained a reputation."

"I'm not sure about that." Youssef didn't feel as though he was being modest, only realistic.

"You may not be sure, but others are. Seize the initiative, Youssef, and make the enemy fear your name."

Now Abisali was dead and Youssef wasn't sure what to do.

There was movement close by and Youssef looked up into the face of Ali. There were others in the shadows behind him.

"Youssef, we will follow you." Ali spoke up. "You are a good leader. You brought us back here alive."

"Do you all feel like that?" Youssef asked.

175

Around the group heads nodded in assent. "Good. I will tell the other leaders and see what they say."

"They had better say yes, Youssef. We won't follow anyone else."

Youssef smiled, but knew that such decisions were not in his gift. He was a servant and had sworn allegiances of his own. He would offer himself as leader, just as Abisali had made him promise, but he would not be making the final decision.

Youssef made his way to a place far enough away for him not to give away the position of their cave, and where he could also get a signal for the cell phone that he used. He would have time for just one text message then he would have to switch the phone off and remove the battery. After that he would find a new location before switching the phone back on to receive the replies, before removing the battery once again. He didn't know how effective the Americans were in tracking mobile phones in this part of Afghanistan, or even if the phone he had been given was known to them, but he couldn't take any chances. He removed a dirt bike from its hiding place and headed off towards an area that neither he nor Abisali had used to make telephone calls before. It would be a lengthy journey.

After they had abandoned their firing positions, as the British had attacked, they had made their way back to where they had concealed their dirt bikes. The throb of the helicopter's rotors had tracked them every inch of the way. They were retreating so the helicopter crew were no longer permitted to fire. How Youssef loved the rules of engagement that the British used. How embedded in fair play they seemed to be. Never hit a man when he's down; never hit him when he's running away. They could never win this war with rules like that, Youssef felt. No Muslim fighter would show such scruples. It was kill or be killed.

After they had mounted their bikes, those that had managed to stay with the group, the helicopter had continued to track them through the night, the heat from the bikes' engines providing an excellent source for the thermal imaging equipment. At last they had found the cave that had been cut through the mountain by some long dried up river. The helicopter couldn't follow but the pilot would keep it orbiting above the entrance until a drone could be directed to the area to maintain the watch until morning. That was when the soldiers would arrive. They would be too late.

Abisali had shown him the route through the tunnels and out the other side, some two kilometres from the original entrance. The solid bulk of the hill blocked their heat signatures from the helicopter, though they could still hear the steady throbbing of the rotor blades as the sound carried through the still night air. Good. That meant that the drone hadn't yet arrived.

The drones flew high enough to be able to see both sides of the hill with their multiple cameras, whereas the helicopter had only one camera with heat sensing capability; The camera that would be kept locked onto the cave entrance so it could see if anyone tried to leave. The party re-mounted their bikes and disappeared into the night.

The soldiers would no doubt blow up the cave entrances to stop them being used again, but it would make no difference. This wild land was riddled with potential escape routes and the local people knew them well. Youssef could hire a guide for ten dollars a day and never have to use the same escape route twice.

The replies to his text message came in as soon as the phone recorded its presence on the network. They all said the same. He should take command, and they would be in touch to arrange a meeting. One message also gave him details of where he could pick up supplies for his men. Youssef was particularly grateful for that. He knew it was common for the fighters to take what food they wanted from the local peasants, but he wanted to avoid that. It didn't feel right to him to steal from Muslims. Besides, it would upset the people and upset people might just choose to betray them to the British.

What they really needed right now was ammunition. Over the months they had used up most of what they had stock piled in the cave. If they didn't get more soon they would no longer be an effective fighting unit.

* * *

Fatima sat at her kitchen table, tears streaming down her face. In front of her lay a copy of that morning's newspaper. They didn't often buy the English papers, preferring the ones produced in Urdu, but as she had passed the newsagent's shop the headlines had screamed out to her.

"Three British soldiers killed in Afghanistan." A sub heading added that several other soldiers had been injured.

A second headline, enclosed in a box beneath the main story, was even worse: "Taliban leader identified as British Muslim."

Fatima was dismayed to find that she knew one of the dead soldiers. A boy by the name of Jason Green, who had been in the same class as her at school. He had been a bit of a bully and a racist, if the truth be told, but her heart sank to think of him dying. That aside, it was the other story that had brought on her tears.

It was apparently based on a press release issued by the MoD which said that in the same action in which Jason Green had died the leader of the Taliban attackers had also been killed. The Yemeni born terrorist was a much prized target and the British were clearly jubilant at having killed him. It also stated that one of the attackers was thought to be British and from the London area. He may now have replaced the dead leader.

Fatima didn't believe that it was a coincidence. There couldn't be two men from London both in Helmand and both fighting the British. Partly she cried because the man she knew was doing something that was totally out of character for him. Youssef wasn't a killer. He wasn't even someone who got into fights. The other part of her cried because it meant that he was in danger. If one leader could die then so could another.

Mrs Rahman tried to comfort her daughter, but her soothing words had little effect.

"You still can't be sure that its Youssef." Mrs Rahman denied.

"Oh, mother, please don't try to fool me that way. How can it not be Youssef? How many British Muslims are fighting in Afghanistan, and of those how many are from London?"

"It still isn't proof." the older woman persisted.

"It's enough proof for me. I have to go to the police."

"And what good would that do?"

"If he is captured he will go to that terrible prison they have over there. Would you want that for

Youssef? Human rights are not something that is high on their agenda. He will be tortured and maybe even killed. If he's identified as being British at least he will be brought back to Britain for trial. He'll be put in a British prison. It may not be much, but it is better than an Afghan prison."

"I think you will be wasting your time. They won't believe you. Worse, they may believe you and then believe that you're involved in some way. Maybe you will go to prison as well."

"Maybe I will, but I must try. It isn't much, but it's all I can do for him."

"Please, Fatima. Don't be hasty. At least sleep on this. Maybe Youssef will contact you, then you can discuss this with him."

"Mother, apart from one 'phone call and that e-mail to father he hasn't been in contact for months. Wherever he is he chooses not to speak to me. But I will wait one day. If he doesn't contact me tomorrow then I'm going to the police."

* * *

Emma handed Sam her cup of tea and then took a seat beside her on the settee. It was quiet now. The CO's wife had finally gone, as had the RSM's wife. They had drunk tea and offered sympathy and held Sam as she wept, but there was no more that could be said or done, and there was still the other grieving widow to go and see. Emma had agreed to stay and hold Sam's hand and to stay the night if necessary.

Emma felt helpless. She had never had to deal with death before. Her grandparents had all died while she was just a child and her own parents had protected her from the events. Emma wished now that they had been more open about it. She might have been able to cope better.

"At least there's one good thing. I didn't have to put on a brave face for Brenda Smith." The tea cup rattled in its saucer as Sam tried to replace it. Emma took it gently from her fingers and placed it on the coffee table.

"No. I think she's got her own problems for a change." The CO's wife had confided that Brenda was on her way to the Queen Elizabeth Hospital in Birmingham to be close to her injured husband.

"Have you spoken to Lofty yet?" Sam asked, trying to focus on the living for a moment.

"Yes, he rang this morning. Just a quick call to tell me he was OK, just in case I saw something on the news."

"That was thoughtful." Sam stifled a sob and took a sip of her tea. "Did he mention Cobber?"

"Of course. He's very cut up about it, I can tell you. You know how close Lofty and Cobber were."

"Yes, they were, weren't they."

"What time do you expect Todd to get here?" Sam's eldest son had been summoned back from university to be with his mother. Sam's daughter Kylie was upstairs in her room, sobbing uncontrollably into the shoulder of a school friend. Emma made a mental note to go up and offer some comfort before too long.

"I think he should be here around seven. Did Lofty say what had happened?"

"Not really. Something about a night attack on the FOB, whatever that is, then a sortie led by the CSM. It was some sort of trap, but of course they didn't find that out till it was too late."

"An FOB is a forward operating base, lovey. Its where the company are based while they're out there." Sam commented absently, her mind automatically dealing with the trivia of army language. "But what the hell was Dave Smith doing leading the sortie? That's what they've got Platoon Commanders for."

"So what happens now?" asked Emma. This was all new territory for her.

"They're sending a car for me and the kids in the morning. Eight o'clock. That will take use to Brize Norton to meet the flight that's bringing them home. Cobber and the other two. Then we'll go to Oxford with them, to the mortuary at the John Radcliff Hospital. We'll get to say our goodbyes to him there. They haven't told me when the funeral will be, but I'll let you know."

"Would you like me to go with you tomorrow?"

"Oh would you love? That would be good. The kids will appreciate it as well."

"Will there be an inquest, do you know?"

"I fucking hope so." Sam spat through gritted teeth. "I want to know what part Dave Smith had in all this and I'm fucking sure the army won't tell me. I also want to know what Cobber was doing getting involved in a night attack. He's a Company QM. He should have been in the magazine counting bullets, not gallivanting around in the dark getting himself shot at." Sam broke down into another series of sobs and Emma leant forward to take her in her arms.

* * *

Kylie had given up her bed for Emma and gone to share with her mother. No doubt the mother and daughter would spend the night sobbing in each other's arms.

Sleep was hard to come by in the Bruce household that night and Emma tossed and turned as well. The shock of Cobber's death had come as a surprise to Emma. She had known him only a few weeks, but he was the sort of man who you felt you'd known all your life. Cheerful, irreverent, chatty and charming, all the things that nice blokes were. And a few not so nice blokes, she had to admit, but Cobber had been one of the good ones, she knew.

Of course she really knew why she had felt Cobber's death so acutely. It could have been Lofty. Lofty had told her that he'd been on the sortie so she had no doubt that it was sheer chance that had taken Cobber rather than her husband.

The implications hit her hard. Here she was living in a place she didn't know, surrounded by people she didn't know, with her own family a hundred miles away. What would have happened if it had been Lofty? Who would have held her in their arms, as she cried for her dead husband.

This was the part of army life that she wasn't prepared for and this was the part of the army she could never get used to. They were out there, the battalion, for the best part of four months yet. How many more Sam Bruce's and Toyah Martin's would there be? And that was just in C Company. There had been other casualties in the other Companies, she knew. Gossip flew round the garrison at an incredible speed, and she heard a lot of it in the Education Centre where she worked.

But what could she do? The army was Lofty's life. It was more to him than just a job, she knew. He wanted to be like his Dad, making a difference. That was what he was doing in Afghanistan, wasn't it, making a difference? She hoped so. But did it have to cost so many lives?

What of her though? Didn't she deserve to have a husband, the man she loved, by her side? Didn't she have the right to go to bed at night and not fear the knock at the door that announced the presence of the officer who would tell her that her husband was dead, or maimed?

But if she claimed her right it meant denying Lofty his right to do the job he loved. He might come to hate her for it, mightn't he? When Sam and she had gone shopping at Cribbs Causeway, the older woman had told her about the woman who made her husband leave the army. They were divorced six months later and the man re-enlisted. Would that happen to Lofty and her if she made him leave? Ten months of marriage hadn't yet granted her the secure feelings she had expected.

There was nothing for it. The next time Lofty was able to telephone her she would have to talk to him about it. It would make no difference to this tour; he would still have to finish that, but maybe he would be prepared to consider the idea that he had done his bit and that in doing it he had made a difference. Maybe it was now someone else's turn.

* * *

"They've identified the man behind Tracey Temple." Debbie told Lofty as they drank a cup of coffee together in the Company Office. "I can't tell you his name but he lives in Preston with his Mum and Dad. Real computer geek apparently. Anyway, according to G2 he's under surveillance now. As soon as we've carried out our operation he'll be arrested."

"That's great. In the meantime I've clamped down on all my blokes and their Facebook posts. I don't want any slip ups."

"That includes you, you know. I heard you talking to your wife about the Brit in the Taliban, and about the Op."

"I know. I'll be careful."

"More careful than the man in Preston, I hope."

Lofty cocked a quizzical eye.

"He thinks he's been clever." Debbie informed him. "Keeps all his files on a memory stick. But every time he plugs it in the contents get sent straight to us. It's a simple little virus, criminals have been using it for years. The thing is, we've managed to disguise it so that his anti-virus software doesn't block it. We've also got his password for his e-mails. He runs several accounts but uses the same password for all of them. Very careless indeed. G2 know everything he's sending out. They've also taken control of about half a dozen Facebook pages and are keeping them updated."

"Won't he get suspicious if the intelligence doesn't pan out."

"Oh it's all genuine intel. He just gets it a little bit too late for them to be able to use it. Hopefully whoever he sends it to won't cop on. We seed it with stuff that's a bit more useful to them as well, but nothing that endangers life."

"You seem to be in the loop on this." Such insider knowledge wasn't common at Company level.

"It's the way we work in the Corps. I was the one that stumbled on the Facebook connection, so I get updates on what's going on. Not all of it, of course. A lot of its above my security clearance, but G2 tells me what they can just in case I find out something else. It helps everyone to keep the dots joined up."

"Pretty good. Well, I'd better get off and brief the troops on tomorrow's patrol. Are you on that one?"

"I wouldn't miss it for the world." Debbie answered, giving him a cheeky grin. "Are you OK?" Debbie was concerned that Lofty might still be affected by Cobber's death.

"No, to tell you the truth, I'm not." Lofty's face showed lines where none had been before. "But the world still turns and my men have still got a job to do. If I'm not there then it will make it harder for them." Lofty turned and left the room.

* * *

In his room Saafir composed an e-mail advising his contacts about what the press were saying with regard to the British Taliban fighter. He had no idea if it was true, but if it was then they had to be told. If this man's family were arrested it would affect his morale and might even make him come home. They needed every fighter they had.

He also added that the news had become the talk of the mosque and a number of young men were wondering how they could go about joining him.

After he had sent the e-mail he went back to his daily routine of checking the Facebook pages of his priority targets: those that were currently 'in theatre'. He was pleased to see that Ronnie King had made a fresh post.

Glossary

Drone   A Remotely piloted vehicle, also RPV. Predator drones are unarmed, while Reaper drones can carry bombs, rockets and/or missiles.

14 - Christmas In Helmand

"Hi Emma, its me." Lofty shouted into the handset.

"No need to shout Darling. It's quite a clear line."

"Sorry. Sometimes it gets a bit crackly. How's that?"

"Better; not so deafening. How are you? What have you been up to?"

Lofty gave Emma an update on what they had been doing, and she reciprocated.

"How's Sam Bruce coping?" Lofty asked, his voice giving away the concern he felt.

"Poor woman's still in bits. She was OK up until to the funeral, probably putting on a brave face, but then she seemed to fall apart. I can hardly recognise her from the woman she was. Todd went back to uni and I think that hit her hard as well. It's just her and Kylie rattling around in that married quarter wondering what to do with themselves."

"Is she getting many visitors?"

"Only me I think. You know how people are with death. They steer clear, as though it's contagious. It's the same with Toyah Martin. I go over as often as I can, but you would think they would see more of the people who have known them for longer. I thought a battalion was supposed to be like a family."

"Usually it is. I'll have a word here, maybe get the husbands to have a word on their next 'phone calls home."

"That would be good. Look, Lofty, I need to talk to you, seriously."

"Sounds ominous."

"Seeing Sam the way she is has made me take a look at us. I'm not sure that I could cope if I was in her position."

"Come on love, I can look after myself, you know that."

"And I'm sure that's just what Cobber told Sam. But we know that it doesn't work like that. It's totally random. Someone gets killed and someone else gets away unharmed and there's no way of knowing who's who. Look at Mickey Flynn. You told me he should have at least been injured in that blast, but he walked away with just a bit of ringing in his ears and a few minor scratches."

"I know, but that's the way things are. There's nothing that I can do to change that. If I could I would, you know that."

"I know that there's nothing you can do on this tour. But if you stay in the army this won't be your last tour, will it? There'll be another one, not necessarily Afghanistan, but somewhere else. Sam told me all the places that Cobber had been and quite frankly I was surprised he had survived for so long."

"So what are you saying?

"When you come back, I'd like you to put in your papers; leave the army."

"That's a big ask love. You know how I feel about this job."

"I know Lofty, and I wouldn't ask if I could feel confident about you coming home every time you go away. But I can't. I've sat for hours holding Sam Bruce's hand, and hours more with Toyah Martin. I can't face the idea of one day having some other soldier's wife holding my hand and trying to comfort me that way."

"But that doesn't make sense. I could get knocked down by a bus crossing Trowbridge High Street."

"At least you've got a chance of seeing the bus before it hits you. You don't have a chance to see the bullet that might kill you. Look, Lofty, I love you so much, and if I thought I could manage then I wouldn't ask this, but I'm not like you. I'm not even like Sam Bruce. I'm not an army wife and I can't face the thought of losing you to some unknown gunman in some arsehole corner of the world where we have no business being anyway."

"Look, I need time to think about this."

"Of course you do. I've rather sprung this on you. But please promise me you'll think about it."

"And what if I decide to stay in?"

"I don't know. I'm not going to lay down any ultimatums over this. Just please think about it."

"OK, I promise. By the way, I just rang to wish you a Happy Christmas. Oh yes, and I want you to make sure you're on your own when you open up your present."

Some of the tension faded from the conversation as Emma asked why.

"You'll see,." giggled Lofty."

"If it's what I think it is you won't have to wait for a Taliban bullet to kill you, I'll do it myself." The full impact of what Emma had just said hit them both between the eyes.

"I'm sorry lofty, I didn't mean that."

"I know, Emms. Look, my time's up, I've got to go."

"Happy Christmas Lofty. I love you."

As the line went dead Lofty added "and I love you too", but it was already too late.

Christmas Day dawn broke bright but cold over Helmand Province. Dogfish Platoon had sentry duty, so it was Angelfish that went out to set up the defensive perimeter in readiness for the arrival of the helicopter. Along the parapet off duty soldiers stood waiting expectantly.

The steady thrumming of helicopter blades indicated that a Chinook was inbound and the troops strained to get a first glimpse of it. At its normal cruising speed of 149 m.p.h. it didn't take long for the aircraft to swoop in over the landing zone and settle onto the ground. The pilot kept the rotors spinning ready for an immediate lift-off should it be necessary, but for once the Taliban seemed to have stayed at home. Dust billowed outwards in the downdraft of the giant spinning blades and soldiers covered their faces with their neck clothes, but it didn't deter them from staying and watching. No seven year olds could have been more excited than the men of C Company.

The rear loading ramp of the helicopter lowered slowly to the ground and Angelfish 3 section sprinted forward to help unload the precious cargo. A Mastiff reversed into position just beyond the reach of the deadly spin of the rotors, ready to accept the packages that were being passed from hand to hand. Mail sacks and boxes of food were stowed into the rear of the vehicle.

At last the cargo was all off-loaded, but still the soldiers remained where they were. A figure was spotted moving through the shadowy interior of the helicopter, then stepped off the ramp into the full glare of the sunshine. A loud cheer sounded from the assembled men and Father Christmas paused to acknowledge it. One hand clamped his cheery red bonnet in place while the other waved to the soldiers. The holstered pistol at Santa's waist contrasted wildly with the season of good will to all men, but in Afghanistan even Santa carries a side arm.

A second figure stepped down, this one unarmed, and the soldiers gave another cheer to welcome the battalion Padre. Hardly had his feet touched the ground before the ramp started to close again and the volume of the helicopter's engines increased as the pilot readied his aircraft to get airborne once again. The air gunner at the forward door gave a cheery wave of farewell.

As the helicopter lifted off a Jackal drove forward to collect Santa. As was suitable for such an occasion the vehicle had been decked out to make it an approximation of a sled, complete with cardboard cut-out Rudolf at the front. The two figures climbed on board and the Jackal followed the Mastiff back into the compound. Angelfish Platoon retreated behind them, still watching the surrounding countryside with suspicion.

Santa and the Padre didn't have a lot of time to spare. The Chinook would return in under an hour to carry them to their next destination, which was the B Company FOB at Camp Charles. The acting CSM fussed over the final arrangements for the visit, while the Padre reached into a briefcase for his vestments and dressed, ready for the Christmas morning service.

Dogfish 2 took over from Dogfish 1 on guard duty and the rest of the company assembled in front of the table that was to serve as an altar. It wasn't a parade and any soldier that didn't want to attend could stay away, but every soldier inside Camp Elizabeth was present, with the exception of those on guard and the RLC cooks sweating over the preparation of Christmas dinner. Even the two Afghani interpreters stood to one side to watch, though they would take no part in the service. The acting CSM pressed a button on a CD player and the sounds of Once In Royal David's City swept over the FOB, amplified through the borrowed PA system. Hymn sheets were passed from hand to hand and the soldiers joined in with the words.

In a Muslim country far from home the British Army did their best to celebrate Christmas. The Padre kept the service as short as was decently possible and as the last notes of Oh Come All Ye Faithful died away Santa strode into the centre of the camp carrying a sack. At the direction of the acting CSM soldiers sprinted to collect the other sacks and Santa started to distribute the contents.

Each soldier was given a box and all the boxes were the same. The contents had been paid for by donations to the Operations Welfare Fund organised by the MoD but paid for by donations from the public. They contained items that the soldiers themselves had said would be welcomed such as books, magazines and toiletries as well as a few oddities that some bright spark in the building on Whitehall thought would be amusing. This year that included a clockwork driven snail which the soldiers were soon using to organise races. Bets were being placed. Tears before bedtime, thought Lofty as he watched. If anything was guaranteed to start a fight it was gambling.

Although it was Christmas the alcohol ration wasn't increased. Two cans of beer per man per day was all that was allowed, and that couldn't be

193

consumed if a soldier was due to do an armed duty. Absolutely no hoarding of the ration was allowed. It had been arranged that each Platoon would stand one six hour duty during the 24 hours. Catfish had stood the midnight to 6 a.m. shift and could now drink their alcohol allowance when they liked. Some of the soldiers took the opportunity to get ahead of the game, others chose to hang onto their beer until they could drink it with Christmas dinner.

Lofty went across to join the re-constituted Catfish 1, mainly made up of soldiers from 1st battalion, rushed out from the regimental depot in North London.

"Everything alright, Mickey?" Lofty asked cheerfully. The Corporal cocked his hand behind his ear, playacting at being deaf. His new section members laughed dutifully.

"Fancy a beer?" Lofty whispered.

"Oh, thanks Sarge." Mickey answered.

"Thought you might hear that. Well you can buy your own. This is mine." He raised his can in salute.

"Everything OK with you guys?" Lofty asked.

There was a chorus of assent.

"Well, make the most of it. We're back on stag tomorrow for a week, then the CO has got some patrols lined up for us. There's been a bit of bother over Zābol way so we're stepping up our profile over there."

There didn't seem to be much more he could say, so he wished them a Merry Christmas and left Mickey to entertain the newcomers in his own way. No doubt a football would be involved at some point.

Lofty went and sat on the front of a Jackal and let the weak Winter sun play on his face as he sipped at his beer.

"Feeling lonely, Sarge?"

"No need to stand on formality. You aren't one of my platoon. Call me Lofty when we're in private."

"The middle of the vehicle park is hardly private."

"It's as close as we're going to get." Lofty said firmly. He didn't want to give Debbie Moon the wrong idea.

"So, who are you missing today?" She asked lightly, as though it was of no real concern.

"My wife, Emma."

"What will she be doing?"

"Christmas with her Mum and Dad and sister I'd guess."

"You can't beat a family Christmas." Debbie took a pull at her can. "What did you get for her?"

Lofty told her of the item he had left for Emma and Debbie laughed. "I also gave her a bottle of her favourite perfume though." He excused himself. "I just hope she doesn't open the other one in front of her family." Debbie laughed again.

"You're looking a bit glum, if you don't mind me saying."

"I rang Emma last night. It was a difficult conversation. She wants me to leave the army. I can understand why, after what happened to Cobber."

"Will you? Leave I mean."

"I don't know. It keeps nagging at me. Emma doesn't understand the army. She's hardly had any contact with it up to now, and then to have something like that happen so soon after she moved down. It must be very worrying for her."

"I'd never ask a bloke to give up something he really wanted to do."

Lofty looked sideways at the woman. Was she trying to tell him something? He had to admit the possibility. She seemed to find excuses to be in his company, like now. Mostly they were good official reasons, to be sure, but most of them could wait or they could be dealt with by one of the other Platoon Sergeants. Was she just being friendly, or was it something more?

"Are you in a relationship?" Lofty asked.

"Was. Two timing bastard. I caught him shagging one of the civvie women in RHQ. I wouldn't have minded so much if she'd been good looking, but she looks like the back of a bus. And she's married!"

"A bit careless of him."

"Well, yes and no. He thought I was safely on my way out here but my flight was cancelled so I was sent back to barracks to wait for the next one. I walked in to the RAO's office to report and there he was, having her over her desk. He hadn't even locked the door. Now that *was* careless." She giggled, able now to accept the absurdity of the situation. "Well, at least I wasn't sat out here like a numpty thinking he was being good and faithful to me, sitting by the fire waiting for me to come home."

Lofty allowed himself a dry chuckle. In his experience girls on the rebound were dangerous. They were prone to throwing themselves at the first bloke they took a fancy to, regardless of their marital status. Well, maybe he was being harsh. There were plenty of women who wouldn't have anything to do with a married man, but he knew from experience that there were plenty who had chased married men as well. Was this Debbie's plan for him?

"So what did you do?"

"I gave her a right hook that Lennox Lewis would have been proud of. Didn't even give her time to pull her knickers up. Then I gave him a few choice words, accompanied by some good hard kicks. I think they got the message. You should have seen his face when I walked in. It was a picture. I'll carry that memory to my grave." She let out a full blown laugh. The beer was clearly taking effect.

"I'm surprised you weren't arrested."

"Oh, there was no way that cow was going to put in a complaint. Her husband would find out what she'd been up to. And Alfie is six foot two. I'm five foot six in my boots. You can imagine the piss taking he'd get if his mates found out I'd given him a kicking. But I was back at Brize Norton again in quick time and had to wait in the transit hotel until my new flight came through. Could have been worse. At least it's got a bar."

"Where are you based?"

"Chicksands, near Bedford. It's our Corps HQ." The girl answered. "Not a bad place. The Yanks had it until a few years ago, so it's in pretty good nick. Anyway, what about you? Will you get to speak to Emma today?"

"Well, I didn't get a place in the draw for a phone call today, so I'll have to wait to talk to her." Everyone wanted to phone home on Christmas Day and there was only one phone that could be used, so the Company Commander had arranged a lottery to keep things as fair as possible. "To tell you the truth I think I'd rather not talk to her today. It's all very emotional, Christmas Day. I might say something I'd regret."

A hand bell was being rung to announce that Christmas dinner was ready, even though most of the soldiers had been sat in the Dining Room for an hour or more holding snail races. "Sorry, but duty calls." Lofty was quite relieved in a way. He wanted time to think about Emma and Debbie would only create a distraction.

The army has many traditions but one of the most popular is that the men of a unit are served Christmas Dinner by their officers and SNCOs. Lofty marched into the dining area where the air was already alive with the din of squeakers and party poppers. As he headed across the room towards his platoon he felt the thump of a minced pie hitting him in the back. He resisted the temptation to turn round and find out who had thrown it. He knew there was far worse to come.

* * *

A third of the world away, Emma did something unusual at her family's house, unusual even at Christmas. She asked them to go to church with her. They had never been a religious family so it caused them some discussion, but when Emma explained why she wanted to do it, they hurried to support her.

As the service progressed and reached the point where the vicar offered everyone the chance to offer up their private prayers Emma screwed her eyes up tight and asked a God she didn't really believe in, to protect her husband.

The family made its way back through the chilly North London streets and Emma's Mum bustled around getting the dinner ready. Before they sat they offered up a toast to the soldiers in Afghanistan and for the memory of those that wouldn't be celebrating Christmas that year.

Christmas Dinner that year was a subdued affair.

* * *

Lofty was sat on his camp bed cleaning his rifle. It was the sort of mundane task that he liked to do when he wanted to think. It helped to keep his hands busy without cluttering up his mind. Emeli Sandé sang into the ear pieces of his MP3 player, soothing him.

What to do about Emma, that was the question on his mind. He was no closer to answering it than he had been earlier. He really did want to be with her for the rest of his life. On the other hand the soldiering out here made him feel alive. The adrenalin rush when they came under fire, the instantaneous decision making that kept his soldiers alive and the enemy dead. Where would he get that in a civvie job? At best he'd have to take up extreme sports and he doubted Emma would approve of that either.

A knock came at the door of his tiny room and he looked up to see Debbie Moon standing in the open doorway. She held two mugs, one of which she was offering to him.

He slipped the ear pieces off and welcomed her. "What's in the mug?"

"You tell me." She grinned at him. He took it and looked inside. An inch of golden liquid sloshed around the bottom. He took a sniff and his nostrils filled with the sharp aroma of good quality Scotch.

"Where on earth did you get this?"

The woman tapped the side of her nose. "Perks of the job. I get a box to pack my office equipment in. It's a big box with lots of space left over."

"You realise this is strictly against standing orders."

She shrugged. "I won't tell if you won't. Besides, it's Christmas. If you can't break the odd rule at Christmas when can you?"

"I doubt if the CO would see it that way." He took an experimental sip of the whisky. It was good stuff. "To what do I owe the honour of sharing in this illegal activity?"

"You looked so fed up. I saw you coming back from the mess hall, covered in custard, and I thought 'there's man who could do with a drop of the hard stuff'."

"Well, you weren't wrong about that." Lofty took a generous pull at the fiery liquor, causing his eyes to water. Debbie sat down on the camp bed, not close enough to invade his personal space, but a little closer than Lofty would have liked. To distract himself he re-assembled his rifle and laid it on the poncho on the floor beside his bed so that he wouldn't undo his work by letting dust contaminate the weapon.

"So, have you decided what to do about Emma?" Debbie asked.

"Have you been reading my mind?"

"I'm in Intelligence, remember. It doesn't take much to see when a bloke has something on his mind, and you clearly had when we were talking this morning."

"Oh, I don't know what to do for the best." Lofty sounded exasperated.

"Well, if you try to please everyone you'll end up pleasing no-one. That's what my Mum used to say." She took a gulp of her own Scotch. "And I'm guessing you'll please yourself least of all." Her words were slightly slurred, suggesting this wasn't her first mug of whisky.

Lofty turned to place the mug on top of the packing case next to his bed. While his back was turned

Debbie took the opportunity to slide along the bed a couple of inches towards him.

"Is there anything I can say that would help?"

"You can give me some other options." he replied.

"How do you mean?"

"Well, at the moment I've got two. Put Emma first and leave the army, or stay in the army and risk losing Emma. Got anything else?"

Debbie seemed to be applying careful consideration to the question. "Perhaps there is an alternative." She stood up and closed the door, shutting out most of the light. In the gloom Lofty could see her hands working on the front of her camouflaged jacket. She slid the sleeves from her arms and dropped the garment to the floor, then started on the buttons of her combat trousers.

"What are you doing?" Lofty protested.

"Shh." She replied. "Someone will hear you." Most of the platoon were sleeping off their Christmas lunches in the barrack room just the thickness of a wall away but it wouldn't take much noise to wake someone.

Lofty stood up and took Debbie's hands from the front of her trousers. "I'm very flattered, but that isn't the answer. You're very nice, and if I wasn't married then…. But I am, and I love Emma very much. This really isn't an option for me." Even in the gloom Lofty could see the sheen on the bare skin of her shoulders and chest, broken only by the dark shadow of her bra. Temptation stirred in his loins. They had been here three long months; Who would blame him? Lofty knew the answer at once. He would blame him.

He bent over to pick up her combat jacket in the cramped space, an action that took him closer to Debbie's bare skin than he really wanted to be. He smelt the clean smell of her soap and his base instincts made another bid for control. With some difficulty he suppressed them again.

"You don't know what you're missing." She purred at him, stepping close enough to make sure that he really did know. Her small breasts pushed against him. Lofty was glad she was still wearing her bra otherwise he might have been tipped over the edge.

"I know, Debbie. But I love Emma and that's that. I'm sorry, and I hope I haven't upset you, but it's not on."

"OK, suit yourself." She shrugged herself back into her jacket and did up enough buttons to keep herself covered. She was glad Lofty couldn't see her face. "If you change your mind you know where to find me."

"I won't change my mind."

Debbie shrugged again and opened the door, not daring to look back at him. A tear shone at the corner of her eye. Lofty winced as sunlight hit his eyes. He watched Debbie's back as she strolled down the barrack room. Half way along she stopped to talk to someone out of Lofty's vision. There was a burst of laughter and Debbie gave a brittle laugh in return, her neck reddening with a blush. Well, it wouldn't hurt his reputation, even if nothing had happened.

Lofty finished the whisky and returned to Emeli Santé while he scraped cold custard off his jacket and mentally struggled once again with his problem.

Mickey Flynn stuck his head round the door frame. "Naughty, naughty." He grinned.

"Don't you start. Nothing happened."

"A bird comes out of your room with half the buttons of her jacket undone and you expect me to believe that?"

"Believe what you like. Nothing happened. She was only in here five minutes. Who do you think I am, Speedy Gonzalez?"

"After three months without you could have a hair trigger. I know I have."

"Then you go and chat her up."

"I might just do that Lofty. Mightn't I just."

He wouldn't have accepted that from anyone else, but a friendship first forged on the football field had stood the test of time off of it. Mickey was a good bloke and meant no harm.

"And lay off the whisky if she offers you any." Warned Lofty at Mickey's retreating back. "We're back on stag tomorrow morning."

"Oh it's not her whisky I'm after Sarge." he guffawed.

Well, Mickey could do a lot worse than Debbie. The thing was, could Debbie do better than Mickey?

Lofty returned to his reverie. In his heart he knew he loved Emma more than he loved the army. But the army was more than just a job.

After his father had died, he and his mother had often been visited by old comrades of his father. They had told him the stories. As they spoke he would stand in front of his father's photograph, taken just before he departed for that final tour in Northern Ireland. Even as a young child he had recognised that his father had been different. The stories the men told showed that.

He had died at the hands of an IRA gunman, out on a routine patrol through the streets of West Belfast. But that wasn't one of the stories the soldiers had told

203

him. They told him how his father had put his section of four men between a Catholic family and a rampaging Loyalist mob intent on burning them out of their home.

They told him about him climbing into the back of a burning Warrior armoured personnel carrier in Southern Iraq to pull out a soldier trapped inside. That had been in the first Gulf War; the one that actually had been justified.

They told him how his father had always put his men first and his own safety second. How he refused to eat until all his men had been fed and how he refused to sleep until all his men were resting.

It was those stories that had inspired Lofty to join the army. He couldn't get his father back, but he could do what his father had done. He could finish the job.

His mother had opposed him joining up. It had taken the combined efforts of his uncles, Dave and Eddie, to talk her round. He was under eighteen, so he needed his mother's signature to join. She had fought against it, getting angry with both his uncles and himself, but they had prevailed with the simplest of arguments. He would be eighteen in due course and could join up on his own signature. If he had to wait he might resent her, and the relationship between them might sour. It had tipped the balance in his favour and she had, reluctantly, signed the forms.

Was that what he was risking now, by putting the army before Emma? Her alienation? He hoped not.

The Stand To alarm wailed into life, cutting off his reverie. He picked up his rifle and body armour, grabbed his helmet and headed out to join his men as they jostled their way through the doors and streamed towards their assembly point. Christmas was apparently over.

Glossary

2IC   Second in command
Chinook   Boeing CH-47 heavy lift helicopter used by the RAF and American armed forces for cargo and troop carrying operations. Its design is distinctive in that it has a tandem rotor arrangement with one rotor mounted over the front of the aircraft and one over the tail, rather than the traditional mid fuselage single rotor blade assembly with a smaller vertically mounted stabilising rotor at the rear.
RLC   Royal Logistics Corps. Formed in 1993 by merging the Royal Army Ordnance Corps, Royal Corps of Transport, Royal Pioneer Corps and Army Catering Corps. The branch of the army responsible for re-supply, transport, catering and pioneer support.

15 - The Trap

The Chinook settled onto its landing pad and the high pitched whine of its engines descended as they slowed and finally stopped. Through the small windows Lofty saw the rotors slowing and eventually come to a standstill. The Loadmaster opened the side door while the passengers undid their safety belts and stood, stretching or reaching for equipment as the need took them.

Lofty followed his platoon and company commanders out of the helicopter and into the sunlit morning. Camp Bastion bustled around them as soldiers, sailors and airmen went about their daily business. Ground crew were already busy re-fuelling the helicopter ready for its next mission.

A Landrover was waiting to take them to the complex of prefabricated buildings that housed Brigade HQ. According to legend the total size of the camp was now equal to the town of Reading. A sizeable part of that was the runway and aircraft dispersals, but the vast American occupation of real estate also added to its breadth.

They were greeted by a major wearing Royal Marines insignia. He introduced himself as Major Munroe, CO of the combined SAS and SBS detachment. After they had deposited their weapons in the safe keeping of a soldier the Royal Marine ushered the three of them into the Brigadier's office. It was actually too grand a title for the cubby hole that was separated from the rest of the building by partitions made from recycled cardboard boxes supported by batons of wood. They were still in their helmets so they didn't salute, but stood to attention until the Brigadier ordered them to stand at ease then take a seat. The Major made the introductions.

"Sorry for the loss of your men in that raid last month." The Brigadier opened proceedings. "I've read the report. I'm afraid Sergeant Major Smith doesn't come out of it too well."

"Will he be disciplined?" The Company Commander asked.

"If I disciplined him then I would also have to discipline others in the decision making chain." The Brigadier looked pointedly at the Company Commander. "I think the best outcome for him would be a medical discharge. He's got six months till he reaches pensionable age. He'll be in hospital and rehabilitation for most of that. If I have a word with the MoD, I can make sure he isn't offered an extension to his service. It won't seem unusual, given the number of redundancies that are being made at present, combined with the longer term effects of his injuries."

"It seems to be a bit of a reward considering that he got three men killed and another five seriously wounded, if you don't mind me saying so Sir." Captain Trent voiced the opinion that Lofty had also formed.

"We can't afford a scandal, I'm afraid. The MoD are already under fire for the number of casualties we've taken recently. It wouldn't look good in the press if we admitted that some of them were the result of a cock up by one of our most experienced NCOs. Now, to the matter in hand."

Politics, thought Lofty, wanting to spit. The CSM would walk free while Sam Bruce and Toyah Martin had to get on with their lives as widows, and while

Justin Green's parents grieved over the loss of their son. Would the truth ever come out?

The Brigadier picked up a pink folder from his desk. "My staff have prepared a plan to entice the Taliban in your area into a trap. We think that if we give them a juicy enough bit of bait we'll attract them like flies round a honey pot. I've scheduled it for March, so it will be your 'Parthian shot'." The battalion was due to start withdrawing from theatre at the end of that month.

He scanned a page within the folder to refresh his memory. "Major Munroe will command the operation, as his special forces team will be the first to deploy. I've assigned B Company of the Royal Warwickshires as one element of the cordon force. One of your platoons will remain behind to guard Camp Elizabeth while the other three platoons from your own Company will form the other half of the cordon force. One of those will be the bait. I assume that you would like that honour, Sgt Lofthouse?"

"I would indeed, Sir." Never volunteer for anything, that was the army motto, but he could hardly tell the Brigadier to stick it. Besides, his men were hungry for revenge on the Taliban and this would be their last opportunity unless the enemy attacked them first. Lofty didn't much like the use of the word 'bait' though. It made him feel vulnerable, like a tethered goat waiting for the arrival of a tiger.

"You'll have air support, of course, and there will be a company of Royal Marines back here in reserve, should you need them. Hopefully you won't. I'll let Major Munroe fill you in on the details, but the essence of the plan will be for your platoon to set up a patrol base in an abandoned village. It's one that your men will be familiar with. We'll be advertising the fact to the Taliban using that Facebook channel your intelligence clerk identified. A good job there, by the way. Please pass on my thanks.

We expect the Taliban to infiltrate into the village and try to attack you. That will be the signal for the net to close. Your other two platoons will be waiting out of sight and will close down the escape route on one side of the village, and we'll drop the Warwickshires behind them by helicopter to close the net. After that you just have to pull the string tight and you'll land them like a net load of cod."

"You mentioned special forces, Sir. What's their role?" ask the Company Commander.

"They will be on the ground a few days ahead of you, keeping an eye on the village. If the Taliban try to sneak in early or plant booby traps they'll be able to tell you where they are. They'll also act as your eyes and ears outside the village to give warning of when the enemy are on their way. Finally, if any holes appear in the net they'll be on hand to plug them. Now, Any questions?"

* * *

"This is outrageous." protested Mr Rahman. "How dare you invade my house in this way?"

"We have a warrant issued under the Prevention of Terrorism Act to enter and search these premises, Mr Rahman." The police officer waved several sheets of paper under Mr Rahman's nose before handing him his copy of the warrant.

"But you didn't have to break the door down. If you had rung the bell I would have let you in. Look at that. Who will pay for that to be fixed?" Mr Rahman pointed at the splintered door jam, caused by the ram that the police had used to gain entry.

The police Inspector had the decency to look slightly abashed by the damage his men had done. Dressed in full riot gear, complete with crash helmet, he felt rather over-dressed when faced with a short, indignant, middle aged Asian man wearing striped pyjamas. The armed police unit was way over the top, he thought, but the Commissioner had insisted. It would look better on TV.

"We did ring the bell, Mr Rahman."

"Yes, but did you give me time to answer it? No you didn't. The first crash on the door was barely a second after the bell sounded. It's five o'clock in the morning. We were all in bed. It takes more than a second to rise and come down the stairs."

"I'm sorry. I'll leave you a form so you can claim for the damages. Now, my men have their duties to perform, so if you don't mind I'll ask you to step aside."

"They may not go near my wife or daughter. Our religion prohibits it." Mr Rahman made further protests.

"Don't worry, Sir. I have female officers who will look after the ladies of the house and search their rooms."

"But I don't understand what all this is about. What are we supposed to have done?"

"We have a report that a person in this house is connected to a suspected terrorist."

"I know that. It was my daughter who made the report. My wife went with her to the police station. Why did you not just come back here and search the house then?"

"That's not for me to say, Sir. Now if you will allow me to get on with my job." The Inspector pushed past him and went through to the kitchen.

"And what about all these reporters and cameramen?" Mr Rahman followed the officer along the corridor, still protesting. "Are they really necessary? Who told them to be here, officer?"

Feet pounded on the stairs. "Daddy, they're taking my laptop. It's got all my college work on it. I won't be able to sit my exams without it."

"In English, please. If you don't mind Sir, Miss."

Mr Rahman turned to deal with his daughter but spoke English as requested. It was easy to forget that they normally spoke Urdu in their home. "Go back to your room child. You aren't dressed to be seen by men." He waved his hand to indicate her pyjamas, including the six inch gap between the top and the bottoms that exposed her tummy. "And your hair is uncovered. Go back to your mother."

"But Daddy…."

"Don't argue child. You are unfit to be seen. There can be no talking about this until you are either properly dressed or until these men have gone."

For once Fatima had to acknowledge that her father was right. It was unseemly for her to be seen in her current state of dress, or rather undress.

But Mr Rahman had taken her protest to heart and continued into the kitchen to challenge the police on the seizure of the laptop.

"I'm sorry Sir, but we have to take it. It needs to be examined to find out what is on the hard drive. Who knows what it has been used for."

"My daughter does, and she uses it for college. How will she study when you have all her notes?"

"I'm sorry Sir, that's not our concern. We are here because we have a duty to protect the public against terrorists."

"But we're not terrorists."

"So you say, Sir, but what proof have we of that?"

"So why haven't you arrested us already?" challenged Mr Rahman.

The officer was taken aback by the unexpected and rather pertinent question, but he hadn't made it to the rank of Inspector without having some intelligence.

"If we find evidence then we will make arrests, Sir."

"So this is just one of the Metropolitan Police's famous fishing expeditions, is it?"

"We have information…"

"Yes, information provided by my daughter who went to a police station of her own free will. And now you use that to justify the invasion of my home."

"I suggest that you let me get on with my job, Mr Rahman." The Inspector's tone had changed from conciliatory to threatening. "Otherwise I may have to arrest you for obstructing the police."

Mr Rahman realised that further argument was futile. Besides, he had stated his case and it had made no difference. This was the police at their most officious and unthinking. He climbed the stairs and went to join his wife and daughter. He found two police women busily going through the drawers and wardrobes.

"Are you happy now?" He said to his daughter. "First they search the Ibrahim's house and now they search ours. I hope you are satisfied."

"Sa'id, that is unfair." Mrs Rahman protested. "How could the child know that the police would behave in this manner."

"She should not have interfered in the first place. What Youssef Haq Ibrahim does is not our concern. She had no need to get involved."

"You fool, she loves the boy, and you know it. How many times have we talked of the possibility of marriage between them."

"That was before. He will not marry my daughter now."

Fatima let out a wail of anguish. "Father, you can't say that. I love him."

"Child, if he returns here then he will go to prison. How can you marry a man in prison?"

Fatima continued to sob into her mother's shoulder. "But what if I go to Afghanistan, or Pakistan?"

Mr Rahman let out a snort of derision. "Do you know what you are saying? Would you give up this" he waved his hands and Fatima was unsure if he just meant their home or the whole of London, "in exchange for a slum in Islamabad, or worse, a peasant farm in Helmand? Don't be such a fool. Love would soon end under those circumstances."

"But I love him." Was all she could reply.

"And that is why people shouldn't marry for love! It makes them do stupid things." Mr Rahman folded his arms and sat on the bed with his back to the two women, making it clear that the matter was closed.

Fatima wept quietly, knowing that in part at least her father was right. She needn't have gone to the police. She had acted out of what she considered to be love for Youssef, but it had all gone wrong.

She had finally persuaded her mother that she needed to do something to protect Youssef. It hadn't just been that, of course. What Youssef was doing was wrong, by any standards. She had been raised to obey the law and to live by it, and protecting Youssef, for whatever reason, would be to collaborate with the forces of evil. She couldn't stop him fighting for the Taliban, but if he was captured then at least she could make sure he was brought back to Britain. So she had gone to the police, and her mother had gone with her to offer support.

For three hours Mrs Rahman had sat on a hard, uncomfortable chair in the front office of the police station while her daughter was interviewed. At first the police hadn't seemed to be interested, but that soon changed.

"I've come to tell you about a British man who might be in danger." She told the civilian receptionist on the front desk.

"In what way?" he had replied.

"He went to Pakistan to study, but his family were killed and things changed. I think he may have become mixed up with the wrong people.

"I don't think that's really a matter for us, Miss. If he's in Pakistan that's not within our jurisdiction to deal with."

"You don't understand. I think he may have gone from there to Afghanistan."

"I realise that might be dangerous, Miss, but there's still nothing we can do."

"There was a report in the papers before Christmas, that the authorities believe that a Taliban group is being led by a British fighter."

"Yes, I'm aware of that story, Miss, but what has that got to do with this man you're talking about?" The penny dropped. "Are you saying that this fighter may be the same man as you were talking about?"

"Yes, that's exactly what I mean."

"Take a seat. I'll give someone a call."

It was fifteen minutes before a harassed looking constable appeared in the reception area. "I'm sorry to keep you waiting, but as you are a Muslim female they had to find a female officer to talk to you, and it took them some time to find me. I'm Detective Constable Theresa Molineux. Now tell me what this is all about."

DC Molineux sat down beside Fatima and her mother and listened patiently to Fatima's story. "How sure are you that this man, Youssef, is the same as the fighter mentioned in the newspapers?"

"I'm not sure at all really. But how can this be just a coincidence? He said he was in the mountains of Pakistan, and that the Taliban were close by. I think he was being untruthful about that. I think he was with the Taliban. And since then I haven't heard from him at all. That can only be because he is in Afghanistan and he can't contact me from there."

"Has there been no contact at all?"

"Just one e-mail sent to my father. That is what worries me more. What he says in his e-mail is so different to what we have talked about before. He sounds so different. I fear he has been radicalised."

"OK, Fatima. I'd like you to come with me and we'll carry out a formal interview and take a statement. Mrs Rahman, I think it would be better if you went home, as this may take some time."

"No. I will stay. Fatima, if you need me I'll be right here."

"Thank you Mummy." Fatima stood and followed the DC through a door into the hidden interior of the building. The door closed with a solid clunk that suggested it would not be opened easily, the thought confirmed by the heavy duty combination lock above the handle.

That was when Fatima started to realise that she might have made a mistake. The quiet consideration shown by DC Molineux disappeared as she was interviewed again and again by ever more senior ranking officers. DC Molineux remained with her as a chaperone throughout it all, but played no further part in the process. She kept her face blank, showing no emotion as ever more bizarre accusations were levelled at Fatima.

"Have you ever been to Pakistan yourself?"

"No."

"So where did you go to be radicalised?"

"I am not radicalised. I am a faithful Muslim who follows the laws of my religion, nothing more. I have no truck with the radicals or those that support the jihad.

"That's easy to say. Have you ever seen any of these men?" She was shown a series of photos of men she had never seen in her life.

"No. I don't know any of them."

"Something else that's easy to say. I think you know these men. Where did you meet them?"

It seemed to go on for hours, and the more she denied their claims the more insistent they became. They simply wouldn't accept that she was just a student worried about her boyfriend. Finally Fatima realised that she didn't need to tolerate their behaviour. She was in the police station voluntarily and didn't have to stay.

"If you wish me to answer any more questions I think I would like a solicitor present."

"Why? We haven't arrested you."

"No, precisely, you haven't arrested me, but I'm pretty sure that the Police and Criminal Evidence Act allows me to have a solicitor present at any time if I wish it." In fact Fatima was very unsure of her rights, but it seemed to do the trick. The officer disappeared and ten minutes later was replaced by a uniformed sergeant.

"That will be all, for now, Miss Rahman. Please let us know if Mr Ibrahim makes any contact with you."

Fatima made a silent vow to do nothing of the sort. If this was how innocent people were treated by the police she had no intention of having anything more to do with them. She would try to find other ways to help Youssef.

Her parents had been right. When the police look at an Asian they don't see a British citizen, they see the people who had forced them out of India. No, worse than that, they see someone who is a terrorist until proven otherwise.

Two days later Mr and Mrs Ibrahim's house was raided by the police, and now their own house was being ripped apart for no good reason.

Fatima started crying again and her mother passed her a box of tissues. There was nothing more that could be said for the present.

Glossary

SAS   Special Air Service, an elite unit in the British Army.

SBS   Special Boat Service, the Royal Marines' equivalent to the SAS.

16 - Ghostville

"What happened here Sarge?" Pvt Dangerfield asked. He was one of the new arrivals and hadn't yet heard the story.

"The Russians happened, lad." Lofty replied. "They were carrying out reprisals for an attack on a convoy that happened a few klicks along the road. They rounded the people up and shot them all, but only after raping the women and girls, in front of their husbands and fathers. The few that somehow survived went elsewhere."

The young soldier let out a low whistle, then stuck his head through the door of one of the houses. It was a basic affair. A single square room with a ladder leading up onto the wooden boarded roof.

"Careful, lad." Lofty warned. "We haven't checked these for booby traps yet."

The soldier withdrew his head sharply and moved along the alley a short way.

"What's this place called." Dangerfield asked.

"No one knows. If it ever had a name then it disappeared with the people. The first Brit soldiers to come here called it Ghostville, and that's what we've marked it as on the maps."

Number 1 Platoon had patrolled Ghostville on a number of occasions. It was an obvious place for Taliban fighters to hole up if they were planning an attack in the area. Traces of them were found quite regularly: cigarette ends, food wrappers, the ashes of cooking fires and midden heaps. C Company commander had asked for the place to be demolished, not the first such request to have been made, but the over worked engineers and pioneers never had the time to get round to it. So now Lofty led the men through the village again.

This time it was a formal reconnaissance ahead of their operation. It had been called Op MANACLE and that was the name the soldiers now used for their task. The full briefing hadn't yet taken place, but rumours regarding the operation and its mission abounded.

The village lay on the side of a small hill, rising no more than a hundred feet above the surrounding plain. A pot holed dirt track joined it to the main highway that passed it by to the East.

At its height it had been home to no more than thirty families, each with their own mud walled house separated from its neighbours by dark, narrow alleys. Its compact size made it easier to protect against bandits. At the highest point of the village, just below the summit of the hill, stood the former home of the headman, distinguished by its location and larger dimensions. Unlike the other houses it was built around a small courtyard.

The house was a rectangular arrangement of rooms which formed the small courtyard in the centre. It was almost a miniature version of Camp Elizabeth. The exterior walls were windowless and pierced only by double doors leading into the courtyard. These now hung drunkenly on their broken hinges. The roof above the rooms was flat, which allowed the occupants to sleep up there during the summer to escape the heat that would build up within the mud walled rooms. It was also the only house in the village to have a proper staircase leading to the roof.

Lofty led Catfish 1 Section up to the house. A search was gingerly carried out for hidden bombs before Lofty climbed onto the roof. As he stood there he concluded that it would make an ideal patrol base. He made a note on his pad to bring the tools necessary to fix the doors.

A patrol base is no more than a temporary FOB. The platoon had set them up before, establishing firing points at the windows and on the roofs of buildings and sleeping on the hard packed earth floors of the rooms. One section would remain on guard while the remainder of the platoon conducted patrols around the local area, either on foot or in vehicles. When they had completed whatever tasks they had been assigned they would withdraw to the security of the FOB once again. A Platoon on its own was too vulnerable to attack to remain in a remote location for more than a few days. Sometimes Afghan security forces would then occupy the patrol base to establish a more permanent security presence. Sometimes it would just be abandoned and returned to its owners.

This time the patrol base would serve a different purpose. It was to form the bait in a trap that was designed to destroy the Taliban in this part of Helmand province. However the plan was for the bait not to get eaten, so 1 Platoon was being meticulous in its preparations.

Climbing down the stairs from the roof, Lofty left Catfish 2 occupying the headman's house and took Catfish 1 back through the narrow streets to find the Platoon Commander. Capt Trent was in conversation with Staff Sergeant Micklin, the acting Company Sergeant Major, as they worked to produce an up to date sketch map of the village.

Capt Trent looked up. "How does it look?"

"It'll be OK, Sir. It'll need some repairs doing to make it more secure, but there are good fields of fire across the village. I think we may need to clear a bit more ground between the house and the rest of the village. An RPG man can get too close for comfort and those walls won't take a lot of battering."

"How hard will it be to do that?" asked the SSgt.

"Not too hard, Sir." Only a few weeks earlier Lofty would have addressed him as Kev, but such was army protocol that this man's temporary promotion now gave him the right to be addressed more formally. His arrival with the company had been a breath of fresh air and he had made the most of the opportunity that had unexpectedly been presented to him. The FOB was now tidier and the defences in better repair. The men benefited from daily PT sessions when they weren't tasked to be on patrol, and he had organised some evening entertainments to break up the monotony. The last had been a sports quiz that Lofty's team had won. There had been a significant improvement in morale since the unlamented CSM Smith had departed on the medevac chopper.

"We'll need some sledge hammers and crow bars, but I think once we can make some holes in the walls we can probably get some chains on them and pull them down using the Mastiffs. It will take some effort to clear the rubble, but nothing that a bit of muscle can't manage."

"I'll need to get clearance from Brigade for that." The Platoon Commander commented. "Technically we can't go destroying buildings, even abandoned ones, in case the Afghan government has plans for them. They could ask for compensation."

Lofty grunted. It was common for the population to ask for money for damages, even a bullet hole in a mud wall was worth a few dollars, so a whole house would be worth a lot more if someone decided to claim. But the paying of compensation was the difference between the British being seen as occupiers, like the Russians, or allies.

"Could we get a section of Pioneers in to help with the demolition work?" asked Lofty.

"I'll look into that as well, but the Pioneers are a bit stretched at the moment."

"Sarge." a voice interrupted their discussion. It was Pvt Richardson, another of the new arrivals. Lofty was still getting to know them, which was why he was keeping close to Catfish 1 while they were in the field.

"What is it?"

"Up there Sarge." He pointed towards the top of the hill.

It took Lofty a few moments to pick out what Richardson was pointing at, but then he saw it. The loose end of a turban cloth blowing in the slight breeze.

"You've got sharp eyes, Richardson. Well done. Looks like we've got company, Sir."

"So I see. Well, in this case that may be a good thing. They'll wonder what we're doing here, and it will support the intel they'll get in a couple of weeks' time." He turned to the acting CSM. "However, discretion is the better part of valour Mr Micklin. I think we'll return to Camp Elizabeth now. Next week we'll come back and start on the work we need to do to strengthen the defences." He led the way down the hill to where Catfish 3 were guarding the vehicles while Lofty called Catfish 2 in from the headman's house.

* * *

"They were drawing maps and pacing out distances, Sheikh." The man reported.

Youssef listened with interest.

"Did it look like they intended to defend the area?"

"I can't say, I have little military knowledge. I have seen them there before though. Then they searched the buildings and left. This time was different. They still searched, but then they started to do the other things. I could pick out the officers quite clearly. They wrote things down and held discussions. You would think that they were back in their own country enjoying a day out."

The British didn't do anything without a reason, Youssef knew, and such a detailed examination of the abandoned village suggested that they had been carrying out more than just a routine patrol. He pulled a few dollar bills off the roll he kept in his pocket and handed them to the man, at the same time instructing him to return if he discovered anything new.

It would be useful for him to conduct his own recce of the place. If the British were to establish a base there then it would be helpful if he knew the layout before they moved in. It might help them if they ever decided to mount an attack.

Youssef's group of fighters had been strengthened by the arrival of some new recruits from Pakistan. Strengthened might not be quite the word he needed to describe them. They were keen enough, but the quality of training had declined. The Pakistani Army had discovered two of their training camps and attacked them, robbing the Taliban of their most experienced instructors. Such men were hard to replace. So Youssef bided his time and invested in his new recruits by providing more training for them, even though they insisted they were ready to fight as soon as he gave the word.

Ali had been given charge of the recruits and now stooped below the rough curtain to speak to his leader.

"They're itching to have a go, Youssef. It will be bad for morale if we don't do something with them soon. There are some new police in Zābol. Apparently they're throwing their weight about a bit. Why not teach them a lesson?"

Youssef considered the suggestion. It might not be a bad idea. He could use a diversion while he conducted the recce on the abandoned village, and the half trained Afghan police would provide him with a good opportunity to test the mettle of his recruits.

"OK, you can lead an attack on them. Make a plan and discuss it with me later. If I think it can work then you can go ahead. But I'm not going to throw those young men's lives away. If I think it's too risky I won't allow it."

Young men, reflected Youssef. The youngest was just a few weeks shy of his own age; the majority were older. But after facing rifle and machine gun fire so many times Youssef now felt ancient. He was almost surprised to remember that he had only just passed his twenty first birthday.

Ali grinned at the prospect of his first independent command. "Don't worry Youssef. We'll give those crusader puppets a good kicking."

Ali admired Youssef's caution, but sometimes wished for the return of Abisali's more flamboyant style. Abisali would have agreed the mission at once. On the other hand Youssef's more cautious style had prevented more of the men becoming casualties and in return the men felt confident in his leadership because of that. While all of them were prepared to become martyrs in the cause of Islam none of them wanted to think their lives were being thrown away.

The man left the corner of the cave that Youssef called his own and allowed his leader to return to his reverie. They were the same thoughts that had plagued him for weeks, even months now. What would happen to Fatima and himself? He was a committed jihadi now. He had no place to call his own, no place he could take Fatima and be with her as man and wife.

Until the war was won there was no place of safety. When that happened things would be different, he had been assured of that. He attended the councils that discussed these matters. His point of view was listened to. He gave wise counsel which was acknowledged by the other leaders. There would be a place for him at the highest level of the Islamic State of Afghanistan. He dared to dream.

But that was a long way off. Dare he phone his beloved, or maybe make some other contact with her? Perhaps he might dare. It would take time, of course, but perhaps he could take a few days and travel down to Pakistan. There he could use the internet, or even the telephone. Would she still be there waiting for him? She was a good Muslim girl; Yes, of course she would still be waiting.

* * *

The small band of fighters crept through the village. It was known to them, indeed they had used it themselves on one occasion, but they had never viewed it through the eyes of their enemy before. How would a conventional military force prepare the place for defence?

Youssef drew the same conclusion as his adversary. The former headman's house was the obvious place to set up a base, and it would require some work to widen the field of fire and remove safe havens for an attacker to fire from. But the rest of the village; What use was that to anyone?

It was deserted, so of no use to the Afghan security forces. No one would put a police station or a barracks in such a place. The population of a village or town was part of its defence. They were its eyes and ears. When an enemy approached the population melted into places of safety, which a policeman or a soldier would note, like startled birds taking to the sky warns of the presence of a cat.

But the man had been quite explicit in describing what he had seen.

In the bright February moonlight Youssef drew some sketches himself. On them he marked the routes that soldiers would take to get to and from the headman's house. He marked the places where the enemy might mount a concealed machine gun, and the route by which it might be approached in a way that wouldn't expose attackers to its fire. He placed himself in the mind of the enemy officer and sited his defences accordingly.

In the training camp they had told him: "To understand how to attack a target you must get inside your enemy's head and work out how he will defend it. Once you have that answer you are assured of victory."

At last Youssef had seen and drawn enough. He whistled a low, quiet note which was repeated by each man who heard it. One by one the fighters withdrew from their defensive positions and gathered round him in the shadow of the headman's house. Quickly he quizzed them. Had they seen anything unusual? Had they noticed anything that might be of use to them if they attacked this place?

There were a few quiet observations which Youssef took note of, then he decided that they had lingered in the place for long enough.

"Return to the caves and get as much rest as you can. When we find out what the enemy are going to use this place for we will come back and take another look. Then we will attack them."

"Are these the ones, Youssef?"

"The nearest kuffar base is the one where Abisali was killed. Yes, I think it is them. He will be avenged here. But first I have a journey to undertake."

"Are you not coming with us?" asked Gamal.

"No. I have something I must do. I'll be gone a few days. No more than seven. When Ali returns obey his instructions like they were my own. Gamal, Taj." He turned his attention to the two men. "Do nothing that would make me ashamed of you. Do you understand?"

The two men said that they did. They looked somewhat sheepish.

"And I command you to make sure no one else does anything that the Prophet, all blessing be upon him, would disapprove of.

I have no idea what is going to happen here, but after it has happened I will take you back across the border. You have fought well and deserve a rest. We will go to Pakistan for a few days and relax. If you want to see your wives or families you may do so. Until then be patient."

Their faces brightened at the prospect of a trip South. As poor peasants from Afghanistan and the North West of Pakistan the concept of a holiday was foreign to them, if not to Youssef. But they understood what a few days of home comforts meant after months of living in caves.

Youssef strode away into the darkness and found his dirt bike. As he rode away into the night he wondered if this was the event Abisali had foretold. The event that would make him a household name in Britain and cause others to flock to the Taliban cause. Would it also be the event that would allow him to avenge Abisali? He also hoped that it would be. Two birds with one stone. He smiled at the thought.

Glossary

Pioneers   Part of the RLC (see below) who carry out a range of operational battlefield support tasks, including construction and demolition.

SSgt   Staff Sergeant – an NCO normally employed on administrative duties within Battalion HQ. Senior to a Sergeant.

17 - Doubts

"Oh Youssef, is it really you?"

From a third of the way round the world Youssef answered. "Yes, Fatima, it's me. How have you been?"

"Worried sick. Everyone has been worried sick. Your aunt and uncle, me, my family, your friends at the mosque. Half of Finsbury has been worrying about you. Where have you been? What have you been doing?"

"I can't tell you that, not over the phone, but you can assume that I haven't been at the Madrassa."

"We know that. We found out months ago that you haven't been near there. Youssef, please tell me. I have to know."

"OK, I'll tell you this much. I've been in Afghanistan."

"So it's true then."

"What's true?"

"We've heard that there is a British born fighter for the Taliban in Afghanistan. We've heard he is now a leader and has attacked the British many times. Is it you, Youssef?"

The line went silent except for some crackling and the occasional hiss.

"Youssef, are you still there?" Fatima pleaded frantically.

"Yes, I'm still here. How did you hear about this?" Fatima noticed that he hadn't denied her accusation.

"It was in the newspapers shortly before Christmas. The soldiers took a prisoner and he told them about the British leader of the Taliban. I hoped it wasn't you. I hoped so much that it was someone else. Tell me it isn't you."

The line went silent again as Youssef considered his response. He was well aware of the possibility of ears listening into the conversation, if not in Pakistan then in Britain or the U.S.A. In the end he decided to remain non-committal.

"Have the police spoken to you?"

"Yes. Rather I went to the police."

"Why did you do that?" Youssef sounded incredulous that she would have done such a thing.

"I was worried about you. I was worried that you might be captured and be thrown into an Afghan prison, or been shot out of hand. At least if the British are looking for you there will be a chance that you will be brought back here."

"And be put in a British prison instead?" he asked scornfully, forgetting the need for discretion as his anger boiled up.

"Which would you rather be in?"

"Neither. I would rather be a martyr."

Oh God no, Fatima thought. The depression phase. "And if you become a martyr, what becomes of me? Have you thought about me at all?"

"Of course I have, my love. I think about you constantly."

Fatima snorted derisively. "You have thought about me so much that you would rather die than return to me. I would rather you had found another woman. At least I would be spared having to grieve for you."

"You don't understand, this is my calling. Allah has called me to wage jihad against the satanic forces."

"And what makes you think Allah has called you?"

"The death of my parents. It was a sign."

"It was an accident. They were aiming at the house next door and something went wrong. It was in the newspapers."

Youssef knew that to be true. "But it was still a sign. I was called to wage holy war against the West as Allah has commanded and as the Prophet told it. We will fight them until every nation of Islam is free from their presence, their interference. Then we will establish one Holy Islamic state, where all Muslim brothers will be free."

"Youssef, do you really believe that?"

"Of course. I have been told it."

"Who by? Who told you such nonsense?"

"Be careful woman. Don't mock me."

"Since when have you addressed me in that way. Is this something else you've been told? Have you been told that I am in some way inferior to you?"

"It is the woman's duty to obey the man."

"I think I had better say goodbye now." Through the ether Youssef could hear the tears in Fatima's voice, the half stifled sobs that were wracking her body. "Call me when you have recovered your wits." Fatima carefully lowered the handset into its cradle, then fled to her room before her parents could discover her distress.

In a semi-darkened room in Cheltenham a signals officer clicked her computer mouse to end the recording of the telephone call, made a note in her log book and then dialled a telephone number in London.

In Pakistan Youssef stared uncomprehendingly at the telephone before replacing it on its cradle. He couldn't believe that Fatima, the woman he loved, had hung up on him. Even worse he couldn't believe that she hadn't supported him in his new vocation as a

232

jihadi warrior. The instructors in the camp were right. No good can come from educating women. Her faith had been contaminated by Western thinking and ideas that she would never have discovered had she stayed at home.

But then he remembered how much he loved Fatima and that he wanted to marry her. Could he deny her simply because she thought differently from him? Yes. She was a woman, one of Shaytaan's temptresses, and that was what she was doing now. She was tempting him away from the true path.

Youssef thrust Fatima from his mind and returned to the Taliban safe house that he was staying in. He would rest another night and then make his way back to Helmand to continue the fight.

* * *

In her room Fatima eventually stopped crying. She tried to rationalise Youssef's behaviour. Grief for his family accounted for some of it, of course, but surely not enough to make a killer out of a man of peace? No. That was the work of others. Youssef hadn't said as much, but he must have attended some sort of training. Perhaps in one of the camps she had heard about on the news.

She had heard of brain washing, of course. In some of her tutorials the subject had been raised, though it wasn't part of the undergraduate syllabus. Not surprisingly psychology students were interested in how someone could be made to change their beliefs not by force but by persuasion. Perhaps she should learn how it was done, so that she could understand Youssef better.

Who could she turn to now? Her mother was clear on the matter. Youssef was no longer a prospective husband and his name would no longer be used in the Rahman household. They had no desire to be visited by the police again. She had no one to confide in at college, no friends that would understand.

As a female Fatima couldn't travel to Pakistan to search for Youssef, and the onward journey into Afghanistan was simply unthinkable in its magnitude. A woman alone would be see as nothing short of a whore, she knew, and would be treated as such. No, that was out of the question.

In a house occupied by the family that loved her, Fatima had never felt so utterly alone.

* * *

After a restless night's sleep, his first in a proper bed for nine months, Youssef was better able to rationalise his feelings towards Fatima. Alone on his bucking dirt bike, heading towards the Afghan border, he had plenty of time for thinking.

Was he really prepared to sacrifice his love for Fatima on the say so of some peasants in a terrorist training camp high in the mountains of Pakistan? Of course he didn't regard himself as a terrorist. He was Taliban, the students who defended Allah. They were the ones who would drive the kuffar from all Muslim lands and establish one giant Islamic Republic dedicated to living life as Allah demanded it.

But who were these people who had taught him this? Fatima was right to challenge that. He should have challenged it himself before now. What education did they have? What insights had they gained through the study of the Koran?

Mohamed Dost Mohamed had explained the justification of jihad to him, and Youssef had re-read the texts over and over again. He had reluctantly concluded that the cleric was right. That had set him on the path of jihad, but what of all the other teaching in the camp. More than half the time he had been there they had attended lectures where men ranted about the degeneracy that had occurred in the true faith and described how only a fundamental change could protect the faithful from themselves.

"How can we expect our children to grow up to respect women when they see women on TV and film disporting themselves naked?" one lecturer had screamed. "We must protect young men and women from this and to do that we must prevent them from seeing it. Only when the control of TV and film is in our hands can that be done."

There had been a similar rant against music. "Music creates the urge to dance, and dancing is lewd. When women dance they are tempting men with their bodies. When men dance they are expressing carnal desires." and so music was also banished.

He thought about these men that had taught him. The weapons and fighting skills, well anyone who knew what they were doing could teach that. But what of the beliefs that underpinned their fight? Which of the Pakistani and Afghan peasants that had lectured them was qualified to speak on behalf of Allah? Surely he had a much better understanding of the issues.

Were these men just parroting the words of others? They quoted passages of the Holy book, the Koran, to support their arguments but he had studied the Koran, both in Britain and in Pakistan. The Imams that had taught him placed different interpretations on the Sura that they recited. He touched his copy of the book, carefully stored beneath his clothing, wrapped in a polythene cover to keep out damp and dirt. It was his talisman and his comfort.

It wasn't just what they taught about the jihad that worried him. It was the other teachings about life and how to live it. Some of it he accepted without question; It was mainstream Muslim teaching. Don't drink alcohol, don't take mind altering drugs, treat women with respect. Worship God and pray five times each day whenever possible, and when five times wasn't possible then do whatever you can. Give to charity, fast during the Holy month of Ramadan and go on pilgrimage to Mecca at least once in your life. Youssef had already undertaken the journey and hoped to do so again.

It was some of the other stuff that he found difficult to accept, especially now he was away from the influence of the camp and the other fighters. Mohamed had been a great champion of women and their rights. Everyone agreed with that and were able to quote examples from the Koran to back this up. But at the same time he was shown other texts that prevented women from making their own choices. Women must obey men, and in return men would protect them. So in preventing a woman from leaving her home without permission a man was only protecting her.

But that pronouncement had been made fourteen hundred years before. How did it apply in the modern world?

Ah, there was the thing. In the modern world. But of course these people didn't live in the modern world. They lived in an agrarian society where a man farmed as much land as he was capable of, kept what he needed to feed his family and then sold the rest at market to buy the things he couldn't make or grow himself. It was a simple life, uncluttered by the need to think on a larger scale.

It was also dangerous country, a woman alone outside her home would be easy prey to anyone intent on doing her harm. So here, in the mountains, much of what they said made sense. It was dangerous for a woman to go out to work, even if she wanted to.

Most of these people had never seen a city, so they couldn't understand that in a city a man couldn't grow food. In a city a man had to earn money to buy food. In a city you couldn't build your own house out of mud bricks and then live in it. You had to buy or rent a house built by someone else. There were some things you could do for yourself, but the rest you had to pay for. That meant employment, and employment meant having to make something, or sell something, or provide a service that people needed.

Of course they understood the existence of commerce and industry, after all someone had to make the dirt bikes, the pick-up trucks and the AK-47s, but they didn't understand the complexity of the societies where these things were made. He had noted that the peasants were far more fanatical in their beliefs than the city people he had met. Was that why? Was it that simple?

If it was that simple it meant that the people who had taught him didn't understand that if women weren't educated and couldn't work then the family was at risk of starving. On a farm a woman could feed the chickens, make the clothes and cook the meals. She didn't have to be educated to do that, so why waste time and money on sending a girl child to school? But in a city a woman who couldn't work held the family back and kept them in poverty.

No, it couldn't be that simple. Foreign fighters came to support jihad, both here and in countries like Iraq and Syria. Many of them knew about modern society and how it worked. So what else was it?

There was a risk that educating women would be to expose them to ideas that might make them dissatisfied with their place in Muslim society, make them think like Fatima thought, but that wasn't the big issue. If I was dying, he thought, would I turn down the chance of being saved because the doctor was a woman? He had to think hard about that one. Allah didn't accept you as a martyr if you threw your life away stupidly, or through ignorance, Youssef felt sure. In London, in his old life, Youssef would have had no doubt about his answer, but that was before he had been enlightened. What would he do now? Would he bleed to death waiting for the arrival of a male doctor?

If work was hard to come by then it made sense for the men to do it. A woman could stay at home and raise babies while the man worked. It was a fair division of labour as far as Youssef was concerned. But where pay was poor, then the woman's wage was as valuable as a man's and just as important for keeping the children fed.

Youssef had been lucky. His father had been a skilled worker whose employment kept the family fed and the business he had eventually inherited meant they were comparatively wealthy. Indeed, as the business was now Youssef's. He was now wealthy. But what about his friend Tariq's father, Mr Jafree? The only work he had been able to get was cleaning at the hospital and it paid badly. His family had nothing.

Tariq wore clothes bought from a charity shop. He had free school dinners and they were the only hot meal he got each day. Even with the state benefits they lived under constant threat of being evicted from their house because they struggled to pay the rent. Youssef shivered at the memory of how cold the house was in winter. Mr Jafree forbad his wife from taking a job. How much easier things might have been for them had he not done so. Was it the will of Allah that they should be poor?

Youssef put his childhood memories to one side and returned to the other things that they had taught him in the camp. The kuffar burnt mosques. Well, he had travelled extensively in Afghanistan over the past few months and he had yet to see a burnt out mosque. He had challenged Abisali on that point, only to be told that it had happened elsewhere, in another part of the country. Then he had been told that the kuffar soldiers raped the Afghan women, but the nearest thing to rape he had seen had been within his own band of fighters.

When he had taken the girl back to her house, he had spent an hour with her family. The rules of hospitality demanded that they offer refreshments and that he accept them. He had talked with the girl's father and discussed the kuffar and their behaviour. The man hadn't said anything bad about them. They had never bothered him. A patrol had come to his house one day. The kuffar had been polite but had left him in peace. They hadn't caused offence by talking to the female members of his family. Perhaps, thought Youssef, he should have asked the man more questions.

Other men had come to the caves, bringing information to sell, or carrying messages. None of them had mentioned women being raped either.

Perhaps that, too, was happening in another part of the country.

Youssef realised that he was nearing the border. The road narrowed to a track and then to a footpath along a ridge, with steep drops to either side. He dismounted from the dirt bike and continued to push it on foot up the hill to find a place to wait until darkness fell.

In the distance he could see the main trunk road that connected that part of Pakistan with Afghanistan. It was busy with the supply trucks that the kuffar rented to bring their war making materials into the country from Pakistan's Indian Ocean ports. He would dearly love to be able to mount an attack on the convoys, but the Pakistani army guarded the road too well, and on the other side of the border the convoys bristled with weaponry as the soldiers provided their own escorts.

As the sun dipped towards the Western horizon Youssef found a place where he could lie down and take a nap before he attempted the night time border crossing. The risk was low. There was no fence and the Pakistani army rarely patrolled at night. Neither did the Afghans, but it was always possible that he might stumble into a kuffar patrol on the other side, so the cover of darkness was essential if he was to enter the country undetected.

High above Youssef's head, invisible to all but the sharpest of naked eyes, a Reaper drone circled, keeping watch for anyone attempting an illegal border crossing. Its cameras were capable of reading a vehicle's number plate from an altitude of 50,000 feet.

At Creech Air Force Base an RAF Navigator of 39 Sqn locked the Reaper's camera onto the lone man he had spotted sitting on the Pakistani side of the border.

As the man raised his face to catch the last warmth of the setting sun the officer froze the frame on his screen and saved the image as a photograph. A few seconds later it was being e-mailed to Camp Bastion, as well as to the MoD in London.

The officer had a brief consultation with the Reaper's pilot and over the telephone with Brigade G3, responsible for operations. It was agreed that the lone man didn't represent a clear threat and was therefore not to be targeted, but he would be watched. As the sun set in Pakistan the officer switched the Reaper's camera to infra-red mode so he could continue to track the man in the darkness. He centred the bright glow of the dirt bike's engine and keyed in the command to lock the camera onto the heat source.

The two RAF officers looked up and greeted their replacements as they entered the flight operations centre. With them was the intelligence analyst assigned to the crew. It took only a few minutes to provide an update on the mission brief, then they vacated their padded leather chairs and allowed the new arrivals to take over the controls. The Officer's Club bar called out to them with a promise of ice cold American beer. The Navigator actually preferred traditional British bitter, but would have to wait for that until their tour of duty in Nevada came to an end. Soon the RAF would leave Nevada to start controlling the drones from their home base in Lincolnshire. The crew would miss the excitement and diversions of Las Vegas, but home was where the heart was.

Glossary

G3	Staff Officer responsible for operations.
Sqn	Squadron. A unit within the RAF, normally composed of 12 aircraft. Because the complexity of modern aircraft requires a larger number of personnel to maintain them a modern RAF Sqn is commanded by a Wing Commander, not a Squadron Leader. Also a unit of cavalry equivalent in size to a company of infantry.

18 - Preparations For Battle

While 1 and 2 platoons, and the Pioneers that had been attached to them, worked on improving the defences of Ghostville, 4 Platoon provided a defensive screen around the village. The air was loud with the sound of sledgehammers pounding on walls and the scrape of shovels on earth as men dug weapons pits or filled sandbags. Spring had arrived in Helmand and the work was making the soldiers hot. A strong breeze whipped up the dust and the combination made them thirsty. Lofty called a break and sent the men to refill their water bottles from the bowser that they had brought with them, towed along behind one of the Mastiffs.

The main weakness of the defences was the ability of an enemy to crawl to the top of the hill up the reverse slope and approach the village undetected. Lofty had decided to build a sangar to fortify the summit and to counter that threat. He walked towards it to see what progress had been made.

"How's it going Mickey?" he called as he approached Catfish 1.

"Bit of a slog, but we're managing. The ground up here is solid rock, so we're having to fill the sandbags down below and drag them up here. It's heavy work though."

"Your brains will never save your legs, will they Mickey? Load the sandbags into the back of a Mastiff and bring them up that way."

"I wanted to do that, but those fucking Lancers told me I couldn't. Scared I'll get their nice clean wagons all covered in muck."

"Well you can go and tell them from me that if they don't want to use the Mastiff then they can help your section carry the sandbags. I think they may change their minds."

Mickey Flynn's face broke into a grin and he swaggered off to relay Lofty's message. Lofty cast an expert eye over the work that had been done. It was a good job. The sandbag wall had been built double thickness to provide extra stability and protection against RPGs and the posts to support the roof were well bedded into the corners.

Standing in the middle of the sangar he looked out over the hillside to assess the view. There were a couple of blind spots where chunks of rock pointed skywards, but they were at a good distance. The occupants of the sangar would have a good 200 metre deep killing zone. Anyone attempting to approach would be seen in good time. Looking through his binoculars Lofty picked out the places where he would site trip flares. Satisfied, Lofty turned and descended the hill again. He allowed himself a smile as he saw a Mastiff reversing towards the men of Catfish 1 where they worked at filling the sandbags.

* * *

"I'm afraid, brothers, that I find this news a little too convenient." Youssef advised the group. They sat in a circle in the comfortable salon of the house's owner, a grower of poppies. Youssef had been summoned to the council of war to discuss interesting intelligence that had been forwarded to them from their agent in Pakistan.

"Would you look a gift horse in the mouth, brother?" Gul Shah asked. As the eldest of the group he had taken the chairmanship of the meeting.

"I have been to this place. It is deserted. I can't believe that the British or the Afghan usurpers have such plans for it."

"The evidence is clear. They are there as we speak strengthening the defences, making it ready to move into."

"I know that brothers. I have my own eyes and ears in the area. I'm sorry, but when the lion opens its mouth it is a very unwise man who decides to put his head between the jaws."

"So what do you think is happening?"

"I fear a trap. We have hurt them badly over the last months. They would want revenge."

"I agree that is a possibility, but look at the source of the information. It is the same as the information that has placed the British in our gun sights so many times since this battalion arrived in our country. Your group has been a major beneficiary of such information. If it is wrong then it is because the people who provide him with the information are wrong."

"How does he get his information?" asked Youssef.

"I'm afraid I don't know. It comes to us through an agent in Islamabad. How he gets it he won't say. But he is never wrong."

"Until now, maybe?"

"Youssef, you are right to be cautious, but if you have no appetite for this mission then we will give it to someone else."

Youssef could see that he had painted himself into a corner. His men were under his command but they did not belong to him. This group could place someone else in command. To refuse the mission would not stop it from taking place, and at the same time it was his duty to lead his men. The fard ayn, the personal obligation, demanded it. Better to give in gracefully than be stripped of his command.

"I accept that the source of the information has never led us astray. I withdraw my objection. Now, what is the plan?"

* * *

Brigade had leaked the intelligence over a number of Facebook posts. Lofty thought it a bit overdone, a bit too elaborate, but then good bait had to smell very strongly if it was to attract its prey.

He read the posts again.

"Going to Ghostville to set up a Patrol Base. Dodgy stuff. Where's my body armour?"

"Stupid place to build a girls' school. And why not let the Afghans protect it?"

"Oh no. I hope we're out of Ghostville before the Afghans take over. Don't trust them as far as I can throw them. Watch your backs guys."

And there were more. Lofty thought it might be an information overload and would give the game away, but G2 had been adamant.

According to the faked posts the Platoon were readying Ghostville in order to establish a permanent Patrol Base there. They would man it at first, then supposedly hand it over to Afghan forces. The need for the Patrol Base was established in a way that the Taliban would find totally offensive to them. The village was going to be turned into a school for girls and the building of the new school would be paid for by a Christian charity. Such an affront to Taliban beliefs would be sure to stimulate pre-emptive action, or so thought the staff at Brigade HQ.

"We've had some more intelligence about the British fighter." Debbie commented as they walked towards the mess hall for the O Group. "A drone got a full face photo of a man crossing the border last week. They used digital scanning to identify him. They have a name and address and everything now. If ever he goes home his feet won't touch."

"Can you tell me who he is?"

"Sorry. They haven't told me. Need-to-know and all that. But apparently he's from London."

"Under different circumstances he might have been one of us." commented Lofty. The Middlesex Regiment recruited from around North London and Southern Hertfordshire, within what would have been the old county boundaries of Middlesex until the Greater London Council had been created in the 1960s. Although no Muslims served with the regular battalions there were a couple of reservists serving with the TA.

"Maybe. But he's a ruthless and quite clever terrorist now. That's all that matters."

Lofty grunted an acknowledgement and pushed the door open. After the darkness outside the bright light made him flinch. Most of the Company were assembled and waiting for the arrival of the officers. Lofty knew the plan already, of course. He had been closely involved in its development, but for the majority of the men present the O Group would finally reveal some of the mysteries surrounding Op MANACLE.

The acting CSM called the room to attention and there was a loud stamping of feet followed by instant silence as the men stood ready for the officers. The Company Commander led the group in.

"At ease, men. Sit down where you can." There was jostling as the men squeezed themselves onto the benches and sat on the dining tables.

"OK, men." Debbie coughed. "Oh, and women. This is going to be our last major operation before we go home and have a well-earned rest." Some of the men let out ironic cheers and the Major paused to allow them to get it out of their system.

"I'd like to introduce Major Munroe who will talk us through most of the brief. He's a bootneck, but please don't hold that against him." A ripple of laughter swept the room. "Major Munroe commands these gentlemen here." He indicated a group of soldiers occupying a corner at the front of the room. "Who will be introduced to you in due course."

The men of the Middlesex didn't need to be introduced. There's an air about special forces personnel that makes them instantly recognisable to other soldiers. Their eyes are keener and they seem to be constantly on the alert, looking for the slightest hint of trouble. Physically they were all well-built and fit looking, but the same could be said of many of the soldiers in the room. It wasn't size that mattered; it was attitude.

The Royal Marines Major stepped forward and started the briefing. Officers and NCO's took notes, while the soldiers looked closely at the maps as the dispositions of the troops was pointed out to them. A hundred miles away in another mess hall an SAS Captain, Munroe's 2IC, was giving a similar briefing to the men of B Company of the Royal Warwickshire Regiment.

* * *

"Hi Emma, just wanted to give you a call to say I love you."

There was something about Lofty's tone that didn't sound right to Emma. He was usually so upbeat when he called, cheerful and full of life, but this time he sounded quite sombre.

"Something's happened, hasn't it?" her mind leapt to a logical conclusions. "Someone else has been killed."

"No, at least not that I know of. Why, have you heard something?" It wasn't unheard of for the folks back home to get to know things ahead of the troops on the ground. Mushroom syndrome they called it. Kept in the dark and fed on shit.

"No, nothing, it's just you don't sound like your normal self."

"Ah, right. Well I have got quite a lot on my mind right now."

"How so? What's happening?"

One of the down sides to being married to a woman as bright as Emma was that she was often one jump ahead.

"Sorry, I can't tell you much. It's all a bit hush-hush."

"Do you think so? It's all over the Facebook that you're going to some place called Ghostville to set up a patrol base."

Shit, of course, anyone back home who was Facebook friends with one of the soldiers supposedly making the posts would know all about it. It must be garrison gossip by now. Oh well, nothing to do but play along.

"You're not supposed to know about that. How did you hear?"

"Well I heard at work. Someone saw it on Facebook."

"Those stupid pillocks." Lofty play acted. "They're not supposed to put stuff like that on the internet."

"I guess they just want their friends to know what you're all doing out there."

"But it could be a problem if someone not so friendly finds out. Not every Facebook friend is a real friend. Never mind that. How are you?"

"Better. But what's puzzling people is how Ronnie King is making posts. He's still in a coma as far as we know down here."

Oops. It was clear that no one at HQ had thought of that. Lofty decided to deflect attention by changing the subject. "How's Sam?"

"She's gone to stay with her sister while the welfare people try to sort out a house for her."

"What are her chances?"

"Quite good, apparently. There's housing association who're specialists in providing houses for soldiers widows and families. Demand is high, especially in London, but they reckon they might be able to find her a place in Enfield. She's a priority, of course. Anyway, with Sam gone I've been able to get on with my own life a little bit more. It sounds selfish, I know, but being the friend of a grieving widow is very demanding."

"Well, that's all good then. But how are you, in yourself?"

"I'm OK. I keep thinking about … well, you know. What I would do if anything happened to you. I hardly sleep any more for worrying. You should see the size of the bags under my eyes. More like suitcases."

"Look, don't you worry. As soon as this Op is finished we start getting ready to go home. The advance party from the Northumberland Fusiliers are already arriving. Of course we can't understand a word they're saying, 'cos they're all bloody Geordies, but at least they've got some boots on the ground. It's the beginning of the end."

"And have you decided yet about what you're going to do."

"I've given it a lot of thought Emma, but I really don't know yet. Let me get this over with. I think things will look different when I get back home."

"OK Lofty. I'll wait for your answer. Now, you take care, you big idiot. I love you."

"And I love you too babe."

As Lofty left the little cubicle that was used to make the telephone calls he spied the Company Commander across the other side of the Company Offices.

"Apparently this Op is the talk of the garrison. We should have foreseen that. It could cause a morale problem. They've also realized that Ronnie King is making posts from his hospital bed, as though he were going out with us." Lofty reported.

"Ah yes. Well, that's one of the penalties of playing these sorts of games. Thanks for the heads-up. I'll make sure that everyone is briefed to play along when they make their calls. It wouldn't do for someone back home to put a post on-line that says we're really setting up a trap."

"I realise that it's not my business, Sir, but I'd be a lot happier if the source of the intel, this Tracey Temple or whoever they are, were safely under lock and key. If King's family and friends have been posting updates on his health then there's a risk this character could stumble across them and put two and two together. If that happens then it's me and my men that will have our bollocks on the barbeque."

"OK, Sgt Lofthouse. You've made your point. I'll pass it up the line."

Lofty had a sinking feeling, as though he was in a small boat that had just sprung a large leak. He really didn't want his life to be at the mercy of a wife or girlfriend several thousands of miles away.

Glossary

Sangar A temporary fortification usually constructed of sand bags. Can have a roof, usually made of canvass or corrugated iron sheets. Generally square in design and capable of housing two to four men. If the floor is dug out to provide extra depth then it may also be referred to as a weapons pit or fire pit.

TA Territorial Army. Volunteers who serve as soldiers on a part time basis. A number of TA soldiers are on active service in Afghanistan.

19 - Betrayal Exposed

In the back of the Panther command vehicle, Capt Trent put down the handset that connected him to Brigade HQ by radio. "The drone has identified several groups of suspected Taliban converging on a point about 20 kilometres North of here. They reckon there could be up to a hundred of them all told."

Lofty let out a low whistle. That was a big concentration of fighters, there hadn't been that many since the early days of the fighting. Since then the insurgents had favoured small groups using hit and run tactics, or to plant bombs and booby traps. Even the fight outside Camp Elizabeth had involved less than two dozen men. When the plan had first been proposed it was assumed that it would only be that group that C Company would have to deal with.

"Well they clearly don't think it's a trap, otherwise they'd be high-tailing it in the other direction."

"Or they do think it's a trap and they're bringing in as many guns as possible to weigh the odds in their favour." responded the Platoon Commander. "We're going to be heavily outnumbered until we spring it."

Lofty leant into the vehicle so that he could see the map that was mounted on a board fixed to the armoured side. "If they're assembling North of here it looks like they're going to come straight down the main road."

"Hmm. Unlikely. They would be too visible. Look here." The Captain traced a finger along the map. "There's a wadi runs parallel to the road and about half a K from it. They can ride their dirt bikes along that and we wouldn't see them until they're almost on top of us. Have we got the exit of the wadi covered?"

A bit late to think of that now, Lofty thought, but resisted the temptation to say it. Besides, the Captain knew the answer. He was just testing Lofty's knowledge of the plan. "There's an SAS sniper team on the high ground above it, just there." Beside the main map was a sketch plan of the village's defences and Lofty was able to point to one of the red dots that showed where the special forces teams were. "They've got visibility about 500 metres along it, then there's a bend. We'll know as soon as they come into view."

The Platoon Commander took a close look at the sketch and tapped a blue dot. "Whose manning that fire point."

The dot indicated the presence of a fire team. "That's Charlie team from Catfish 3. Davie Tomlinson. I'll take a wander down and make sure he knows what to expect."

Lofty strode off towards the village, leaving the relative security of the headman's house behind him. He sprinted across the open ground to the edge of the village, zigzagging to disrupt the aim of any potential sniper. He slipped into the shadows between the houses. He had to assume that they were being watched and he didn't want to give away the carefully concealed defensive positions.

They had been in the village for two days now, and had carefully crafted the false routine that they wanted the Taliban to accept as being true. Each morning the Jackal and two Mastiffs would depart, apparently taking two sections out on a patrol of the local area. However the Mastiffs were empty except for their crews, and they went only as far as the concealed positions where Dogfish and Angelfish waited to be called into action. The two sections that were supposed to be inside the Mastiffs were instead in concealed firing positions carefully sited around Ghostville, ready to repel any attack.

Lofty tapped the butt of his rifle twice on the mud wall of a house, paused then tapped twice more. Satisfied that the defenders now knew the person entering their position was a friend and wouldn't blow his head off he lay on his belly and crawled under the camouflaged scrim net and into the weapons pit.

"Alright Davie?" he greeted the Corporal in a hoarse whisper.

"Yeah thanks Sarge. Bit tedious though."

"This sort of thing always is. Your lads behaving themselves?"

"They've been OK, but I can tell that the boredom's getting to them."

Lofty was aware of the problem. He'd had to take one of the lads from Catfish 1 aside and give him a talking to for putting out spoof radio messages on the net. Lofty had to laugh at the memory.

"I'm bored." The voice on the radio had said.

"This is Sunray. Who's that?" The platoon commander had demanded to know.

"I'm the one that's fucking bored." The voice had replied.

"This is Sunray, I want the name of the man that said that."

"I'm fucking bored, not fucking stupid." The voice had said before going silent.

Lofty had recognised the voice of Pvt 'Billy' Mitchell, who owned up when Lofty threatened to discipline the whole of his fire team.

"I think that will change soon enough." Lofty told Cpl Tomlinson what he and the Platoon Commander

255

had discussed. "If we're right, they'll appear right there." He pointed towards the dip in the ground that showed where the banks of the wadi ended. "Don't worry, I'll make sure that you get plenty of supporting fire from our HQ. We've got two jimpies up there, an HMG and a mortar."

"But a hundred of them Sarge. That's quite a lot of small arms fire."

"Don't worry, your Delta team will have them inside their arc of fire as well, so you've got quite a lot of fire power and you're in a good cover here. They'll be in the open. As soon as the first shot's been fired I'll get a platoon of the Warwickshires into the wadi behind them. With you in front and them behind, the rag heads'll almost certainly run sideways, down the hill that way. That will take them straight towards Dogfish and Angelfish."

"I hope to fuck you're right Sarge."

Lofty hoped he was as well. A hundred fighters was far more than they had prepared for. The sensible thing at this point would be to call in the Royal Marine reserves from bastion, but that action could give the game away, Lofty realised.

"Make sure you get plenty of rest." He noted that two of the fire team were dozing at the back of the weapons pit while the other two kept watch. Good soldiers can sleep anywhere, and Pvts Scott and Ridley were proving it.

* * *

As soon as news of the kuffar arrival in the village had come through Youssef had dispatched scouts to keep an eye on what was happening.

"They patrol in their armoured trucks during the day, and at night they lock themselves away in the big house at the top of the village. I have counted three machine guns on the roof of that house."

"Where are the vehicles kept when they aren't being used."

"They're parked along the walls of the house, so the sentries can keep watch over them."

"And have you seen anything else? Any signs of other positions?" He wished he'd gone himself, but someone had to organise the fighters as they arrived and he was the leader of the operation.

"No, Youssef, but I couldn't get close. They have built a weapons position on the top of the hill, so I had to approach from the side. I couldn't get close without giving myself away." The man didn't know it but he had crept within feet of an SBS sniper. Had he discovered the marine he wouldn't now be alive to tell what he had seen.

"Well done Taj. Go and get some food and try to sleep. We have a long night ahead of us."

Concealed around them in the hills were the other groups of fighters, some of whom had come a long way to take part in the attack on the patrol base. Youssef raised his eyes to the sky trying to see if there was a drone above them, but if there was then it was beyond the power of his eyes to see it. He had dispersed the men into whatever concealment was available, but the threat from the sky was something that was difficult to guard against.

Youssef called to one of his men. "Gamal, go and gather the other group leaders together. It's time to decide on our plan of attack."

He sat in the shadows and waited for the half dozen men who had led their small bands of fighters to this place.

* * *

"But I say that we should come from the East. That way the rising sun will be in their eyes." The man's name was Kamal and it was the third time he had made this statement.

"It is a fair point, Kamal, but not a practical one. The ground on the Eastern side is open. Their sentries will see us coming."

"Not with the sun in their eyes." He insisted.

"They will see us while it's still dark. They have night vision glasses.

"But we will wait for the sun to rise before we try to approach."

"And by the time we get close enough the sun will have risen above our heads and they will be able to see clearly again. There is more than a kilometre of open ground to cross if we approach from that side. We must come from the North, down the wadi."

He realised that his command over them was only nominal. They could obey him or they could ignore him as they saw fit. He had a feeling that there would be a lot of discussion before they were finished. Already they had been talking for nearly two hours without reaching any sort of agreement. Youssef envied his enemy's command structure that allowed for clear cut decision making; the ability of a commander to guillotine extended discussions and give an order.

"Who agrees with this boy?" Kamal's insult was calculated. The older man was in his forties and had been fighting the kuffar since their arrival in their country. He may even have fought against the Russians.

"I have to say I prefer the route that gives greatest concealment." One of the older men spoke up. "While your idea has merits, my brother, it is also the longest route. The wadi starts just beyond the hill there and we can ride the bikes most of the way."

Kamal glowered, not happy to be obstructed from this new direction. "Very well, I will take my men by myself. When I hear the shooting start I will come upon the enemy from where they least expect it, and with the sun in their eyes." He stood up abruptly and stalked off to gather his men and start their journey South and East.

Youssef was relieved to see that none of the other leaders rose to follow Kamal. With him gone the plan took shape more quickly. The main problem was the exit from the wadi. So many men in so confined a space made a large target, ideally suited to the enemies mortars and heavy calibre machine guns. They finally agreed a way of reducing the risk and splitting the enemy's firepower.

As the leaders made their way back to ready their groups to prepare for the attack Gul Shah moved to sit closer to Youssef.

"I sometimes wonder if our cause is really as just as we claim?" he said in a low voice, not wanting to be overheard expressing his doubts.

"You're having doubts?"

"Yes. We attack the enemy but they get stronger while we get weaker. Surely that cannot be in Allah's plan. We are having trouble finding new recruits. There are plenty who want to stay and terrorise small villages in Waziristan, but few who wish to face a martyrs' death here."

"Hypocrites. We should do something about them."

"Perhaps you are right. But our funding is starting to disappear as well. Our supporters seem to think they will get a better return on their investment in Cairo, or Baghdad or Damascus."

"They are hypocrites too."

"Maybe, but they are hypocrites with money. We need them. Perhaps if this attack is successful we can attract them back again."

"'Insha'Allah." replied Youssef. "Perhaps I should take you to meet the Egyptian that persuaded me to join the jihad. He is a great cleric who studied at the University in Cairo. Abisali introduced us."

Gul Shah gave Youssef a quizzical look. "An Egyptian you say. What was his name?"

"Mohamed Dost Mohamed. Do you know of him?"

Gul Shah roared with laughter and slapped himself on his thigh. So loud was he that it caused the men around them to peer at them with curiosity. Levity before a battle was unusual. Youssef had often heard the expression to roll around with laughter, but had never expected to see it actually happen.

"I'm sorry, Gul Shah. Have I said something funny?"

"You most certainly have, young Youssef. If Mohamed Dost Mohamed ever set foot in the University of Cairo it was to try to sell them a carpet." He roared with laughter again, this time at his own joke.

"You mock me. Why do find this so funny?"

"Mohamed Dost Mohamed is no cleric. He was a carpet trader in Cairo." Mohamed slapped his thigh again, but his laughter had diminished to loud chuckles.

"But Abisali told me that he had upset the Mubarak regime and had to flee."

"Oh, he upset *someone* in the Mubarak regime right enough. He persuaded some big-wig to invest in a load of Bokhara rugs. When they arrived they turned out be worthless fakes. Even the stupidest tourists wouldn't buy them. The big-wig wanted his money back and was prepared to take it out of Mohamed's hide if that was the only way. That is why he fled Cairo. He fetched up here and attached himself to Osama Bin Laden's group."

Gul Shah stopped to release another fit of giggles before taking up his story again.

"Like most traders he was good with words so they gave him a job indoctrinating recruits. When the kuffar came he fled to Pakistan. He continued to work in the training camps for a while, but then came into some money. Probably not legally I might add. He retired and bought himself a couple of young wives. I haven't seen him for a while, but I knew him well enough."

Youssef sat stunned as Abisali's manipulation and betrayal was exposed to him. Gul Shah rose and walked slowly away, still chuckling. The last thing Youssef heard him say was "Silver tongued old faker."

Youssef felt the world crashing about his ears, even though nothing actually changed. Abisali had betrayed him; told him lies. But to what purpose?

Of course, Abisali would know that it would become public knowledge that a British born Muslim was fighting with the Taliban. Perhaps it would encourage others to join, if not here, then in the other places where Muslims were fighting against the kuffar. A thought crossed Youssef's mind. Did Abisali have

261

some spectacular martyrdom planned for him, that would draw recruits from across Britain to avenge him? Was that the idea? And had it been forestalled only by Abisali's own death? But Abisali had encouraged him to undertake a great mission to strike fear into the hearts of the kuffar. Was it the intention that he should survive and become well known, or to die and become even better known?

Youssef could believe just about anything of Abisali at that point. He had lied to him all along, about pretty much everything.

So what now? Youssef looked around him where his men were preparing themselves for that night's attack. Those men still looked to him for leadership, and he couldn't avoid that obligation. Their lives depended on his clear thinking. He couldn't let them down.

After that, if he still lived, he would consider what he should do.

* * *

Most of the men around Youssef were praying, as was right and proper before fighting an enemy. If it was Allah's will that one becomes a martyr then it is best to be spiritually prepared. Once they left this place they would have no opportunity to pray, so it had to be done now.

Youssef delayed his act of worship. There was one thing he had to do before he could talk to his God. From his small rucksack he pulled out one of the purchases he had made while he had been in Pakistan; a bundle of pre-paid sim cards. He inserted one into his mobile phone. If the number he was about to call was being monitored then there was little he could do, but at least the new number he was about to use wouldn't be on any list. His phone made a connection via satellite and in distant Britain he heard the ring tone.

"Fatima, it's me. Please don't hang up."

"Youssef. I'm sorry, we parted on bad terms when we last spoke. I didn't want that. I had waited so long to speak to you."

"Please, don't apologise. It was my fault. Out here it's hard to remember what life is like in Britain. Out here life is so simple. You have an enemy and you must fight him. I hardly thought anymore about why I was fighting. You made me think about it again and I think that some of the things you said were true."

"Oh, Youssef, does that mean you will come home now?"

"I don't think I will ever be able to come home again. I think the British would put me in prison. We'll have to talk about the future when I have more time. Today I just wanted to say I'm sorry and that I still love you and want to marry you."

"Youssef, I love you too and I want to marry you. But my father won't let me marry you. Not now."

"Look, I have to go now, but I will call again. Perhaps you could think about how we might be together again, but outside of Britain. I don't know how that will work, but if we're to be together we have to find a way. Allah will show us a way."

"I understand. I love you Youssef."

"And I love you too." With tears in his eyes Youssef broke the connection. Now it was time to pray.

Back in London Fatima wept, but this time they were tears of happiness. At last he seemed to have reached the end of the cycle: Acceptance. Of course it wasn't yet over. He was still out there in that dangerous foreign country, but he had spoken of their future together, and that was what counted. He had no intention of becoming a martyr.

Glossary

HMG   Heavy machine gun. 12.7 mm calibre belt fed. Can be mounted on a tripod or fixed to a vehicle. Has an effective range up to 2 km.

Scrim   Also scrim net. A net with a mesh about the same size as that used for a football goal, with scraps of coloured material attached to provide camouflage. The net is draped over poles above and around objects to disguise their shape and colour and to help them blend in with their background.

20 - The Final Battle

Captain Trent came onto the radio net. "All stations this is Sunray. Air observation shows the enemy is on the move. At their present speed we can expect them around 04.00 hours."

The section commanders acknowledged the message in turn.

The drone would have no problem tracking the heat signatures given off by the engines of the insurgent's dirt bikes. It would get more difficult to track them when they stopped and continued their journey on foot; when their individual heat signatures wouldn't be so bright.

Lofty climbed to the roof on the Northern side of the compound to make sure that Catfish 2 were alert and ready. In addition to their normal weaponry they had been lent a heavy machine gun and gunner from Heavy Weapons Platoon to increase their firepower. He went to make sure that the weapon was correctly aligned on the mouth of the wadi. He didn't want the gunner to waste a second in bringing the gun's power to bear on the enemy.

He toured the rest of the positions and spoke a few words with each of the soldiers. There wasn't much he could say to bolster their morale and fighting spirit, but he could share a joke and remind each man of how good a soldier he was. In any battle the defending side has the advantage providing the defences have been correctly sited. Lofty was reasonably confident that he and the Platoon Commander had done a good job. The men seemed to be in good form and one or two even managed a joke, though Lofty knew that they were nervous.

Returning to the command vehicle, parked in the middle of the building's small courtyard, Lofty waited to find out what would happen next. It had been difficult to reverse the Panther into the tight space, but it was the only way to protect it. It carried all the communications that the platoon needed to co-ordinate its activities with those of the other units, and it was no use to them if the enemy could bring fire to bear on it.

The rear doors were still open so Lofty stuck his head inside. "How do you think they'll do it, Sir?"

"If I was leading the attack I'd come as far down the wadi as it was safe to do, perhaps stop about three klicks away, then send small groups out to the sides. Then they can advance on a broader front. The mouth of the wadi is a natural murder hole, so if it gets congested it would be slaughter."

"I walked some of that ground this morning. It was pretty rough going."

"But that means it also provides some cover. That will help the enemy. It's a good job we've got the special forces teams out there to spot for us."

The handset for the radio on the Brigade net gave a chirp and the Captain picked it up. After listening for a few moments he acknowledged the message with a curt "Roger." and replaced the handset in its rest.

"The images from the drones show they've stopped about 4 klicks away, just a bit further away than I expected. Smaller groups have split off from the main body and are advancing down both sides of the wadi. That gives them a frontage of about two to three hundred metres."

A hundred men about two metres each apart. Not an easy target. Fire teams worked best when they were able to concentrate their firepower onto a small target area. This dispersal meant that the defenders would have to concentrate on an individual target until it fell and then move onto the next. That provided opportunities for individuals and small groups to break through the defences and perhaps get into the village. Well, they had always known of that danger and had planned for it.

The defenders did have some advantages. With the night sights on their weapons they would be able to see the enemy while the enemy wouldn't be able to see them. Well, not all the enemy, anyway. He remembered the set of British Army issue night vision goggles that had been recovered from the body of the dead Taliban leader when they attacked Camp Elizabeth.

Lofty turned towards the East and saw a thin pale band above the horizon. Dawn wasn't far away. That was good. Daylight suited him and his men just fine.

* * *

The Taliban fighters crept forward as quietly as the terrain allowed. The hillsides were strewn with rocks that turned ankles and rattled along the ground when they were kicked. Their determination to reach the target was absolute. The kuffar were offering a singular insult to Allah with their plan to build a school for girls. Such an insult couldn't go un-avenged. Youssef's own group had a more personal motivation to add an additional spur. All except for the betrayed Youssef himself. His motivation now was to save the lives of as many of his men as possible without jeopardising the attack itself. A tricky business.

Youssef stopped and waved the nearest men to crouch down. The signal was passed along the line. He lowered the goggles over his eyes and allowed time for them to adjust to the green glow. The device was good, but its breadth of vision was limited. He had to sweep his eyes slowly from left to right to see what lay ahead of them. They were still a kilometre from the village and at this distance he didn't expect to encounter any opposition, but he was an experienced enough fighter to know that his expectations could be wrong. A bold commander might well place a patrol forward of his main defences in order to provide warning of an attack.

Satisfied that all was well he led his men forward once again.

* * *

"Oscar one and Oscar two both report sighting groups of the enemy." Capt Trent advised his subordinate.

Lofty instinctively turned to the sketch map of the village and located the two call-signs on the map. They were the two special forces sniper teams nearest to the wadi. At least the enemy were conforming to expectations.

"Sunray to Oscar one and Oscar two. Hold your fire. Let the Tangos pass you. Don't open fire until Catfish three opens fire on them."

The two snipers acknowledged the platoon commander's message with a double click on the switches of their radios. Their proximity to the enemy meant that spoken responses were inadvisable. Even a whisper might give away their positions.

Letting the insurgents get past them before opening fire also protected the sniper teams. With such a large force arrayed against them they risked death or capture if they gave away their positions too early.

"Catfish three, enemy approaching to your front. Stand by. Await my orders."

Lofty heard Davie Tomlinson acknowledge the order. "Time for me to take up my position, boss." he announced.

"OK Lofty. Good Luck." It was unusual for the platoon commander to call him by his nick name rather than his rank. A sign of his own nervousness perhaps? Capt Trent was a laid back sort of officer, but even he must suffer from nerves sometimes, Lofty concluded.

Lofty sprinted up to the roof of the house and took up a position next to the HMG. Using the night vision sights on his rifle he scanned the ground to his right, towards the mouth of the wadi. Nothing in sight so far. He looked the other way, West towards the sangar on top of the hill. Best to make sure that the Delta fire team were awake.

"Catfish two two, this is Sunray minor. Keep your eyes peeled on your side."

"Roger Sunray minor." The curt tone suggested that LCpl 'Larry' Grayson didn't think he needed the reminder.

Lofty resisted the temptation to call the other two sections, split into their fire teams around the perimeter of the village. They would have heard the exchange. On the roof with him was the Charlie team from Catfish two section while Catfish one were in two weapons pits on the South and South East sides of the village. Catfish three were still facing the enemy on the North and Northeast. They had an all-round defence, just as the military manuals dictated, but they were very thinly spread. Once the shooting started Capt Trent would direct the Jackal and the Mastiffs to move out to add their firepower in support of the fire teams, but until then they were parked impotently beside the walls of the house below Lofty, part of the bait that was supposed to suggest a poorly defended patrol base where the only people awake were the sentries.

* * *

Youssef crept slowly forward by himself. As good as Taj's reconnaissance might have been he wanted to see the village for himself before committing his men.

He found cover behind a pair of rocks, the small gap between them giving him a view of the Northern side of the village. He swept his goggles across the vista, starting from the sangar at the top of the hill to the West and finishing with the open plane in the East. He saw nothing untoward, but the definition of the glasses wasn't good at that distance so he swept back again more slowly. His eyes paused on a gap between two houses. There was something wrong with the shape.

He let his eyes settle and gave his brain time to process the visual information piece by piece. That was it. The gap between the walls of neighbouring houses didn't extend all the way to the ground. There was something obstructing the entrance. From his own visit to the village a few weeks earlier he knew that shouldn't be. He let his eyes pick out more details. A breeze fanned across his face and he saw movement. There! Some sort of screen was filling the gap. Scrim net, he was sure. And what was beneath it? He could only guess, but whatever it was meant he had to be cautious. Camouflage was designed to conceal, and what it was most likely to conceal was a weapons pit.

He let his eyes travel further West and saw another bulge at the side of a house where a bulge shouldn't be expected. Another position, probably.

It was a pity that Taj had been unable to get closer when he had carried out his reconnaissance. Advance notice of the position of the weapons pits would have been useful. But they accorded with his own thinking with regard to the defence of the village when he had carried out his own recce. Now he had to find out how strong they were, and if there were any others on this side of the village.

There was one way to find out for sure. Youssef spoke into his radio, then waited. It was a few minutes before he was joined by Ali. Youssef explained what he wanted and Ali nodded his understanding. Carefully he took aim then squeezed the trigger on his RPG launcher. The rocket blasted away from the tube towards the houses of the village.

The range was far too great for the weapon to be fired accurately, but that wasn't what Youssef wanted. The rocket fell fifty metres short, as anticipated, and exploded in a cloud of dirt and rock fragments.

* * *

As the grenade exploded the tension snapped in the weapons pits.

"Holy shit." A voice blurted out in the darkness. At once the night air was shattered by the rattle of automatic gunfire as Catfish 3 reacted to the attack.

* * *

Rifle and machinegun fire crackled from the two positions Youssef had identified as defensive points and tracer rounds stitched daisy chains of light across the night sky. From the roof of the HQ building the deeper boom of a heavy machine gun joined in. He heard the supersonic cracks of bullets zipping above his head and instinctively pressed his body closer to the ground. Bullets whined as they struck the ground and ricocheted skywards

* * *

"Cease fire, cease fire. All Catfish call signs cease fire." Lofty shouted into his radio. Releasing the toggle switch he cursed his men for being so trigger happy. At once he relented. They had waited all night for the enemy to arrive, nerves stretched to breaking point. It should come as no surprise that they should open fire at the first sign of trouble, but it meant they had given away their positions to the fighters. Doubtless that was what the enemy commander had intended.

* * *

As the last echoes of the shooting died away Youssef allowed himself a small smile. He had been right, there were at least two fire teams deployed right in front of him, with another on the roof of the headman's house. He clapped Ali on the back in congratulations. "OK, go back to the others." he commanded.

Ali didn't move. Youssef gave him a firm shove but there was still no movement from the man beside him. He shuffled sideways a few inches and rolled Ali onto his back. Where his forehead should be was a fist sized hole. Youssef recognised the exit wound of a high velocity bullet.

It took Youssef's brain a moment to understand the significance of the wound, but then he realised. Ali's death wasn't caused by some lucky shot from the defences. If the exit wound was in the front of Ali's head then the entry wound must be at the back. And that meant that he had been shot from behind.

Youssef froze. Somewhere in the darkness behind him he now knew that there was a sniper. His skin crawled as he imagined the cross hairs of the weapon's telescopic sight settling on his body, or maybe his head, ready for the sniper's next shot. He had heard no shot, which suggested that the sniper was using a weapon with a silencer fitted.

Youssef braced his muscles, focusing all of his strength into his arms and legs. He pushed hard and vaulted the two low rocks in front of him, landing with a bone jarring thud. He heard the smack of the bullet into the rock and then the whine as it span off into the night. A fraction of a second later he heard the crack of the shot as the sound of its sonic wave caught up with the bullet. Youssef hunkered down behind the small safety of the rocks. He cursed himself. His AK-47, his constant companion and second only in importance to his copy of the Koran, was still lying on the ground on the other side of the rocks. Fortunately he still had his radio in his hand and the night vision goggles on his head. But now he was unarmed and an unarmed man in battle was usually also a dead man.

The best way of saving his life now was to call up the rest of his force and start the attack. In the midst of the fighters he would be just one target amongst many. The first fighter to fall would also provide him with a replacement weapon. Youssef sent back the information regarding the enemy defences then gave his instructions about how they were to organise the attack.

The plan was simple and he saw no need to change it now. They would use the gap between the village and the HQ building to divide the enemy force. Once in the shelter of the houses they would be able to fire at the enemy while remaining in cover. Part of his force could take the enemy weapons pits from the rear. He reckoned that would leave just one section in the HQ and one in the sangar. A small force against his much larger one. They would pound the walls of the house with RPGs until they fell or at least created gaps large enough to enter through. That would signal the beginning of the end for the kuffar soldiers.

They had to be quick though. Once dawn arrived they would be vulnerable to air attack. It was the one thing they couldn't defend against. The rockets and chain guns of the Apache helicopters would blast through the mud walls of the houses and strip away their defences bit by bit. It would also delay the attack long enough for enemy reinforcements to arrive. It would take perhaps sixty minutes for a large enough force to be assembled at the nearest FOB and perhaps another sixty minutes for them to travel to the village. That was more than long enough for his men to destroy the kuffar, provided they could survive an aerial bombardment.

Boots crunched across the ground interspersed with the occasional slap of sandals. The RPG explosion had done away with any need for a covert approach. The enemy knew they were here, although their overwhelming strength would still come as a surprise to them.

* * *

"Sunray minor this is Sunray. The drone has been withdrawn. They can't track the targets well enough to be able to help us anymore."

"Roger Sunray." Lofty acknowledged. Well, that was part of the plan. A Reaper wasn't much use once the enemy was firing at them, and they were a scarce resource that could be better used elsewhere. The Reaper's Hellfire missiles were an expensive way of dealing with the terrorists, compared with the price of small arms ammunition. They had been lucky to have had one assigned to the operation in the first place.

Now that the battle lines had been drawn they could expect helicopter support to fill the gap, or maybe even a couple of American Harriers. A pair of fast jets screaming across the plain at zero feet always put the fear of God into the attackers and bolstered the morale of the defenders. Lofty spared time to curse the lack of foresight of the British politicians that had resulted in the disbanding of Britain's own Harrier force.

Lofty's rifle sight filled with figures emerging from the darkness of the wadi and the slopes on either side of it. They ran forward singly, in pairs and in small groups. A fighter snagged his foot on an invisible wire and a trip flare lit up to illuminate him and the men closest to him.

Lofty spoke a command into the mouthpiece of his radio and heard a cough behind him as a mortar was fired. It exploded exactly in the centre of the wadi's mouth claiming at least two victims. There were more coughs and more explosions before the mortar crew switched ammunition to parachute flares, their light adding to that already provided by the flares on the ground.

The thud of a sniper rifle sounded and one figure fell, then came the crackle of SA80's and LMGs splitting the night as the two fire teams of Catfish 3 started shooting from their weapons pits. Lofty tapped the HMG gunner on the shoulder and he added to the noise, firing three and four round aimed bursts into the running ranks of the insurgents. More flares burst, keeping the scene illuminated for the defenders.

"Sunray this is Sunray minor. Tangos are advancing from the North. Estimate eighty to ninety. Over."

"Roger Sunray minor. Can you tell what their intentions are?"

The line of fighters was splitting, with half heading towards the nearest end of the village and the remainder heading for the Eastern end, taking casualties as they had to pass in front of the Catfish three's Delta fire team on the North-eastern corner. If they managed to get into the village they could advance down the middle and split it in half.

Figures fell in the open killing ground between the mouth of the wadi and the village. At least a quarter of the attackers must have fallen already, Lofty estimated. This wasn't soldiering, this was slaughter, his mind registered. Poorly armed peasant fighters up against modern sophisticated weaponry, and that was even before they brought air power into play.

Lofty reported the facts to his OC. "Suggest we implement phase two." He added. If the next two phases went to plan they would have the enemy trapped, and hopefully they would surrender and end the killing. Lofty offered up a silent prayer in the hope that Allah might guide the thinking of the enemy leaders and save the lives of some of their men.

* * *

In weapons pit 3 Charlie Davie Tomlinson was having problems.

"Get up you bastard." He shouted at Pvt Scott, who was cowering behind the sandbagged wall of the pit. Scott just whimpered in reply. Tomlinson aimed a kick at the man, connecting with his thigh. It must have hurt but Scott didn't react to the pain.

Pvts Ridley and Cook continued to pour concentrated automatic fire on the advancing enemy, but Scott had taken refuge as soon as the first AK-47 rounds thumped into the sandbags.

An RPG round exploded against the wall of the nearest house, showering Charlie fire team with debris and leaving a gaping hole in the wall.

Tomlinson lowered his weapon and pointed it at Scott. "If you don't get back on the wall I'll shoot you myself, you cowardly bastard." But Scott stayed resolutely where he was.

Tomlinson shifted his aim slightly and fired his rifle, sending a bullet thudding into the sandbags just a few inches to the right of Scott's head. He flinched as the heat of the discharge hit his face, but otherwise remained still. Sand trickled out of the hole and onto Scott's shoulder.

Somewhere in the back of his mind, Tomlinson thought, he knows I won't actually kill him. Not much to be done then.

He grabbed Scott's weapon off him and returned to his own place on the wall. He heard a scurrying noise behind him and turned just in time to see Scott wriggle out of the back of the weapons pit. Well, that was game over for Scott. He couldn't avoid a court martial now.

Setting his own weapon down on the top of the sand bagged parapet Tomlinson raised Scott's rifle and checked the load. Finding that it had a grenade in the under-slung launcher he fired it towards the advancing Taliban. The grenade exploded with a loud crack and Tomlinson saw two men fall, but the others continued to advance. He took aim and emptied the rifle's magazine in a single long burst, watching the enemy scatter into what limited cover there was. He put Scott's weapon to one side and picked up his own, taking snap shots as targets revealed themselves.

* * *

In 3 Delta weapons pit things were slightly less fraught. Pvt Griffiths on the LMG fired a three round burst then shouted to his companion, Nosey Parker. "That's two, that's a tenner you owe me."

Parker took a lead on a group of three running men and pulled the trigger, allowing the men to run into his stream of bullets. He had first learned to shoot on a farm and could pick a crow out of the sky as easily as hitting double top on a dart board. Two of the fighters fell and the third dived for cover behind his two fallen comrades.

"And that's two to me. All square bro. And when this other fucker tries to move I'll have him as well and it'll be your turn to owe me."

On the other side of the weapons pit LCpl Jim Jones and Pvt Scott Campbell stared out into the night. Their arcs of fire covered the Eastern approaches and so far they had no targets.

Jones was worried about the growing light on the eastern horizon. In a few minutes the sun would rise and send shafts of light towards them, effectively blinding him. Neither his night sight nor his day sight would be of any further use to him. It would be sun glasses on and hope for the best.

A trip flare popped into bright light and Campbell and Griffiths both turned their weapons on the new threat. Figures dived for cover, trying to find the shadows. Jim Jones could see that an attempt was being made to outflank his weapons pit. He put out a radio call for mortar bombs and more flares. It would take a few moments for the weapon in the HQ building to be re-aligned, so they would have to rely on the meagre light of the trip flare in the short term.

It seemed to take an age for the mortar to fire its first round. It exploded in a bright flash but Jones couldn't see what damage had been done. A second bomb exploded before a flare burst into light above them to reveal the new threat. The ground seemed to be alive with wriggling bodies, squirming their way towards the end of the village. Two more flares followed the first as the figures on the ground froze, trying to escape detection. Campbell and Griffiths needed no further invitation. They opened fire and sprayed the area, sending tracer rounds arcing and ricocheting across the 200 metre gap between them and the enemy. A man tried to stand up and run forward, but he fell to the ground and flailed around for a few seconds before finally lying still. The remainder of the fighters started to wriggle backwards to escape from the withering rain of automatic fire.

The weapons pit fell silent as its occupants realised they had nothing more to shoot at. They heard the deeper sound of diesel engines roaring into life, audible above the crackle of gun fire from the other weapons pit.

"I reckon you owe me a tenner." Griffiths punched Parker on the arm and held out his hand. In return Parker raised his hand, middle finger extended.

* * *

"Catfish one this is Sunray. Fall back to Bravo positions. All Catfish vehicles, advance to position Charlie and provide supporting fire."

Almost at once the vehicles parked in the shadow of the walls began to move. They took up a position between the HQ and the Western end of the village. Their LMGs and jimpies barked into life, pouring fire into the flanks of the closest enemy groups as they ran to try to reach the safety of the houses. Lofty saw half a dozen more fall to the concentrated fire of the machine guns.

Raising the sights of his weapon Lofty saw movement on the roof of the houses that sat between the two Catfish three weapons pits. The round tops of their helmeted heads showed them to be soldiers. Good. Catfish one had withdrawn from their positions on the South side of the village to protect the rear of Catfish three, firing down into the narrow gaps between the houses to prevent any attackers from approaching the rear of the weapons pits.

"All Catfish units this is Sunray. Friendly forces are approaching from the East. Repeat, friendly forces approaching from the East."

That would be Dogfish and Angelfish platoons in their armoured vehicles. The plan was for them to provide cover along the East and South of the village, closing off any escape route along those sides.

Helicopter rotors thudded overhead and in the dim light of the growing dawn Lofty made out the silhouette of a Chinook. He expected to see three of them, each carrying a full platoon of the Royal Warwickshires. A second silhouette passed, then the third, which banked left and headed along the line of the wadi. The presence of the Warwickshires behind them would force any straggling fighters to seek refuge in the village.

"Catfish 1 and Catfish 3 this is Sunray. Withdraw to position Yankee two and Yankee three. Catfish one alpha and Catfish three alpha proceed to RV with your sections."

That was the signal for the two remaining sections within the village to withdraw and complete the cordon. It left the insurgents in control of the village, but with an overwhelming force surrounding them, ready to shoot anyone who showed themselves. The net had closed. Unfortunately not all the insurgents were inside it.

"All Catfish call signs this is Sunray. Oscar five reports Tangos to the East of us. Angelfish will advance to contact."

While the battle in and around the village had been raging another force of Taliban had been creeping up from the Eastern side of the village across the open plain. A sniper, devoid of any other employment in his position, had spotted them creeping forward.

The sun rose above the horizon and Lofty had to quickly search for his sunglasses to cut out the glare as he stared over the rooftops to try to make out the new enemy. The glasses didn't help. The enemy were hidden in the bright shafts of light that flooded the Eastern horizon. Looking to his right he saw the three Mastiffs of Angelfish platoon advancing towards the enemy. At some unheard command they drew into a line and Lofty saw their occupants spilling out to take up firing positions.

From the North a black shape resolved itself into an Apache helicopter. From his angle of attack the pilot wouldn't be hampered by the sun's bright rays. A jet of smoke emerged from the underside of the machine as the chopper's chain gun started to fire. Moments later Lofty heard the familiar chainsaw buzz of the weapon's discharge.

The chopper overshot its target then made a tight banking turn to return for a second pass. Again the chain gun fired. For a brief moment Lofty felt pity for the fighters. Caught on the open plain they would have nowhere to escape from the chain gun's heavy calibre onslaught.

Lofty saw the men of Angelfish stand up and form a skirmish line, advancing towards the enemy which were still invisible to his eyes. Two of the Mastiffs moved to the outer ends of the line to protect the flanks, while the remaining one followed in the centre of the line, firing over the heads of the infantrymen. The platoon advanced in fire teams, the four man groups leapfrogging past each other. All the time the staccato chatter of machine guns drifted back to Lofty's ears on the early morning breeze.

Firing started up closer to Lofty and he realised that the insurgents had taken up defensive positions on the roofs of the houses. A bullet cracked past his ear and he ducked behind the safety of the parapet. The HMG gunner turned his attention to the village and swept the barrel of his gun from right to left, firing off bursts as the gun came to bear on targets, then returning through the same arc to repeat the pass.

An RPG round arced across the gap between the village and the headman's house and exploded against a wall with a crash that threw Lofty off his feet.

Standing up again Lofty saw a man slump over the parapet of the nearest house, the victim of one of the special forces snipers that were still concealed in the rocks and hills around the village. A salutary lesson for any of the fighters that might try a similar shot.

Silence fell. The British soldiers had nothing to fire at and the Taliban were in no position to try and fire on their enemies without risking their own lives. It was, for the moment, a stalemate. Lofty reported the situation to his platoon commander. The sound of hammering came from the village as the new occupants tried to dig out loopholes through which they could fire their weapons with greater safety, but until they succeeded there would be no more firing.

The double doors of the headman's house swung open and the Panther command vehicle crept slowly into the open and towards the nearest end of the village. It drew to a standstill thirty metres from the nearest house. The driver would clearly be able to see the streak of blood running down the wall from the dead RPG man.

A voice bellowed from a speaker mounted on the top of the Panther, speaking in Pashto. A pre-recorded message called on the insurgents to surrender.

"Men of the Taliban, you are surrounded. Further resistance is futile and will only result in your deaths. Surrender and you will be treated as prisoners of war.

Lay down your weapons and come out with your hands up."

The message was repeated then silence fell once again as it came to an end. In the village no one moved. Lofty didn't expect them to. It didn't work like that. Somewhere within the village the Taliban leaders would assemble to discuss the offer. Some would want to accept it and some would want to fight on. It would take time to reach a decision.

* * *

As the fighters rushed past him to start the attack Youssef leapt to his feet to join them. He expected to feel a sniper's bullet slam into his back but none came. Of course, if the sniper was close, near enough to be detected by the fighters, then firing now would give away his position and allow his men to kill or capture him. Youssef had made a good decision.

Curses ripped the night as flares popped and fizzed close to his men. Youssef hadn't expected that. Now his men would have to advance silhouetted by the bright light of the burning phosphorous. Machine guns opened fire from the edge of the village and the killing started.

A mortar bomb exploded and Youssef felt the wet splatter of shredded flesh land on his face. The blast of the explosion threw him forward so that he staggered, but he managed to retain his balance.

"You there." Youssef called to a man carrying an RPG launcher tube. "Fire on that house to the West. Silence their mortar." he commanded. Before the man had time to reply the tube fell from his lifeless hands and he collapsed onto the ground. Youssef quickly ran on, trying to make himself a small target.

Other men began to fall, some dead but others only wounded. They would have to fend for themselves. To stop and tend them invited more bullets. Youssef called a command and led his men at an angle to the village, aiming for the gap between the headman's house and the houses in the village closest to it. There didn't seem to be any firing coming from that area. That made sense. It wasn't a big village but it was big enough to stretch a platoon to its utmost. A man fell in front of him and Youssef bent down to pick up his AK-47 and strip the satchel of spare magazines from him. He hardly broke his stride.

Bullets buzzed around him and he stopped, calmly knelt down and fired a burst of automatic fire towards the headman's house. Standing up again he sprinted after his men. Adrenalin carried him forward, making him run faster and then faster still. He forced himself to slow down in order to avoid looking as though he was panicking.

Spotting a gap between the end house and the one next to it Youssef threw himself into the darkness, hoping that the enemy hadn't had the forethought to block it with barbed wire. No, it was OK. For the moment he was safe. For the first time he realised how hard his heart was pounding. He fought to get his breathing under control. The coppery taste of adrenalin burnt the back of his tongue. Bodies struggled past him into the darkness of the alley.

Something was wrong, he realised at once. The kuffar platoon was at full stretch, he knew, so it was important that they protect their flanks and leave no gaps that he and his men could exploit. Gaps between houses, for example. This alley should have been filled with the wicked razor wire that the kuffar always surrounded themselves with. He had even made some of his men carry wire cutters to counter the threat. So why wasn't it?

As more bodies pushed past him Youssef realised that they were meant to gain entry to the village. He felt a sickening lump build in his throat. The enemy had led him into a trap. He couldn't yet be sure, but that was what the evidence pointed towards. For the moment he would keep his suspicions to himself. No point in alarming his men. It was still just about possible that the enemy had made a fatal error which he could exploit.

Youssef felt his way along the wall until he found a doorway and entered the house. Carefully he navigated across the room until he found the ladder that led to the roof. He realised that men had followed him and he directed one to climb the short flight. At the top the man opened a trap door then ducked back down, but no challenge came; no shot rang out. Youssef could hardly believe their luck. They had a defensible position from which to fire on the HQ.

A man jostled his way through the crowd. "The soldiers on the North are pulling back. They are joining those on the South side. I'm going to take my men and try to get close enough." He pulled back a fold in his salwar kameez to reveal a string of grenades suspended from a leather strap.

"Be careful." Youssef told the man in a hoarse whisper. "I think something may be wrong." Youssef told the man of his suspicion with regard to the lack of razor wire.

"A little late to think of that, Youssef. We are here and the enemy are there. We fight until we either win or until we become martyrs."

The man turned and left the house and half the men in the room followed him. Youssef searched out the man he wanted and beckoned him forward. In his hands he cradled the launch tube of an RPG. Extending above his shoulder were the rockets held in a rucksack on his back.

"Come Masood. I have work for you." Youssef led the way up the ladder. Hunching down they scuttled crablike across the roof and dropped behind the protection of its wall. "Your target is the door to the house. I want you to blast a way in for us."

The slope of the hill meant that Masood only had to raise his head slightly above the parapet to gain a clean shot at the headman's house. He lined himself up and nodded at Youssef. Youssef pulled a rocket from his rucksack and handed it to him. The man slid it into place then raised the sight to his eye. Youssef could practically feel the tension in Masood's legs as he braced himself for the shot. He took one more glance the house, adjusted his position slightly then pulled the trigger. There was a hair's breadth of a pause and then the projectile whooshed from the tube towards its target.

As the rocket exploded Masood abruptly stood up, as though pulled from above, then he sank downwards as his legs buckled, tipping him forward slightly to hang over the wall. The launcher tube clattered down the outside of the wall and crashed onto the ground. If the sound of the rifle that had fired the bullet reached him Youssef didn't hear it as the echoes of the RPG explosion still vibrated through his head. Youssef threw himself to the floor. He rarely swore but on this occasion he allowed himself an Anglo Saxon expletive. "Fuck! Fucking snipers."

Youssef stayed prone and crawled slowly back to the trap door. A head popped through to ask what had happened and Youssef explained. If they were to break into the headman's house then this wasn't the way to do it.

"Get the men digging loop holes in the walls. This side" he indicated the wall nearest to the headman's house, "and that side, the one that faces outwards from the village. Send word to the other groups to do the same. We are in a fortress. Let's make use of it."

The air above his head vibrated and Youssef heard the distinctive sound of helicopters. Damn, how had they got here so fast? He slipped headfirst through the trapdoor, grasping the rungs of the ladder and lowering himself down to floor level, then turned around to stare back up at the night sky, already getting paler with the dawn. It was a Chinook, he saw.

This wasn't air support called up by a commander who had unexpectedly been attacked. This was reinforcements called in by a commander who knew he would be attacked and had made his preparations. So it was a trap. The knowledge that he had been right gave him no pleasure. It did fill him with dread.

Youssef sat cross legged on the floor of the house's single room and analysed the situation. News filtered in as runners were sent between the commanders to keep them informed of their changes in fortune. The British had withdrawn from the village, surrendering it to his fighters, but at the same time the kuffar had an impenetrable cordon around them.

The sound of a heavily amplified voice drifted through the open trap door and Youssef climbed the ladder to listen to it.

* * *

"I fear we have no alternative, my brothers. If we stay in here we die. We die of thirst or we die of hunger or the kuffar come in and kill us. The outcome is the same." It was Gul Shah who spoke, as the eldest of the Taliban leaders it was his place to voice his opinion first. "Surely we would take a few of them with us, but the price is too high. We would not be martyrs, we would be suicides."

"That isn't an option for me. I am British. If I'm captured I will be sent back to my home country and I'll spend the rest of my life in a kuffar prison. You must do as you see fit, but I will stay here until I die or until they kill me." It was a stark reality for Youssef to have to admit, but he knew that if he left the village with his hands up he would be in Belmarsh Prison before the week was over. "Any who wish to stay with me may do so, but I won't criticise any who go."

"I'm staying." A voice came from the back of the crowded room. Youssef recognised it as being that of Gamal. "Me too," stated another. That was Taj. That was unexpected. The two men had no reason to stay loyal to him, Youssef thought. They weren't the same nationality. They had disagreed on many things, not least the attempted rape of the young Afghan girl. Two others, Hamid and Latif also announced their intention to remain with him.

"If you wish to stay, brothers, you are welcome, but I can promise you nothing more than death."

"We have no wish for anything more, Youssef. We will become martyrs alongside you."

"It's settled then." Stated Gul Shah, flatly. "We will give you what water we have and any food. You will have all our weapons and ammunition. You can make a good fight of it."

"Thank you my brothers. When we next meet it will be in Paradise."

"Insha'Allah." Gul Shah rose and the two men embraced. The other fighters in the room stacked their weapons in a corner and lowered their satchels of magazines and grenades onto the ground before following their leaders out to accept their fate.

Alone at last Gamal asked the question. "What do we do now?"

"We prepare a defence. It won't take long for the kuffar to start searching the village. Once they believe that all our brothers have left they will start. There is the chance for us to send a few of them to join Shaytaan before we go to join Allah in Paradise. Come, follow me. I know the place where we will make our stand."

21 - Cordon and Search

The fighters walked from the village in a long line. Less than half the number that had come out of the wadi were able to make the short journey. Some were supported on the shoulders of others and one was carried bodily between two men. They were ordered to lay down with their hands behind their heads while pairs of soldiers stepped forward to conduct body searches. Once they were certain that the prisoners had no weapons on them their hands were secured with cable ties and they were allowed to sit cross legged to await the vehicles that would transport them to imprisonment.

Two helicopters droned into sight, a Merlin of the RAF with an Apache in close formation for protection. From the Merlin descended two soldiers. As the chopper lifted off again they walked forward looking for the officer in command. Recognising Major Munroe they stepped forward to greet him.

Major Munroe introduced the officers to C Company's commander.

"Major Hardcastle, this is Lieutenant Ashwood and Captain Trelawney of the Intelligence Corps. They will make a start on interrogating the prisoners."

"This was no place for civilians so we didn't bring any interpreters." Commented the Company Commander. "First thing we need to know is if anyone is left in the village. Wounded men or fighters who don't want to surrender."

"Good point." Ashwood responded. "Just because some of them gave up it doesn't mean that they all did. They're an independent lot. They'll follow their own leaders into the jaws of hell but will ignore someone who's from a different tribe, even though he may be able to save their life. Some of them will even take up old feuds if the mood takes them."

Trelawney broke in. "Our main purpose is to extract any intelligence they may have on other groups. Once the news of this gets out they'll run for cover, so we have to get the jump on them. We're also looking for 'Arsenal'."

"What?" The Catfish Platoon Commander broke in, confused by the football reference.

"Sorry. That's the code name for the British fighter that was thought to be leading this attack. Apparently he lives close to the Arsenal ground so it seemed an apt code name for him. Though I can't see him amongst the prisoners."

"He may be among the dead." Major Munroe spoke. "Two of my snipers reported having him in their sights but he managed to get behind cover before either of them could pull the trigger. He was last seen on the roof of one of the houses in the village."

"He may also be alive and preparing for a final stand. From intercepts its apparent that he knows we're onto him. He may not relish the idea of a life spent at Her Majesty's pleasure." drawled Ashwood.

"Trouble is, we don't know how many made it into the village, so we don't know how many may be left behind."

"Leave that to us. The leaders are unlikely to give anything away, but some of the pond life usually let something slip. Some of them are so grateful just to be alive that they'd sell their own mothers in exchange for a couple of cigarettes. They're not all committed to the jihad. Can we borrow a couple of your men to act as guards, and we'll get started? If we may we'll use your HQ as an interrogation centre."

"Make yourself at home, gentlemen." Major Hardcastle offered. "Sgt Lofthouse, will you assist these officers with whatever they need."

Lofty accompanied the two Int Corps officers as they headed to the headman's house and started to unpack their brief cases onto a makeshift table made of packing cases. Lofty commented on the contents.

"Ah, yes. We video all interrogations now. We don't want to be accused of torture in some human rights court a few years down the line. We also tape everything, partly so that it can be heard that what was revealed was done so freely, and partly so that translators can go back over it all later and make sure we didn't miss anything. We both speak Pashto, but not fluently enough to capture all the subtleties. It saves a lot of writing as well, of course."

Lofty detailed two of Catfish 2 section to act as guards and the remainder were put in charge of escorting the prisoners to and from the temporary interrogation room.

The leaders of the insurgents had been identified. They had been quite happy to reveal their importance, one of them speaking a few words of English and interpreting for the rest. With the priority being given to finding out if there were still any fighters in the village Lofty started picking men at random from the lesser fish in the net.

It wasn't long before Lt Ashwood emerged from the house and sauntered across to the Company Commander's Panther.

"Some of them stayed behind. One has been identified as Arsenal and the others are from his group.

If they've stayed behind voluntarily they'll be prepared to die to protect Arsenal."

"Any idea where they are or how many."

"Not really. The bloke we questioned said he thought three, maybe four or even five. They'll tell us a lie just as easily as telling the truth so it could be any number. They're in a house near the West end of the village." He pointed. "That end, nearest us. But I doubt they would still be there. They'll know that we'd interrogate prisoners, so they'll anticipate someone talking. We'll see if we can pin down the numbers better from some of the other prisoners."

"OK, thanks. We'll take it from here."

The Int Corps officer returned to the headman's house and Major Hardcastle summoned his officers for an impromptu O Group.

"The Warwickshires are engaged in searching the surrounding bondu, so we'll have to carry out the search of the village. From what the Int guys tell us there may be up to five fighters still holed up in there. Our primary mission is to find them and either kill or capture them. Capture is the preferred option. So it's going to be a house to house slog. Catfish Platoon, you've had a pretty rough night so I'll put you on cordon with Dogfish while Angelfish conduct the search."

"With respect, Sir." Lofty found himself saying. "We'd like to see this through to the end. It was us they beat up at Camp Elizabeth, and the bloke we're looking for was responsible. With the Captain's agreement we'd like to do the search."

"Not a problem for me, Sir." Capt Trent chipped in. "The men are tired though Sergeant. Are you sure they're up to it?"

"I've not spoken to them individually, but they're good lads and they want to see this through to the bitter end. They'll do what's asked of them."

"That's settled then." continued the Major. "But I don't want anything untoward going on. Strict Geneva Convention rules. Got it?"

"Understood Sir." Lofty assured him. Silently he hoped his soldiers would abide by their orders. When friends get killed people harbour grudges and soldiers were only human, himself included.

"I suggest you split the men into fire teams and assign a house to each team. As they clear each one mark it off on the map and move onto the next one. Start at the West end of the village and work your way down to the East. Make sure that the men move forward together, so no fire team ends up isolated and allows the buggers to sneak in behind them. All clear?"

Lofty had lost count of the number of 'cordon and searches' they had practiced during the training period, but he refrained from commenting on the superfluous instructions he was being given. Officers love to show that they're in charge and that was one of the ways they did it.

* * *

Youssef and Gamal watched the soldiers deploying ready to start the search of the village.

"Here they come. Better warn the others. I'll see you at the first rendezvous point."

Gamal scurried off to do as he was bid. There had been plenty of time to make their preparations and their traps were laid. Youssef climbed down from the roof of the house and made his way down an alleyway. The soldiers would enter from the West end and the first trip wire lay just a few metres in, just where the shadows were deepest. It would take time for the kuffar's eyes to adjust to the change in light and it was unlikely that the tripwire would be spotted. He took up his firing position and waited.

An object was extended into the Western entrance to the village. A flash of light showed that it was a reflective surface of some sort. Clever, a mirror on the end of a stick so they could look down the alley without exposing themselves. The mirror was withdrawn and a head showed itself briefly. As no shot rang out the head appeared again and took a longer look. Satisfied, the figure entered the alley and crouched down, hugging the left hand wall. A second figure entered and moved along the right hand wall until it too crouched.

As the first figure edged along the wall it was replaced at the entrance by a third soldier and the manoeuvre was repeated until four soldiers were gathered in the narrow space. They crept forward until they were opposite the first door. A hand reached inside the owners jacket and withdrew an object. The soldier rested his rifle across his legs as he used two hands to manipulate the object. The grenade gave up its safety pin and was thrown through the door as the soldier pressed himself back against the wall out of the line of the blast.

It must have had a short fuse because there was a sharp crack almost as soon as it was thrown. A flash of light silhouetted the soldiers. A stun grenade; lots of flash and bang but no flying fragments. Not lethal but it would disorient anyone inside the building. Interesting. Its use suggested they were more interested in taking prisoners than creating corpses.

Two of the men threw themselves into the house while the other two stood outside, ready to fire if an enemy emerged. There was a chorus of shouting and the rattle of feet on the rungs of a ladder. Youssef heard the crash as the trap door to the roof slammed open, then made out the word 'clear' before the two soldiers re-joined their colleagues in the alley. They repeated the operation on the house on the other side of the alley.

With two houses clear the lead soldier inched forward once again, approaching the gap that separated them from the next house. The mirror was withdrawn from the belt and a check was made to make sure that the cross route was clear in both directions. Youssef held his breath.

"Grenade!" The shout was clear along the alley as the soldier threw himself backwards and onto the ground. At once the men behind him dropped to the floor.

Triggered by the jerk of the trip-wire as the soldier walked forward the small bomb exploded, the alley concentrating the noise and making it far louder than normal. Dust and flakes of dried mud pattered down. Youssef let loose a volley of shots from his AK-47 and heard others join in from the roofs above him. Chunks of mud flew from the walls of the building. Answering shots came back, but they were fired wildly and none came close.

A smoke canister bounced along the alley. Good, the enemy was so predictable. It landed a few metres away and the grey fog filled the space between the buildings, blinding both attackers and defenders. Youssef shouted a command and he and his followers retreated to their next strong point, hidden by the enemy's own smoke.

* * *

"Man down. This is Catfish one five. Catfish one two is down."

The report of a casualty forced Lofty to go forward and take personal control of the search. He had warned the men to be on the lookout for booby traps but obviously his words hadn't been heeded.

He edged into the alley and crept forward until he reached the four men. LCpl Roberts was dabbing at a gash on his face with a field dressing while the other three members of the fire team kept up a steady fusillade along the narrow passage.

"Roberts you dick-head, I told you to watch for booby traps." Lofty barked.

"Sorry Sarge. It was all so quiet, I just got a bit carried away after we cleared the first houses. I got a bit pumped up, you know."

Lofty took pity on him. He had learnt his lesson the hard way. "Alright. Let me take a look at that." He pulled Roberts' hand away from his face and examined the wound. "That's going to need stitches. You get back to the Command vehicle and get that dressed. I'll take over here."

The soldier looked downcast, and appeared ready to protest but Lofty's stern expression made him think better of it. Picking up his rifle he turned and jogged from the alley, one hand still held up to his face.

"All Catfish call signs listen in." Lofty commanded. "There are booby-traps. Proceed with caution. Sunray this is Sunray minor. Catfish one two is on his way back to you. Minor injury. No other casualties. I am taking command of Catfish one two's fire team."

As the smoke started to drift away their position became more exposed. Lofty asked the other soldiers where the shooting had come from, then moved them into the cross route on either side so that they could observe the way ahead without keeping them exposed. When he stuck his head round the corner no shots rang out. He looked again, taking more time. Still no shots.

"Looks like they've pulled back. No point in trying to clear these houses while there are booby traps around. We'll have to clear the route first. The other sections haven't reported any movement so we must assume that they haven't circled round behind us. We'll move forward house by house and clear the route. When we reach the end of the village we'll turn back and then start to search each house in turn, working our way back to here. OK?"

The three soldiers nodded their assent. The risk was the terrorists emerging from a house after they had gone past, able to fire into their exposed backs. It meant two men having to walk backwards all the time to watch their rear. Lofty briefed the rest of the platoon over the radio.

Ahead of them the alley bent in a gentle arc, concealing what was beyond. Lofty concluded that the attack must have come from close to that bend so that the enemy could take advantage of it as they withdrew. From his jacket pocket he took a pen like object. He pulled on one end and extended it like the telescopic aerial of a radio. He handed it to Catfish one six.

"Ghost walk." he instructed.

Richardson extended his arm in front of him and used the pointer to feel for a trip wire, starting from the ground and raising his arm until the tip of the pointer was above his head, then lowering his arm again.

Satisfied that there were no trip wires immediately in front of him he shuffled three feet forward and repeated the test.

Slowly the fire team made its way along the alley towards the bend. Lofty found a scattering of spent bullet cases where at least one of the fighters had fired from. The curve of the alley provided just enough cover to keep a man concealed, especially in the gloom. The only time this place saw sunlight would be in the middle of the day when the sun was directly overhead.

Lofty held Catfish one six back and extended the mirror around the bend. The next twelve or so feet of passageway appeared to be clear. He tapped the man on the back again and they moved their way forward painfully slowly once again.

Lofty saw the tip of the pointer stop, snagged on something not quite visible. Richardson withdrew the thin length of metal and knelt down to feel with his fingers about six inches above the ground. Ankle height.

"Trip wire." he reported.

Lofty pulled him back and stepped forward into his place. He lay flat on the ground and felt for the wire. Feeling its smoothness he concluded that it was fishing line, not that it made a difference. Wire might reveal itself with a glimmer of reflected light, but the dark green nylon filament wouldn't.

He traced it to where it was anchored into the wall by a spent bullet casing hammered into a crack in the dried mud. Nothing on that end. He tried the other way. The wire disappeared into a heap of mud flakes and dust. Carefully Lofty swept it away to reveal the hand grenade bound to another spent bullet casing with more fishing line. The pin was pulled almost fully from the safety lever. A jerk on the wire of less than an inch would have completed the task, pulling the pin free so that the safety lever flew off and allowed the grenade to arm. If the fuse had been instantaneous, rather than delayed, Frank Roberts would now be dead or crippled.

Almost absentmindedly Lofty identified the grenade as a Russian F1, known as a limonka or little lemon. They were provided to a number of Middle Eastern countries but this one could have come from anywhere, including being a left over from the Soviet occupation.

Lofty released the wire from the far wall by pulling out the securing bullet case. With a sigh of relief he pushed the pin safely back to lock the grenade's safety arm in place.

Looking up and along the alley Lofty saw a shadow flit across his narrow field of vision. Someone had just crossed the gap between the houses, As he had detected the booby trap the enemy must have decided that another ambush wasn't viable in this place and so was moving to a new position. Lofty radioed a warning to the section covering the houses to his right and left, then moved his own section forward, yard by patient yard.

A black dot landed in front of Lofty, dropped from above. It rolled towards his feet. The frustrated ambusher had decided on another form of attack.

"Grenade" Lofty shouted, warning his three companions. He heard them drop flat behind him. Without thinking he stepped forward and launched a mighty kick at the object. Adrenalin rushed into Lofty's body and he re-lived the experience of time slowing down.

* * *

On the roof of the house Gamal watched with grim satisfaction as the leader of the soldiers stood and watched his grenade roll towards him. This time there would be no mistake. His expression turned to a grin of delight as he watched the man try to kick the grenade away.

* * *

The strike was worthy of Beckham at his best. The grenade arced upwards. As it reached its zenith the fuse ran out and the grenade exploded with a vicious crack, scattering shrapnel in all directions, but not far enough to reach Lofty."

"Good shot, Sarge." a voice said from behind him.

"Lucky shot more like." another voice added.

"Quiet you lot." barked Lofty, unnerved by how close he had come to death. All those hours of football practice over the years had finally paid off with something tangible; his life.

Lofty signalled the men forward again.

Reaching the next gap between the houses Lofty used the mirror to check that the way was clear. To his right the alley widened out and the light levels increased. He could see the edge of the village on the North side. Rifle fire started up and the muzzle flashes showed him a loophole dug out of the far corner of the house in front of him. Across the alley from that the final house on that side of the village had a similar loophole. Sticking out of it was another rifle muzzle blasting out fire along the alley parallel to them. Mickey Flynn's fire team were trying to advance along that alley and Lofty heard the familiar crack of SA80's as they returned fire.

Lofty called up a mental picture of where they were in the village. If he was right then they were close to one of the weapons pits on the North side of the village. If the Taliban fighters withdrew to that they could make a final stand with 270° arcs of fire towards the open ground, and a shooting gallery down the alley behind them. It would be difficult to dig them out. The weapons pit had been designed to stop an RPG grenade, so it would defeat most of their own armaments. They would have no choice but call in a missile strike from a helicopter, and that meant there would be no chance to take the fighters alive.

Lofty withdrew the mirror and thought for a moment. These were the only pre-prepared defensive positions the enemy fighters had used, which suggested that they were the places chosen for an extended fight. He pulled his sketch map of the village from his jacket pocket and checked their position, at the same time confirming his previous assumptions. It didn't take him long to formulate his plan of attack. He called the three members of the fire team to him.

"This is what we're going to do." he announced. After briefing the men he issued some commands over the radio, requesting support from the platoons forming the cordon.

Lofty carefully led his men over the cross route and into the shelter of the wall of the house. Catfish one five slung his weapon over his back while Catfish one six took hold of the butt of his rifle so his partner could take the muzzle.

"Remember, keep your eyes peeled for more booby traps." He gave a final whispered warning to the three men. He slung his own rifle across his back so it wouldn't get in his way. He would effectively be unarmed if he now became a target.

Lofty placed one booted foot onto the centre of Catfish one six's rifle. "Lift." He breathed, not that a voice would have been heard above the cacophony of gunfire. The two soldiers heaved him upwards until his feet were level with their shoulders. They pushed again, grunting with the effort needed.

Grabbing the top of the wall Lofty pulled, at the same time swinging one leg sideways until the toe of his boot caught on the top of the wall. With muscles screaming in protest he levered his body onto the parapet and rolled onto the roof, dropping a short distance to land on his hands and knees. Recovering his slung rifle Lofty spotted a man in the far corner of the wall. He rolled away to avoid the bullets that must surely be fired at him, but the man didn't move.

Carefully Lofty crawled forward until he was able to check the man over. The crater sized hole in the man's head showed the work of a sniper. With alarm Lofty realised that he might be the next target.

"Sunray this is Sunray minor. Request the sniper teams cease fire."

"Roger Sunray minor. What's your position?"

Perilous, thought Lofty, but instead he replied, "Sunray, I'm on the roof of the house that one of the Tangos is using." He read the house's grid number off of his sketch map.

"Roger Sunray minor. Wave your rifle in the air." Lofty did as he was instructed. There was a pause before Sunray spoke again.

"Sunray minor Oscar two has you identified. Proceed as planned, he will watch your back."

Satisfied he was now safe from being shot by his own side Lofty half stood and duck walked his way towards the open trap door that led down into the interior of the house. His feet made the roof boards creak and he could only hope that the firing of weapons in the house below had numbed the insurgent's hearing.

Lying flat on his stomach Lofty craned his neck to see inside. In the near blackness he was able to make out a single man in the corner of the room, firing his AK-47 through the loophole. The loud hammering of his firing stopped for a moment as the man swapped an empty magazine for a fresh one. A dozen more were piled beside him. The number of magazines told Lofty how long the man was prepared to remain in this refuge. No man could run away carrying a dozen loose magazines.

Lofty was about to lower himself through the trap door when something else caught his eye. Lying like a broken doll in the far corner of the room was a figure. At first Lofty thought it must be a fighter but then he recognised the camouflaged uniform. It was a soldier.

Lofty peered into the gloom to try to identify him. He wasn't wearing his osprey armour or helmet, Lofty could see that, and there was no sign of his weapon. A dark stain spread across the neck and shoulders of the his jacket. It could only be blood. Lofty realised that the strange angle of the soldier's head was caused by the fact that it was barely attached to its body. Lofty gagged as he realised what must have happened. A soldier caught by himself, captured and executed when the Taliban had reached the village. But none of the platoon had been reported missing.

Lofty realised his mistake. In the aftermath of the battle he hadn't conducted a roll call, and none of his subordinates had reported anyone missing. Lofty sat stunned, wondering if he could have been saved. At last Lofty put a name to the bleached white face below him. Pvt Scott.

So many questions sprung unbidden into Lofty's mind, but he had to push them to one side. He still had a Taliban fighter below him that he had to try to capture, if at all possible. Just as Lofty was about to lower himself through the trap door a figure rose on the roof of the neighbouring house. He was advancing towards the far corner to bring his weapon to bear on the Dogfish section that was advancing on the house from outside the village, just as Lofty had ordered. Lofty started to raise his weapon to take a shot at the man but the movement caught his attention and the insurgent whirled round, raising his AK-47 and spraying a burst of fire towards him.

Lofty followed the sweep of the weapon as he raised his own. He knew he had only one shot before the arc of bullets found their target. The SA80's sight was in front of his eye and the circle of light was filled with the stained brown of the terrorist's Salwar Kameez. Lofty squeezed the trigger and the rifle bucked in his hand.

Chips of mud peppered Lofty's face as a bullet struck the mud brick parapet, but it was the last bullet that the terrorist ever fired. As Lofty lowered his rifle again the roof of the house on the other side of the alley was clear. Lofty stayed in his kneeling position, waiting for his heart to stop hammering. It seemed to take an eon to do so.

Nausea swept through Lofty's body. He had never killed before. He had fired his rifle often enough, but towards fleeting targets. If he had hit them he had never known it. This time there was no doubt. He crawled to the parapet and stared across the narrow gap into the dead man's sightless brown eyes. This was it, Lofty thought. This is what it all comes down to. Kill or be killed, and for what? What did that man just die for?

Lofty shook his head, trying to dislodge the thoughts that galloped through his mind. First Scott and now this unknown gunman. Time for that later. Right now he had a job to do and if he failed then more men might die, and they were men that he actually cared about. He took a deep breath. For the second time that morning he had come within a heartbeat of dying. Would he be allowed a third escape? Much as he tried not to, he couldn't prevent the intrusion of an image of Emma sitting on the settee that they had bought only a few months earlier, drinking tea and being comforted by... by who? He squeezed his eyes shut and created a picture of him striding across the tarmac at RAF Brize Norton into the waiting arms of his wife. It helped, but not much.

Eventually Lofty felt able to shuffle forward and silently lower himself onto the ladder that provided the route to the ground floor of the house, then crept carefully down rung by silent rung. With his back to the ladder and his hands holding his rifle it was an awkward manoeuvre. The constant bark of the rifle would cover any noise he made, Lofty felt sure, but he took no chances. Stepping off the bottom rung he raised his rifle and took careful aim.

It didn't feel right, shooting a man in the back. If he was facing him Lofty knew he wouldn't hesitate to pull the trigger, just as he had done on the roof a few moments before, but this felt cowardly. Shifting his aim Lofty squeezed the trigger. His single shot cracked out, blasting chunks of baked mud from the wall beside the Taliban fighter's head.

The man whirled round seeking the source of the threat. Spotting Lofty's aimed weapon he raised his AK-47 to try to get off a burst of fire before he died.

"Surrender!" Lofty barked at the man, but the rifle kept on rising. Lofty felt his finger tightening on the trigger of his own weapon. At this range he couldn't miss.

An explosion rocked the house and mud bricks flew. One caught the insurgent on the back of his head, throwing him to the ground, his AK-47 spinning away into the corner to lie next to the dead Pvt Scott. Lofty stepped forward, knowing as he did so that he should really be seeking the safety of the undamaged rear wall of the house, but his first instinct was to help the casualty.

Glossary

Bundu   Often spelt and pronounced as bondu. Slang for any uninhabited and non-cultivated land. Probably originating in South Africa from a Bantu word meaning wilderness

Int Corps Intelligence Corps. The branch of the British Army responsible for the gathering and analysis of military intelligence. Also takes the tri-service lead on security matters.

Lt   Lieutenant

Merlin   Augusta Westland AW101 medium lift helicopter. Originally purchased as an anti-submarine platform for the Royal Navy it was drafted into RAF service as a stop gap to make up for the perceived shortfall in helicopter capability in Iraq and Afghanistan.

22 - An Ending

The Gods laugh when mortals make plans. Lofty had heard someone say that, sometime in the past. The army version says 'no plan survives first contact with the enemy'. He wondered how long he had been lying under the rubble of the house. Five minutes? Five hours? After being knocked unconscious he couldn't be sure.

So this was how it was going to end. All soldiers have to face the possibility of dying and when Lofty had considered it, he had always seen himself going in a blaze of glory, attacking a machine gun post single handed or carrying a wounded comrade from the battlefield. But here he was lying under tons of rubble slowly having the life crushed out of him. Was this how it had felt for his father? Had he lain in the street after being hit by the IRA sniper's bullet, with the life ebbing out of him? Was this why he had joined the army, Lofty asked himself, before another spasm of pain pushed the thought from his mind. A groan escaped from his lips.

"Is that you, soldier?" the voice came from the darkness. What was that accent. It sounded so familiar. It certainly wasn't the voice of someone who had learnt their English as a second language. The familiarity was stark. Had he not known better it could have been one of his own platoon speaking.

"Who are you?" Lofty called.

"I'm the man who's been trying to kill you for the last six months. It looks like I may yet succeed." The words were followed by a rasping cough as dust entered the man's throat.

"You're the British terrorist we've all heard so much about."

"It would appear that my fame precedes me. My name is Youssef, by the way. Youssef Haq Ibrahim."

"Well, if I die I reckon you'll be dying too, chum. I'm Lofty. Well, that's just a nickname but everyone calls me that, even my Mum."

"I'm ready to die, Lofty. I will be a martyr and will go straight to Paradise. It is written. Are you ready to die?"

The crackle of gunfire filtered through the debris that buried them both as the battle continued without them.

"The others must still be alive." Youssef's voice in the darkness let the comment hang in the air. Right on cue there was another explosion and the rattle of small arms fire increased. Lofty knew it had to be a head on assault, and also knew that the surviving Taliban were about to die, regardless of whether they were the attackers or the defenders.

"What happened to Scott? Lofty demanded.

"Who? Oh, the dead soldier. One of my men found him cowering in here. He put him out of his misery."

"A bullet would have been kinder."

"A bullet would have given away our position. He was unarmed by the way. He couldn't protect himself. I don't have enough men to take prisoners."

Lofty couldn't quite bring himself to hate the man for what he had done. Scott shouldn't have been there and he certainly shouldn't have been unarmed. He should have been with his section. More questions for later.

Lofty tried to remember what had happened before the blackness had descended on him and he woke up with a searing pain where his legs should be. Bit by bit the events came back to him.

After boosting him onto the roof the other three member of the fire team would have skirted round the outside of the house to block any escape towards the empty weapons pit. Lofty had already asked for sections of Dogfish platoon to move in to block the side exits from the village. With Mickey Flynn in front and a section of Angelfish coming in from the South all the possible escape routes from the two houses had been sealed off.

Lofty remembered the explosion, probably an LASM rocket, shook the house and threw the terrorist off his feet. Something must have hit Lofty on the head as well, maybe there had been a second rocket blast, and despite the protection of his Kevlar helmet he had lost consciousness. When he woke, it was to feel pain coursing through his lower limbs and rubble piled up around and over him, cutting out the light. He must have groaned, and that was when the insurgent made his presence known, trapped by the same collapsed roof and walls.

Lofty felt with his hands and identified a heavy beam lying across his pelvis. One of the beams that supported the roof.

"Where are you from?" Lofty called.

"London, Finsbury Park. And you?"

"Me too. Lennox Road."

"Durham Road." replied the terrorist. "It's a small world, it seems."

"Yeah, but you wouldn't want to have to paint it." Lofty replied sardonically. He would have laughed at

312

his own joke, but knew it would hurt so he stifled it. "We could have stayed at home and killed each other." Lofty had to suppress his wit, he decided.

The two men lay in silence for a while, each wrapped up in their own thoughts. For Lofty the searing pain in his legs told him that he may never get the chance to make his decision about whether or not he would leave the army and be with Emma. Strange to think that here he was lying under a heap of rubble with a man he might have passed in the street back home. What sense did it make that they were now in a foreign country trying to kill each other?

Youssef lay preparing himself for martyrdom. Now that he was here it didn't seem nearly such an attractive prospect. A bullet followed by instant oblivion, and the Prophet's face welcoming him to Paradise. That was how it was supposed to be.

An image of Fatima's face, framed by her hijab, drifted across Youssef's mind. He felt a pang of pain that had nothing to do with his injuries. He had never seen her without the concealment that the garment gave. He had never seen the flow of her hair around her face. He only knew that her hair was long because she had told him. The only time he had seen her hair was in a school photograph taken when she was nine years old; before she was regarded as being a temptation to men.

He had let Fatima down, hadn't he? All she wanted was to marry him, and all he had ever wanted was to marry her. Oh, he had a vocation, he knew. He had really believed that he should become an Imam. That dream would die with him too, but it was marrying Fatima that had shaped his life above all else.

"Hey, soldier. Lofty. Have you got a girlfriend?"

313

"No, a wife."

"I have a girlfriend. We were going to get married if our parents agreed."

Lofty's vision darkened and for a moment all he could see were the staring brown eyes of the dead gunman. In that instant Lofty realised what was most important to him. Why had it taken so long for him to see what was so obvious now?

"I don't think I'll be getting married now." Youssef's voice croaked from the darkness.

"Why not?"

"I don't think she would like Afghanistan very much. It wouldn't fit in very well with her plans." Fatima's plans now seemed to be so important. Perhaps because Youssef no longer had any plans of his own.

"What brought you out here in the first place?" Lofty asked. Talking might help to stop him from losing consciousness again. The Taliban leader gave him an edited version of the story.

"I'm sorry about your family." Lofty said, thinking of the loss of his own father.

"I have had my revenge now."

"Oh, how's that?"

"I have killed so many of you."

"How many of my unit do you think you killed?"

"A dozen, maybe more."

"You've killed three. Then Lofty remembered Pvt Scott. "No, make that four. There are half a dozen more who will never return to active duty, but you only killed four."

"You lie. You kuffar always lie?

"Why should I lie to you? Besides, if I wanted to lie I would tell you that you didn't kill any of us. How many of your family died?"

314

With a lurch to his heart Youssef realised that more of his family had died than he had managed to kill. So much for an-eye-for-an-eye. He still wasn't avenged and it seemed now that he never would be. If he didn't die here he would be rescued and sent to prison. And of course it hadn't been just his family that had died. Across the ground outside, and in other places, lay an unknown number of his dead comrades. What price revenge?

"Tell me something, Youssef. When you pray you pray to Allah you call him the Great, don't you."

"We call him the *Greatest*." corrected Youssef.

"OK. So if Allah is the Greatest, how come you aren't winning this war?"

"Because we fight against the forces of Shaytaan, and he is cunning." Despite his own misgivings now that he knew that Mohamed Dost Mohamed was a fake, Youssef still felt the need to defend the jihad.

"Interesting. I'm no theologian, but that argument doesn't hold up."

"This is hardly the place for theological debate." Youssef stated scornfully.

"Have you anything better to do?"

The truthful answer was that there wasn't anything else to do, but Youssef didn't really want to be drawn into a debate with a kafir. The forces of Shaytaan will tell you a million truths in order to disguise the one big lie. On the other hand, it might be interesting to see things through the eyes of the enemy, and it would help to pass the time while he waited for Allah to take him.

"OK, so what are you saying?"

"If Allah is the Greatest, then why are the forces of Shaytaan winning?"

"He is cunning. He will use people and then throw them away. That is why there are so many of you fighting us. You can't do it with small numbers the way we can. We fight and hope to become martyrs, but you fight in the hope of surviving. So we will always be more determined to win than you."

"But surely, if Allah is the Greatest then he can defeat us any time he wishes. Why prolong all this suffering and death? Why make his own people suffer, like he did in Iraq, or Egypt or Syria or any of the other places where Muslims mistreat Muslims. You also call Allah the most compassionate and the most merciful, but surely he is neither if he allows Muslims to kill Muslims."

"You misuse our words, soldier." snarled Youssef, wishing he could reach his gun and shut this kafir up. But at the same time a seed of doubt had already been sewn by the discovery of Abisali's betrayal.

"Maybe I do. Look, I don't pretend to know much about your religion. But I do know that when it comes to a fight the man with the best weapons always wins."

"Vietnam?"

"Very good. OK, I'll give you that one. But where else?"

"The mujahedeen chased the Russians out."

"True, but they needed American weapons to do it. Besides, the Russians had other problems at the time. History will show that they decided the war was costing them too much at a time when the political map was changing. Have you never heard of Glasnost?"

"We beat the British, twice!"

"Who's this we? You were born in Britain."

"If I was born in a barn it wouldn't make me a cow."

"And as for those two wars. They were small forces and poorly led. I'll give you two in return. The siege of Malta and Khartoum. At Malta a tiny force held out against a massive Turkish attack because they had better defences. At Khartoum a modern army beat a force made up of men with muskets. Things are a bit different now. If Allah is Greatest why hasn't he given you helicopter gunships and strike-attack aircraft? You can't win a war without them."

"And sometimes you can't win a war even if you have them. We do what Allah commands us as it is written in the Holy Book.

"Evil men have often twisted religion to make it suit their own purpose. History has shown us that. Look at the crusades. Men put crosses on their clothes and said they were doing God's work when all they were really interested in was land and plunder. Europe became rich from what it stole from the holy lands. Religious wars split Europe for 200 years over who should rule the Christians; the Pope or our own Kings and Queens. We stopped fighting about it a long time ago, once we put religion into its proper place in our world." Lofty remembered his father's death. "Well, almost. We're not here because of our religion. We're here because we're afraid of what's being done in the name of your religion."

The image of the twin towers in New York leapt unbidden into Youssef's mind. He remembered he had been shocked at such a callous and indiscriminate act. He'd only been ten years old, but even then he knew it was wrong. He had got into a fight at school with another Muslim boy who was gloating over it. But now he had taken part in meetings where similar atrocious acts had been discussed. How many people did Allah want him to kill? How many people had to die before someone said 'enough'; before Allah said 'enough'?

In the darkness Youssef thought on what the soldier had said. He had to admit that he had a point. So what was the one big lie? Could it be that others were telling him the small truths to disguise it? The ranting men in the camp? Well, if they were all as unqualified as Mohamed Dost Mohamed then it is likely that they had no real knowledge of the words of the Prophet. He remembered his life before and his certainty that Allah would never ask him to kill, yet here he was killing.

The Islamic religion was a simple one. He had always been told that. Obey the rules as laid down in the Koran, because they were the words of Allah. But this soldier had just made it very complicated. Who stood to gain from this war? The country would be returned to Allah again, and so the souls of the people would be saved. But as he thought it he realised he was wrong. People like Gul Shah would rule if the current government were to be overthrown. Peasants who knew how to use a gun and who quoted the words of the Prophet. That didn't mean they would rule wisely. They would be vulnerable to the lies of the people who would exploit the country. People like the opium growers. People like the lying Mohamed Dost Mohamed, the carpet seller. If it could happen in the West with well-educated leaders then how much more easily could it happen when the country was led by illiterate peasants?

He realised the truth of his own thoughts. A clever man had once come to Afghanistan and persuaded the peasants of the Taliban to give him a safe haven. From that small seed of Muslim hospitality this whole war had grown.

"It is easy for you, a well-educated man who lives in a rich country, to argue against us."

"I may live in a rich country, but I'm not rich and I'm not well educated. I left school with a couple of GCSE's in art and design, and a bit of knowledge about history. That doesn't make me a mastermind. It taught me to ask questions though. It's not the answers that are important, it's the questions.

"And what questions do you ask?"

"I ask who pays for your guns and ammunition?"

"Our supporters are generous."

"I'm sure they are. And have they said what they want in return?"

Youssef realised that he didn't have an answer for that. He remembered what Gul Shah had said about their backers and their desire for a return on their investment.

"They give because they believe in our cause." Youssef persisted.

"And how many of them are here fighting alongside you?"

Youssef knew then what Lofty had meant by the questions being more important than the answers.

Youssef's silence spoke volumes. "Yes, they support your cause so much that they let you do the fighting and dying for them. They buy your lives and pay for your deaths."

"And what of your leaders, where are they?"

"Doing what they're paid for. That's the deal. They get paid to lead us, and we get paid to do the fighting. If I choose not to fight then I have to find something else to do for a living, that's all."

319

"So this is just a job for you?"

"I used to think it was more, but I was wrong."

"When did you find that out?"

Deep brown eyes in a dead face. "Not long ago. If I live I don't think I'll be a soldier for much longer."

Lofty realised that the shooting had stopped. "It's over." He stated flatly, if somewhat ambiguously.

There was the sound of rubble being moved. Lofty gathered his strength in the hope of staying alive long enough to be rescued, but he had over-exerted himself in arguing with Youssef. Blackness slipped over him.

* * *

"And that was it. Once we had taken out the last rag heads we started digging for you."

Cpl Mickey Flynn sat on the edge of Lofty's bed and offered him another chocolate. Lofty declined so Mickey helped himself again. The box was nearly empty and Lofty hadn't eaten a single sweet. Visiting the field hospital to have his hearing checked, Mickey had dropped in to see his old friend, bringing with him the chocolates he had bought in the NAAFI shop and which he was now scoffing.

"Who fired the LASM? Don't worry, I won't thump them."

Mickey gave a rueful grin. "First one was me. Second one came from Dogfish. They were trying to blast a way into the other house but they missed and hit the one you were in again."

"Dogfish always were rotten shots." was all Lofty could say. "And you owe me a pint or three for doing it as well."

"I have to say, for an invalid you're looking pretty well." continued Mickey. "What have they said, about your legs I mean?"

"Oh, they'll be OK. There are several breaks, and they've filled me so full of metal, I'll never get through airport security again, but they think I should be fit for duty again eventually. That's if I want to stay in the army."

"I heard about your brilliant bit of football. Nice one mate. And do you? Want to stay in the Army I mean."

"No, I don't think I do. Somehow in the end, in the darkness, it didn't feel right anymore. I mean, what right do we have being in this country?"

"Sorry, Lofty. You've got me there. You know I'm better at sports than philosophy." chuckled Mickey.

"Well, Emma wants me to leave the army, and I think maybe she's right. Did they find Scott, by the way. He was in the same house that fell on me."

"Yeah. When the wall came down he was left sitting in the rubble."

"Did they find out what he was doing there?"

"Yeah. Davie Tomlinson told the whole story. He's in trouble for not reporting it straight away, though it wouldn't have stopped them killing Scott." Mickey went on to repeat the story of Scott's panic stricken flight from the weapons pit.

"What happened to the other guy?"

"What other guy?"

"The guy I went into the house after. He was trapped in there with me. Quite a chat we had."

"Well, we found one body lying on top of the rubble, half buried. His face was missing. To tell you the truth we didn't really look any more than that. Once we found you and Scott and got you out we started on the clean up so we could get back to Camp Elizabeth."

Lofty wondered if he had imagined it, the whole conversation. No, he was sure the man was there. It was too real. But if he was there, then he wouldn't have been lying on top of the rubble, he had been under it, no more than a few feet from himself.

"How many bodies did you find?" asked Lofty, suspicions building in his mind.

"I'm not sure. My section found one. I think Dogfish found a couple more."

How many should there have been? Had the Int Corps officers said?

"Debbie came up in the chopper with me. Had some business with G2. Do you want to see her?"

"If she wants to say hello then I won't mind. It's never a problem seeing a pretty face."

"I'll let her know when I catch up with her. Just you make sure you keep your hands to yourself. She's spoken for now."

Lofty laughed his agreement to behave.

"The Company fly out on Monday, then we get a week of decompression in Cyprus before the next flight to Brize."

"I'll be home before you then." said Lofty. "They fly me to Birmingham tomorrow." Decompression, thought Lofty. The week long, officially sanctioned, letting off of steam in the British garrison on Cyprus, just to make sure that the returning soldiers didn't run amok through the towns of Wiltshire. It seemed to work.

"Anyway, I must be off now." They said their farewells and Mickey left, the empty chocolate box still lying on the starched bed sheet that covered Lofty's shattered legs. He was just drifting off to sleep again when he felt a presence. He looked up to see Debbie Moon smiling at him.

"So how's the wounded hero?"

"OK, I think. I'll walk again but I think the battalion football team will have to find another captain."

"Football. Is that all you men ever think about?"

"Oh, we think about other things as well." Lofty grinned at her. "How are you and Mickey getting along."

"Not bad. He's got some rough edges to knock off but I enjoy a challenge."

"Is it serious?"

"I don't know. Being out here it's a bit like a holiday romance. We'll have to see how things are once we're back home. Anyway, I just came in to let you know that they've arrested the guy in Preston. You know, the one who was Tracey on Facebook."

"Have they got enough evidence for a conviction?"

"Plenty. You know I told you about how he kept his files on a memory stick? Well, apparently the spyware they got onto his machine didn't just allow them to read the files, it also copied them onto his hard drive without him knowing. He managed to destroy the memory stick, but it made no difference. The evidence is all there. He's not as clever as he thinks he is. The Pakistanis have also arrested his contact in Islamabad. They were able to trace him though his IP address."

"What about the terrorist, the British one."

"Well, you should know. He was found in the rubble with half his head missing. You killed him."

"No I didn't. I was just about to shoot when the LASMs hit the house. He was buried under the rubble with me. We had a bit of a chat. Then I blacked out and woke up in here."

"Well if you didn't shoot him who did?"

"I don't think anyone did. I think the body you're talking about was the man on the roof."

"What are you talking about. No one mentioned a man on the roof."

Lofty swore and told her about the insurgent he had found on the roof. "One of the SAS snipers got him. I took out another one on the roof of the neighbouring house, then I went down stairs and found Youssef."

Debbie Moon's head jerked round as he used the name. Lofty shouldn't know the man's real name. "What do you know about Youssef?"

"Like I told you. We had a chat. He said his name was Youssef Haq Ibrahim and he was from Durham Road in Finsbury Park."

"You're sure about that?"

"As sure as I can be after having a house fall on top of me."

"Fuck. We'll have to go back and search the rubble again. I hope to God we find a body, or we'll never know for sure whether he's dead or alive." She stood up and patted his shoulder. "Sorry Lofty. I've got to go."

"No problem. Look after Mickey for me, won't you." She smiled her farewell and hurried from the hospital ward.

* * *

"What's that music?" Emma asked, as the band marched past the saluting dais, the soldiers of the battalion following behind in column formation.

"It's the Regimental March Past." Lofty replied. "It's a mash up of two old tunes. One is called Sir Manley Powers and the other, the one that sounds a bit Irish, is called Paddy's Resource."

Outside Inglis Barracks the families of the soldiers had assembled to watch the home coming parade. Mixed in with them were a crowd from the local population, drawn to the sound of the music or wishing to greet their local heroes.

On the saluting dais stood the Mayor of Barnet alongside the General Officer Commanding London District. To their right was a short line of wheelchairs bearing those soldiers from the battalion who had been injured, but who were fit enough to attend the parade with a little help. Behind one of them stood Emma, her hands resting on Lofty's uniformed shoulders.

Lofty turned and smiled at his wife, then looked back to watch the marching soldiers, searching back along the parade route to get the first sight of C Company. As he did so his eye caught the gentle, almost invisible swelling of Emma's tummy. He wasn't a religious man, but he uttered a short prayer to anyone who might be listening, in thanks for his almost safe return and the safe birth of his first child.

After the parade the General would present the soldiers with their campaign medals for Afghanistan. Lofty could feel the weight on the chest of his uniform jacket where his medal, awarded four years earlier after his first tour, sparkled above his breast pocket. He had been told that it would soon be joined by a Military Cross, awarded in recognition of his leadership in the counter attack against the Taliban when they had attacked Camp Elizabeth back before Christmas. The

MoD needed a hero from that affair and Lofty fitted the mould.

* * *

In the watching crowd Youssef stood with Fatima at his side supporting him. His legs and ribs were still painful and he was still suffering headaches from his head injury. He wondered if he would ever walk properly again. The medical treatment he had received was hardly first class.

After the soldiers had rescued their sergeant Youssef had lain alone in the darkness. The thin chink of light that had told him he was still alive gradually grew darker as night fell. For two days and nights he had lain there.

It had been a harder journey back to London for Youssef than it had been for Lofty. In the darkness he had been able to listen to the faint sounds of the soldiers moving around him, dismantling the village's defences so they couldn't be used by other insurgents. The soldiers were buoyant, happy to have survived the small battle and looking forward to returning home. Dimly Youssef heard that the advance party would leave for England at the end of the week.

At last silence had descended on the village, at least for a few hours. Youssef made some experimental efforts to move but pain shot through his body and he had to give it up. He resigned himself, ready to die of thirst, then he heard the children's voices.

With the soldiers gone it was time for them to scavenge. Spent brass bullet cases were worth money as scrap metal and there were thousands lying on the ground just waiting to be picked up. If a complete weapon could be found then the child's family would at once become wealthy. Sometimes the soldiers left behind ration packs and items of equipment that had been set to one side and then forgotten. Youssef filled his lungs with dusty air and shouted for all he was worth. His Pashto had become good, but he still had to hope it was good enough for the children to understand.

He coughed, his lungs protesting over the amount of debris he had subjected them to. Pain coursed through him again and he felt faint, too weak to make a second attempt.

There were screams of alarm then silence fell once again. Youssef cursed himself. Instead of summoning help he had scared it away. The children must have thought he was a ghost or a jinn.

Allah favoured him. After a few hours he heard the sound of an engine followed by the heavy crunch of feet and knew that an adult must be close. He called again and this time his call was answered. Hands scrabbled at the rubble and as his face was uncovered he saw the gap toothed grin of an Afghan farmer. Behind him, smiling shyly past her father's shoulder, was a pretty young girl that Youssef had once taken home. Behind them both a young boy bobbed his head, trying to see what his father had found.

For the promise of hard American dollars the man took him to his house and Youssef instructed him in how to make contact with people that he could trust. A sympathetic volunteer from the Red Crescent provided some basic medical care before Youssef was smuggled across the border into Pakistan where a proper doctor was able to attend him, though hospital treatment was deemed to be too risky for fear of awkward questions being asked.

After some negotiation with the Taliban leadership it was agreed that Youssef had suffered enough for the jihad. He could return home if a way could be found and the Taliban sympathisers would pay for his travel. It was made clear that it was a favour he might be called on to repay some day. The thought made Youssef shiver with fear.

Arriving back in Britain, Youssef made covert contact with Fatima and the two of them finally met up in the safe house where Youssef was staying, chaperoned once again by Fatima's bemused aunt. Her parents had opposed the meeting, but the hard glint in Fatima's eye had told them that they were fighting a losing battle. She would meet Youssef despite their wishes, so it was better done in an appropriate manner.

Tearfully Fatima asked Youssef how he had managed to get back home.

"It wasn't easy, especially as I was still injured. The Ta... the people who I was with, provided me with documents that said I was going to Spain for treatment for my injuries. Once there I was provided with another set of papers, this time saying that I'm an Irish citizen of Pakistani parentage. There is actually someone in Ireland who has my real identity." Youssef offered Fatima a handkerchief. She took it from him and dabbed at her tears while he continued. The cost of those documents, Youssef knew, was enormous and a measure of the debt he might one day be asked to repay.

"From there it was easy. There are no border controls between the Republic and the North, not even a customs post. I took the train from Dublin to Belfast. I got a bit of a fright when I got off the train though. There were a couple of policemen coming straight towards me, but they were interested in the man behind me. It seems that it helps to have a brown face in Belfast if you want to pass unnoticed by the police.

Anyway, from there it was a taxi ride to catch the ferry across to Stranraer. After that it was all trains until I arrived here. These people look after me. I'm doing some clerical work in a warehouse owned by one of their uncles, just to pay my way."

"There is to be a 'homecoming parade' for the battalion, you know, the Middlesex." Fatima told him.

Youssef looked up in surprise. "Why do you tell me?"

"I thought you might like to see the people who you tried to kill, and who tried to kill you." Fatima kept her tone level, not allowing any expression of emotion. While she was so happy to see her boyfriend again she knew that he wasn't the young man who had left for Pakistan over a year before. She would have to get to know this new Youssef and she might not like him as much. Only time would tell. The first step was to gauge his reaction to the news of what amounted to a victory parade.

Youssef said in a quiet voice. "There was man buried with me. His friends pulled him out of the house. They left me to die."

Now Youssef stood concealed by the crowd and watched his former adversaries being cheered by their people. There would be no cheers for his men. They now either lay in shallow graves in the cemetery of the abandoned village or in the cells of Bagram prison. He was lucky not to be in either place with them.

"Do you still feel hate for them?" asked Fatima, gently squeezing his hand.

"No, not any more. I don't wish them well, and I wish them out of Afghanistan and every other Muslim country where they have set their feet, but I don't hate them anymore."

"So why did you do it? Why did you abandon your studies and fight them?"

"I thought it would make me feel better. I thought I would be doing Allah's work."

"And do you feel better?"

"No."

"And were you doing Allah's work?"

Youssef turned and hobbled away from the parade without answering.

* * *

From across the road Emma watched as Fatima's back disappeared into the crowd. There weren't many Asian faces in the crowd, so the couple stood out. The young woman seemed vaguely familiar to Emma, but the distance was too great and the memory too faint. The young man who hobbled beside her was in obvious pain. Poor bloke, wonder what happened to him?

As the parade passed through the gates of the barracks Emma pushed Lofty's wheel chair through after it. That night a fleet of coaches would take the battalion and their families back to Wiltshire, but Lofty would stay here at the depot. In a few weeks' time he would walk out of the gates as a civilian and they would start a new life together.

The End

Glossary

LASM   Light Anti-Structure Missile. An unguided rocket fired from a single shot telescopic tube. The rocket buries its head in the wall of the structure before the explosive warhead detonates, which makes a bigger breach than if it exploded on impact.

Appendix A

On The Structure Of Units In The British Army

To the lay person the British Army is a strange and mysterious place. Its structures and terminology provide a common frame of reference for those inside the organisation, but are a foreign language to those who are unfamiliar with the military way of life. This Appendix and the Glossary below it are aimed at assisting the lay person to understand the jargon and the organisational structures that are used in this book. This explanation is based on current British Army practice and some ex-servicemen may see differences from the time when they served.

The smallest recognised formation in an infantry unit is the section. It's made up of eight men split into two fire teams of four men each, a Charlie team led by a Corporal and a Delta team led by a Lance Corporal, who is also second in command of the section, or 2IC. Both fire teams are similarly equipped with the Corporal/Lance Corporal plus one rifleman armed with 5.56 mm SA80 rifles, another rifleman armed with a 7.62 mm light machine gun and the fourth rifleman with a 5.56 mm light support weapon.

Three sections combined make up a Platoon of 24 men, which is commanded by a junior officer with a sergeant as his 2IC. Junior Officers are, in ascending order of rank, Second Lieutenant, Lieutenant and Captain. For identification purposes platoons are traditionally numbered 1 to 4.

A Company is made up of four Platoons, with a Major commanding it. He will be assisted by a Company Sergeant Major and may have runners, a driver and a Quartermaster Sgt at his disposal. His second in command is the senior most Platoon commander who is usually a Captain. Across the companies will be a spread of specialist teams such as mortar, machine gun and reconnaissance platoons. In addition there will be individual soldiers trained to carry out specific tasks, such as snipers, first aid and EOD.

A Battalion is made up of four rifle companies, identified as A, B, C and D, and a headquarters company. The commanding officer is a Lieutenant Colonel, assisted by his 2IC who will be a Major, the Regimental Sergeant Major, responsible for discipline and ceremonial, and a wide range of specialist trades such as medical, intelligence, technical, communications, quartermaster and administration. Armoured units are called regiments rather than battalions and their companies are called squadrons.

Confusingly an infantry regiment is one that has one or more battalions. In this story C Company is part of the 2nd Battalion the Middlesex Regiment, which implies that there is also a 1st Battalion Middlesex Regiment. An infantry regiment is commanded by a Colonel, which is an administrative and ceremonial role rather than an operational command and is often combined with another duty, such as Staff Officer or Garrison Commander. A complete regiment will often include battalions made up of reservists, part time soldiers who are members of the Territorial Army.

In operational terms two or more battalions under the same command make up a Brigade, commanded by a Brigadier. To assist him he will have a Chief of Staff, usually a full Colonel who is also the 2IC. The Chief of Staff leads a number of staff officers, designated G1 to G9. G1, for example, is responsible for personnel, G2 for intelligence and security, etc. In some circumstances one officer may combine two or more staff responsibilities. The Brigadier will also have direct command over a number of embedded units such as artillery, logistics, communications and engineers.

Brigades are normally designated mechanised or armoured. A Mechanised Brigade is made up of at least two mechanised infantry battalions and one armoured regiment, while an Armoured Brigade has at least two armoured regiments and one infantry battalion. Mechanised means that the soldiers are equipped with armoured fighting vehicles that transport them to the battlefield, though to win the battle they will inevitably have to put 'boots on the ground'.

Two or more Brigades under a single command form a Division, commanded by a Major General. The Divisional headquarters is organised in a similar manner to a Brigade though the staff officers will usually be of more senior rank. The Divisional Commander will also have additional resources available to him, including units from the Army Air Corps who will provide aerial reconnaissance and ground attack capability. Divisions are designated as Armoured or Infantry depending on the mix of brigades that make them up.

At the time that the story was set in, the end of 2012, there was one Mechanised Brigade deployed in Afghanistan. It was made up of four infantry battalions plus an armoured regiment operating in an infantry and reconnaissance role. There were also a wide variety of embedded and support units. To enhance its capabilities the Brigade also had command over units normally seen only at divisional level, such as helicopters and the field hospital. The Royal Air Force and Royal Navy also had a considerable presence in the country, bringing the total strength of British forces in theatre to around 9,500.

Communications

In the fog of war it is important that everyone is able to communicate with and identify everyone else, especially over the radio where voices might not be immediately recognisable. In times past a platoon might only have one radio available to communicate with higher authority, but with the advent of more modern communications equipment all soldiers in a unit now carry a personal role radio (PRR), allowing 100% levels of communications. Command vehicles and Headquarters units have the capability to communicate both upwards and downwards along the chain of command using different radio networks.

To reduce confusion over identities there is a call-sign system. For the purposes of this story the C Company call-sign is Shark. The platoon call-signs are: 1 Platoon: Catfish, 2: Dogfish, 3: Swordfish and 4: Angelfish. The three sections within 1 Platoon are designated Catfish 1, 2 and 3. Within the sections the soldiers are each numbered off with the Corporal being 1, the Lance Corporal being 2, and the six privates being 3 to 8. For the purposes of this story the two man crew of the section Mastiff vehicle are designated alpha and bravo. To identify themselves over the radio each soldier will refer to himself by the section call-sign plus his own number, eg Catfish one one, Catfish one two, etc. Call-signs are also sometimes used in everyday conversation as a form of shorthand to indicate which bit of the organisation is being discussed or to identify an individual or group.

Glossary

2IC   Second in command

AK-47   An assault rifle capable of single shot or automatic fire. 7.62 mm calibre fed from a thirty round magazine. The weapon of choice of most of the world's terrorist groups.

Apache   Boeing AH-64 ground attack helicopter used by the British and US armies. It's capable of carrying rockets and anti-tank missiles and is equipped with a 30 mm calibre M230 Chain Gun.

Barracks   The permanent base of a military unit, comprising domestic accommodation for both single and married soldiers, administration and training buildings, armoury, storage buildings and workshops. Very often named after a significant military figure, eg Wellington Barracks in London. A building providing domestic accommodation for unmarried soldiers is a barrack block, while SNCOs and Officers live in the Sergeants and Officers messes respectively.

Boot Neck   British Army slang for Royal Marines, originally used by sailors referring to the high leather stock that formed part of the marine's uniform in the 17th and 18th centuries.

Bundu   Often spelt and pronounced as bondu. Slang for any uninhabited and non-cultivated land. Probably originating in South Africa from a Bantu word meaning wilderness

Capt	Captain.
CCTV	Closed circuit television.
Chinook	Boeing CH-47 heavy lift helicopter used by the RAF and American armed forces for cargo and troop carrying operations. Its design is distinctive in that it has a tandem rotor arrangement with one rotor mounted over the front of the aircraft and one over the tail, rather than the traditional mid fuselage single rotor blade assembly with a smaller vertically mounted stabilising rotor at the rear.
Civvie(s)	Slang: civilian personnel. Often used as a derogatory term. Can also be applied to a soldier's non-uniform clothing as in 'wearing his civvies'.
CO	Commanding Officer, normally of a battalion or regiment.
COS	Chief of Staff, the chief administrator in a Brigade or Divisional HQ.
Cpl	Corporal.
Crabs	Slang name used by the Army and Navy to refer to the Royal Air Force.
CSM	Company Sergeant Major, Warrant Officer II rank.
Drone	See RPV.
EOD	Explosives ordinance disposal - bomb disposal.
FOB	Forward operating base.
G2	Staff officer responsible for intelligence and security.
G3	Staff Officer responsible for operations.
Garrison	A geographic area providing infrastructure, eg barracks, for a large number of soldiers,

usually in different units. It may consist of a number of different estates spread around the geographic area and can be quite extensive. Catterick Garrison, for example, houses around 12,000 soldiers and their families.

Glasshouse Slang name for a military prison. The only one remaining in Britain is at Colchester Garrison.

GPMG General purpose machine gun, 7.62 mm calibre, belt fed. See also jimpy

Hesco ™ Large diameter wire mesh baskets, 3 to 4 ft tall, that can be filled with rubble to form a defensive barrier.

HMG Heavy machine gun. 12.7 mm calibre belt fed. Can be mounted on a tripod or fixed to a vehicle. Has an effective range up to 2 km.

HQ Headquarters.

IC When used by officers it mean 'In Command'. When used by an NCO (see below) it normally means 'in charge'.

IED Improvised explosive device, which includes roadside bombs and booby traps. There is no set design for an IED and each bomb maker will design his own.

Int Corps Intelligence Corps. The branch of the British Army responsible for the gathering and analysis of military intelligence. Also takes the tri-service lead on security matters.

Intel Intelligence – information on enemy forces: strength, leadership, weapons, tactics, training and morale and also on the operational environment: terrain, infrastructure, local population etc. all of

	which supports the commander in his strategic or tactical decision making.
ISAF	International Security Assistance Force, forces from countries across the world that have agreed to provide military support to the Afghan government. The USA and Britain are the two largest contributors.
Jackal	A lightly armoured patrol vehicle with a crew of two, a driver and a gunner and room for a passenger.
Jimpy	Slang for GPMG (see above).
Klik(s)	Slang for kilometre(s), sometimes also abbreviated as 'k'.
LASM	Light Anti-Structure Missile. An unguided rocket fired from a single shot telescopic tube. The rocket buries its head in the wall of the structure before the explosive warhead detonates, which makes a bigger breach than if it exploded on impact.
LCpl	Lance Corporal.
Lt	Lieutenant
LMG	Light machine gun, 7.62 mm calibre, magazine fed.
Long	Also 'The Long'. Nickname for the L115A3 Long Range Rifle used by snipers in the British Army. 8.59 mm calibre, bolt action, capable of a range of 1,100 metres, about three times the effective range of an SA80 rifle.
LSW	The SA-80 A2 LSW is a light support weapon with a 5.56 mm calibre. It differs from the standard SA-80 rifle (see below) by having a longer barrel length and a bipod stand to provide greater accuracy.

Mastiff	An armoured truck capable of transporting a complete section. It also has a crew of two, a driver and a gunner.
Medivac	Medical evacuation.
Merlin	Augusta Westland AW101 medium lift helicopter. Originally purchased as an anti-submarine platform for the Royal Navy it was drafted into RAF service as a stop gap to make up for the perceived shortfall in helicopter capability in Iraq and Afghanistan.
MoD	Ministry of Defence, the arm of Government responsible for administering the British armed forces.
Mortar	A small bomb fired from a tube that has its base resting on the ground. The bomb has a small explosive charge in its base to act as its propellant. The bomb is dropped down the barrel of the mortar tube and the striking of the cartridge on a firing pin fires it. Especially useful for indirect fire over objects such as walls, or for firing out of a trench. Mortars come in three calibres: 51 (obsolescent), 60 and 81 mm. The last is a specialist weapon and wouldn't be expected to be seen at battalion level. They can be used to fire explosive, smoke or illuminating rounds (flares). Ranges extend from 800 metres to around 5,500 metres depending on calibre.
MP	Military Police. On military bases they have similar powers to civilian police officers. Off base in the UK they would normally act through the local constabulary.

NAAFI   Navy, Army and Air Force Institute. A 'not for profit' business employed by the MoD to provide bars, cafeterias and shops for service personnel. Now mainly operating on overseas bases and replaced in the UK by contract catering companies.

NCO   Non Commissioned Officer. There are seven NCO ranks in the army which are, in ascending order: Lance Corporal, Corporal, Sergeant, Staff Sergeant, Colour Sergeant, Warrant Officer II (CSM, see above), Warrant Officer I (RSM, see below)

OC   Officer Commanding, usually of a formation smaller than a battalion.

O Group Orders Group – a briefing for soldiers about to take part in an operation.

Op or Operation Anything from a minor combat or non-combat mission up to a major on-going conflict may be called an operation. Usually assigned a code word (see Op HERRICK below) to disguise the meaning and also to provide shorthand for everyday use. The code words themselves are often unclassified but security caveats, eg 'Secret', may be applied to their meaning. Operation names are usually printed in block capitals so they stand out in written communications. To differentiate an operation from an exercise the latter are assigned two word codenames.

Op HERRICK The codename applied to the overarching military operations being conducted by British forces in Afghanistan.

OpSec   Operational   Security;   the   security arrangements for operating in the field including radio protocols.

Orderly Officer A   Warrant   Officer   or   junior commissioned officer who takes effective command of the unit outside of normal working hours. It is normally a 24 hour duty allocated by rota.

PAF   Pakistan Air Force.

Panther   An armoured command vehicle.

Pit or pit space   Slang: the bed space that a soldier has allocated to him in a barracks.

Pioneers   Part of the RLC (see below) who carry out a range of operational battlefield support tasks, including construction and demolition.

Pvt   Private, the lowest rank in the army. Trooper is used for cavalry soldiers and there are other terms that stem from the specialist nature of the soldiers work, eg Sapper for an engineer, Signaller for a member of the Royal Signals, etc. There are also terms used as a matter of regimental tradition, eg Fusilier for soldiers in Fusilier regiments.

QM or Quartermaster   The officer in a unit, usually a Major, responsible for providing the equipment that soldiers require to live and fight.   He   is   also   responsible   for accommodation and catering. QMs are often long serving soldiers promoted from the non-commissioned ranks. Most units also have a quartermaster of Sergeant rank in each company to allow them to operate independently.

R & R   Rest and recreation. A short period of rest away from the battle front, usually no longer than a week.

Rag Heads   Derogatory term. Originally used to refer to Iraqis it is now also used to refer to Afghan insurgents.

RAO   Regimental Administration Officer or Regimental Administration Office.

RAF   Royal Air Force

Redcaps   Slang: Military Police. So called because their peaked caps have a bright red covering. When they wear a beret it is crimson in colour.

Recce   Reconnaissance. The process of gathering intelligence through direct observation of the enemy or terrain.

RHQ   Regimental Headquarters

RLC   Royal Logistics Corps. Formed in 1993 by merging the Royal Army Ordnance Corps, Royal Corps of Transport, Royal Pioneer Corps and Army Catering Corps. The branch of the army responsible for re-supply, transport, catering and pioneer support.

RoE   Rules of Engagement. A set of rules based on British and International law that describes the circumstances under which British forces may use deadly force. Other nationalities in ISAF may use different RoE based on their own law.

Roulement   The routine deployment of troops on operational duties, usually to relieve a unit already in place.

RP   Regimental Police. Members of the battalion given some police training in order to act as constables within the barracks. They hold powers of arrest over military personnel of junior rank but not civilians.

RPG   Rocket propelled grenade. An unguided explosive projectile fired from a tube that is rested on the shoulder for firing. Originally of Russian manufacture it is in common use by terrorist groups.

RPV   Remotely piloted vehicle, a drone. Predator drones are unarmed, while Reaper drones can carry bombs, rockets and/or missiles.

RSM   Regimental Sergeant Major, the senior most NCO in a battalion or regiment. He is responsible for discipline within the unit and also for the organisation of ceremonial occasions.

RV   Also RVP, rendezvous and rendezvous point. A place to which soldiers will return if they are separated from each other.

Sangar   A temporary fortification usually constructed of sand bags. Can have a roof, usually made of canvass or corrugated iron sheets. Generally square in design and capable of housing two to four men. If the floor is dug out to provide extra depth then it may also be referred to as a weapons pit or fire pit.

SAS   Special Air Service, an elite unit in the British Army.

SA80   The SA80 A2 rifle is the standard infantry weapon used by the British Army and can be used to fire single shots or in automatic mode to fire bursts. It has a 5.56 mm calibre and is fed from a magazine holding 30 rounds. The

SA80 A2 UGL is fitted with an under slung grenade launcher. Each fire team will have one of these issued.

SBS   Special Boat Service, the Royal Marines' equivalent to the SAS.

Scrim   Also scrim net. A net with a mesh about the same size as that used for a football goal, with scraps of coloured material attached to provide camouflage. The net is draped over poles above and around objects to disguise their shape and colour and to help them blend in with their background.

SDU   Situation display unit, a TV screen inside a Mastiff vehicle that the section commander uses to display views from any one of six external cameras, including infra-red capability for night use.

Sgt   Sergeant.

Shell scrape   A shallow earth work, usually dug in haste, which provides a modicum of protection against enemy fire.

SIS   Secret Intelligence Service, also known as MI6, the foreign intelligence gathering arm of the British security services.

SNCO   Senior Non-Commissioned Officer, NCOs (see above) of Sergeant or higher rank.

Sqn   Squadron. A unit within the RAF, normally composed of 12 aircraft. Because the complexity of modern aircraft requires a larger number of personnel to maintain them a modern RAF Sqn is commanded by a Wing Commander, not a Squadron Leader. Also a unit of cavalry equivalent in size to a company of infantry.

SSVC	Services Sound and Vision Corporation. An MoD owned organisation that provides radio, TV and cinema to military personnel serving overseas.
Stag	Slang. Sentry duty.
SSgt	Staff Sergeant – an NCO normally employed on administrative duties within Battalion HQ. Senior to a Sergeant.
Sunray	Radio call-sign used to identify the local commander. Sunray Minor identifies the second in command. These may be used with or without the unit's own call-sign, eg Catfish Sunray or just Sunray.
TA	Territorial Army. Volunteers who serve as soldiers on a part time basis. A number of TA soldiers are on active service in Afghanistan.
Tango	Radio code word for target.
Theatre	The main geographical area where military operations are being carried out, eg Iraq, Afghanistan.
VCP	Vehicle Check Point.
WO	Warrant Officer, also WOI and WOII. The senior most non-commissioned ranks. Although not commissioned Warrant Officers are addressed as Sir by junior ranks and may be addressed as Mr by officers.

NEXT...

The following Prelude and Chapter 1 are from 'The Warriors - Mirror Man' the sequel to the book you have just read...

* * *

Prelude - A Fallen Warrior

The battered van bounced over the rough ground, then through the open gates into the farm compound. The trailing dust started to settle back onto the road as a child hurried to close the gate to shut out any prying eyes.

Conscious of the ever present risk of surveillance drones, the driver of the van didn't stop until the vehicle was under the protective matting screens that served as a rough and ready car port.

The two men from the front hurried to the rear doors, then opened them so that the precious cargo could be unloaded. A third man climbed stiffly from the rear of the vehicle. The three exchanged a few words before they slid a crude stretcher out, one man supporting the end while one pushed and pulled it far enough along the vehicle bed to allow the third man to grasp the handles. Between them they hefted the load, testing it to make sure they would be able to bear its weight, before lifting it free and hurrying through the rear of the car port and into the dim interior of the farm house.

Inside a man waited, his medical instruments laid out on a sterile cloth lying on the bare earth floor. Hot water steamed in a basin next to them. The stretcher bearers laid their burden down in front of the man, as though he were a high priest and they were delivering the sacrificial offering. They rose, then backed away, as if expecting the man on the stretcher to suddenly rise from it. The third man joined them. They gazed down on the battered young man lying on the floor.

"He's in a bad way." One of the men offered his opinion.

"I can see that." The doctor started picking at the bloody dressings that were wrapped around the injured man's lower body and legs.

"You would be in a bad way if you had been buried under a house." One of the stretcher bearers snapped at his colleague.

"Gentleman, please." The doctor chastised them. "This man is ill. By the look of him he's hardly a man at all, more like a boy. Let's not make him wish he was actually dead by quarrelling over him." As if in agreement the patient let out a low moan as the doctor tugged at a blood encrusted and particularly stubborn bit of bandage, stuck to the skin. He used a water soaked swab to dampen the blood and soften it so that the dressing could be freed without hurting the patient any more than he had to.

"Who provided the First Aid?" The doctor inquired.

"We don't know his name. We were told he was from the Red Crescent."

"He did well with limited resources. I won't be able to do a great deal more. Not without taking him to a hospital." With the leg wounds exposed the doctor started to probe at the bandages that swathed the casualty's head.

"No hospitals." The men protested as one. One of them, probably the leader, continued the protest. "The government watches the hospitals. There is too much risk of betrayal. We didn't bring him this far just to have him arrested and handed over to the British.

"Why would the British want him?" The doctor ask, his curiosity piqued.

"Do you not know who this is?"

"I was told only that there was a badly injured fighter who needed my medical attention. So what makes this one so special, apart from his youth of course?"

"He is Youssef Haq Ibrahim. He is a British born fighter for the Jihad. For months he has been leading a band of our people against the kuffar soldiers in Afghanistan. The British. That's how he was injured. There was a big battle. Many of our fighters were killed or captured. We thought Youssef had been as well, until some children found him lying in the rubble of a house."

"He is a lucky man. He would have died of his injuries had he not been found, of that there can be no doubt. Well, I can stitch up his wounds and dose him with morphine for the pain, but I can't set his bones without the benefit of X-Rays. The head injury appears to be superficial: More blood than anything, but to be sure I would need that to be X-Rayed as well. For a full recovery he would need to be in hospital. There is a danger he will be crippled for life without the treatment they could provide."

"No hospitals." One of the leader repeated. "Do the best that you can for him."

The doctor sucked air through his teeth, wishing he had the authority to insist that they take the patient to a hospital, frustrated that he could only comply with their order. He was used to being obeyed, not obeying. Slung over their shoulders the three men had AK-47 assault rifles, the rusted magazines already attached. The threat was clear. If he argued they might decide that he was too much of a risk and that would put his life in danger as well. He wasn't prepared to risk his life any further for a foolish boy who had been carried away by the romance of the Jihad.

"OK, that I will do. I can straighten his legs and apply splints, but if his pelvis is broken then that is the end of the matter. His legs will heal but there's no way of knowing if he will ever walk. And if the head wound is worse than it looks then he may never function as a human again. If that is the risk you want to take then I will do what I can with splints, stitches and bandages."

"It is the will of Allah." One of the men said. The others mumbled their acknowledgement of their God's powers. The doctor was as good a Muslim as any of the three fighters but he knew that Allah always welcomed a helping hand when it came to healing people. However, he kept his own counsel.

"What will become of him?" the doctor asked, inserting a needle into one of the boy's veins and injecting morphine.

"We are in contact with people in Islamabad who will take care of him. They will find a way of getting him back to Britain, if that's what he wants. Or they'll find somewhere safe for him here in Pakistan.

"I hope he isn't in a hurry. It will be a while before he is fit to travel."

"He can stay here for a few days, we've been promised that."

"A month, minimum, if you want him to live and to walk. And then he will need to be carried to his next destination. It will be months before we will know if he will walk or even talk again."

"However long it takes, he will be looked after."

"Good. Now, I have injected enough morphine into him to sedate an elephant for a week, so now I need your help to straighten his legs and get them into splints. I will get plaster of paris when I return to the city and return and set his bones properly later."

* * *

1 - A Deadly Cargo

Mehmet steered his 38 Tonnes of lorry off of the M40 and towards the town. The name of the town was vaguely familiar to him, but he had no interest in it. He would be there for less than an hour and then continue to his ultimate destination.

Looking at the piece of paper with the sketch map on it he prepared to navigate the roundabout ahead of him. He had been told that the handover point was no more than a mile from the motorway and already he could see the roofs of the warehouses rising above the trees.

The gates stood open and a large sign on the side of the building proclaimed it to be To Let. The road around the warehouse took him to the rear, out of sight of anyone passing along the service road. They had chosen well, just as they had in France.

A plain coloured van, devoid of markings, showed him where he was expected to stop. Switching off the engine and applying the parking brake Mehmet climbed stiffly from the cab to meet his contact.

"Have you got a light?" The man asked, putting a cigarette between his lips. Mehmet fished in his pocket for his plastic lighter.

"What brand do you smoke?" Mehmet asked, going through the ritual as instructed. His English wasn't good and he'd had to memorise the words parrot fashion.

"I prefer Rothmans, but these are Dunhill. What do you smoke?"

"I only smoke Samsun, they're a Turkish Brand."

"Keys." With the bone fides of both parties established the man stuck out his hand. Mehmet handed them over. The man passed Mehmet an envelope, which the lorry driver stuffed into the bib pocket of his dungarees. He would check the contents when he was alone, so as not to cause offence. "Now take a walk." The man commanded.

When given that instruction in France Mehmet had considered it a bit rude, but this time he was ready for it. He wandered off to the distant corner of the building and walked round it. A blank wall extended away from him, with a narrow gap between it and the perimeter fence. A thick hawthorn hedge grew on the outside of the fence providing concealment from the neighbouring buildings. Mehmet took the opportunity to empty his bladder, after which he leant against the wall and lit a cigarette before taking the envelope from his pocket and counting the thick wad of Euro notes. His instructions were clear, given to him in his native Turkish so there could be no ambiguity. "Wait until you hear the sound of a vehicle horn, two long blasts and one short. Then you may return to your truck. Have no fear, your cargo will be intact and will match the manifest exactly."

At the back of Mehmet's lorry three men were unloading the rearmost stack of cardboard shipping cartons. They weren't heavy but lifting them down from the rear of the trailer was difficult. They were meant to be handled by fork lift truck, so didn't have any hand holds. With the second row of boxes visible they had only one more to lift backwards and to the side before they had access to the one they were looking for.

To the naked eye it looked just like its neighbours, but the difference was apparent to the men who were trying to move it. It was considerably heavier and had to be half dragged and half lifted to the rear lip of the trailer's floor.

The man on the ground backed the van up to the rear of the lorry and positioned it so that the box could be lowered directly from the trailer into the van. One man remained in the trailer while the other dropped into the van to provide more muscle at the lower level.

With some cursing and a lot of conflicting instructions the load was finally transferred, and the van visibly sank on its suspension. All three of the men then manoeuvred it into the centre of the load space so that the van would be evenly balanced.

It didn't take long to replace the containers into the back of the lorry, along with the extra box that the men had brought with them, delivered from France by a different route.

The leader secured the back of the lorry and dropped the keys on the driver's seat of the cab, before taking his place behind the wheel of the van and giving the pre-arranged signal. He put the van in gear and drove from the warehouse yard without looking back.

Mehmet returned to his vehicle and checked it over, opening the back of the trailer to make sure that the cargo had been left secure. Climbing back into his cab he placed the envelope into his rucksack alongside its twin, the first instalment that he had been given in France. He had no idea what had been put in his lorry and cared even less. He was a Turkish driver working for a Bulgarian haulage company driving a lorry with Czech number plates. Why should he care what these people got up to? He was just happy to take the money and return to his family.

He had another four hours of driving before he could deliver the lorry's cargo, then he had to cross the Pennines to pick up his return load. Only then could he start the long journey home to enjoy the fruits of his labour. He waited in the yard, drinking coffee from a flask, until his statutory forty five minute rest break had elapsed, then continued his journey.

* * *

And Now

Both the author Robert Cubitt and Ex-L-Ence Publishing hope that you have enjoyed reading this story.

Find Robert Cubitt on Facebook at www.facebook.com/robertocubitt and 'like' his page; follow him on Twitter @robert_cubitt and visit Robert's website www.robertcubitt.com where you can read his weekly blog and learn more about his other books.

Please tell people about this eBook, write a review on Amazon or mention it on your favourite social networking sites.

For further titles that may be of interest to you please visit the Ex-L-Ence website at www.ex-l-ence.com where you can optionally join our information list.

Lightning Source UK Ltd.
Milton Keynes UK
UKOW05f0257260417
299914UK00001B/1/P